W9-BSX-337

tiger's voyage

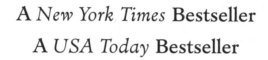

A *New York Times* Bestseller
A *USA Today* Bestseller

"Epic, grand adventure rolled into a sweeping love story . . ."
—Sophie Jordan, author of *Firelight*

"An epic love triangle that kept me eagerly turning the pages!"
—Alexandra Monir, author of *Timeless*

". . . high adventure ensues. As in *Tiger's Curse* and *Tiger's Quest*, this story is part action-adventure and part romance . . . the novel will satisfy the saga's fans, who will be delighted by the prospect of a fourth volume."

—*Booklist*

PRAISE FOR OTHER BOOKS IN THE SERIES:

Tiger's Curse

"A sweet romance and heart-pounding adventure. I found myself cheering, squealing, and biting my nails—all within a few pages. In short, *Tiger's Curse* is magical!"

—Becca Fitzpatrick, *New York Times* bestselling author of *Hush, Hush*

"One part Rick Riordan, two parts Twilight . . ."

—*Newsday*

"Colleen Houck's debut *Tiger's Curse* has it all: paranormal, romance, fantasy, adventure, historical fiction."

—*USA Today*

"One of the best books I have ever read. An ultimate thrill ride. A roller-coaster ride from the beginning to end, this book has action, history, poetry, romance, magic—everything you could ever want. A book with so much passion and thrills you won't be able to put it down. This saga is going to be one of the best yet."

—*RT Book Review*

tiger's quest

"Forget vampires and werewolves, tigers are the new hottest thing. The second book in Houck's Tiger's Curse series features a love triangle, passion and nonstop action. It's a guaranteed page-turner with a huge twist at the end that will leave you breathless."

—*RT Reviews*

". . . shocking, heart-rending, soul-tearing . . ."

—*Kirkus Reviews*

tiger's destiny

"Ablaze with fiery passions—and sheets of actual fire, too—this conclusion to the Tiger's Curse quartet brings Oregon teenager Kelsey and the two Indian were-tiger princes who have divided her heart through a climactic battle to a final, bittersweet mate selection. . . .[Readers] are sure to be left throbbing and misty-eyed."

—*Kirkus Reviews*

"Kelsey, Ren, and Kishan return in this final volume in Houck's popular Tiger's Curse series. [Houck] tells a good story that will appeal to both action-adventure and romance fans."

—*Booklist*

tiger's voyage

by COLLEEN HOUCK

SPLINTER

New York

SPLINTER

An imprint of Sterling Publishing Co., Inc.
387Park Avenue South
New York, NY 10016

SPLINTER and the distinctive Splinter logo are trademarks of Sterling Publishing Co., Inc.

© 2011 by Colleen Houck

Author's Note originally written by Colleen Houck for RTBookReviews.com. Used with permission. All rights reserved.

All rights reserved. No part of this publication may be reproduced, stored in a retrieval system, or transmitted in any form or by any means (including electronic, mechanical, photocopying, or otherwise) without prior written permission from the publisher.

ISBN 978-1-4549-0357-4

Library of Congress Cataloging-in-Publication Data

Houck, Colleen.
  Tiger's voyage / by Colleen Houck.
    p. cm. -- (Tiger's curse ; [3])
  Summary: After battling the villainous Lokesh, Kelsey and the Indian princes Ren and Kishan return to India, where Kelsey learns that Ren has amnesia, and five cunning dragons try to keep the trio from breaking the curse that binds them.
  ISBN 978-1-4027-8405-7 (alk. paper)
  [1. Tigers--Fiction. 2. Blessing and cursing--Fiction. 3. Amnesia--Fiction. 4. Dating (Social customs)--Fiction. 5. Immortality--Fiction. 6. Orphans--Fiction. 7. India--Fiction.] I. Title.
  PZ7.H81143Tiv 2011
  [Fic]--dc23
                                                                                        2011017812

Distributed in Canada by Sterling Publishing
c/o Canadian Manda Group, 165 Dufferin Street
Toronto, Ontario, Canada M6K 3H6
Distributed in the United Kingdom by GMC Distribution Services
Castle Place, 166 High Street, Lewes, East Sussex, England BN7 1XU
Distributed in Australia by Capricorn Link (Australia) Pty. Ltd.
P.O. Box 704, Windsor, NSW 2756, Australia

For information about custom editions, special sales, and premium and corporate purchases, please contact Sterling Special Sales at 800-805-5489 or specialsales@sterlingpublishing.com.

Manufactured in the United States of America
Lot #:
2 4 6 8 10 9 7 5 3 1
03/14

www.sterlingpublishing.com

Some of the terms included in the book may be trademarks or registered trademarks. Use of such terms does not imply any association with or endorsement by such trademark owners and no association or endorsement is intended or should be inferred. This book is not authorized by, and neither the Author nor the Publisher is affiliated with the owners of the trademarks referred to in the book.

R06020 42339

For my parents, Bill and Kathy—
who put off all their adventures
to raise a brood of seven

contents

forget thee?

by John Moultrie

Forget thee? If to dream by night and muse on thee by day;
If all the worship deep and wild a poet's heart can pay;
If prayers in absence breathed for thee to Heaven's protecting power;
If winged thoughts that flit to thee a thousand in an hour;
If busy fancy blending thee with all my future lot—
If this thou call'st forgetting, thou, indeed, shalt be forgot!

Forget thee? Bid the forest-birds forget their sweetest tune;
Forget thee? Bid the sea forget to swell beneath the moon;
Bid the thirsty flowers forget to drink the eve's refreshing dew;
Thyself forget thine own dear land, and its mountains wild and blue.
Forget each old familiar face, each long-remember'd spot—
When these things are forgot by thee, then thou shalt be forgot!

Keep, if thou wilt, thy maiden peace, still calm and fancy-free,
For God forbid thy gladsome heart should grow less glad for me;
Yet, while that heart is still unwon, oh! bid not mine to rove,
But let it nurse its humble faith and uncomplaining love;
If these, preserved for patient years, at last avail me not—
Forget me then; but ne'er believe that thou canst be forgot!

blood in the water

behind the thick glass of his Mumbai penthouse office once again, Lokesh tried to control the incredible rage slowly circling through his veins. Nothing had gone according to plan in the Baiga camp. Even the villagers had turned out to be weak and disloyal. True, he had captured Dhiren, the white tiger-prince, and taken a vital piece of the Damon Amulet from the girl, but he hadn't been able to finish what he'd started.

Breathing deeply to calm his rage, he pressed his fingers together and deliberately tapped them against his bottom lip as he pondered the fight. *They'd possessed special weapons. His underlings had discovered that the weapons were somehow tied to the goddess Durga. Clearly, there was some kind of magic involved, and it wasn't the weak country magic of the tribe.*

Magic was a tool, a gift to be used by those wise enough to understand and manipulate it. A trick of the universe that only a few sought and even fewer could harness. Lokesh had it, and he would use it to bring him even more power. Others thought him evil. He didn't believe in good and evil—only in powerful and powerless. Lokesh was determined to be the former.

Why Durga? Perhaps the goddess is somehow guiding them.

Like good and evil, he didn't believe in gods. Faith was a crutch, a convenient way to control the masses who would become mindless slaves, choosing not to use whatever meager intellect they possessed.

Believers sat at home and wept and prayed, prostrating themselves for divine assistance that would never come.

An intelligent man takes matters into his own hands. Lokesh frowned as he remembered the girl slipping from his. To her, it must have seemed like he ran. He'd sent in reinforcements, but the idiots had returned empty-handed. The command center had been destroyed. The cameras and video records were missing. The Baiga, the tiger, and the girl were nowhere to be found. It was extremely . . . vexing.

A chime rang as his assistant entered the room. Lokesh listened as the man nervously explained that the tracking device he'd implanted in the prince had been found. The man opened his shaking hand and dropped the smashed remains on the desk. Without a word, Lokesh picked up the broken chip and, using the power of the amulet, threw it and the quivering assistant out of the sixtieth-story window. He listened to the assistant's screams as he dropped floor by floor. Just when the man was about to hit bottom, Lokesh murmured a few words that opened a hole in the ground under his assistant and buried him alive.

Disappointing distractions dealt with, he pulled his hard-won prize from his pocket. Wind whipped through the broken window, and the sun rose higher above the bustling city, casting a beam of light on the freshly acquired fourth piece of the amulet. Soon, he would unite *all* the pieces of the amulet and would finally have the means to accomplish what he'd always dreamed of since he'd learned of the amulet's existence. He knew that the completed amulet would fashion him into something new . . . something . . . more. Something . . . perfect. Though he had deliberately prolonged starting the process and relished the anticipation almost as much as the victory, it was time.

The moment had arrived.

A crackle of pleasure raced through his blood as he touched the fourth segment to his precious amulet collection.

It didn't fit.

He turned, twisted, and tilted the wedge, but it would not mold to the others. *Why? I snatched it from the girl's neck in the Baiga camp. It was the same amulet piece she had worn in both visions.*

Instantly, a heavy black shadow of loathing fell upon him. Gnashing his teeth, he crushed the offending amulet imitation and let the powder trickle through his tight fist as each cell of his body burst with a blazing tempest. Sparkles of blue light popped and crackled between the digits.

Waves of anger washed through his mind, pummeling against the thin barrier of his skin. Without an outlet to assuage his violent urges, he clenched his fists and buried the power deep within him. *The girl! She tricked me!*

Anger pulsed at his temples as he considered Kelsey Hayes. She reminded him of another from centuries ago: Deschen, the tigers' mother. *Now there was a woman full of fire*, he remembered—unlike his own wife whom he had killed when she bore him a girl, Yesubai. He'd wanted a son. An heir. *My son and I would have ruled the world.*

After his disappointment with the birth of his daughter, he'd come up with a new plan—kill Rajaram and take Deschen for his own bride. Part of the fun would have been breaking her spirit. The fight would have been exquisite.

Deschen was long gone now, and fortunately, the tigers had brought him Kelsey. She was more than he bargained for. *Much* more. Slowly, his seething rage transformed into something else. It cooked and bubbled in his mind, thoughts forming and bursting like cankerous blisters until his determination boiled down to a dark, maddening desire.

Kelsey had the same fiery bravery that Deschen had possessed, and he would have a perverse pleasure taking her away from the sons of Rajaram. Suddenly, his fingers itched to touch her fine skin again. How pleasant it would be to put his knife to her flesh. As he pondered that thought, he ran a finger along the sharp edge of the broken glass window. *Perhaps* he would even let the tigers live so he could revel in the turmoil it would cause them. *Yes. Caging the princes and making them watch as I subdue the girl will be highly pleasurable. Especially after* this.

So long. I've waited so long.

Only one thought calmed him: The battle was far from over. He would find her. His team was already searching all over India, monitoring Durga's temples, and watching every transportation hub by land, air, and sea. He was a man who took no risks and left no stone unturned. He would strike again. After all, she was only a girl.

Soon, he thought. Lokesh shuddered as he imagined touching her again. He could almost sense her. *I wonder what she'll sound like when she screams.* It surprised him that he was almost looking forward to capturing the girl more than to obtaining the amulet. The need to have her was vicious. It tore through him as his fingers itched again. Soon he would have the girl and unite the pieces of the amulet. *Once I get my hands on her though, I'll have to be patient. Rushing things has been my downfall.*

He twisted one of the rings on his finger. Perhaps he shouldn't have expected grappling with the tigers to be easy. They'd caused so much trouble the first time. However, they weren't the only predators in India. He too was a creature to be feared. He was like a shark, cutting silently, swiftly, and fatally through the water.

Lokesh smiled. Sharks were creatures to admire, the ultimate predator, the dominant fish in the ocean. In the animal world, predators are born. However, a man chooses to be a predator, ripping to pieces those who stand against him, cracking the backbones of all who would oppose, and swallowing his enemies. He chooses to be the predator, or he chooses to be the prey.

Long ago Lokesh had decided to be at the top of the food chain. Now there was only one family and one young girl left that stood in his way. *And no girl stands a chance after I catch the scent of her blood in the water.*

Lokesh thoughtfully stroked his beard and smiled as he pictured circling her. The waters were chummed. They would never see him coming.

living without love

Is he going to do it?

I stared at Ren, searching for a hint of emotion.

A full minute ticked by. The second he made his choice, I knew it. Ren stretched out his hand to make his move.

"I win." He smiled as he knocked Kishan's pawn off the board and moved his HOME. He sat back in his chair and folded his arms across his chest. "Told you," he said. "I never lose at Parcheesi."

It had been more than a month since we rescued Ren from being tortured and held prisoner at Lokesh's Baiga camp and three weeks since my terrible birthday party—and life was purgatory. Even though I gave him my journal and used up all the flour baking my mom's famous double-chocolate peanut-butter cookies, Ren sadly had no memory of me. Something had happened with Lokesh to cause Ren's amnesia. Now we were reunited, but we weren't together.

Still, I refused to give up hope that somehow he might miraculously recover our past, and I was determined to free him. Even if Ren could never be mine again, I had made a commitment to seek the other two gifts to fulfill the goddess Durga's prophecy and break the tiger's curse so that both princes could once again be normal men. The least I could do for the man I loved was to not let him down.

Every day being near Ren but not being *with* him was harder than the last. Mr. Kadam did his best to distract me, and Ren's brother, Kishan, respected my feelings and stood by me as a supportive friend, though every look and touch made it very clear he was still interested in something more.

Neither Ren nor I knew how to act around each other. The four of us seemed to be walking on eggshells, waiting for something, anything, to happen. Only Nilima, Mr. Kadam's great-great-great granddaughter seemed to keep us all breathing, eating, and sane.

One particularly tear-filled night, I found Mr. Kadam in the peacock room. He was reading a book by the soft light of a lamp. I sat down next to him, put my head on his knee, and cried softly. He patted my back and hummed an Indian lullaby. Eventually, I calmed down and shared my fears. I told him I was worried that Ren was lost to me and asked him if a broken heart could really heal.

"You already know the answer to that, Miss Kelsey. Was your heart full and happy when you were with Ren before?"

"Yes."

"Your heart wasn't too damaged to love Ren because of your parents' death?"

"No. But those are two different kinds of love."

"It's different in some ways but the same in others. Your capacity for love does not ebb. You love your parents still, do you not?"

"Of course."

"Then I would suggest that what you are feeling is not the scarring or the diminishing of your heart, but the absence of your loved one."

I looked at the wise Indian businessman and sighed. "It's pretty sad when I feel the absence of my loved one while he's standing in the same room."

"It is," Mr. Kadam admitted. "Maybe it would be best to do nothing."

"You mean let him go?"

He patted my arm and, after considering a moment, said, "One of my sons once caught a small bird with an injured wing. He longed to care for it and keep it for a pet. One day he brought his bird to me. It was dead. He explained that the bird had healed and flapped its wings. But my son panicked and caught the bird before it flew away. He held it so tightly it suffocated.

"The bird may have chosen to stay with my son or may have flown away. Either of those events would have led to a happier conclusion. If the bird had left, my son would have been sad, but he would have remembered it with a smile. Instead, my son was devastated by the death of his pet and had a very hard time recovering from the experience."

"So you *are* saying to let Ren go."

"What I'm saying is . . . you will be happier if *he* is happy."

"Well, I definitely don't want to smother Ren to death." I sighed and tucked my legs under me. "I don't want to *avoid* him either. I like being around him and avoiding him would make finishing Durga's quest together difficult."

"May I suggest trying to be his friend?"

"He was always my friend. Maybe if I could get that part of him back, I won't feel like I've lost everything."

"I think you are right."

Friends with Ren? I pondered as I pulled out the ribbon holding my braid and climbed the stairs to turn in. *Well, something is better than nothing, and right now I have a whole lot of nothing going on.*

The next day Mr. Kadam and Nilima had set out a brunch. They'd already come and gone, but I found Ren in the kitchen piling a plate high with fruit and sweet rolls. He looked more like himself every day. His tall frame was filling out, and his dark hair had regained its glossy sheen. His gorgeous blue eyes watched me with a concerned expression as I took a plate.

When I got to the strawberries, I bumped him with my hip and he froze.

"Can you move down a bit please?" I asked. "I'd like to have a go at those cheese Danishes before Kishan gets here."

Ren snapped out of it. "Sure. Sorry."

He set his plate on the table, and I took the seat across from him. He watched me as he slowly peeled the paper away from a muffin. My face burned slightly from his attention.

"Are you okay?" he began haltingly. "I heard you crying last night."

"I'm fine."

He grunted and started eating but kept his eyes on me. When he was half finished, he looked away.

"Are you *sure*? I'm sorry if I upset you . . . again. I just don't remember—"

I stopped him right there by raising my hand. "How you feel is how you feel, Ren."

"Still, I apologize for hurting your feelings," he said softly.

I stabbed my melon with a fork. Despite my protestations and my attempt to be nonchalant, I was having a hard time following Mr. Kadam's advice. My eyes felt hot.

"Which time? On my birthday when you said I'm not attractive or that you can't stand being in the same room with me or when you said Nilima is beautiful or—"

"Okay, I get the point."

"Good, because I'd like to drop it."

After a moment, he elaborated, "By the way, I didn't say you weren't attractive. I just said you're young."

"So is Nilima by *your* standards. You're more than three hundred years old!"

"That's true." He grinned lopsidedly in an attempt to get me to smile.

"Technically, you should be dating a very old lady." A tiny smile passed my lips.

He grimaced. "I also want you to know that you're perfectly easy to be around and very likeable. I've never had this reaction to anyone before. I get along with almost everyone. There's no legitimate reason why I should feel the need to escape when you walk into a room."

"Other than the pressure to remember, you mean?"

"It's not the pressure. It's something . . . else. But I've decided to ignore it."

"Can you do that?"

"Sure. The longer I stay near you the more intense the response. It's not talking with you that's hard; it's just being in close proximity. We should try talking on the phone and see if that makes a difference. I'll just work on building up immunity."

"I see. So your goal is to build up a tolerance for me." I sighed. "Okay."

"I'll keep trying, Kelsey."

"Don't strain yourself *too* much, because it doesn't matter anymore. I've decided to just be friends with you."

He leaned forward and said conspiratorially, "But aren't you still, you know, in love with me?"

I leaned forward too. "I don't want to talk about that anymore."

Ren folded his arms across his chest. "Why not?"

"Because Lois Lane never suffocated Superman."

"What are you talking about?"

"We'll have to watch the movie. The point is, I'm done holding you back, so if you want to date Nilima, go for it."

"Wait a minute! You're just going to cut me off?"

"Is that a problem?"

"I didn't say it was a problem. It's just that I've been reading your journal, and for a girl who's supposed to be crazy about me, you're sure giving up pretty quickly."

"I'm not *giving up* anything. There's nothing *between* us now *to* give up."

He stared at me as I speared another piece of fruit.

Rubbing his jaw, he said, "So you want to be friends."

"Yep. No pressure, no tears, no constant reminders of things you forgot, no anything. We'll just start over. A clean slate. We'll learn how to be friends and get along despite your inner trigger to run. What do you say?" I wiped my hand on a napkin and held it out. "Want to shake on it?"

Ren considered, smiled, and took my hand. I pumped his up and down once.

"What are we agreeing on?" Kishan asked as he walked into what was the longest conversation Ren and I had had since before he was captured.

"Kelsey just agreed to give me a demonstration of her lightning ability," Ren smoothly lied. "Being able to shoot fire from your hand is something I've got to see."

I looked at him with a raised eyebrow. He smiled and winked, then stood and took both of our plates to the kitchen sink. Kishan's golden eyes cast a doubtful glance at me, but he sat down and snatched the remaining half of my cheese Danish. I smacked his hand playfully before picking up a towel to help Ren. When we were finished, he swiped the towel from me, snapping it lightly against my thigh. I laughed, enjoying our newfound repartee, and turned to find Kishan frowning at us.

Ren put his arm lightly around my shoulder and dipped his head closer to my ear, "'Yond Cassius has a lean and hungry look. He thinks too much; such men are dangerous.' Better keep an eye out for him, Kelsey."

I laughed, glad that he remembered his Shakespeare, if not me. "Don't worry about Kishan, Caesar. His growl is worse than his bite."

"Has he bitten you lately?"

"Not recently."

"Hmm, I'll keep an eye out for you," Ren said as he left the room.

"What was all that about?" Kishan growled, giving me a brief glimpse of the fierce black tiger hiding behind his eyes.

"He's celebrating his emancipation."

"What do you mean?"

"I've told him that I'd like to be friends."

Kishan paused, "Is that what *you* want?"

"What *I* want is irrelevant. Being my friend is something he can do. Being my boyfriend is not in the stars right now."

Kishan kept thankfully silent. I could tell he wanted to offer himself as a replacement, either seriously or in jest, but he bit his tongue. Because he did, I kissed his cheek on my way out.

With the ice finally broken between Ren and me, we all could finally move on and soon settled into a routine. I checked in with my foster parents, Mike and Sarah, every week, telling them virtually nothing but that I was fine and busy assisting Mr. Kadam. I assured them that I'd finished my freshman year at Western Oregon University online and that I'd be spending summer break doing an internship in India.

I practiced martial arts with Kishan in the mornings, had late breakfasts with Ren, and helped Mr. Kadam research the third part of Durga's prophecy in the afternoons. In the evenings, Mr. Kadam and I cooked dinner together—except when he wanted to make curry. Those nights I made my own dinner, using the Golden Fruit.

After dinner we played games, watched movies, and sometimes read in the peacock room. Kishan stayed in the library only if I was

telling a story, and then he'd curl up at my feet as the black tiger. We began reading *A Midsummer Night's Dream* together. Mr. Kadam bought several copies of the play so we could take different parts to read. I liked being able to share those times with Ren.

Mr. Kadam had been right, as usual. Ren did seem happy. Everyone responded to his improved mood, including Kishan, who had somehow changed from a brooding, resentful younger brother into a confident man. Kishan kept his distance, but his golden come-hither eyes made my face burn.

Sometimes in the evenings, I'd find Ren in the music room playing his guitar. He'd strum through songs and laugh when I requested "My Favorite Things" from *The Sound of Music*. One such night, Ren played the song he'd written for me. I watched him carefully, hoping a memory might be coming back. He was concentrating deeply as he picked softly through the notes. He kept getting stuck and started over again several times.

When he caught my gaze, he dropped his hands and grinned sheepishly. "I'm sorry. I just can't seem to remember this one. Do you have a request this evening?"

"No," I said curtly and stood.

Ren took my hand but dropped it quickly. "What is it? You're sad. More than usual."

"That song . . . it's—"

"The song? Have you heard it before?"

"No," I lied and smiled sadly, "It's . . . lovely." I squeezed his hand and stumbled away before he could ask any more questions. I wiped a tear from my cheek as I climbed the stairs. I could hear him working on the song again, trying to figure out where the notes belonged.

Another evening, I was relaxing on the veranda, smelling the night jasmine, and looking up at the stars when I overheard Kishan and Ren talking.

"You've changed," Ren pointed out to his brother. "You're not the same man you were six months ago."

"I can still whip your white hide if that's what you're getting at."

"No, it's not that. You're still a powerful fighter. But now, you're more relaxed, more certain, more . . . composed." He laughed. "And much harder to get riled up."

Kishan replied softly, "She's changed me. I've been working hard to become the kind of man she needs, the kind of man she already believes me to be."

Ren didn't respond, and the two entered the house. I sat quietly, thinking deeply about Kishan's words. *Who knew life and love would be so complicated?*

getting reacquainted

A few days later, Mr. Kadam called us together in the dining room. As we all took seats around the table, I secretly hoped this wasn't bad news and that Lokesh hadn't found us again.

"I'd like to propose an idea," Mr. Kadam began. "I've figured out a way to make sure we can find one another if, perchance, someone is abducted again. It won't be comfortable, but I feel a little discomfort is a small price to pay to make sure no one is lost."

He opened a box and took out a bubble-wrapped package. Inside was a black velvet bundle that unrolled to reveal five thick syringes with needles the size of a giant porcupine quill.

Nervously, I asked, "Umm, Mr. Kadam? What exactly do you mean by a *little* discomfort?"

He opened the first syringe and took out a bottle of saline solution and some alcohol wipes. "Have you heard of RFID tags?"

"No," I responded with alarm as I watched him gently take Kishan's left hand, swipe the area between his thumb and forefinger with an alcohol wipe, and then dab a yellow topical ointment in the same place.

"It stands for Radio Frequency Identification tags. They're used in animals."

"You mean to track whales and sharks? Things like that?"

"Not exactly. Those are larger and drop off after they lose power."

Ren leaned forward and picked up a chip about the size of a grain of rice. "It looks similar to what Lokesh implanted in me."

He set the chip down and rubbed his hands together slowly, looking off into the distance.

"Did it hurt? Could you feel it inside your skin?" I asked tentatively, trying to bring him back from whatever dark place he had gone.

Ren let out a breath and gave me a small smile. "The pain was minimal at the time, but yes, I could feel it under my skin."

"This tag is slightly different." Mr. Kadam hesitated and added, "We don't have to use them, but I think they will be a protection for all of us."

Ren nodded in agreement, and Mr. Kadam continued, "These are somewhat similar to RFID tags which are used in pets. They emit a frequency, usually a ten-digit number, which can be scanned through the skin.

"The chips are encased in biocompatible glass to prevent them from coming in contact with moisture. RFID tags for humans are not commonplace yet but are beginning to be approved for medical purposes. They identify medical history, allergies, and the types of medication a person is currently taking."

He drew some saline solution into the syringe and replaced the smaller needle with the giant one. Then he placed a tiny chip into the needle's groove. He pinched the skin between Kishan's thumb and finger and carefully inserted the needle. I looked away.

Unperturbed, Mr. Kadam continued, "Now for the large marine animals you were speaking of, researchers use satellite tags that transmit anything from the current location in longitude and latitude, to the depth of the animal, the duration of the dive, and the swimming speed. That type of tag is external and is attached to a battery that eventually is used up in the transmission of information. Most of them last only

a short time but some of the more expensive ones can last for a few months."

He pressed a cotton ball to Kishan's hand, removed the needle, and covered it with a Band-Aid. "Ren?"

Kishan and Ren switched places, and Mr. Kadam began the process over with Ren.

"There are a few internal tags put into marine animals that can record the heart rate, the temperature of the water, the body temperature, and the depth of the animal. Many of them transmit information to satellites when the animal surfaces."

He selected a new syringe, drew a bit of saline solution, replaced it with the larger one, and placed another chip into the needle's groove. When he pinched the skin and moved closer, I grimaced. Ren looked up and made eye contact with me. He smiled and said, "Easy as peach pie."

Peach pie. The color drained from my face.

He tried to reassure me, "No, really. It's not that bad."

I smiled weakly. "I'm not sure your tolerance for pain and mine are the same, but I'll survive. You were saying, Mr. Kadam?"

"Yes. So the problem with the RFID chips and the satellite tags is power. What we have here is technically not on the market and will likely never be, due to the general public's fear of identity theft and having government agencies monitor them.

"Almost every technological development can be used for either the benefit or detriment of mankind. I understand the fear associated with such a device but there are many valid reasons for exploring technologies such as this one. Luckily, I have military contacts, and they often walk where others fear to tread. Our tags can do all of those things and much, much more, transmitting data constantly even well above and below sea level."

He finished with Ren and looked at me. Hesitantly, I pushed back my chair and switched places with Ren. When I sat down, Mr. Kadam patted my hand briefly. I found myself staring fixedly at the needle as he switched needles again. He chose the hand not marked by Phet's henna tattooing and repeated the wipe-ointment process.

"I'm giving you a topical medicine that will numb the area slightly, but the injection will still hurt."

"Okay."

He placed a chip into the tip of the large needle. When he pinched my skin, I shut my eyes and drew in a tight breath through clenched teeth as he found the right spot.

Kishan's warm hand took mine, and he said tenderly, "Squeeze as hard as you need to, Kells."

Mr. Kadam slowly inserted the needle. It hurt. It felt like he was shoving one of my grandma's giant knitting needles through my hand. I squeezed Kishan's hand and started breathing fast. Seconds ticked by that felt like minutes. I heard Mr. Kadam say he had to go a little deeper.

I couldn't bite back the whimper of pain and wiggled in my chair as he twisted the needle and pushed it farther. My ears started ringing, and everyone's voices became thick. I was going to faint. I never thought of myself as wimpy, but needles, I realized, make me sick. About to keel over, I cracked my eyes open to look at Ren.

He was watching me with concern. When our eyes met, he smiled my favorite lopsided grin, the sweet expression he used only with me, and for just a moment the pain disappeared. For that brief instant, I allowed myself to believe he was still mine, and that he loved me. Everyone else in the room vanished to leave only us.

I wished that I could touch his cheek and brush back his silky black hair or trace the arch of his eyebrow. I stared into his handsome face and let those feelings overwhelm me, and in that fleeting time, I felt the ghost of our emotional connection.

It was just a mere whisper, like a scent on the breeze that blows past too quickly, bringing with it a memory of something you can't quite grasp. I wasn't sure if it was a trick of the light, a flicker of something real, or something I fabricated, but it captured all of my attention. My entire being was focused on Ren, to the point that when Mr. Kadam pulled out the needle and replaced it with a cotton ball, I realized that I'd dropped Kishan's hand completely.

Voices rushed back into my consciousness. I nodded in answer to Kishan's question and looked from my hand to Ren again, but he'd left the room. Mr. Kadam asked Kishan to assist him in placing his own device. He began explaining the difference between our technology and the others he'd described.

I only half-listened, but I did hear him say that we could access one another's tags with new cell phones, which he then distributed. He explained how the power source worked. I sat nodding slightly but snapped out of my trance when Kishan stood up several minutes later. Mr. Kadam offered me some aspirin and water. I swallowed the pills and headed to my bedroom.

Restless and uncomfortable, I lay on top of my covers unsuccessfully trying to fall asleep. My hand was sore and sleeping with it tucked under my cheek was out of the question.

I heard a soft knock on the door. "Come in."

"I heard you wiggling around and guessed that you were still awake," said Ren, closing the door softly behind him. "I hope I'm not bothering you."

I sat up and clicked on the bedside lamp. "No. It's fine. What's the matter? Do you want to go out onto the veranda?"

"No. Kishan seems to have taken up permanent residence out there."

"Oh." I looked through the window and saw a black tail hanging over the edge of the loveseat twitching lazily back and forth.

"I'll talk to him about that. He doesn't need to babysit me. I'm perfectly safe here."

Ren shrugged. "He likes to watch over you."

"So what did you want to talk about?"

He sat down on the edge of my bed. "I . . . I'm not sure exactly. How's your hand?"

"It stings. How's yours?"

"Mine's healed up already." He held up his hand for inspection.

I took his hand in mine and studied it. I couldn't even tell anything was under his skin. He wrapped his fingers around mine briefly. I blushed, and he brushed the backs of his fingers lightly against my warm cheek, which caused my skin to burn even hotter.

"You're blushing."

"I know. I'm sorry."

"Don't be sorry. It's . . . quite becoming."

I sat very still and watched his expression as he concentrated on my face. He lifted his hand and touched a strand of my hair. He trailed his fingers down the length of it. I sucked in a breath, and he did too—but for a different reason. A bead of sweat trailed from his forehead down his temple when he pulled back.

"Are you alright?"

He closed his eyes and took a deep breath. "It's worse when I touch you."

"Then don't touch me."

"I need to get past this. Give me your hand."

I placed my right hand in his, and he covered it with his left. He closed his eyes and held my hand for a full minute. I felt a light tremor in his arm as he cupped my hand gently between his. Finally, he let go.

"Is it time for you to change back to a tiger?"

"No, I have time left. I can remain in human form for twelve hours now."

"Then what is it? Why are you shaking?"

"I don't know. It feels like something's burning me when I touch you. My stomach cramps, my vision blurs, and my head throbs."

"Try sitting over there." I pointed to the couch.

He stubbornly sat on the floor with his back to the bed and brought up a knee to rest his elbow on.

"Is that better?" I asked.

"Yes. The burning is gone but the blurry vision, headache, and stomach heaving is still there."

"Do you feel pain when you're in another part of the house?"

"No, only touching you causes the blistering pain. Seeing you or hearing you brings on the other symptoms in varying degrees. If you're sitting far enough away, it's barely a twinge. It's merely uncomfortable, and I have to fight the urge to get away. Holding your hand or touching your face is like handling red hot coals."

"When you first came back and we talked, you put my foot in your lap. Didn't that hurt?"

"Your foot was on a pillow. I touched it for only a few seconds, and I was in so much pain at the time anyway that I barely noticed more."

"Let's test it. Stand over there by the bathroom door, and I'll go to the other side of the room."

He moved.

"So right now, how do you feel?"

"I feel like I need to get out of here. The discomfort has lessened, but the longer I stay, the worse it will get."

"Is the need to leave a creepy feeling, like you need to run to save your life?"

"No. It's a desperation that builds . . . like when you hold your breath underwater. It's fine at first, maybe even nice, but soon it feels like my lungs are screaming for air, and it's all I can do not to claw my way to the surface."

"Hmm, maybe you have PTSD."

"What's that?"

"Post-traumatic stress disorder. It's a condition you get when you've been exposed to terrible trauma and high stress levels. Soldiers in combat usually have it. Remember when you told Kishan that when you heard my name, all you could picture was Lokesh torturing you, questioning you?"

"Right. There's still some of that, I guess. But now that I know you better I don't associate you with him as much anymore. I can distance that from you now. It wasn't because of you that it happened."

"Part of your symptoms with me might still be related to that. Maybe you need a therapist."

Ren chuckled, "Kelsey, first of all, a therapist would put me in an asylum for claiming I was a tiger. Second, I'm no stranger to bloody battles or pain. It wasn't the first time Lokesh has tortured me. It was definitely an experience I wouldn't want to go through again, but I know that you are not to blame."

"It doesn't make you less of a man to ask for help once in a while."

"I'm not trying to be heroic about it if that's what you're getting at. If it makes you feel better, I've already started talking with Kishan about it."

I blinked. "Has he been helpful?"

"Kishan is . . . surprisingly sympathetic. He's a different man now. He said he's changed because of you. You've influenced him. Brought out a side of him I haven't seen since our mother died."

I nodded. "He's a good man."

"We've talked about many things. Not just about Lokesh but about

our past too. He told me about Yesubai and about how the two of you have become close."

"Oh." For a panicked moment, I wondered if Kishan had shared other things with Ren, things like maybe his *feelings*. I wasn't sure I wanted to broach that subject, so I changed it. "I don't want you to feel pain or suffer when you're near me. Maybe it would be better for you to avoid being around me."

"I don't want to avoid you. I like you."

"You *do*?" I couldn't help but smile.

"Yes. I imagine that's why I dated you," he said dryly. He slid down to the floor and rested his back against the bathroom door. "Let's see how long I can last. Come closer."

Obediently, I took a few steps forward. He gestured to me again. "No. Closer. Sit on the bed."

I got on the bed and watched his face for pain. "Are you okay?"

"Yes." He stretched out his long legs and crossed them at the ankles. "Tell me about our first date."

"Are you sure?"

"Yes. It's tolerable now."

I scooted to the edge of the bed farthest away from him, crawled under the covers, and put my pillow in my lap. "Okay, our first date would probably be the one you tricked me into."

"When was this?"

"Right after we left Kishkindha. In that restaurant at the hotel."

"The restaurant? Is that the one right after I got six hours back?"

"Yes. What do you remember about that?"

"Nothing, except eating dinner for the first time in centuries in a nice restaurant with a table full of food. I felt . . . happy."

"Ha! Well, I imagine you *did* feel happy. You were very smug, and you flirted shamelessly with the waitress."

"Did I?" He rubbed his jaw. "I don't even remember the waitress."

I snorted. "How is it you always know the right things to say even when you can't remember anything?"

He grinned. "Must be a gift. So about the waitress . . . was she pretty? Tell me more."

I described our date and how we'd fought over dinner. I told him about how he'd ordered a feast and tricked Mr. Kadam into bringing me there. I described how handsome he looked, about how we'd argued, and how I'd stomped on his foot when he winked at the waitress.

"What happened after dinner?"

"You walked me back to my room."

"And?"

"And . . . nothing."

"Didn't I at least kiss you goodnight?"

"No."

He raised an eyebrow. "That doesn't sound like me."

I laughed. "It's not that you didn't want to. You were punishing me."

"Punishing you?"

"In a way. You wanted me to admit my feelings."

"And you didn't?"

"No. I'm pretty stubborn."

"I see. So the waitress flirted with me, huh?"

"If you don't stop grinning at the thought of the waitress, I'm going to punch your arm and make you physically sick."

He laughed. "You wouldn't."

"I would."

"I'm too fast for you to even come close."

"Want to bet?"

I crawled across the bed while he watched me with an amused expression. I leaned over the side, made a fist with my good hand, and swung, but he quickly spun away, got to his feet, and was now standing at the foot of the bed. Getting off the bed, I walked around the side, trying to corner him. He laughed softly and motioned me closer. I stalked toward him slowly.

He stood his ground with a soft smile of confidence and let me approach him. When I was five steps away, he lost his smile. At three steps, he grimaced. At one step, he groaned and staggered. He moved several feet away and clutched the back of the couch for support as he took some deep breaths.

"I think that's all I can handle tonight. Sorry, Kelsey."

I took several steps backward and said softly, "I'm sorry too."

He opened the door, and gave me a small smile. "I think it was worse this time because I touched your hand for so long. The pain built up too quickly. Normally, standing next to you doesn't affect me so strongly."

I nodded.

He grinned. "Next time I'll just have to remember to touch you at the end of the evening. Goodnight."

"Goodnight."

A few days later, our tiger's curse adventure started up again. We set off to visit the shaman Phet who had finally replied to Mr. Kadam's courier and indicated that he wanted to see "Tigers, Kahl-see, and Durga's special gifts." He was adamant that just the three of us make the journey.

Although I didn't voice the thought, I hoped Phet, with his odd, mystical ways and herbal potions, would be able to reverse Ren's memory loss.

Even though Ren and I were on much better footing and both brothers seemed to get along since our last road trip, I still felt a bit uneasy about being trapped in a small space with two hot-headed tigers.

Well, if they act up, I'll just blast them with a little lightning burn. That'll teach them not to fight when I'm around, I thought with a grin and stepped into the morning sunshine.

The men were standing by the newly washed and gassed-up Jeep when I walked out the front door. Mr. Kadam placed the backpack full of weapons on the backseat, winked at me, and hugged me. I swung another bag containing my grandmother's quilt, which had so far proven to be lucky, next to our weapons.

We were all wearing hiking boots and smooth seamless cargo pants that Ren had made with the Divine Scarf. He had looked up styles on the Internet and had the Scarf create them in multiple colors. He claimed my apple-green shirt would protect my body from UV rays and could wick moisture away and be breathable at the same time. I had to admit the shirt was comfortable, and to show him how much I liked it, I had twisted my hair into two long French braids and tied an apple-green ribbon to the bottom of both tails.

Kishan wore a brick-red shirt of the same fabric, but it had a pocket on the side seam, while Ren wore a seamless cerulean-blue shirt that clung to his muscular frame. He was still thin, but he'd started to gain weight back in the weeks he'd been home, and his daily workouts with Kishan were showing results. It obviously didn't take long for his muscles to make a comeback.

"Can you even breathe in that shirt, Ren?" I teased lightheartedly. "You probably could have gone a size up."

Ren replied, "The shirt is tight so it doesn't inhibit movement."

My snort turned to a giggle. Then, spurred on by Kishan, the giggle changed to loud peals of laughter.

"It's not like there are any pretty waitresses out there in the jungle, Ren. There's no reason for you to show off your muscles."

Still laughing, Kishan claimed the driver's seat.

As I grabbed the door handle, Ren leaned over and murmured in my ear. "In case you didn't notice, your shirt is pretty tight too, Kelsey."

My mouth dropped open.

"And there it is."

I punched him on the arm and hissed, "There *what* is?"

He winced and rubbed his arm, but grinned. "Your lovely blush."

He hopped into the car and playfully shoved Kishan aside so he too could listen to Mr. Kadam's driving instructions along with his plea that Kishan maneuver carefully and not crash the car.

I got in the back and clicked on my seatbelt, deciding to ignore the brothers' antics. They tried to bring me into the conversation, but I paid no attention to them, burying my nose in a book instead.

They talked the entire way, and I was fascinated by their conversation. I'd never heard them speak to one another so . . . *civilly* before. Ren told Kishan about the first time we'd visited Phet and politely asked me to fill in the blanks. He remembered a lot of it. He just somehow forgot anything that applied to me.

I spoke of the amulet around my neck, the henna hand tattoo that Phet had given me, and of how we figured out it gave me the power to access the mythical cities. Ren didn't remember that at all and had no idea how he got into places with me out of the picture. He just drew a blank.

By the time we arrived at the Yawal Sanctuary, Ren was pretty desperate to get out of the car and away from me. He took off on foot, walking through the trees.

Kishan watched him go and reached around me to grab the big backpack with all the weapons. He slid it over his shoulders before he locked the Jeep.

"Shall we?"

"Sure." I sighed. "He's pretty far ahead now, isn't he?"

"Yes. Not too far though. I can easily follow his trail."

We walked silently for a few minutes. Teak trees loomed over us, which was nice, because they provided shade from the hot sun.

"We'll hike to Suki Lake and then have lunch and rest during the hottest part of the day."

"Sounds good."

I listened to the crunch of my steps as I walked over the bracken covering the jungle floor. Kishan was a silent, steady presence beside me.

"I miss this," he said.

"Miss what?"

"Hiking through the jungle with you. It's peaceful."

"Yeah, when we're not running from things."

"It's nice. I miss being alone with you."

"I hate to break it to you, but even now, we're not alone."

"No. I know that. Still, it's more alone than I've been with you in weeks." He cleared his throat. "I heard you the other night when Ren came to your room."

"Oh. Then you know he gets sick around me. He can't touch me."

"I'm sorry. I know it causes you pain."

"More like it causes him pain."

"No. He's only hurting physically. You're hurting emotionally. It's difficult to go through that. I just wanted you to know that I'm here if you need me."

"I know you are."

Kishan reached over and took my hand as I looked up into his golden eyes and asked, "What's that for?"

"I wanted to hold your hand. Not everybody cringes in pain when touching you, you know."

"Thanks."

He smiled and pressed a kiss on the back of my hand. We walked another couple of hours in silence, holding hands the entire time. I reflected again on the differences between Kishan and Ren. Ren was always talking or writing. He liked to think out loud. He said that not communicating was the most frustrating thing about being a tiger.

In Oregon, Ren would bombard me with questions every morning. He'd answer questions I'd long forgotten and talk about things he'd been thinking about all afternoon as a tiger and couldn't tell me.

Kishan was the opposite. He was still, silent. He liked to just *be*, just *feel*, just *experience* the things around him. When he drank a root beer float, he delighted in the experience and gave 100 percent of his attention to it. He soaked in his environment, and was happy keeping to himself.

I was comfortable with both men. I could appreciate the quiet and the nature more with Kishan. But with Ren near, I was so busy talking with him and, *I'll admit*, staring at him that everything else diminished.

As Suki Lake came into view, we found Ren standing at the water's edge skipping pebbles across the surface. He turned to us with a smile and saw our clasped hands. His grin faltered briefly, but then he teased me and smiled again. "It's about time you two caught up. You're slower than honey in the refrigerator. I'm starving. What's for lunch?"

I shrugged off my backpack. My shirt was stuck to my skin. I peeled it away and crouched down to unzip the pack. "What would you like?"

Ren crouched down next to me. "I don't care. Surprise me."

"I thought you didn't like my cooking."

"Nah. I like it fine. I just didn't like all of you staring at me while I ate, expecting each bite to jar a memory. In fact, I wouldn't mind some of those chocolate-peanut butter cookies."

"Okay. Kishan? How about you?" I shaded my eyes and looked up at him. He was watching Ren.

"Just make me the same thing you make him."

The brothers went off to throw pebbles across the lake and I could hear them laughing as they competed with each other. I asked the Golden Fruit to create a picnic basket for us filled with lemonade; fresh hot biscuits with butter and an assortment of jams and marmalades; a cold pasta salad with olives, tomatoes, carrots, and a lemon vinaigrette; a giant box of tangy Hawaiian BBQ chicken; and my chocolate-peanut butter cookies.

I used the Divine Scarf to create a red-and-white-checked blanket and spread it under a tree. Our picnic was ready.

"Lunch is served!" I shouted.

The brothers wasted no time. Kishan reached for the chicken, and Ren, the cookies. I smacked their hands away and handed each one a bacterial wipe.

Kishan grumbled, "Kells, I ate my food raw off the ground for three hundred years. I really don't think a little dirt's going to kill me."

"Maybe not, but clean hands make me feel better."

I handed them the giant box of chicken and took a biscuit out of the basket, buttered it, and spread marionberry preserves over it. Leaning back against the tree, I watched the dappled sunshine through the leaves as I slowly ate my biscuit.

"How far to Phet's? It only took Ren and me a day or so to hike out there last time."

"We'll have to sleep in the jungle tonight," Kishan answered. "We're on the far side of Suki Lake."

"Oh. Hey! Save some chicken for me!" I cried as the box was quickly emptying. "How can you two wolf down that much chicken in just a couple of minutes?"

"Serves you right for staring into space," Ren said.

"I wasn't staring into space. I was appreciating the environment."

"I noticed. Gave me a good opportunity to 'appreciate the environment' myself," he smirked, teasing me.

I kicked his foot. "You should have at least saved me *something*."

Ren grinned and handed me one of the last drumsticks. "What did you expect? Two or three *tiny* chickens to feed two hungry tigers? We need something at least the size of . . . what would you say, Kishan?"

"I'd say something the size of a small buffalo."

"A small buffalo *would* be good or maybe a goat or two. Did you ever eat a horse?" Ren asked.

"Nah, too stringy."

"What about a jackal?"

"Nope. Killed several though. They liked to hang around and wait for me to be done with my kill."

"Boar?"

"At least one a month."

"What about a . . . are you okay, Kelsey?"

"Can we change the topic of conversation?" The chicken leg drooped in my fingers. I stared at it and imagined the animal it used to be. "I don't think I can eat this anymore. In fact, no more talk about your kills at the dinner table. It's bad enough I had to see you two hunt."

Ren chewed and teased, "Now that I think about it, you're just about snack-size. Don't you think so, Kishan?"

Kishan studied me with a teasing glint in his eye. "I've often thought Kelsey would be fun to hunt."

I glared at Kishan. He bit into a biscuit and winked.

Ren pulled his knees up to his chest and laughed. "What do you say, Kelsey? Want to play hide-and-seek with the tigers?"

"I don't think so," I said haughtily as I carefully cleaned my fingers with another wipe.

"Aw, come on. We'd let you have a head start."

I leaned back against the tree trunk. "Yes, but the question remains . . . what would you do when you caught me?"

Kishan buttered another biscuit while he tried unsuccessfully to hide a smile.

Ren leaned back on his elbows and tilted his head as if seriously considering the question. "I guess that would be up to the tiger that caught you. Wouldn't you say, Kishan?"

"She won't run," he said.

"You don't think so?"

"No." Kishan stood and suggested we walk another hour or two then set up camp for the evening. He crouched down next to me and touched my shoulder. "It's pretty hot now. Let me know when you get tired," he said and walked off into the jungle to find the trail.

"Kishan's right. I won't run," I affirmed as I sipped my lemonade.

Ren sighed. "That's too bad. Most of the time the fun is in the chase, but I suspect with *you* the capture would be equally interesting." He stretched out a finger and brushed it against my cheek. "Made you blush again."

"I suspect it's a sunburn," I said and glared.

He stood and offered his hand to pull me up. Once upright, I let go immediately.

Grabbing the box of cookies, Ren said softly, "It's *not* a sunburn."

He swung my backpack onto his shoulders and strode off after Kishan. With nothing to carry, I mentally instructed the Golden Fruit and the Divine Scarf to make our picnic scraps disappear and trotted after Ren.

We hiked another two hours before I had to call it quits. Ren leaned up against a tree a few feet away, and Kishan used the Scarf to create a small tent.

"That's not big enough for two tigers, Kishan."

"We don't need to sleep next to you, Kells. It's hot. We'll just make you miserable."

"I don't mind it, really."

Kishan wet a cloth and touched it to my face.

"That feels good," I said gratefully.

"You're overheated. I shouldn't have made you walk so far in one day."

"I'll be fine. Maybe I should make up a magic milk bath with the Golden Fruit, huh?" I laughed.

Kishan considered and grinned. "A giant bowlful of milk with you in the middle might be a little too much for us cats to resist."

I smiled but was too exhausted to come up with a flip response.

"I want you to relax now, Kelsey. Take a nap."

"Okay." I went into my tent to bathe my arms and the back of my neck with the wet cloth. The tent was so stifling, I was soon back outside. The two tigers—one black and one white—were resting in the shade of a tree nearby. I heard the soft gurgle of a stream. The heat was definitely making me drowsy.

I sat down between the tigers with my back to the tree. After my head dropped for the third time, I cushioned it on Kishan's soft back and fell asleep.

Fur tickled my nose. I mumbled and turned my head. I heard the call of a bird, blinked open my eyes, and saw Kishan sitting with his back against the tree, watching me quietly. He was barefoot and wearing the black clothes that appeared every time he changed back from a tiger.

"Kishan?" I lifted my head, confused, knowing I had fallen asleep on his soft, sable fur. My hand was pressed against Ren's white shoulder. "Ren?" I quickly scooted back next to Kishan, who put his arm around my shoulders. "Ren? I'm sorry! Did I hurt you?"

I watched as Ren's tiger body morphed into his human frame. He pushed up from all fours into a crouch. The late afternoon sun glinted off his white shirt while he considered me musingly. "It didn't hurt."

"Are you sure?"

"Yes. You moved in your sleep. It didn't burn or cause me any pain at all."

"How long?"

"A little over two hours."

"You didn't feel the need to escape? To get away from me?"

"No. It felt . . . good. Maybe I need to be a tiger around you more often."

He smiled, switched back into a tiger, walked up to me, and stuck his nose in my face. I laughed and awkwardly reached up behind his ear and scratched. He made a rumbling sound in his chest and collapsed at my side, twisting his neck so I could reach the other ear.

Kishan cleared his throat, stood, and stretched. "Since the two of you are . . . getting reacquainted, I'm going to stretch my legs a little, maybe do a little stalking just for fun."

I stood up and put my palm on his cheek. "Don't get caught in a trap."

Kishan lifted his hand, placed it on top of mine, and smiled. "I'll be fine. I'll be back in an hour or two around sundown. You can practice tracking me on the new cell phones if you want."

Kishan morphed into the black tiger. I stroked his head briefly before he ran into the jungle.

I settled down next to Ren with the cell phone tracker. It took me the better part of an hour to figure out how it worked. The screen looked like a Google map. I was the dot marked *Ke*. Ren was *R*. Kishan was the *Ki* dot, and I could see his blip move around the screen. He was about two miles away, quickly moving east.

Widening the map, I figured out how to zoom in on Mr. Kadam and Nilima's location. If I clicked on one of their dots, a small window popped up telling me the exact latitude and longitude, as well as their vital signs. *Pretty cool little device.*

I petted Ren's fur absently and explained how everything worked. His ears flicked back and forth attentively. Then suddenly he sprang to his feet and stared at the darkening jungle.

"What? What is it?"

Ren changed to a man. "Go inside the tent and zip it up."

"It doesn't have zippers. The Scarf can't make them. What's out there?"

"A cobra. Hopefully it will move on and leave us alone."

I went into the tent while he switched back to the tiger.

Ren padded in front of the tent and waited. I peeked out and saw a giant black-and-olive green snake slither out of the jungle. Its head was disproportionately bigger than its body. When it saw Ren, it stopped to taste the air. Ren growled softly, and the snake's head shot up, which showed the pale yellow skin of its belly. As its hood opened and it hissed a warning, I realized I was looking at a king cobra.

Ren didn't stir. The snake would likely move on if we were quiet. It slowly lowered its head and slithered forward a few more inches, but then I saw Ren shake his head just before a loud tiger sneeze tore through his body. The snake lifted its upper body again and spat twin jets of poison from its fangs about nine feet. The stream didn't hit Ren's eyes, fortunately, or it probably would have blinded him. The cobra moved a bit closer and tried again.

"Ren! Move back! It's aiming for your eyes!"

Something moved in my bag. It was another snake! A golden head slipped through the tiny gap in my backpack and shot out of the tent.

Fanindra?

Ren backed up, and I untied a couple of knots so he could come into the tent with me. We watched from inside.

Fanindra wound her way right up to the king cobra, raised her head, and opened her hood. Her jeweled emerald eyes twinkled despite the diminishing sunlight. The king cobra swayed back and forth, tasted the air, and then lowered his head under hers. She slowly dropped her head to rest it on top of the cobra's, which ran its head down the length of her body, turned, and slid off quickly through the jungle. Fanindra returned to the tent, wound her body into a coil, tucked in her head, and became inanimate.

Ren changed to a man. "We got lucky. That was an angry snake with an attitude."

"She calmed him down pretty quickly."

The tent had become dark. Ren's blue eyes and smile flashed in the dimness. I felt a light touch on my jaw. "Pretty women have that effect on men."

He changed back into a white tiger and sat at my feet.

Kishan soon returned and made a throaty, rattling sound as he entered the camp. After changing from a tiger to a man, he ducked his head into the tent. "Why are you guys hiding?"

I stepped outside and told him about the snake. "What was that noise you just made?" I asked as I started to prepare dinner.

Ren switched to a man and sat across from me. I handed him a plate as he answered for Kishan. "It's called chuffing. It's a tiger hello."

I blinked and looked at Ren. "You never did that."

He shrugged. "Never wanted to, I guess."

Kishan grunted. "Is that what it's called?" He elbowed Ren. "Now I guess I know what all those lady tigers were saying. Where did you learn that?"

"The zoo."

"Huh."

Ren grinned. "So . . . you and lady tigers, eh? Is there something you want to share, Kishan?"

Kishan shoved a forkful of dinner into his mouth and mumbled, "How about I share my fist with your face?"

"Wow. Sensitive. I'm sure your lady tiger friends were all very attractive. So am I an uncle?"

Kishan growled angrily and set down his plate. He morphed into the black tiger and roared.

"Alright. That's enough," I threatened. "Ren, do you want me to share your white tiger breeding program story with Kishan?"

Ren paled. "You know about that?"

I smiled naughtily. "Yes."

Kishan switched back, picked up his plate, and smiled. "Please go on, Kells. Tell me all about it."

"Fine," I sighed. "Let's get this all out in the open. Kishan, did you ever engage in any . . . promiscuous activities with female tigers?"

"What do you *think*?"

"Just answer the question."

"Of course not!"

"That's what I thought. Ren, I already know you didn't either, though the zoo tried very hard to get you to breed. Now no more teasing or fighting about that subject, or I'll shock you with lightning. I expect you both to be on your best off-the-leash behavior." I grinned. "Hmm . . . perhaps we should invest in shock collars for the two of you. Nah, better not. It would be *way* too tempting for me."

They both snorted but soon settled down and had about five plates of dinner each.

After we ate, Kishan started a fire to keep animals away, and I shared the story of the lion and the mouse but changed it to a tiger with a porcupine quill. This led to a conversation about hunting and the brothers' greatest kill stories, during which I squirmed and tried to ignore them.

As we watched the sunset, Kishan put his arm around me and described the changes he could feel in the jungle as day turned to night. It was fascinating but also frightening to know just how many creatures began to move through the trees at sundown.

Later that sweltering evening, I climbed into my tiny tent and lay down on top of my bedroll, twisting the lighter blanket around me mummy-style.

Ren ducked his head in to check on me and laughed. "Do you always do that?"

"Only when camping."

"You know bugs can still get in there."

"Don't say that. I like to live in ignorance."

I heard his soft laugh as he knotted the ties for me.

After I'd spent a restless hour tossing back and forth, Kishan appeared at my tent door. "Can't sleep?"

I leaned up on my elbow. "I'd really prefer to have a tiger near me. It helps me sleep in the jungle."

Kishan sighed. His golden eyes shone in the moonlight. "Alright, scoot over."

I happily shifted to made room for Kishan. He switched into a black tiger and pressed his body up against my back. I'd just settled down when I felt a wet nose on my cheek. Ren had squeezed his giant body into the miniscule space between the tent wall and me and lay down— half on top of me.

"*Ren!* I can't breathe. And my arm is trapped under you."

He rolled over and licked my shoulder. I pushed his heavy body and twisted away.

Exasperated, I said, "Divine Scarf, can you make the tent big enough for all of us, please?"

I felt the tent shake lightly and heard the whisper of threads as they

shifted. A short time later, I was pressed comfortably between both my tigers. I rolled to one side, kissed Kishan on top of his furry head, and petted his neck. "Goodnight, Kishan."

Then I rolled to the other side and came face-to-face with my blue-eyed white tiger. I patted his head and said goodnight before closing my eyes. Soon I felt fur tickling my nose. Ren's head was pressed up against my face. I knew what he wanted.

"Fine." I kissed his head too. "Goodnight, Ren. Go to sleep."

He started purring and closed his eyes. I closed mine too and smiled into the darkness.

3

phet

the next morning, we decided to set out early. The temperature had dropped overnight, and the jungle was relatively cool and fragrant. I took a deep breath, stretched, and inhaled the spicy, sweet smell of the olibanum trees. After breakfast, Kishan headed off into the jungle to dress in the new clothes he'd created with the Divine Scarf.

Ren stirred the cold black ashes of our fire with a long stick. I stood a good enough distance away so my presence didn't bother him. This new "being friends" thing was awkward. I wasn't really sure how to talk to him. This is who Ren was before me. I wanted him to be like *my* Ren. In many ways he was. But how can you be the same person with a chunk of your life missing?

Ren was still charming, kind, and sweet. He still loved all the same things, except he wasn't as self-assured. Kishan had always been the follower and Ren the leader, but their roles were now reversed. Kishan was confident; he had direction. Ren had been left behind, like he no longer had a place in this century.

Ren didn't seem to know who he was anymore or how he fit into this world. It was startling for me to realize that his sense of belonging was gone. He didn't seem to want to write poetry anymore. He seldom played his guitar. He read literature only when encouraged by Mr. Kadam and me. He'd lost his sense of self, his conviction.

In making decisions, Ren didn't seem to care about much of anything and was happy to do whatever or go wherever Kishan wanted. Visiting Phet was just an activity rather than a way to get his memory back or break the curse. Ren didn't resist it, but he wasn't pursuing it either. It was sobering to recognize that losing me had changed him that dramatically. I was worried about him.

I crouched down across from him and smiled. "Aren't you going to change clothes too? We've got another full day of hiking planned."

Ren threw the stick into the fire circle and looked up at me. "No."

"Okay, but your bare feet aren't going to feel too good after a while. The jungle is full of sharp rocks and prickly thorns."

He walked over to the backpack, took out a tube of sunscreen and handed it to me. "Put this on your face and arms. You're turning pink."

I dutifully started rubbing it into my arms and was surprised to hear him say, "I think I'll be a tiger today."

"What? Why would you do that? Oh. It's probably more comfortable on your feet. I don't blame you. If I had the option, I'd probably be a tiger too."

"It's not because of the hiking."

"No? Then why?"

At that moment, Kishan emerged from the jungle with his hair slicked back. Ren took a step closer as if he wanted to say something more, but Kishan's appearance caught my attention.

"No fair! You took a bath?" I asked with only a tiny hint of jealousy in my voice.

"There's a decent stream out there. Don't worry. You'll have a nice bath when we get to Phet's."

I smeared sunscreen across my nose. "Okay." I smiled in anticipation at the thought. "I'm ready, then. Lead on, Lewis and Clark."

I turned to Ren, who had switched into a tiger and sat watching the

two of us. Kishan raised an eyebrow and worked the muscles of his jaw as he stared at his brother.

"Is something wrong?" I asked him.

Kishan turned to me with a smile and offered his hand. "Nothing at all."

I took it, and we started off. We'd walked only a minute or two when I felt Ren's furry body brush against my other hand. The thought occurred to me that Ren might be more comfortable as a tiger, much as Kishan had been for all those years. I bit my lip, worrying, and massaged the ruff of Ren's collar, then pushed the thought to the back of my mind and told Kishan all about frankincense.

We walked all morning and then stopped to rest and eat. After napping through the hot afternoon, we hiked another couple of hours and finally came upon Phet's clearing. The shaman was outside working in his garden. He was on his hands and knees, pulling weeds and talking to his plants as he carefully tended them.

Before I even called out a greeting, I heard him holler, "Hallo, Kahlsee. Joyous meetings happen with you!"

Kishan stepped over Phet's stone wall, then lifted me over, and set me gently down on the other side. Ren leapt over easily next to us.

I rushed up to the garden. "Hello, Phet! It's so nice to see you too!"

Phet peered at me over a lettuce plant and cackled with delight. "Ah! My flower grows hardy and strong."

He stood up, dusted off his hands, and embraced me. A small puff of dust floated into the air. He adjusted his robe and shook it out. Clumps of rich, fertile dirt fell off the front where he'd been kneeling.

Phet was about my height but his back was hunched, probably due to age, so he appeared shorter. I could clearly see the shining bald spot gleaming in the center of his wiry bird's nest of unruly gray hair. He looked at Kishan's hiking boots and let his gaze travel slowly up Kishan's tall frame until his shrewd eyes stopped at the younger brother's face.

"Considerably sized man travels by you." He took a step to stand toe-to-toe with Kishan, put his hands on Kishan's shoulders, and tilted his head up as he peered into Kishan's golden eyes.

Kishan patiently withstood Phet's scrutiny.

"Ah, I see. Deep eyes. Many colors there. The father of many."

Phet turned around to pick up his garden tools while I gave Kishan a surprised expression and mouthed, "The *father* of *many*?"

Kishan shifted uncomfortably. Color flooded his neck as I elbowed him and whispered, "Hey, so what do you think he meant by that?"

"I don't know, Kells. I just met the guy. Maybe he's crazy," Kishan said nervously as if trying to hide something.

I pressed, "What? What is it? Wait a minute. You're not *already* a father, are you? Did you and Yesubai—"

"No!"

"Huh. I've never seen you look so disconcerted before. There's something you're not telling me. Well, doesn't matter. I'll weasel it out of you sooner or later."

He leaned over and whispered in my ear, "I eat weasels for breakfast."

I whispered back, "I'm pretty wily. You won't catch me."

He grunted in response.

Phet chanted singsong, "Crazy, crazy. Lazy, daisy," then hummed happily as he ducked into his hut.

"Come, come, Kahl-see," Phet announced. "Talk time."

Ren changed to a man and touched my arm briefly, but then took a few steps back. "Phet's not crazy," he said to Kishan, and then turned to me and grinned. "'Better a witty fool than a foolish wit.'"

I smiled at him and countered his Shakespeare with an African proverb. "'When the fool speaks, the wise man listens.'"

Ren bowed gallantly. "Shall we?"

Kishan grunted and shoved Ren aside. "Ladies first. After you, Kelsey."

Kishan put his hand on my back and ushered me inside, not moving it from my waist. I got the distinct impression he was trying to prove something. I turned to see Ren grinning good-naturedly as he followed us in and sat on the bed.

Bustling around in the kitchen, Phet began making us a meal. I tried to tell him it wasn't necessary, but he insisted and soon set large platters filled with a spicy vegetable stir-fry and eggplant fritters on the table. Kishan filled a plate for me before preparing his own.

I took mine to Ren, who accepted it with a cocky smile and winked. I stumbled as I walked back to the table, feeling his eyes on me. Ren sat on the bed and watched me openly as he ate by himself.

Kishan had already filled another plate for me after glaring at Ren. I thanked him and then Phet, who dismissed my gesture.

"Phet knows you coming, Kahl-see." He touched his nose and winked, "Bird's soft voice to Phet's ear. Tell me tigers approach soon nearing."

I laughed. "How did you know it was the right two tigers?"

"Birds glimpse the whole lot. Birds are knowing many thing. Say two tigers smitten. Only one garl." He laughed uproariously and then smiled and patted my cheek happily. "Be-u-ti-full flower captivate many. Beforehand petite bud. Now bud is ajar, half-blossom. Next, the rounded bloom come into flower. Then the perfect bloom and flower life complete."

I patted his brown, papery hand and laughed. "Phet, would you mind if I took a bath after dinner? I feel sticky, dirty, and tired."

"Yes. Yes. Phet talk tigers."

After the dinner dishes were cleaned, I laughed softly as I saw Phet waggle his finger in Kishan's face and point sternly at the door. Ren shot

a grin over his shoulder at me, and the two men followed Phet outside, closing the door quietly behind them. Hearing Phet direct them to take over the weeding made me smile.

Kishan had been kind enough to fill the bucket dozens of times at Phet's kitchen pump so I would have a full bath. I shrugged out of my dirty clothes and asked the Divine Scarf for new ones as I slipped into the tub. Scrubbing my skin with a bar of Phet's homemade lilac soap, I listened to him chastise the brothers as I soaped through my hair.

He was gruff with them. It sounded like he was giving them a stern lecture. Frustrated, he said, "You must take *care* fragile flower! Delicate and fine petals damage easy, bruise. Spoil it and harm it. Garden is no mischief! Rough handling, battle for flower destroy it. Cut the stem, the flower dies. Needs flourish be radiant for admire. Love is look, no pluck. Endeavor gather before harvest ready is waste energy, lost everything. Remember."

I tuned him out and enjoyed my bath, thinking that scented water beat a buttermilk bath any day. Then I remembered Kishan's milk-bath comment, which made me blush furiously.

Phet's voice carried through the walls again. *He sure is raking the guys over the coals about his flowers. Funny, I didn't notice any flowers*, I thought and sank lower into the tub.

After my thorough soak, I had the Scarf make me a couple of soft fluffy towels and wrapped one around my wet hair and the other around my body. I stepped out of the tub onto a woven bamboo mat and slipped on a set of comfortable, thin cotton pajamas. The T-shirt said:

I ♥ TIGERS

The bottoms had pictures of black and white cartoon tigers snoring peacefully away. I frowned.

I didn't remember asking the Scarf for tiger pajamas, but my thoughts must have drifted when I was creating them. I asked the

Scarf to get rid of the tigers, and the fabric shimmered as the black and white threads changed to baby blue to match the top. I created some blue cashmere socks and slipped my feet inside, sighing happily.

By the time the men came in, I was sitting on the bed with a pillow on my lap reading, my long wet hair in a braid down my back. It was dark, so I'd lit the lamp and wished up a snack from the Golden Fruit. Both Ren and Kishan made eye contact with me briefly, gave me weak smiles, and headed to the table. Their downtrodden expressions made them look like they'd just been chewed out for an hour by their grandfather. I stayed on the bed so Ren wouldn't be too uncomfortable. Phet bustled in last and hung a straw hat on a peg.

"Ah. Kahl-see. You clean? Feel refreshed and invigorated?"

"Yes. I feel 100 percent better. Thank you. I made you a snack. It's from Shangri-la."

He approached the table and sat next to the boys. I had created a tea party of Shangri-la delicacies: honey–cherry-blossom tea, buttery peach fizzy tarts, cinnamon-sugar crumble clusters, mushroom-acorn butter spread between layers of cheesy crisps, delicate berry crepes with sour cream sauce, and blueberry dip with sweet fairy crackers.

Phet rubbed his hands together, delighted, and smacked Kishan away before he could grab the peach tart. The shaman filled his plate, ate the tasty morsels with pleasure, and grinned at me with his funny gap-toothed smile.

"Ah. Phet no go Shangri-la long time. Scrumptious foodstuffs there."

Kishan asked, "Want some, Kells? Better speak up now."

"No, thank you. I'm still full from dinner. You've been to Shangri-la, Phet?"

"Yes, yes. Many year ago. Many hair ago," he cackled.

For some reason, I wasn't surprised. I closed my book and scooted forward on the bed. "So, Phet, you wanted to talk with us? Can you help Ren?"

Ren's bright blue gaze turned to me. He stared at me thoughtfully while Kishan slowly tore a crepe into pieces. Phet dusted powdered sugar off his hands.

"Phet long time thinking this. Fix maybe or maybe not. Tomorrow best time looking tiger's eyes."

"Looking into his eyes? Why do you need to do that?"

"Eye is glass. Not mirror. Inside eye is buzz like a bee. Skin is flesh? Not important." He grabbed a fistful of his wiry hair. "Hair is nothing." He smiled at me. "Teeth and tongue? No buzz. Words is no buzz. Only eye is talk."

I blinked. "Are you trying to say that the eyes are the windows of the soul?"

Phet laughed happily. "Ah! Very good, Kahl-see. Smart garl!"

He slapped the table and pointed at the boys. "I tell you, young mans. My Kahl-see vastly quick."

I stifled a snigger as Ren and Kishan nodded their heads like chastised schoolboys.

"Okay, so you want to give him a checkup tomorrow," I continued. "We brought you Durga's weapons. You asked to see them, right?"

Phet stood up, pushed in his chair, and waved his arms. "No, no. Tomorrow is time for weapon. Tonight is for gifts. Gifts for be-u-ti-full goddess."

"Oh! You want the gifts. Okay." I dug through my backpack. "It will be hard to give them up. They do come in handy. Having the Fruit means I have to carry around a lot less as we walk through weeks of jungle, plus we don't have to eat power bars all the time. But, technically they don't belong to us. They're for Durga."

I pulled the Golden Fruit and the Divine Scarf out of my backpack, set them carefully on the table, and then quickly backed away when Ren shifted uncomfortably in his seat.

Phet cupped his hands around the Golden Fruit which began to shimmer in the flickering light of the hut.

"Splendid gift. *Ama sunahara*."

He stroked the skin of the Fruit and murmured to it softly as it glowed under his attentions. Then he turned to the Scarf. He stretched out his fingers, gently touched the iridescent fabric, and said, "*Dupatta pavitra*."

The threads at the edge stretched out toward Phet's palm and began weaving between his fingers as if they were the warp on a loom. The Scarf attached itself to his hand while he cooed over and petted it, and then the colors swirled faster and faster. It sparkled and crackled until it burst like a tiny nova and the material became pure white.

He spoke to the Scarf like he had to the Fruit, murmuring words and clicking his tongue as the Scarf slowly unwound itself from his hand and resumed its resting shape. Orange, yellow, and red shapes poked through the white surface like gleaming fish bodies in a clear ocean. The colors darted more rapidly until the white was overrun and it assumed its normal form, settling on a golden orange color. The fabric seemed to vibrate or hum with contentment as he stroked it idly with his hand.

"Ah. Phet missing gifts long time. Very, very good, Kahl-see. Gift as good for you. Bestow two gift, acquire two gift."

He picked up the Golden Fruit and placed it in Ren's hands. Then he picked up the Scarf and gave it to Kishan. The Scarf immediately shifted color, turning green and black. Phet looked at the Scarf then pointedly at Kishan, who blushed and folded the Scarf, setting it on the table in front of him.

The shaman cleared his throat loudly. "Phet assign to you for a second time. Relieve, make easier for you."

"You mean you want us to keep using them?" I asked.

"Yes. Now Phet present fresh offering to you."

He stood up and gathered several herbs and jars of liquid. Placing spoonfuls of ground herbs into a cup, he trickled in several drops from different jars and then ladled in some steaming water. He stirred it slowly and sprinkled in some white granules. I couldn't really see what he was doing, but I was curious.

"Phet? Is that sugar?"

He turned to me with a gap-toothed grin.

"Sugar as sweet. Drink bitter, sugar better."

He laughed as he stirred and began humming and singing "medicine bitter, sugar better" over and over. After he was satisfied, he scooted the cup over to Kishan who, with a puzzled expression, shifted it over to Ren.

Phet clucked his tongue, "No, no, tiger of black. Is yours."

"Mine? I don't need any medicine. Ren's the one with the problem."

"Phet knows all problem. For you, this drink."

Kishan lifted the cup, sniffed it, and made a face. "What will it do to me?"

"Nothing and everything." He laughed, "Give you what most in world your desire and leave you lacking, not including what most want."

Ren was studying Phet intently. I tried to figure out what Phet meant too.

Kishan picked up the cup and hesitated, "Do I *have* to drink it?"

Phet threw up his hands and shrugged his shoulders. "You choice. Choice always drink, not drink. Eat, no eat. Love, no love." He raised a finger in the air. "But you choice, shape many."

Kishan peered into the cup and swirled the liquid then looked at me. His eyes tightened, and he lifted the cup to his lips and drank it down.

Phet nodded, pleased. "Gift one, one another give you now."

"That was a gift?" I asked.

"Yes. Two and two."

"But you gave us back the Fruit and the Scarf. You're still giving us two gifts?"

He nodded.

"If that drink was a gift for Kishan, what was it?" Ren asked.

Phet leaned back in his chair and, with an odd expression on his face, said, "*Soma.*"

Kishan began coughing violently and Ren froze.

"What's *soma*?" I asked.

Ren turned to me. "*Soma* is the Hindu version of ambrosia. It's the drink of the gods. In the modern world *soma* is also a hallucinogenic."

"*Oh.*"

Phet grunted. "My *soma* no dream."

"Does that mean he becomes a god?" I asked Phet.

The brothers were staring at Phet too.

He just shrugged his shoulders. "Phet not know everything, only some thing. Now gift other one."

He picked a jar from his shelf that had a sticky, clear, pink substance in it.

"You, white tiger, sit here."

He directed Ren to sit in the middle of the room and lean his head back. Then he scooped up a palm full of the pink goo and smeared it into Ren's hair. Ren stood up immediately.

"No! No! Phet no done. Sit, tiger!"

Ren sat and Phet hummed as he scooped another palmful and slicked Ren's hair back with it. Soon his entire head was covered with the sticky stuff, and Phet began massaging it into Ren's scalp like a bizarre hairdresser. Kishan leaned his chair back to watch with a mocking grin on his face. Ren seemed irritable. I couldn't help but laugh at him, which made him scowl even harder.

"What is this supposed to do?" he asked Phet warily.

Phet completely ignored him and was now clawing through Ren's hair like a monkey looking for nits. Blobs of pink stuff coated every inch of his scalp. Finally, Phet announced he was finished.

"Now time sleep."

"You expect me to sleep like this?"

"Yes. All night time sleep. Witness what take place mornings."

"Great."

Kishan laughed outright. Phet went to the sink to wash his hands. Ren stared at me with sullen unhappiness, like a wet dog with soap on his hair sitting in a tub staring moodily at the master who put him there. I stifled a giggle and had the Scarf make a towel. He sat there with his arms folded and a scowl on his handsome face. I approached him with the towel as a giant blob of the stuff dropped onto his nose and slid off onto his cheek.

"Here, let me help. I'll try not to touch you."

He nodded, which caused another blob to start making its way down his neck. I grabbed my comb and drew it through his black hair, slicking it all back from his face and collecting the excess goo in the towel. When that was done, I summoned another towel, wet it, and cleaned the back of his neck, his ears, and then his face, starting at his hairline, moving down his nose, and across his cheeks.

I was gentle but thorough. As I slowly swiped the towel across Ren's cheek, I absently stroked his skin with my thumb. Something inside me switched on. A tender emotion slowly rose to the surface of my mind. My hand trembled, and I froze. The room had become silent. All I could hear was the hitch in my breathing as my heart began to beat faster.

I felt him cup my wrist, and slowly, I shifted my gaze to his eyes. He stared into mine with a tender smile. I lost myself in his eyes until he softly said, "Thank you."

Abruptly, I pulled the towel away, and he let go of my wrist. I saw him rubbing his fingers with his thumb. *How long was I staring at him like an idiot?* It must have burned him terribly. Quickly, I lowered my gaze and stepped away. Everyone was watching me now. I turned my back on them and arranged the bed. By the time I turned back around, I'd composed myself.

I smiled brightly. "Phet's right. It's time for bed."

Phet clapped his hands. "Kahl-see in house. Tiger outside. Phet," he grinned, "with Scarf."

He cackled with glee and created a nice tent for himself. Then he opened the door and waited stubbornly for the tigers to leave.

Kishan touched my cheek, said, "Night, Kells," and ducked under the door awning.

Ren followed but paused at the door and gave one of his traffic-stopping smiles. My heart burned with a hopeful pain. He inclined his head roguishly in my direction and stepped outside. I heard Phet murmuring directions to both of them as they settled down for the night.

The next morning, I woke to Phet humming in the kitchen.

"Kahl-see! Awake. Eat!"

His little table was full of a variety of dishes. I joined him and scooped up fruit salad and something that looked like cottage cheese. "Where is everyone?"

"Tigers have a bath by means of river."

"Oh."

We ate in silence. Phet studied me and gently grasped my hand in both of his. He twisted it and stroked it in different places. When he touched the skin, the henna markings he had given me on our first visit surfaced and glowed red for a short time before disappearing.

"Hmm. Ah. Hmm." He picked up a slice of apple and bit into it juicily, keeping his eyes on my hand while he smacked his mouth.

"Oh, Kahl-see, you set eyes on many thing, go a long way away places."

"Yes."

He peered into my eyes.

"Are you staring into my soul?"

"Huh-uh-huh. Kahl-see extraordinarily depressing. Why damage?"

"What's my damage?" I laughed dryly. "It's mostly emotional. I love Ren, and he doesn't remember me. Kishan loves me, and I don't know what to do about that. It's one of those awful love triangles in which no one is happy. Everyone is miserable. Except for Ren, I guess. He can't remember if he's miserable or not. Any advice?"

Phet considered my question seriously. "Love resembling water. Water on all sides of us everywhere. Ice, river, cloud, rain, ocean. Some is big, some is tiny. Some good drink, some too salty. Every one usefulness for earth. For all time be in motion cycle. Necessitate water to endure. Woman like earth; need immerse water. Water with earth sculpt each other, grow.

"Earth change for river, make waterway. Lake bed know how to hold water in basin, all contain. Ice water is glacier; move earth. Rain make mudslide. Ocean make sand. Always two: earth and water. Need each other. Become one together. You be required to choose. Soon."

"What if I can't choose or don't get to choose? What if I make the wrong choice?"

"No wrong choice. Your choice."

He went to his bed and picked up two pillows. "You be fond of round pillow or square pillow?"

"I don't know. They're both pillows."

"You like round? Choose round. You like square? Choose square.

Not matter. You want sleep, use pillow. You pick rock? No! Pillow is good. Same water. You choose ice? River? Ocean? Is all good. Pick ocean, you change sand. Pick river, you grow to be silt. Pick rain, you are garden soil."

"Are you saying I choose the man based on what I want to become? What kind of life I want to have?"

"Yes. Both man put together your life special. Choose ocean or choose river. No matter."

"But—"

"No but. *Is.* Kahl-see back is sturdy. Can embrace many burden, many duty. You like earth. Your back transformation shape to be same with man your picking."

"So basically what you are trying to tell me is that Ren and Kishan are both pillows in a world of rocks and that I'd be happy with either one?"

"Ah! Smart garl!" Phet laughed.

"The only problem is . . . one of *them* is not going to be happy."

Phet patted my hand. "You no be troubled. Phet be of assistance tigers."

The brothers stomped noisily into the hut a half hour later. They both greeted me politely: Kishan squeezed my hand, and Ren nodded to me from the table.

I quietly asked Kishan, "Did it work? Does he remember?"

He shook his head no and retreated to the table to help Ren quickly polish off every dish that Phet had created. Their hair was slicked back and wet. Ren had gotten all the pink stuff out.

I smirked, thinking, *either that, or it had been absorbed into his brain overnight.*

While the brothers ate, I thought about what Phet said. *Could I*

really be happy with either one of them? Could Ren and I fall in love again? And if so, what would we do about our physical relationship? Would I ever be able to touch him again without inflicting pain? I'd never really considered a future with Kishan before. I was always so sure about my relationship with Ren. Now that his memories of us were gone, I didn't know if it was even possible to get back what we'd lost.

I caught Kishan watching me from time to time as he listened to Phet. Could Kishan have been right? Was losing Ren somehow part of my destiny? Was Kishan the person I was supposed to be with, was meant to be with? Or, as Phet said, am I just supposed to choose which one I want to be with? Which one I want to make a life with? I just didn't see how I could be happy when one of them wasn't.

After breakfast, Phet asked to see the weapons. I dug the *gada*, the *chakram*, Fanindra, and the bow and arrows out of the backpack and handed each to Kishan, who deposited them on the table. Every time his fingers brushed against mine, Kishan smiled. I smiled back, but my happy expression wavered when I saw Ren quickly look away with disappointment.

Phet studied each intently before handing it to the person Durga had originally given it to.

"How did you know?" I asked incredulously. "How did you know the bow and arrows were mine and the *gada*, Ren's?"

"Snake make clear to me."

As if in response, Fanindra uncoiled, stuck her head in the air, hood open, and stared into Phet's eyes. He began singing and moving his head. She started rocking back and forth as if under the spell of a snake charmer. When he stopped singing, she lowered her head and rested again.

"Ah, Fanindra declare be partial you, Kahl-see. You good woman and show consideration for her."

He picked up Fanindra and handed her gently back to me. I pulled a round pillow over and set her in the middle of it. *Huh. I like round pillows. I wonder which man the round pillow represents.*

Phet announced it was time to look into Ren's eyes. He pulled two chairs away from the table and set them across from each other. Ren sat in one; Phet, in the other. Kishan joined me on the bed and reached out to hold my hand. Ren's eyes darted over to us.

Phet slapped his hand. "Glimpse my eye, Tiger!"

Ren growled softly as he turned to face the old monk. Phet peered into Ren's eyes and clucked his tongue while turning Ren's head to several different angles as if Phet was adjusting the rearview mirror in a car. Finally, he was satisfied, and the two men froze in place for several minutes while Phet just stared. I bit my lip nervously as I watched.

After an uncomfortably long silence, Phet jumped up out of his chair. "Can't patch up."

I stood. "What do you mean?"

"Tiger vastly stubborn. Block me."

"Block you?" I turned to Ren. "Why would you block him?"

"I don't know."

"Phet," I asked, "can you please tell us what you know?"

Phet sighed. "Fix it the hurting of knife and cage. Evil black at this time gone. But remembrance is jam, have trigger, only white tiger be acquainted with it."

"Okay, to clarify, you were able to fix the PTSD, the pains, and memories of the torture? All the trauma of Lokesh is gone now? Can he still remember it?"

"Yes. I still remember it. I'm right here, you know," Ren grumbled.

"Okay, but Phet says he took the blackness away. Do you feel differently about it?"

He concentrated. "I don't know. I guess we'll see."

I looked at Phet again. "But his memory is still blocked? What do you mean there's a trigger?"

"Means tiger hinder himself. No from criminal one, evil one. From tiger mind. Only he be capable of fix."

"Are you saying he's deliberately doing this to himself? He's blocking his memories of me on purpose?"

Phet nodded.

I gaped at Ren, stunned. He looked at Phet dumbfounded; then knit his brows together in confusion and stared at his hands. Tears filled my eyes.

In a tiny voice, I choked out, "Why? Why would you do this to me?"

He worked the muscles of his jaw and looked up at me. His blue eyes were bright with emotion. He opened his mouth to say something . . . then closed it. I backed toward the door and pushed it open.

Ren stood. "Kelsey? Wait."

I shook my head.

"Please don't run," he softly pleaded.

"Don't follow me." I shook my head, tears dripping down my cheeks as I ran off into the jungle.

4

prophecy

I sat in the jungle with my back against a tree. I was tired of running away from emotional turmoil. The reasonable part of my brain told me that Ren most likely had a perfectly legitimate reason for purposefully forgetting me. However, there was another side that doubted him, and that voice screamed louder. It hurt. If someone had asked me before he was taken if I trusted Ren, I would have said yes. I trusted him absolutely, 100 percent. There was no question in my mind that he was sincere.

But. A negative voice picked away at me, telling me I wasn't really right for him anyway and that I should have expected this. It said that I never deserved him in the first place and that it was only a matter of time before I lost him. I'd always considered him too good to be true. I never wanted to be right, but there it was.

That he took himself out of the picture made it worse. Much worse. *How could I have been so wrong about him?* I'd been naive. I wasn't the first girl to have her heart broken, and I wouldn't be the last. I'd trusted him. I believed his professions of love.

Before the visit with Phet, I could tell myself that Lokesh had done this. That it wasn't Ren's fault. That somewhere deep inside, he still loved me. Now I knew that he deliberately wanted to forget me. He wanted to cast me aside and had somehow found a very convenient way to do it.

How nice it must be to just erase your mistake. Pick the wrong girl? That's okay. Just highlight and delete. Those pesky memories won't bother you anymore. You could sell that pill and become a billionaire. So many people have done things and been with people they'd like to wipe out of their memory. To forget completely. Expunge your memory! Buy one, get one free! Limited time offer!

After an hour of feeling sorry for myself, I returned slowly to the hut. When I walked through the door, all talking ceased. Both brothers watched me while Phet started busily grinding spices.

Ren stood and took a step toward me. I looked at him dully, and he stopped in his tracks.

"There's nothing else you can do for us, then?" I asked Phet.

Phet turned to me and tilted his head. Soberly he said, "Phet regretful. No can help this."

"Okay." I turned to Kishan. "I'd like to leave now."

He nodded and began filling the backpacks.

"Kelsey," Ren stretched out a hand and then pulled it back when I stared at it like it was a foreign object, "we need to talk about this."

"There's nothing to talk about." I shook my head and took Phet's hand. "Thank you for your hospitality and for everything you've done for us."

Phet stood and hugged me. "You no worries, Kahl-see. Don't fail to remember water and earth is contented all together."

"I remember, but I think this time I'm like the moon. No water for me."

Phet pressed his hands on my shoulders. "Is water for Kahl-see. Moon maybe, but moon pull tide anyway."

"Okay." I said softly. "Thanks for the optimism. I'm sure I'll be fine. Don't worry about me," I assured him as I hugged him back. "Good-bye."

Phet said, "Future time pay a visit you happier, Kahl-see."

"I hope so. I'll miss you. Sorry to leave so abruptly, but I'm suddenly anxious to get this curse over and done." I grabbed my backpack and headed out the door.

Kishan gathered his things quickly and caught up to me.

"*Kells,*" he started.

"Can we just walk for a while? I don't feel like talking."

His golden eyes perused my face until quietly he said, "Okay."

Before I'd taken many steps the white tiger was walking next to me, butting his head against my hand. I refused to look at him, clutched the straps of the backpack, and purposefully moved to Kishan's other side. Kishan looked at my tight expression and then at the white tiger, who fell back and walked behind us. Soon he was far back enough that I couldn't see him anymore.

I relaxed my stance and hiked without speaking and without stopping for food or rest until I couldn't walk another step. Creating a small tent with the Scarf, I fell on top of my sleeping bag, skipped dinner, and let the brothers fend for themselves. They left me alone, for which I was both grateful and disappointed, and I fell into a deep sleep.

I woke when the sky was still dark and checked my phone for the first time in days. No calls from Mr. Kadam. It was four in the morning. I didn't feel like sleeping anymore so I popped my head out of the tent and saw the weak flames of a dying fire. Neither Ren nor Kishan were around. Placing a couple more logs onto the fire, I built it up until it was crackling again and wished up a hot chocolate. I sipped my drink slowly as I stared into the flames.

"Have a nightmare?"

I whirled around. Ren was leaning against a tree. I made out his white shirt but his face was in the shadows.

"No." I stared into the flames again. "I just slept enough, that's all."

He stepped into the firelight and sat on a log across from me. The flickering flames made his golden-bronze skin glow warmly. I tried not to notice. *Why does he have to be so good-looking?* His blue eyes studied me intently.

I blew on my cocoa and looked everywhere but at him. "Where's Kishan?"

"Out on a hunt. He doesn't get to do it very often anymore, and he enjoys it."

I grunted. "Well, I hope he doesn't expect me to pick out the porcupine quills. If he gets those, he's on his own." I took another sip. "Why didn't you go with him?"

"Because I'm watching over you."

"You really don't need to. I'm a big girl. Go hunt if you want. In fact, you probably should. You're still too skinny."

"Nice to know you've been looking. I was worried you'd forgotten all about me."

I raised my eyes to his and sputtered with anger. "Forgotten all about you? *Me?* Forget about *you?* I . . . you know what? You're really starting to annoy me!"

"Good. You need to get it all out."

I set down my mug and stood. "Oh, you'd like that, wouldn't you? You'd love to have me profess my undying love for you while you laugh in my face and mock me!"

He stood too. "I'm not mocking you, Kelsey."

I threw my hands into the air. "Well, why not? You might as well. You took away everything in the world that was important to me! You plucked out my heart, squeezed it in your hands, and gave it to the monkeys to play with. I shouldn't have trusted you! What an idiot I was to believe that you actually had feelings for me. That you cared about me. That we belonged together. You're just a . . . just a square pillow. And I've recently discovered that I like round ones!"

He laughed, which irritated me even more.

"I'm a square pillow? What does that mean?"

"It means we aren't meant to be together, that's all. I should have known that you'd trounce all over my heart. All those things you said, all those poems you wrote—they meant nothing to you. When we get home, I fully intend to give back every one of your poems."

He stiffened. "What do you mean?"

"I mean, they don't matter anymore. They might as well be thrown into the fire because that's the only warmth they'll ever offer me."

"I don't believe you'd do it."

"*Watch* me."

I retreated to the tent, grabbed my journal, and quickly leafed through the pages until I found the "Pearl without Price" poem. Running to the fire, I ripped the page from my book and stared at it.

"*Kelsey.*" My brown eyes met his blue ones. "Don't."

"What difference does it make? The man who wrote this is dead at best, a pretender at worst."

"You're wrong. Just because I don't remember you now doesn't mean that what I felt for you before was a lie. I don't know why or how I did this to myself or why I forgot you. It doesn't make sense. But I can assure you that I'm not dead. I'm alive and standing right here."

I shook my head. Denying his words, I said, "You're dead to *me*," and dropped the page. I stared at it as it spun in the air. A tear coursed down my cheek as I watched the corner of the page catch on fire.

Faster than lightning, Ren grabbed the page out of the fire and crumpled the burning edge in his fist to put out the flame. He was breathing heavily, obviously upset. His hand quickly healed from the burn while I stared mutely at the charred edge of the precious poem.

"Were you always such a stubborn, blind, obtuse girl?"

"Are you calling me stupid?"

"Yes, but in a more poetic way!"

"Well, here's a poem for you. Get lost!"

"I'm already lost! That much should be obvious! Why can't you see what's right in front of you?"

"What am I supposed to see? A tiger who happens to be a prince? A man who happens to hate me so much that he purposefully erased me from his brain with a magic spell? A man who can't tolerate being in the same room with me for more than a few minutes? A man who can't stand touching me? Is that what I'm supposed to see? Because if so, then I've got a pretty good view!"

"No, you *hotheaded* girl! What you're not seeing is this!"

He grabbed me, yanked me up against his body, and kissed me. It was fiery and passionate. His lips were hot as they melded against mine. I didn't even have time to react before it was over. He backed away and bent over, clutching the trunk of a tree. He breathed heavily, and his hands shook.

I folded my arms as I watched him recover. "What exactly were you trying to prove by doing that?"

"If you have to ask, then obviously I failed in my effort."

"Okay, so you kissed me. So what? It doesn't mean anything."

"It *means* everything."

"How do you figure?"

He took a big gulp of air and leaned against the tree. "It means that I'm starting to develop feelings for you, and if I feel them now, the likelihood of me feeling them before is pretty strong."

"If that's true, then remove the block."

"I *can't*. I don't know what it is or how it got there or what this trigger might be. I was kind of hoping kissing you would do the trick. Apparently, that's not it."

"So . . . *what*? You thought you could kiss the female frog and turn her into your fairy princess? Well, I hate to burst your bubble, but what you see is what you get!"

"What on earth would make you think I wouldn't be interested in what I see?"

"I really don't want to hash that out with you again. We've been over it before even though you can't remember. However, in the short-term memory that you *do* possess, you might remember saying that Nilima was beautiful."

"Yes. I remember saying that. *So what?* How does saying that she is beautiful mean you're not?"

"It's all in the way you said it. *'Too bad I wasn't in love with Nilima . . . she's beautiful.'* Which implies I'm not. Don't you know anything about women? Never call one woman beautiful in front of another."

"I didn't. You were eavesdropping."

"The point is still valid."

"Fine! Then I'll tell you what I think, and may I go without another meal if I'm lying! *You* are beautiful."

"That train has already zoomed on by, buster, and you didn't have a ticket."

He combed his fingers through his hair in frustration. "Is there anything I can say to fix this?"

"Probably not." I put my hands on my hips. "I just can't understand why you would *do* this. If you really loved me, then why would you choose this? The most logical conclusion is that you didn't really love me. I knew you were too good to be true."

"What do you mean?"

"You said it yourself to Kishan. You couldn't imagine loving someone like me. See? Even you knew we didn't fit together. You're Mr. Perfection and I'm Miss Average. Anyone can see that, and those *were* your true feelings right after we rescued you."

He laughed bitterly. "Believe me, I am far from perfect, Kelsey, and you are no more *average* than Durga is. I barely knew you when I said those things, and you're misinterpreting my words anyway!"

"How so?"

"I . . . what I meant was . . . what I said was . . . look! You're not the same person I thought you were then."

"I'm exactly the same person!"

"No. I was avoiding you. I wasn't getting to know you. I was—"

I ripped out another page.

"*Kelsey!*" Ren ran over and yanked the journal from my hands, groaning with the effort of being so close to me. "Cut it out! Don't even *think* about burning another page!"

I grabbed the journal and tugged. "They're mine to do with as I please."

He yanked back. "You need to stop judging me based on things I said right after I got back! I was still traumatized, and I wasn't thinking coherently. I've had time to get to know you, and . . . I like you!" he yelled. "I like you enough that I think I even understand why I loved you, despite how frustrating you are!"

I pulled on my book. "You like me . . . *enough*? Enough! Well, *enough's* not good enough for me."

He wrenched the journal again. "Kelsey, what else do you *want* from me?"

I tugged again. "I *want* my old Ren back!"

He stiffened and growled, "Well, I don't know what to tell you. The old Ren may be gone forever. And . . . this new Ren doesn't want to lose you." He glowered at me sullenly, moved his hand up to my wrist, and tugged me closer this time instead of the book. Then he said, "Besides, *you* said we could start over."

"I don't think that's really possible." I gave a final tug as he let go and moved away a few steps.

Ren dropped his hands to his sides and clenched his fists. In a dangerously low voice he said, "Then *make* it possible."

"You expect too much."

"No. *You* expect too much." He took a step closer. "You're *not* being reasonable. You need to give me *time*, Kelsey."

I looked up, and we locked eyes. "I would have given you all the time in the world until Phet said you did this to yourself."

"'How poor are they that have not patience! What wound did ever heal but by degrees?'"

"Shakespeare isn't going to save you this time, Superman. Your time's run out."

He scowled. "Perhaps I should have been studying *The Taming of the Shrew*!"

"Okay, then here's your first lesson: 'My tongue will tell the anger of my heart. The door is open, sir; there lies your way.'"

"I don't need a lesson. I already know how it ends. The guy wins. 'Think you a little din can daunt mine ears?'" He crooked his finger and beckoned me closer. "In fact, come on over here and kiss me, Kate."

I narrowed my eyes. "You botched the line, and you'll find I'm not as easily won over as Katherine."

Ren's face tightened, and he threw up his hands in disgust. "Fine. You win. If you insist on giving back all my poetry then do it. But *don't* burn it."

"Fine! I'll agree not to burn it, if you agree to leave me alone for the rest of this trip."

"*Fine!* And incidentally, I don't understand how I could have believed you were a warm, affectionate, and tenderhearted person! You're obviously as prickly as a porcupine. Any man who comes close to you will end up with a face full of quills!"

"That's right! A girl needs to have *some* defenses from the men who want to devour her for lunch. Especially when those men are wild tigers on the prowl looking for trouble."

He narrowed his eyes, grabbed my hand, and nipped the inside of my wrist lightly before kissing it, though I could tell it caused him pain.

"You haven't seen just how wild I can be, *subhaga jadugarni*."

I rubbed his kiss off dramatically. "What does that mean?"

"It means . . . 'lovely witch.'"

"Flattery gets you nowhere, and a backhanded compliment gets you less than nowhere. I'm well versed in your verbal tricks."

He smiled mischievously, snickered, and dropped his gaze deliberately to my lips. "They must get me *somewhere*, or you wouldn't have a journal full of poems."

"Don't you have something to chase?"

"Sure. I'll give you a head start."

I glared at him. "Not in this lifetime, pal."

He folded his arms across his chest and grinned at me.

"Don't do that. It just makes me angrier."

I'd lied. Ren's smile didn't make me angrier. In fact, it was the opposite. It made me miss him. I felt sadness creep in around the edges, cooling my wrath down to a simmer.

"You never called me that one before."

"What? *Subhaga*? Did I have other nicknames for you?"

I paused and answered slowly, "Yes."

"What did I call you?" He tilted his head and appraised me in a mocking way. "I *probably* called you stubborn, close-minded, irritable, impatient—"

The unquenchable rage returned in a mighty blaze and burned so hot it bubbled over. I wanted to hurt him. "That's it!" I pressed my hands against his chest and shoved as hard as I could but he was immovable and just laughed at my puny efforts, so I gave him a little zap.

"Ow! Alright, kitten, you show me your claws, and I'll show you mine." He pressed both of my hands against my hips, trapping them. I

was mashed up against his chest, and his arms moved to become iron bands around my body. He kissed my neck and murmured softly, "I *knew* you couldn't wait to get your hands on me."

I gasped in outrage. "You . . . you . . . deserter!"

"If by deserter, you're asking if I'll have you for dessert, I'd consider it. Of course, I'd have to sweeten you up a bit first." He laughed as he kissed my neck again.

I pushed myself away from him, quivering with frustration—*at least, I think it was frustration.* I was seriously considering shooting enough voltage through his body to make his hair stand on end and wipe the infuriatingly smug smile off his face when Kishan crashed through the trees.

"What's all the yelling about?" Kishan asked.

"Would you please tell your sorry excuse for a brother that I'm not talking to him anymore?"

Kishan grinned. "No problem. She's not talking to you anymore." He laughed. "I'd been worried you two were getting along *too* well. I should have known better."

Ren's smile faltered. He frowned at his brother and narrowed his eyes at me. "Not talking to you is fine because at least that means I won't have to listen." With a sarcastic bow he added, "And with nothing else to say, I'll gladly accept your terms of surrender."

"I'm not surrendering *anything*, oh, Prince of the Battle of the Five Horses. And it's *fine* with me, because I don't expect you to listen to me anyway!"

"That was *Champion* at the Battle of the *Hundred* Horses!"

"Fine! Then why don't you gallop on back to the Jeep, *Champion*?"

"*Fine!* Then I will!"

I spat with barely controlled rage. "Good! And don't let the jungle hit you on the way out!"

He stared into my eyes as he stalked past me. He was breathless with anger and frustration, and, heaven help me, all I could think of was grabbing him and kissing him.

He spoke softly as I glared back at him. "I pity poor Kishan, who has to walk the rest of the way back with you."

"I'm sure he'll survive," I replied acerbically.

He glanced at Kishan, and looked his brother up and down coldly. "No *doubt*. I'll meet you back at the Jeep."

Kishan nodded, and Ren hesitated.

I folded my arms. "Well? What are you waiting for? A good-bye kiss?"

His eyes darted to my lips. "Careful what you wish for, *mohini stri*."

For a brief second, I panicked thinking he'd accept that challenge, but he tilted his head, smiled an infuriatingly knowing smile, leapt over the fire, and was gone.

Kishan stared at the hole in the forest where Ren had disappeared. Then he turned to me and put his hands on my shoulders.

"I've never seen you so angry before."

"What can I say? He brings out the best in me."

Kishan frowned. "It would appear he does."

"What did those words mean?"

"*Mohini stri*? They mean 'siren,' or 'fascinating woman.'"

I grunted. "Figures he'd take the opportunity to mock me further."

Kishan gave me a puzzled look. "I don't think he's mocking you."

"Of *course* he is. And I'm warning you right now: I'm not in the mood to start another tiger fight, so if you want to take off after him, then by all means feel free."

"Kelsey, I have no intention of leaving you alone. And I don't want to fight with you."

"Well, at least one of you is a gentleman," I muttered as I started gathering my things to leave. I picked up the crumpled poem and

smoothed the paper regretfully as I slipped my abused journal carefully into the backpack.

"Kelsey, despite what you think, Ren wouldn't have left you alone either. If I wasn't here, he would have stayed."

"Yeah. Right. I could walk off the side of a cliff for all he cares. Why are you defending him anyway? I thought you wanted him out of the picture!"

"That's not . . . exactly true."

"Oh! I see. So *Kelsey* is the one at fault. *Kelsey* misunderstands everyone's intentions. Then let me make sure I understand *your* motives. Do you still want to be with me, or don't you?"

He scowled. "You know the answer to that."

"Fine. Then now's your chance! Kiss me."

Kishan studied my face carefully and shook his head. "No."

"No? Don't you want to?"

"Yes, but I promised that I wouldn't kiss you until I knew you and Ren were over. And I don't think you are."

"Ha! Oh, I think we *are*."

"No. In fact, your little tirade proves that you're not."

I stood up on my toes as high as I could, getting as close to being nose to nose with Kishan as was possible. "*Fine*. Then neither one of you needs to walk me back."

I grabbed my backpack and left him standing in shock. I stomped through the jungle, letting my anger guide me for several moments before I slipped my phone out of my pocket and searched for Ren's dot on the map. I could see Kishan's dot following me at a distance. He was far enough back that I couldn't see or hear him, but he was near enough to close the distance if I needed him.

Walking through the jungle relatively alone was good for me. It gave me time to cool down. I was still angry and muttered to myself the entire

way, but at least my blood pressure normalized, so I didn't have to worry about having a stroke. And when I realized that I had possession of the Golden Fruit and the Scarf, I grinned wickedly thinking about the two of them starving or having to hunt. In fact, I made myself a big ice cream cone and soothed my temper with chocolate brownie and mudslide as I walked.

Several hours later, I found Ren leaning against the Jeep, which was parked in the shade of a tree. He watched me as I tromped through the undergrowth. He'd probably heard me coming for the last ten minutes. He looked behind me, surprised that I was alone, then glared, changed into the white tiger, and walked between some bushes so he wasn't in view anymore.

I studiously ignored him, sank down to the dirt with my back against the Jeep, and took a long drink of sugar-free lemonade from my canteen. I would have preferred water, but we'd run out and the Golden Fruit couldn't make plain old H_2O.

Kishan emerged from the jungle and briefly stared at me with a fathomless expression before unlocking and opening the Jeep doors. Ren emerged from the bushes and silently leapt into the backseat. I wasn't about to cozy up next to Ren so I chose the passenger seat, cranked up the air conditioning, made a pillow, and leaned my chair back. It was a very quiet ride home.

The second the Jeep stopped in front of the house, I leapt out of the car, slammed the door, and stomped inside.

"We're home, Mr. Kadam! I'm taking a shower!" I yelled and disappeared into my room.

Finally feeling refreshed and almost human again a few hours later, I whipped up a bowl of mixed fruit and a chicken salad sandwich and looked for Mr. Kadam in the peacock room.

"Mr. Kadam? I can't tell you how much I missed being around a gentlema—" I said, stopping abruptly when I saw he was with a freshly showered Ren.

"Miss Kelsey, come in," Mr. Kadam beckoned, approaching me with open arms.

I took an awkward step forward, hugged Mr. Kadam, and glared at Ren. His hair was wet and slicked back, and he was wearing a fitted V-neck shirt in dragonfly blue over a pair of straight-legged gray herringbone designer pants. He was barefoot, and he was the most gorgeous thing I'd ever seen. He folded his arms across his chest, which made his arm muscles bulge. I scowled at him.

"I'll leave you two alone," Ren said with a mocking flourish and left, deliberately brushing his arm against mine as he passed.

"I hope that hurt," I muttered quietly and heard his soft laugh as he went into the kitchen.

Mr. Kadam seemed completely oblivious of our exchange. "Miss Kelsey! Come and sit with me. I have something to show you!"

"What is it?"

"I've finally finished decoding the third prophecy, and I'd like to hear what you think," Mr. Kadam said and slid his translation across his desk.

The words were written in beautiful calligraphy. I read:

> Lustrous gems of blazon black
> Once graced her satin'd skin.
> A ruthless knave her neck ransack'd;
> The strand sank deep within.
> Now beads hide buried in the sea;
> A brave one brings them out.
> Deadly monsters bite and sting—

Too horrible to rout.
But trident wield, kamandal imbibe,
And the lady who weaves the silk
Will guide and guarantee you lay
The wreath on sea of milk.
Seek dragon kings of oceans five
From cardinal compass as you dive:
Dragon of Red—Unveils the stars that move in astral time;
Dragon of Blue—Bestows the range that straightly points the way;
Dragon of Green—Prepares the mind to see right through the clime;
Dragon of Gold—Watches the town that's hid beneath the waves;
Dragon of White—Unlocks the doors which lead to icy lights.
Take her arms and wield them well
Her unblemish'd prize to win.
Capture the string with fluid power;
Head homeward once again.
Cool India's lands with precious dew;
River, stream, the rain will fill.
The dry land and the heart renew,
Else healing pow'r is latent still.

I let the page fall gently to my lap and looked at Mr. Kadam with a newfound horror. "Dragons?" was all I could mutter.

preparation

"Dragons?" I repeated.

Mr. Kadam chuckled sympathetically. "I believe the dragons will be helpful. I don't think you have to fight them."

"I sincerely hope you're right about that. So, I assume you've looked into what some of these things are?"

"You assume correctly. Some I know, and some will need a bit more research. Would you like to assist me?"

"Definitely. It will be a good distraction for me."

"Excellent! But first tell me what Phet said."

We talked for a couple of hours. Kishan approached, saw me, and quickly departed again.

Mr. Kadam finally noticed the obvious tension. "Did the brothers do something to upset you?"

"Don't they always?" I asked dryly.

"What happened?"

I shifted nervously in my seat. "They didn't do anything, really. It's just that Ren and I argued about his amnesia. It was a really intense fight, and Kishan heard at least part of it. Phet said they were both pillows, which is true, but that doesn't make it easier."

Mr. Kadam drummed his fingers on his thigh. He should have been frustrated with my vague babblings, but he picked through my disjointed thoughts and asked, "What did Phet mean? How are they both pillows?"

"Basically, he said they were both pillows in a world of rocks, which I think means they are both good guys, and I would be happy no matter which one I choose."

"I see. It's been obvious to me that Kishan has developed feelings for you. Is this what you were fighting with Ren about?"

"No. Kishan was just . . . a convenient target. I was mad at Ren for blocking me out. For forgetting me."

"We still don't know why that happened."

"I know." I picked at the hem of my sleeve and sighed. "But my old insecurities surfaced, and I just got mad. He pushed the right buttons, which he seems to have a knack for, memory loss or not. He makes me so angry sometimes that I could just shake him."

"If he stirs that much emotion in you, then it should be obvious which one you should pick."

"Right." I sighed. "That means I should pick Kishan. I'd have a much more peaceful life with him."

Mr. Kadam leaned forward. "That's not what I meant, but that decision I will leave entirely up to you. Phet seems to believe that you cannot make a wrong choice?"

I nodded glumly.

"Hmm. That's interesting. A stress-filled visit indeed. If I might be so bold, I would encourage you to try to set aside your differences and learn to trust both of them. It will be much easier to focus on the task ahead if we all work in harmony. We are already halfway to breaking the curse. Finding Durga's third gift will be our biggest challenge yet."

I sighed and put my head in my hands. "You're right. I'll apologize to both of them for my outburst, but I'm waiting until tomorrow. That will give me time to cool off."

"Good. Now what would you like to have for dinner?"

"How does humble porcupine pie sound?"

He laughed. "Don't tell me. I don't want to know. Shall we check the cupboards for porcupine then, Miss Kelsey?"

I laughed. "I wonder what spices go well with quill soup. I get to grind this time."

"It's a deal."

The next morning, I found Kishan doing chin-ups in the gym, which was his favorite place to be other than in the kitchen or on my veranda. I watched him through the window, covertly admired his muscles, and considered what Phet had told me.

Could I really learn to love Kishan? It wouldn't be too difficult. What would be difficult would be forgetting about Ren. Maybe I never would. My parents only dated each other. Do you ever forget your first love? How do people do that anyway? Could I look at Kishan with the same affection I felt for Ren?

I guess lots of people do. People all over the world can move on from one love to another. I just never figured I'd be one of them. I thought once I'd found Ren, I'd never have to look at another guy again. Phet seems to feel a choice is looming in the near future. I bit my bottom lip. *There's still hope that Ren will somehow remember me. But what if he doesn't? What if he can't ever touch me again without pain? Do I just give up and say, "Thanks for the memories"? How can I be with one when the other is still around?*

I heard a grunt from Kishan, and my eyes drifted back to him.

What's my problem? Poor me. Having to pick between two of the best looking guys on the planet. Good, sweet, honest men who both truly care for me. Both handsome princes. Kishan would be good to me. Would love me. A girl could do worse. Much worse. I should remember that.

I opened the sliding glass door and sat on a chair. Kishan let go of the pull-up bar and dropped to the ground. I was amazed that he could land without making a sound, as large as he was.

"Hi," I said lamely.

He pulled up a chair across from me and sat, assessing me with his pirate-gold eyes. "Hi, yourself."

"I just wanted to say I'm sorry for yelling at you earlier. I . . . well, there's no excuse, and I apologize."

"You don't have to apologize. You were just frustrated. It's an emotion I've become very familiar with in the past few weeks."

"I want all of us to focus on breaking the curse. If there are unresolved issues, we'll be distracted and someone could get hurt."

"And, uh, how exactly do you plan to *resolve* these issues?"

"That's a good question. I guess the best thing to do is to get things out in the open."

"Are you sure that's what you want to do right now?"

"Yes. It's probably for the best."

"Fine. Then you start." He folded his arms across his chest. "How do you feel about me?"

I sucked in a breath and muttered, "Well, why don't we just go ahead and dive right into *that* hornet's nest? Okay. Open and honest, right?" I tucked my hair behind my ear and sat back in the chair. "Here it is. I rely on you. I like having you around. I feel . . . more for you than I should. More for you than I want to, which makes me feel incredibly guilty. And Phet said . . ."

"Go on."

"Phet said that I'd be happy with either one of you, and that I would soon have to make a choice."

Kishan grunted and studied me. "Do you *believe* him?"

I twisted my fingers and mumbled, "Yes."

"Good. I'd like to think I could make you happy. Is it my turn now?"

"Yes."

"Fine. To be blunt, Kells, I want you. I want to be with you more than I've ever wanted anything. But I see how you look at Ren, even now. You still have feelings for him. Strong ones. And I don't want to be your backup boyfriend. If you choose to be with me, I want it to be because you *love* me. Not because you can't have *him*."

He stared at me with his intense golden eyes, and I dropped my gaze under his scrutiny.

"What if it ended up being both?" I asked softly.

"I think I could live with that as long as I had your heart in the end. One more thing . . ." He picked up my hand between his and traced imaginary lines along the back of it. "If you do choose Ren, it's okay. The main thing is . . . I want you to be happy."

"You mean no more catfights?"

"Ren and I have spent a lot of time together lately," Kishan shrugged. "He's forgiven me for Yesubai and for all of the other things I've done. If you two end up together, I'll just have to live with it."

"He's right. You *have* changed."

"I like to think I've just become better with age."

"Well, you have."

As I stood to leave, Kishan wrapped his hand around my wrist and pulled me back. He trailed his fingers down my bare arm, causing goose bumps to rise.

"That doesn't mean I've given you up, though. I still plan on winning you for myself, *bilauta*."

He kissed my fingertips before letting me go. I stumbled back and braced myself to have a sit-down with Ren.

The problem was . . . I couldn't find him. I searched the pool, the grounds, the kitchen, the music room, the media room, and the library. There was no sign of him. I knocked on his bedroom door.

"Ren? Are you in there?" No answer.

Twisting the knob, I found it unlocked. I sat at his desk. Poems were spread all over, some in English and some in Hindi. A book of Shakespeare quotes was open and flipped upside down. I sank into his leather chair and picked up the page he'd been working on.

Remembering

Where is The X?
A pirate's treasure lay hidden
But the map is faded
The burned edges charred and unreadable
The chest is buried and locked
And the key is missing
The ship drifts alone
The island is gone
How would he find it?
Unearth the precious charms?
The sun kiss'd jewels
Lips of sparkling ruby
Golden-brown doubloons of hair
So much it could spill through his hands
Silken fabrics to wrap around soft pearly skin
A maiden blush of Mandarin garnet
Shining topaz eyes that burn and
pierce like fiery diamonds

A perfume—subtle and clean and enticing
A rich man indeed
If he could but find
The X

I'd just finished reading the poem a second time when it was snatched from my hand.

"I thought you hated my poems. Who invited you in here anyway?" Ren spoke sharply but raised his eyebrow and smirked calculatingly as if he was looking forward to another verbal spat.

I replied, "The door was unlocked. I was looking for you."

"Well, you found me. What do you want? More poems to burn?"

"No. I told you I won't burn your poems."

"Good." Ren glanced at the poem in his hand and relaxed. "Because this is the first one I've been able to write since my liberation."

"Really? Maybe it's because Phet got rid of the PTSD," I ventured.

Ren slid the poem into a leather notebook and leaned against the bedpost. "Maybe, but I suspect not."

"Well, then what got you writing again?"

"Apparently, I have a muse. Now *why* are you in my room?"

"I wanted to talk with you. Clear the air."

"I see." He walked along the bed and sat back against the headboard, patting the space next to him. "So sit here and talk."

"Uh, I don't think we should be so close."

"We'll kill two birds with one stone. I need to test my endurance." Ren patted the bed again. "Closer, my *subhaga jadugarni*."

I folded my arms across my chest. "I'm not especially fond of that nickname."

"Then tell me what else I used to call you."

"You called me *priya, rajkumari, iadala, priyatama, kamana, sundari,* and most recently, *hridaya patni.*"

Ren stared at me with an unreadable expression. "I . . . called you all of those names?"

"Yes, and probably a few more that I can't remember."

He watched me thoughtfully. Then in a quiet voice said, "Come here. *Please.*"

I obediently walked closer to him. He wrapped his hands around my waist, careful not to touch my bare skin, and lifted me over his body onto the other side of the bed.

"Perhaps I should come up with a new nickname," Ren suggested.

"Like what? And no *siren* or *witchy woman* kind of name."

He laughed. "How about *strimani*? It means 'the best of women' or 'a jewel of a woman.' Is that alright with you?"

"How did you come up with that one?"

"I was recently inspired. So what did you want to talk about?"

"I wanted to get things out in the open, so we are more comfortable around each other. That way we can work together, and things will go smoother."

"You want to get things out in the open? Like what kinds of things?" Ren studied me intently with his gorgeous blue eyes. Involuntarily, I leaned toward him but caught myself and snapped back, banging my head lightly on the headboard.

"Umm . . . maybe this isn't a good idea. It worked with Kishan, but something tells me it's not going to go so well with you."

His amused expression quickly faded, and he clenched his jaw. "*What* worked with Kishan?"

"We . . . talked about our feelings."

"*And?* What did he say?"

"I'm not sure I should share that with you."

He growled softly and mumbled something in Hindi. "Okay, Kelsey, you wanted to talk, so talk."

I sighed and shifted down on the bed, tucking a pillow under my head. It smelled like him: waterfalls and sandalwood trees. I inhaled deeply, smiled involuntarily, and then blushed when I noticed he was watching me curiously.

"What are you doing?"

I stuttered, embarrassed. "If you must know, the pillow smells like you. And I happen to like the way you smell."

"Really?" He grinned.

"Yes. See? Everything is all out in the open."

"Everything isn't out yet. I'll make you a deal. Tell me what Kishan said, and you can share everything we talk about with him. No secrets."

I thought about what Kishan's reaction might be. He'd probably agree with Ren.

"Alright."

I began hesitantly, slowly warming to the topic. I told Ren all about my discussion with Kishan and left nothing out. It was nice talking to him this way again. I'd always been able to tell him anything, and he still listened as attentively as he used to. I even told him about things he'd missed out on while he was a prisoner, then waited and watched as he processed the information.

I ended by saying, "And as far as you go, I just want to say I'm sorry for yelling at you in the jungle. I know I've been a pain to be with lately, and I apologize. I was angry and hurt, and I blamed you."

"Perhaps I *deserved* the blame." Ren raised an eyebrow and then his expression changed to a wide grin. "So you're here to kiss and make up?"

"Uh, try make up."

"Okay, let me get this straight. Kishan promised not to kiss you until he's sure we're over."

"Yes."

"Did you ever make any promises to me when we were dating? Like, for example, not kissing other men?"

"I never promised anything about kissing, specifically. But after we were together there was never anyone else I *wanted* to kiss. If I'm being completely honest, there was never anyone before you I wanted to kiss either."

"Right. Did I ever promise you anything?"

"Yes, but it doesn't matter anymore, because you're not the same person."

"Get it out. I want to know exactly what I've done to hurt you, other than the obvious amnesia."

"Okay." I blew out a breath. "Do you remember my birthday party?"

"Yes."

"You gave me socks."

"Socks?"

"On Valentine's Day you gave me your mother's earrings. I told you that you could have given me socks. You said, and I quote, 'Socks are hardly a romantic gift, Kells.' On my birthday you said you didn't care for peaches and cream ice cream, but in Tillamook you chose peaches and cream because you said it smelled like me. You also said you liked Nilima's perfume better than my natural scent."

"Is there more?"

"Yes. You told me you'd never dance with Nilima again and when you talk about her it makes me jealous. And, speaking of jealousy, you never get jealous anymore. You used to *always* get jealous, and now you don't care—not even about Kishan's flirting. Kishan has been making a play for me since Shangri-la. Normally you would be extremely upset about that. All of this has been bothering me since we've been back.

"I told you once that I chose you—not Kishan. But now Phet says I'd be happy with him too and that I will have to make a choice soon. In some ways, that's nice to know because if I can't be with you and can't make you happy, at least I could potentially make *him* happy, though I can't see *me* being happy without *you*."

My voice cracked. "And as long as we're confessing everything . . . I *love* your poems. They're more precious to me than anything else I own. And . . . I miss you. It's hard and awkward and emotional to be around you and not *be* with you. Oh, and another thing: That song—the one you can't remember—is one you wrote for me. And I promised . . . I promised never to leave you again."

I lowered my gaze and trailed off. When I finally dared to peek through my lashes, I found Ren's blue eyes watching me intently.

After a moment of deep consideration, he said, "Well, that was quite the confession. I guess that means it's time for me to share." He paused briefly. "I only *feel* when you're around."

"What do you mean?"

"I mean, most of the time I feel numb. I only come alive when you're near me. I can't play music, read, study, or write unless you're some-where nearby. You're my muse, *strimani*. It seems I don't have much of a life without you. And because we're being open, I'll say that I'm fairly certain I'm falling in love with you again. As for the jealousy, I would say that emotion is definitely making a comeback. I'm sorry for the socks. No one told me we were celebrating until the last minute, and Kishan tossed me the gift, which I now think he might have done on purpose.

"I do like your scent. Now that you mention it, peaches and cream is an apt description. Sorry about the ice cream, but I do like peanut butter–chocolate better. I promise not to dance with Nilima. I think you're beautiful, and if you don't believe me you can read my poem again. It was you I was describing. I think you're interesting, sweet, clever, and compassionate. I even like your temper. I think it's cute. And if it wouldn't make me violently ill, I'd be kissing you right now."

"You would?"

"Yes. I would. Does that about cover everything?"

"Yes," I whispered quietly.

"Are you sure there's nothing else I promised you? Is there anything else you've been angry about?"

I hesitated. "Yes. There's one more thing. You promised me once that you'd never leave me."

"I didn't have a choice. I was taken. Remember?"

"You chose to stay behind."

"To save your life."

"Next time, don't. I want to stay and fight with you."

"I don't think I can promise that one. Your life is more important than my desire to have you around. But I'll stay with you as long as I can. Is that good enough?"

"That sounds like *Mary Poppins*. You'll only stay until the wind changes. But I suppose that's the best I'll get."

Ren turned to face me. "There's one more thing I want out in the open."

"What is it?" I asked.

"Do you still . . . *love* me?"

I looked at his handsome face and was overwhelmed with emotion. My eyes filled with tears. I paused only for a heartbeat before nodding once. "Yes, I still love you."

"Then damn the consequences." He cupped my chin lightly with a shaky hand and touched his lips to mine. He wrapped his arm around me and drew me over so I was stretched out almost on top of him. He murmured against my lips as he kissed me, pressing his hands against my back. "If I . . . don't touch your skin . . . it's not that bad." He trailed brief kisses from my mouth up to my ear.

I tentatively stroked his hair. "Does it hurt if I touch your hair?"

"No." He smiled and pressed his lips to my T-shirt–covered shoulder.

"Is it worse when I kiss *you*?"

I kissed him at his hairline then moved my lips to his forehead and pressed a couple of light kisses there.

"When you kiss my hair it doesn't hurt at all, but when your lips touch my skin, it burns. Almost in a good way."

He grinned lopsidedly. I lowered my gaze to his lips, and he crushed me to his chest and kissed me again. It was passionate and sweet, and I returned his ardor. All too soon, though, his body began to shake. He tore his lips from mine, gasping in pain.

Ren panted, "I'm sorry. Kelsey. I can't. Be near you now."

I shifted away from him and moved far back against the headboard. Ren sprang up and to the veranda door where he took several deep breaths. He smiled at me weakly, his face pale, and his limbs trembling.

"Are you going to be okay?"

He nodded and said, "I'm sorry. I can't be near you now." Then he disappeared.

I sat on the bed for a while and breathed in his scent from the pillow. I didn't see Ren the rest of the day but found a note on my bed. It read, "Who could refrain that had a heart to love, and in that heart courage to make love known?"

Who indeed?

Mr. Kadam, determined to uncover Ren's memory trigger, spent many hours with him trying to figure it out. Ren dedicated himself to that effort with a fervor he hadn't possessed before. Kishan always took those opportunities to lure me away. We either watched movies or went for walks or a swim.

When I spent time with Ren, we just talked or read. He watched me often, and his face lit up with a smile whenever I looked up to see what he was doing. He often switched into a tiger and sat with me, napping

in the afternoons. I was able to hug him then. He would rest his head in my lap while I stroked his fur, but he didn't try to kiss me again. It must have been a painful enough experience that he didn't want to repeat it just yet. I stubbornly ignored the voice in my mind that wondered what I'd do if his pain *never* went away.

I helped Mr. Kadam research the third prophecy for the next few weeks. It was obvious we'd be going to a temple of Durga again and would be receiving two more weapons—this time a trident and a *kamandal*. Mr. Kadam and I read a few bits out loud, and I took notes on important facts. During one session, I discovered something interesting.

"Mr. Kadam, this book says a *kamandal* is a vessel typically used to hold water, but in myths, it is said to hold the elixir of life, or holy water, and is also a symbol of fertility. The sacred Ganges is said to have originated in a *kamandal*. Huh. Do you have any water from the Ganges? It says here most Indian households keep a vial in their home, and they consider it sacred."

Mr. Kadam sat back in his chair. "No, I don't, but my wife did. The Ganges *is* very important to the people of India. It's as religiously important to Hindus as the Jordan River is to Christians. It's as economically important as the Mississippi is in America or as the Nile in Egypt. People believe the Ganges has curative properties, and the ashes of the dead are sprinkled in its currents. When my wife died, her ashes were spread on the Ganges, and I always thought mine would be spread there as well, but that was a long time ago."

"Were Ren's parents cremated?"

Mr. Kadam sat back in the chair and rubbed his palms in slow circles. "They were not. When Rajaram died, Deschen began to grieve. I had planned to cremate his body and take the ashes to the Ganges, but she wouldn't let me. She couldn't bear to be so far away from him. You see, the Hindus believe that the soul immediately departs the dead.

They cremate the body as soon as possible so there is no temptation for the soul to linger among the living.

"But Deschen was Buddhist, and in her culture, the dead body is left in repose for three days in the hope that the hovering spirit might change its mind and decide to reunite with its body. Together we watched and prayed over Rajaram, and when three days had passed, I dug a grave and buried him near her garden.

"She spent all her time in the garden working and speaking to Rajaram as if he could hear her. When Kishan wasn't hunting, he rested near his mother and watched over her. She soon became ill and as I cared for her, I carved a marker for her husband's grave out of wood. By the time I finished the marker, I knew I'd soon have to create another one.

"I buried them side by side near our little house. It's not too far from the waterfall Ren took you to. Shortly after that, I left in search of Ren. Their jungle is a peaceful place. I've been back several times to lay flowers on their graves, and I've replaced the wooden markers with permanent headstones. Though Rajaram's burial did not reflect his beliefs, I do know he would have given anything, done anything, to make his wife happy. I suspect, had he been able, he would have asked me to do exactly as I did to give her a sense of peace."

He blinked unshed tears from his eyes and shifted a book on the table. "Ah, I apologize. I did not mean to get so emotional."

"You loved them."

"Yes. I've often thought I might like to be buried near them when I die. I wouldn't presume, of course, but it's a . . . special place for me. I've often knelt at their graves and talked of their sons. It's not something common in Hindu culture, but I find it . . . comforts me."

Mr. Kadam pulled himself out of his melancholy mood. "Now then, we were speaking of the Ganges. Incidentally, there is some basis in fact of the healing properties of the river."

"If it's all the same to you, I'd rather not go for a swim, if we don't have to."

"I don't think you'll have to swim in the Ganges. However, the prophecy specifically mentions diving, which is why I've arranged diving lessons."

"Are you sure it doesn't mean something else? Like the Ocean Teacher thing?"

"No. I'm fairly certain we'll be on the ocean this time. The other two prophecies were based on the elements of earth and air. I believe this prophecy has a water theme—and possibly an underwater theme."

I groaned. "That doesn't bode well, especially the bit about creatures that bite and sting. I can think of lots of things in the ocean that I'd rather not encounter. Plus tiger power is pretty much nonexistent in the ocean, and I'm not sure my lightning power works underwater."

"Yes. I must admit, I've thought of that myself. The good news is that I believe I know what we are looking for this time."

"Really?"

Mr. Kadam thumbed through a book and found what he was looking for. "That is what we are seeking," he said with a flourish. "Look at her neck."

I looked down at the book. Mr. Kadam was pointing to a beautifully artistic rendering of Durga. The goddess was wearing a stunning wide necklace of diamonds and black pearls.

"The necklace? You think we're looking for that? And it's hidden somewhere in the ocean? No problem." I said incredulously.

"Yes. Well, at least we know *what* we're looking for this time. Her necklace is said to have been stolen centuries ago by a jealous god— which, by the way, leads me to my second discovery."

"And what is that?"

"The place where we will begin our search. We will be going to the City of the Seven Pagodas."

"What's that?"

"Ah, I will reveal all tonight," Mr. Kadam concluded mysteriously. "I'll tell you the whole story after dinner."

Despite my pleading to know our destination immediately, Mr. Kadam insisted we continue our research on the prophecy. We spent the rest of the afternoon deep in study. Mr. Kadam focused on the city while I tried to learn more about the dragons.

After gulping down the fastest dinner in history, we gathered in the peacock room. Kishan sat next to me. He stretched his arm out behind me and cheekily slipped it onto my shoulders when Ren took a seat across from us. Finally, Mr. Kadam came in, settled himself, and began to tell the story of Durga.

"Durga is known by many names," he began. "One of them is Parvati. Parvati's husband, Shiva, became angry because she did not pay him the attention he felt he deserved. Shiva cast her to the world below to live as a mortal in an obscure fishing village. The people, though poor, were faithful and had built many temples.

"Even though Parvati lived as a human, she retained her heavenly beauty, and many sought her hand. Shiva soon missed her and became jealous of the attentions other men paid to her. He sent his servant Nandi to the fishing village.

"Nandi secretly stole her necklace and told the villagers that the beautiful maiden's Black Pearl Necklace had been hidden beneath the waves and that it was protected by a fierce shark. The man who could kill the shark and find the necklace would be able to win her as his bride.

"What the men didn't know was that Nandi had taken the form of that shark. He was ruthlessly protecting the necklace for his master Shiva, who had plans to sweep in to save the pearls and let the other men die trying. He hoped this gesture would be sufficient to win back the affections of his wife.

"Many men tried and failed. Some sought the necklace by trickery.

They tried to lure the shark away with bloody carcasses and then seek the pearls, but Nandi was no ordinary shark. He was clever and hid. He waited for the men to dive and then he struck. Soon all the eligible men had been killed and eaten by the shark or were too afraid to try.

"Parvati despaired over the senseless loss of life. Nandi the shark patrolled the waters, causing fear and havoc as he ruthlessly tore through fishing nets and snapped at anyone who dared set foot into the water. The suffering village became desperate.

"But there was another, lesser god who loved the city. Many of its temples were built in his honor. He was the god of lightning, thunder, rain, and warfare, and, in fact, had given Parvati the thunderbolt power she possessed. His name was Indra. He'd heard about the terrible plague that had come upon his people and decided to investigate.

"Indra looked upon the beautiful woman and didn't recognize the goddess for who she was. Indra had always had a reputation for being amorous, and he immediately fell in love with the goddess. He decided to win her hand by disguising himself as a mortal and slaying the shark himself. This was the very same thing that Shiva had thought to do, and he wasn't happy to have another man, a god no less, come forward.

"The two gods, disguised as men, began their quest, both seeking to slay the shark and find the hidden treasure. Indra held the power of weather and caused great storms and waves that confused Nandi the shark. While Indra kept the shark busy, Shiva searched the ocean for the necklace and soon found it. He returned to land just as Indra dragged the carcass of the slain monster on shore and claimed the goddess was his, for he had slayed the great fish.

"Shiva revealed who he was and told Indra that the fish wasn't really slain but was his servant Nandi. The dead body of the shark shifted and changed into the living body of Nandi. Then Shiva lifted the Necklace over Parvati's head. When the Necklace settled, Parvati remembered who she was and embraced her husband. Indra was wroth and asked the villagers to pass judgment as to who the winner would be.

"Put in an uncomfortable position, the people chose Shiva as the victor. They were grateful to Indra for slaying the shark, but the love between Shiva and Parvati was obvious to everyone. Shiva would have killed Indra then, but Parvati stayed his hand. She begged for his life, saying that there had been enough death caused by her. Shiva agreed and whisked her back to his kingdom. The people rejoiced and began to prosper once again now that the terror of the sea was gone.

"But Indra didn't forget his shame and the tricks that had been played against him. One night he snuck into the home of Shiva and Parvati and stole the necklace. He used his power to call upon the waves and the winds to flood the village that had betrayed him, sinking all of the temples under the water except the one that had been dedicated to Shiva and Parvati. He left it there as an empty monument, a reminder that now there was no one left to worship them. Then he hid the Necklace once again and took the form of the shark himself so he could always watch over his stolen prize and imagine Shiva's anger every time he looked at his wife's bare throat."

"Wow," I said. "That story is disturbing on so many different levels. One thing that's mystifying about Indian mythology is how often the names change. The skin color changes—she's golden, she's black, she's pink. Her name changes—she's Durga, Kali, Parvati. Her personality changes—she's a loving mother, she's a fierce warrior, she's terrible in her wrath, she's a lover, she's vengeful, she's weak and mortal, then she's powerful and can't be defeated. Then there's her marital status—she's sometimes single, sometimes married. It's hard to keep all the stories straight."

Ren snickered. "Sounds like a normal woman to me."

I glared at him while Kishan laughed in agreement.

"And *sharks*? Please, please tell me there isn't a shark guarding the necklace."

"I'm not sure what there will be. I sincerely hope there isn't one," he answered.

"Are you frightened, Kelsey? You don't have to be. We'll both be with you this time," Ren said.

"Let me sum it up for you with a Shakespeare quote, 'Fishes live in the sea, as men do a-land; the great ones eat up the little ones.' And I'm a little one. Tigers can't fight sharks. That being said, I better practice underwater lightning power." I bit my lip. "What if I just end up electrocuting myself?"

"Hmm. I'll give that some thought," Mr. Kadam said.

I gripped Kishan's hand tightly. As he squeezed back, I continued, "If I had to pick, I'd rather take on the five dragons."

Mr. Kadam nodded solemnly. Ren and Kishan were quiet, so Mr. Kadam went on, "Would you like to know where we're going?"

"Yes," the brothers said in harmony.

"We'll be going to Indra's city. It's called the City of the Seven Pagodas. This city was famous for having seven pagodas, or temples, each one domed with gold. It was an ancient port city built in the seventh century. It's near Mahabalipuram on the east coast of India. Incidentally, many scholars didn't even believe it existed until an earthquake swept through the Indian Ocean in 2004. It caused a tsunami that uncovered sand deposits and revealed an elaborate underwater city.

"Before the tsunami hit the coast, the water receded and people high above the waterline reported seeing the remains of buildings and large stones, but the water rushed back in and covered everything again. Those city walls have since been rediscovered about a half mile from the coast.

"Statues of elephants, horses, lions, and deities have now been found. The only building left above water is the Shore Temple. Fishermen had

passed down stories of the city for centuries and told tales of seeing the sunken city sparkling beneath the waves, of giant fish that swam through the ruins, of winking jewels left untouched because anyone trying to dive there would be cursed to never rise again."

"That sounds like a fabulous place," I said acerbically.

"It caused enough of a stir that several books were written about it, and many archaeologists have studied it. In one book, I read that Marco Polo made note of the city on his visit there in 1275 and said the copper-domed tops of the temples were a landmark for navigators. Many dismissed his claims or thought he spoke of another city. I feel this is the place we need to go to seek out the Black Pearl Necklace."

I blew out a breath and stood. "Okay. Bring on the diving lessons."

"First, I think we should relocate."

"Relocate to where?" I asked, confused.

Mr. Kadam clasped his hands together and answered matter-of-factly, "Relocate to the yacht, of course."

the star festival

"Nilima has been getting the ship ready in Mumbai," Mr. Kadam explained. "We'll sail around India and stop in Goa to pick up our diving instructor. He will remain on board until we drop him off in Trivandrum. It will take you most of the trip to become a proficient diver, and time is of the essence."

"So you're ready to go? Just like that? Don't we have a lot more research to do first?" I asked.

"We will be traveling fairly slowly, and I've already stocked the boat's library with all the research materials we need, so we can work as we set sail. The yacht is capable of making twenty knots and could get us there within a few days if we traveled by night, but I prefer to go much slower. There are stops we must make along the way, to a temple of Durga, for example, and I also want you to have plenty of time for practice dives before we get to the City of the Seven Pagodas."

I fidgeted nervously. "So when do we leave?"

"After the Star Festival next week," Mr. Kadam stated, as calm as ever.

Ren sat up. "Do they still celebrate that here?"

Mr. Kadam smiled. "Yes, though the traditions have changed somewhat over the years."

"What's the Star Festival?" I interrupted.

Ren turned to me and explained, "It's the Chinese equivalent of Valentine's Day."

"And India has a festival for that?"

Mr. Kadam clarified, "Japan and even Brazil celebrate a similar holiday. It's not exactly the same as Valentine's Day in America. The festival that takes place here is the remnant of a holiday begun by this family."

Kishan added, "My mother loved the holiday and wanted to celebrate it in India, so my father established it in his kingdom. Apparently, they've been doing so ever since."

"What happens during the Star Festival? What are the traditions?"

Mr. Kadam stood. "I believe I'll let Ren and Kishan tell you about that. Goodnight, Miss Kelsey."

"Goodnight."

I looked from Ren to Kishan and waited for one of them to say something. They stared at each other. I elbowed Kishan. "Well? Tell me."

"Keep in mind that I haven't attended the celebration for a few centuries, but if I remember correctly, the city has a party with fireworks, food, and lanterns. The girls all dress up. There's dancing and music."

"Oh. So it's not like an American version of Valentine's Day? Is it about love? Are there chocolates, flowers, and cards?"

"Well, there are flowers and cards, but they're not store-bought."

Ren interrupted. "It's also an opportunity for someone to wish for the person they want to marry."

"But I thought most of your marriages were arranged."

"They are," Kishan said. "It's just an innocent way for a maiden to express herself. I'm curious to see how the customs have changed since our time. I think you'll enjoy yourself, *bilauta*." He squeezed my hand and winked at me.

Ren cleared his throat. "In China it's called the Night of Sevens and is supposed to occur on the seventh day in the seventh month of the year, but the date isn't as important as the stars. The celebration occurs when the stars Orihime and Hikoboshi align, so when you write your wish, you are literally wishing on a star. I don't know the English names for those stars. You'd have to ask Mr. Kadam."

"What am I supposed to wear?"

"Do you trust me?"

I sighed. "Yes. Your taste in clothing is usually better than mine."

"Good. I'll get you something appropriate. If the celebration is true to tradition, a maiden stays near her parents and is allowed to be escorted to certain activities or games only with the permission of her father. It would be customary for you and Nilima to remain close to Kadam. However, because you're not Indian it really wouldn't matter. You could roam freely if you wish."

"Hmm. I'll think about it."

The next week was bustling with activity. Mr. Kadam and I went through the library book by book, packing up anything we thought might be useful on the boat. I researched on the Internet for hours about the dragons of the five oceans. I also spent a lot of time with Kishan and Ren, though more with the latter.

Ren was beginning to seem like his old self. We read together often. He liked being in the same room with me, albeit at a distance. He frequently asked me to sit with him while he played music or wrote poetry, and he'd ask my opinion about certain phrases or lyrics.

He teased and joked with me and tried to hold my hand but it seemed that there was no building up a tolerance, despite his efforts. It hurt him and he got sick every time. He tried not to let it show, but I knew. Still, he seemed happy to be with me, and I contented myself with whatever time I could spend with him.

I often reached out to touch Ren's arm or his shoulder but then pulled back, knowing it would hurt him. He insisted touching his clothing didn't hurt; he just felt the pressing need to escape, and he said he was getting used to the feeling. But still, our relationship felt very limited.

I wasn't exactly sure what he was *feeling* or *thinking*. It seemed as if he was making a great effort to spend time with me despite the side effects. We didn't talk about our feelings again, but he seemed determined to get closer, to *be* closer to me. He tried all sorts of things to find the trigger that would turn on his memory, and started leaving me flowers and poems through the day, much as he did in Oregon. It was *almost* enough.

I didn't give the festival another thought until Ren found me writing on the veranda one early afternoon.

"I brought your dress for the festival."

"Oh, thanks," I said distractedly. "Would you mind leaving it on the bed? I'll put it away later."

"Put it away? The festival is tonight, Kells. And what on earth are you writing?"

"What? How did a week go by so quickly?" I clutched my book to my chest as Ren tried to peek over my shoulder. "If you must know, Mr. Nosy, I'm writing a poem."

He grinned. "I didn't know you wrote other than in your journal. May I take a look?"

"I'm still working on some of the words. It's not as good as yours. You'll laugh."

Ren sat down across from me. "Kelsey, I won't. Please? What's it about?"

"Love." I sighed. "You're going to sit here and pester me until I show you, aren't you?"

"Probably. I'm dying of curiosity."

"Alright, fine. But it's my first one, so be nice."

Ren bowed his head. "Of course, *strimani*. I am always the perfect gentleman."

I smirked at him but handed it over and sat biting my nails while he read through it once quietly. Then he read it out loud.

Love Is about Grooming

Love is about grooming

It starts . . .

Sweet smelling lotion is smoothed over rough skin

Cologne is splashed on freshly shaved cheeks

Shiny faces, starched shirts, short skirts

Colored lips, cheeks, and hair

We glisten

We are plucked, plumed, perfumed, and powdered

We buy flowers, chocolates, candles, and jewels

It's not real

Real love is drab, rough, stubbly

It's mothers changing diapers

It's toenail trimming, nose wiping, morning breath

Trade in your high heels for tennis shoes and house slippers

Mousy manes

Tangled tendrils

Love's chap-lipped, ear waxy, prickly bearded,
and jagged nailed
It's a back scratching, hairy legged, there's something
between your teeth, Dear, feeling

Real love
Is plucking hairs from your husband's back
Emptying Grandpa's bedpan
Wearing sweats on a Friday night
Saving money, not spending it
Wiping feverish faces with cool towels

Lionesses lick clean their cubs
Monkeys pick bugs off backs
Humans wash dead mothers' hair before burial

Love is about grooming

Ren sat silent for a time as he stared at the paper. My foot tapped nervously.

"Well? Might as well get it out."

"It's a bit . . . morose. But I like it. Though technically, monkeys don't pick bugs off for love. They do it for afternoon snacks."

I snatched my notebook back. "And that kind of snacking dedication *is* love, a dedicated love for the snack."

He looked at me curiously. "You've experienced all these forms of love, haven't you?"

"Most of them, I guess. Though I have to admit I've never emptied a bedpan."

"Or plucked hairs from your boyfriend's back, I assume."

"Nope, your back is perfect."

He studied me under his long, sooty lashes. "You have a great capacity for love, and you've been hurt. I'm sorry I added to that."

"Don't worry about it."

Ren touched my hand briefly before withdrawing. "It's the only thing I ever think about. See you tonight." He turned before he disappeared into the hall and grinned. "And save me a dance."

After he left, I walked over to my bed and pulled back the gift's tissue wrapping. Inside was a gorgeous silk Chinese dress. I carefully held it up to me. It was Ren's favorite color. The dress was a blue gradation that started with a soft royal tone from the neck to mid-chest and changed to a dark zodiac blue—the color of the sky at night.

Stars, moons, planets, and fierce dragons were embroidered in gold and silver threads all over the dress. The symbols were interspersed with looping vines and flowers, also in silver and gold. The neck was mandarin style with a small keyhole opening and a silver frog clasp. The dress stopped at mid-calf, and I was just raising my eyebrow at its incredibly long side slit when I noticed the tag.

Ren bought this. He didn't make it with the Divine Scarf.

Just then, Mr. Kadam knocked on my door and delivered two boxes. "The dress is lovely, Miss Kelsey. I brought your shoes and hairclips, which just arrived. Nilima said to tell you she'll be up in an hour to help you with your hair.

"I've never seen a dress as beautiful as this. Why did he buy it? He could have made it with the Scarf."

Mr. Kadam shrugged. "The dress is called a *qipao*. It's traditional in Chinese culture. His mother often wore similar clothing. You might see some here at the party in India, but it's probable you will see the more traditional Indian clothing. You will likely stand out, which, I imagine, is the reason he bought it."

"Oh. Well, thanks. I'll see you in a couple of hours, then."

"I look forward to the celebration."

As promised, Nilima knocked on my bathroom door an hour later as I was finishing straightening my hair.

"Ah, perfect. I have a certain style in mind and it requires smooth hair."

I sat on a cushioned chair in front of the wide mirror and looked at Nilima. She was already dressed in a burnt orange *lehenga* with a velvet blouse that had silk appliqué. Crystals, beads, sequins, and cut glass embellished her skirt and *dupatta*. The slim Indian woman's long dark hair was curled and fell attractively down her back. The sides were held back loosely with gold and orange butterfly clips, and she wore heavy gold earrings and bracelets.

"You look beautiful, Nilima."

"Thank you. You will look lovely as well."

"Well, if your hair is any indication, I'm sure I'll pass for acceptable."

She laughed as she sectioned off my hair. I tried to pay attention, but her hands moved quickly. She neatly parted my hair to the side and began combing out and rolling sections to tuck into an elaborate bun at the nape of my neck. When she was satisfied, she removed an assortment of combs from one of the boxes Mr. Kadam had brought earlier. The jeweled combs were made of sapphires and diamonds, shaped like stars, moons, and flowers.

A pair of dangling earrings was included. A glittering royal blue oval stone was the center and dark blue stones fanned out like crescent moons. A star of diamonds hung in the middle and small glass droplet beads in royal blue, dark blue, gold, and silver hung below it.

Nilima tucked the combs into my hair around the elaborate style she'd done and pronounced me presentable. I asked for help getting into my tight dress. Without the garment's slit I could not have moved without popping a seam.

Nilima told me it looked fine, but I was sure I'd be tugging at my dress all night trying to keep my leg modestly covered. The other box Mr. Kadam had left held a pair of shoes—heeled slippers in silver with gold-braided trim around the top.

I stood in front of the closet's full-length mirror to get the whole picture. I was shocked that the girl in the mirror was me. I looked exotic. A long bare leg peeped from the slit, and with the heels on, I looked even taller.

I'd firmed up from all my workouts with Kishan, and it showed. My waist was smaller, and my arms were toned. My hips were still about the same size, which made me look curvier. Nilima had outlined my eyes with dark blue liner and dusted my lids with sparkling gold shadow. I looked like a woman, not a girl anymore. I felt . . . desirable. I stopped tugging at my dress, dropped my hands, and smiled.

I'd never thought of myself as beautiful. I always chose comfort over style. But tonight, I was pleased enough with my appearance that I might even be able to stand up to Ren and Kishan. With that thought, I picked up the gold-painted fan that came with the hair combs, looped its cord around my wrist, and walked confidently down the stairs.

I was met by Nilima and Mr. Kadam, who looked dashing in a simple white suit and a mallard-green silk shirt.

"Oh, Mr. Kadam! You look nice. But where are Ren and Kishan?" I asked.

"They went ahead. They'll meet us at the fountain." Mr. Kadam offered us each an arm and continued, "Thank you for the compliment, but nothing compares to you ladies. I'll be the envy of every man at the festival."

Mr. Kadam helped us both into his Rolls and complained only briefly that we couldn't take the McLaren, as it only seated two. Soon we were whisked away to the Star Festival, and I felt like Cinderella arriving at the royal ball.

The town was brightly lit, and people roamed the streets in colorful clothing. Wires with brightly colored paper lanterns ran between the buildings. Papier-mâché globes with long, dangling streamers hung over the entrance arch to the festival, and garlands of flowers and strings of lights were draped around an open-air dance floor.

Nilima and I each took one of Mr. Kadam's arms. With the air of a proud father, he walked us to the wishing tree, picked up two colored strips of paper, and handed us each one.

"Write your wish on the paper, and tie it to the tree," he instructed. "If you make a wish at the festival and you have the proper faith in the stars, your wish will be granted this year."

I wrote my wish and followed Nilima to the tree, which was adorned with thousands of colorful papers. We found a good spot to attach ours. Then, it was time to meet the brothers and get something to eat.

We wandered among the groups of people as we headed toward a large fountain in the center of the town. It shot water in high arcs and was lit with rotating colored lights. It was beautiful. Mr. Kadam led us through the crowd, parting the throngs of people so Nilima and I could follow.

Kishan greeted Mr. Kadam and Nilima and then turned to me, exhaling in a husky breath, "You look . . . lovely. I have never seen anyone quite so beautiful."

He wore dark navy slacks and a long-sleeved burgundy shirt with

thin navy vertical striping. His dark rakish hair and glinting golden eyes were magnetic, instantly drawing the attention of several young women nearby.

Kishan bowed his head and offered his arm. "May I escort you?"

I laughed. "I would be delighted to be escorted by such a handsome young man, but you'll have to ask Dad."

Mr. Kadam smiled. "Of course. As long as you bring her back before the lantern ceremony."

As Kishan pulled me away, I asked, "So . . . where's Ren?"

"He took off when we got here. Said he had to do something."

"Oh." I couldn't help feeling slightly disappointed even though I was in perfectly good company.

"Come on. Let's get something to eat," he said.

We walked past stand after stand of delicious foods. Everything imaginable was being sold, even candy. One woman had an entire stand of candy roses. Many of the vendors were offering little tastes or appetizers like tapas. We chose treats from several places.

We had spicy peach chutney on crackers, samosas, and little cups of *baigan bharta*, which turned out to be eggplant charred over a flame, peeled, and mashed with yogurt and spices. There was also a variety of Chinese appetizers, egg rolls, wontons, and dim sum. I even found curried popcorn—but turned it down.

Kishan laughed as I wrinkled my nose. "How can you enjoy India when you hate curry? It's like living in China and hating rice."

"There are plenty of other foods and spices here that I like, just not curry."

"Okay, but that leaves me with very few options left for feeding you."

"It's probably better that way. I don't want to pop out of my dress."

"Hmm," Kishan looked at me and teased, "perhaps you need to eat more, then."

Soon we ran into Mr. Kadam and Nilima. Ren, however, was still missing.

Nilima took my arm. "Let's go to the lantern ceremony."

"What do we have to do?"

"You'll see," Nilima said with a laugh. "Come on."

A crowd of people had gathered by the bridge already. The local festival organizers stood on a raised platform and welcomed the crowd. Mr. Kadam translated.

"They bid us welcome and hope we enjoy the festivities. Now he's talking about the great history of our town and of the accomplishments we've made this year. Ah!" Mr. Kadam clapped his hands. "Now it's time for fathers with eligible daughters to come and pick a lantern. Stay here. I'll be right back."

Boxes of flower-shaped lanterns were opened and handed out to fathers with unmarried daughters. Mr. Kadam brought back two. He handed a pink one to Nilima and a white one to me.

"What do I do?"

"You describe the man you wish to marry," Mr. Kadam explained.

Panicked, I sputtered, "Out loud?"

"No, on paper or in your mind, if you wish. Then each maiden takes a turn and places the lantern in the fire if she feels the man she seeks is near or on the water if she feels he is far away."

I glanced up at Kishan, who winked at me meaningfully.

"Oh," I swallowed thickly.

Nilima turned to me. "Are you ready, Miss Kelsey?"

"Yes."

"Good. Because the announcer has just asked all single women to step forward."

Nilima caught my arm, and we walked together to the front where all the girls were standing. At the ring of the bell, everyone lit their lanterns with tiny candles. When the bell rang again, the throng of giggling women moved forward and one by one made a choice in front of the cheering crowd.

A wooden aqueduct had been set up near the fire; its stream of water carried the lanterns to the nearby river. Nilima said the aqueduct was built recently so the women's fancy shoes wouldn't get muddy. It also made the choice more dramatic because no one watching knew whether the fire or the water would be picked until the last minute.

I stood in line and scanned the crowd for Ren but still didn't see him anywhere. Kishan was all grins though. Nilima went first and placed her lantern in the water. I watched it float down the channel and then stepped forward and deliberated on the significance of my choice. *Fire or water?* I thought briefly about Li in Oregon and sighed thinking how easy my life would have been had I chosen him, but then I remembered why I didn't. Li was not the man I loved.

I would do anything to go back and relive that time with Ren. How desperately short those happy weeks were. I looked at Kishan again and smiled back at him. I knew my choice was in India. The man I would pledge myself to was here. I threw my lantern into the fire with conviction and heard Mr. Kadam and Kishan cheer.

After the ceremony, Kishan asked me to dance, and Mr. Kadam and Nilima joined us. Dancing with Kishan this time was much different than when he first came home. Though still unpolished during the faster songs, he was a very smooth slow dancer. He cradled me close, holding me possessively while swaying, barely moving to the music. There was nothing for me to focus on except him, and I found it hard to resist the handsome man and the sparkling invitation in his eyes.

Kishan scowled unhappily when the dance was over and explained it was the local custom to dance with a girl for only one song, return her to her father, and then get back into line so that other aspiring suitors would have a chance to impress the girl's parents too. Nilima had a group of men clamoring for her attention, but to my surprise, there were also several young men lined up for *me*. That made Kishan very grouchy.

Mr. Kadam seemed happy to orchestrate the whole affair and introduced me to several people, translating when necessary, which wasn't often. Most of my "suitors" spoke English. Kishan stood near Mr. Kadam and glared at the men, which scared many of them off. He danced with me as often as he could and tried to intimidate everyone else who tried.

It didn't look like Ren was going to come. I resigned myself to that and resolved to be happy without him.

Kishan brought me back after our fourth dance and then asked Nilima for a turn. As Mr. Kadam left to get me a drink, my golden fan slipped off my wrist. I looked at it on the ground and stamped my foot in frustration. There was no way I could bend over in my tight dress to pick it up.

A warm voice behind me purred silkily, "Allow me."

"Ren!" I turned to him with a smile and sucked in a breath. He wore white slacks and a fitted blue pinstriped shirt open at the throat. The shirt was night-sky blue, the same color as my dress. He smiled, and my heart started thumping.

He walked a few steps and crouched down to retrieve my fan—then froze in place. His eyes followed the slit of my dress. Though he didn't touch me, I felt his gaze caress me, moving up my bare leg slowly and purposefully from my ankle to the top of my thigh. I swayed, feeling a little light-headed. What Kishan could accomplish by holding me close, Ren could do with his eyes alone. He stood slowly and openly admired the rest of my costume, before finally settling on my face.

"That dress . . . was a very, *very* good decision. I could write an entire poem on the virtues of your legs alone. *You* are a feast for the senses."

I smiled softly. "I don't know about a feast. Maybe just an hors d'oeuvre."

Ren wrapped my hand around his arm. "Not an hors d'oeuvre. The dessert. And I plan to spoil my appetite."

He started to pull me off in one direction when Mr. Kadam approached. Ren spoke softly to him and then quickly returned to me.

"What did you say to him?"

"That I'd be keeping you occupied for the rest of the night. We'll drive back in the Jeep."

"Kishan won't be very happy."

Ren growled softly. "Kishan has had you all to himself for more than half the night already. The rest of the evening is mine. Come on."

We started walking away when I heard Kishan shout. I turned, shrugged my shoulders, and smiled. He started after us, but Mr. Kadam put his hand on Kishan's arm. Ren tugged me enthusiastically.

"Let's go!"

He wove between some people and started moving faster. I had to run in my heels to keep up. I laughed as he pulled me along, my hand still clutching his arm.

"Where are we going?"

"You'll see. It's a surprise."

We ducked under a flower garland, around groups of people who gaped at us as we rushed past, and through a park gate. As we neared the grassy center, he asked me to close my eyes.

When it was time to look, I found myself near a wooden bench. Lanterns cast their soft yellow light from the trees nearby, and in the center of a stone patio grew an old mango tree. Little colored paper wishes hung all over the tree, flapping in the light breeze. Ren handed me a sprig of lilac, tucked a few of the flowers into my hair, and touched my cheek.

"You're a breathtaking woman, Kelsey," he grinned, "especially when you blush like that."

"Thank you." I smiled back. Distracted by the flutter of paper, I said, "The tree is beautiful! There must be hundreds of wishes on it."

"There are. My hand is still cramping."

I laughed. "You did this? What on earth for?"

"Kelsey . . . has Mr. Kadam told you anything else about the Star Festival? I mean, how it originated?"

"No. Why don't you tell me?"

Ren urged me to sit and took a seat next to me, stretching his arm behind my back. Scanning the sky, he pointed up. "There. Do you see that star?"

I nodded.

"That one is Vega and the other one next to it is Altair. The Chinese version of the story is that Vega and Altair were lovers who were kept apart by the Sky King. He created a great river, the Milky Way, to separate them. But Vega wept so much for her lover that the Sky King took pity on them and allowed them to come together once a year."

"On the seventh day of the seventh month."

"Yes. So when the two stars come together, we celebrate their romantic union by placing wishes on a tree, hoping that they will look down upon us in their happiness and grant us our wish."

"That's a lovely story."

He turned to me and lightly touched my hair. "I filled the tree with my wishes, which are all variations on the same theme."

"What's your wish?" I asked softly.

Ren twined his fingers with mine, though I knew it burned him. "My wish is that I can find a way to cross that river and be with you again." He raised my hand to his cheek.

I brushed a strand of his hair gently away from his forehead. "That's my wish too."

Ren slid an arm around my waist, drawing me closer.

"I don't want to hurt you," I whispered.

"Don't think about it," he replied. He cupped my face and kissed me tenderly—just barely brushing his lips against mine—but I felt his arm tremble and gently pushed him away. "You're getting sick. You can stay near me longer if you move away a little."

"Don't you want me to kiss you?"

"Yes. I want it more than anything, but if I have to choose, I'd rather have you near than kiss you briefly and have you leave."

He sighed. "Okay."

"You'll just have to woo me with words instead of kisses this time."

Ren laughed wryly. "'As soon go kindle fire with snow, as seek to quench the fire of love with words.'"

"Well, if anyone can do it, you can, Shakespeare. May I read some of your wishes?"

Ren smiled. "If you do that, they won't come true. Don't you believe in wishing on a star?"

I stood, walked to the tree, and plucked a leaf. "Shakespeare also said, 'It is not in the stars to hold our destiny but in ourselves.' We'll make our own destiny. We'll shape our lives the way we want. I want you in my life. I chose you before, and I choose you again. We'll just have to deal with the physical barriers. I'd rather be around you like this than not at all."

He walked up to me and wrapped his arms around the fabric of my dress. I laid my head on his silk shirt.

"You may accept this now, Kelsey, but in the end you might choose differently. You will want to have a family, children. If I can't get over this, we could never be together that way."

"What about you?" I mumbled against his chest. "You could be with another woman and have those things. Don't you want that?"

He was quiet for a long minute. "I know that I want to be with you. Kishan was right when he said that you are the perfect girl for me. The

truth is we can wish all we want to, *strimani*, but there are no guarantees in this life. I don't want you to sacrifice all those things, to sacrifice happiness, to stay with me."

"I would be sacrificing happiness if I *left* you. Let's not talk about it tonight."

"It's something we're going to have to talk about eventually."

"But you don't know what will happen. You could get your memory back when we find the next object or complete the four tasks. I'm willing to wait that long. Aren't you?"

"It's not about me. It's about you and what's best for you."

"You're what's best for me."

"Maybe I was once."

"You still are."

Ren sighed and stepped away. "Shall we head back?"

"No. You promised me a dance."

"So I did." He held out a hand and asked gallantly, "May I?"

I nodded, and he wrapped both his hands around my waist and kissed the top of my head. I cuddled against him, and we swayed to the music.

When the fireworks began, we sat on the bench and watched the brilliant colors spark against the dark sky. Ren kept an arm around me but was careful not to touch my skin. At the end, I said, "Thank you for the tree and the flowers."

Ren nodded and lightly touched one of the blooms in my hair. "They're lilacs. When a man gives a woman a lilac, he's asking her a question: Do you still love me?"

"You already know the answer to that."

"I'd like to hear you say it."

"Yes. I still love you." I plucked a lilac from the sprig he'd given me and gave it back to him.

He took it and twirled it thoughtfully in his fingers. "As for me . . . I don't think I ever stopped." He touched my cheek and trailed his fingers down to my jaw. "Yes, I love you, Kelsey. I'm glad we found each other again."

"That's all I need to know."

He looked at me and smiled sadly. "Come on, Kells. Let's go home."

"Wait. I'm taking some of your wishes."

Ren nodded as I pulled five papers from the tree and took his arm. When we drove home, we were both quiet. He helped me out of the car, escorted me to my bedroom door, and pressed a warm kiss on the top of my head before saying goodnight.

After I changed into my pajamas and climbed into bed, I turned on my lamp and read Ren's five wishes.

I want to give her the best of everything.

I want to make her happy.

I want to remember her.

I want to touch her.

I want to love her.

7

the yacht

r. Kadam announced that we'd be leaving for Mumbai early the next morning, so we should enjoy our last day relaxing on solid ground before we got down to business again. We all slept late. When I finally opened my bedroom door, I found Ren waiting on the other side.

He smiled and said, "I thought you might like to eat together. Want to grab breakfast?"

"Sure." I smiled back shyly. "Chocolate chip, peanut butter, banana pancakes it is."

He blinked. "Do I like those?"

"We've had lengthy discussions on your pancake preferences. Come on, Tiger."

We made a thorough mess of the kitchen, but it was worth it to see the look of ecstasy on Ren's face when he took his first bite.

"If I didn't love you before, this would have shot me over the edge," he mumbled with his mouth full. "What can I do for you to equal this? Surely there must be something."

"They *are* pretty good. Definitely worth a trade. Hmm, you know what I miss? Your massages. You give the best back rubs on the planet, but it would hurt you too much now. Maybe I'll ask Kishan. He's pretty good at it too. I think I slept on my neck wrong last night."

Ren set his fork down and frowned at me. "I don't want Kishan putting his hands on you. I'll suffer through it."

"You don't need to. He's perfectly capable."

"Kishan is capable of a great many things, and girlfriend stealing is at the top of his list of skills."

"So is that what I am? Your girlfriend?"

Ren searched my face with his blue eyes. "Don't you want to be?"

"I didn't think you were ready to define us yet."

"Labels aren't as important to me as knowing how I feel. I know I want to be with you, and the farther away Kishan is, the better I feel."

"Are you jumping the gun with this because Kishan is interested? Leap on the deer before the other tiger does? That sort of thing?"

"That may be a part of it," he confessed. "But that doesn't mean I'm wrong to move ahead in this relationship. You just *feel* right. In *every* way possible." He grinned. "So? *Will* you be my girlfriend again?"

"I never really stopped being your girlfriend. I've always belonged to you."

Ren gave me one of his heart-stopping smiles and said, "That's exactly what I needed to hear." He took my hand, kissed it, and then happily dug into his pancakes again.

I frowned and swirled my fork in the syrup. "I'll have to talk with Kishan."

"When are you going to tell him?"

"I think the sooner the better. He's probably still mad about me ditching him last night."

"Right. Okay, meet me back here in an hour or so. I'll clean up. You go talk."

"Why? What are we doing in an hour?"

"I have plans to spend the day with you . . . as a tiger. The benefit is I can spend hours with you with no side effects. And if you feel the urge to stroke my back, scratch my ears, and kiss me? All the better."

I laughed. "Okay, it'll be just like old times. I'll see you later."

Kissing the top of his head, I set out to find Kishan.

I had to use my phone's GPS tracker to locate him. He was in the woods behind the house using the *chakram* to level a tree. I heard the *thwang* of the returning disc and ducked in automatic response. He spoke without turning.

"What brings you out here? Isn't Ren keeping you entertained enough?"

"You're mad at me."

He sighed. "It's not that I'm mad. I'm just . . . I'm unsettled."

"Can we talk?"

He finally turned around and looked at me. He was unhappy, but he nodded and held out his hand. I took it, and he led me to a log where we sat down, resting our backs against it.

"First, I'm sorry I ditched you last night. Ren planned this big thing, and he worked really hard at it."

Kishan threw a rock against a tree which thumped before falling to the soft ground. "I'm pretty sure I can figure out why."

"Right," I went on. "But I really enjoyed the time I spent with *you*."

"Kells, stop. You don't have to explain anything. You wanted to be with him, so you went. End of story. You haven't made any promises to me, and you don't have to feel guilty about it. If I got my hopes up, it was my own fault, not yours. I read too much into your actions."

"What do you mean? What actions?"

"When you threw your lantern into the fire and smiled at me, I thought maybe, just maybe, it meant you were considering me."

"That's true, sort of. I didn't float my lantern on the water because I know that the man I'm going to end up with is here."

"Right, Ren."

"I *hope* it will be. We talked last night, and he says he loves me. He wants to try to be with me again."

"So you're back together?"

"As much as we *can* be. And I *was* thinking about him when I threw the lantern. But I was also thinking of you."

"Thinking of me how?"

I sighed and drew my knees up. "I guess I thought of you because I know that if, for some reason, I can't be with Ren that I would choose you."

"So I'm your runner-up? Your backup plan?"

"I wasn't thinking of it like that. You're not a second choice, or a lesser choice, or a wrong choice. You're a different choice. I guess it's not so much that I felt as sure of the man as I felt sure of this family. I belong here. I'm a part of you."

He grunted. "That much is true. If Ren lets you go, I sure as hell wouldn't let you walk away."

I nodded. "I guess I just felt a strong conviction that I belong with the tigers."

"You belong *to* the tigers." Kishan put his arm around me and pulled me closer.

"I don't know how all this is going to play out. I promised you a happy ending once, and I'm still hoping we all get one."

"I don't think that's possible, but thanks for not dashing all my hope."

"I'm not sure I did you any favors."

"You did. You committed yourself to us. No matter what happens, you belong to Ren and me. I'll always have you around, and that's nice to know."

"And I know I'll always have you two."

I nestled my head on his chest, winced, and rubbed my neck.

"I slept wrong last night."

"I can massage it for you."

"Ren will be mad. He wants you to keep your hands off."

"What he doesn't know won't hurt him. Turn around."

After a thorough neck massage, I wandered back to the house to find Ren waiting for me in the library. True to his word, he morphed to a tiger and made himself comfortable on my lap. I'd made him promise no tiger kisses, but he still licked my arm anyway. I stroked his back and read poetry to him while he dozed on and off.

He stayed a tiger, even following Kishan and me into the theater room to watch a movie later that evening. I sat on the floor next to him and fed him popcorn, letting him lick the buttery snack from my palm. Then I rested my head on Kishan's knee and fell asleep.

When I woke in the middle of the night, I was lying on my bed covered with my grandma's quilt. I kicked off the blanket in the pitch-black room and swung my legs over the side of the bed. My feet struck a furry body on the floor.

"Ren? Is that you?"

The tiger purred in response. *Ren.*

I smiled and kissed the top of his head on my way to the bathroom. After brushing my teeth and putting on proper pajamas, I headed to bed and saw a pair of golden eyes staring at me from the veranda. Opening the door, I petted the black tiger.

"Thanks for carrying me to bed. Goodnight." I kissed the top of his head too and went back to sleep.

The next morning, I heard a knock on my door and muffled words. I promptly fell back asleep until I felt Ren's light touch on my forehead.

"Time to wake up, sleepy girl. We're going to the yacht."

I rolled over and mumbled into my pillow, "Five more minutes. Okay?"

"I'd love to give you five more minutes, but Kadam is ready."

I groaned and shook my head as Ren smoothed the tangled hair away from my face. "You're so cute when you're whiny. Come on, *iadala*. We need to be on our way."

"Ren? You never call me *iadala* anymore, which proves I'm still dreaming. Let me sleep."

"Okay, *strimani*, then."

"Nuh-uh. I like *iadala* better."

"Okay, meet you downstairs."

By the time I'd showered, dressed, and grabbed my bag, everyone was already packed into the car. Mr. Kadam was behind the wheel next to Kishan, and Ren was in the back. When I threw Kishan a puzzled expression, he smiled sadly, indicating I should sit in the back. Ren was all grins as I hopped in. He pressed a quick kiss on the top of my head, morphed into a tiger, and put his head in my lap.

Mr. Kadam looked back to check on us. "Is everything alright, Miss Kelsey?"

"Sure. Did you happen to bring breakfast to go?"

"I have the Golden Fruit in my bag," Kishan said. "Wish for whatever you like."

I made a blueberry smoothie for myself. Ren looked at my smoothie, interested.

"No way, Tiger. Last time was a sticky, tiger-saliva mess. Is there something else you'd like?"

He huffed and lowered his head again.

"Fine. If you get hungry later, let me know."

Mr. Kadam, Kishan, and I talked about the prophecy the entire way, and I was so engrossed in the conversation, I was surprised when we merged into Mumbai traffic. Ren softly purred and slept on my lap. It was nice to be able to touch him even if it was just his tiger half.

I stroked his head and buried my fingers in the soft fur at his neck, massaging lightly, which put him into a kind of tiger trance.

I rolled down my window and smelled the ocean and the spicy scent of Mumbai. Mr. Kadam navigated his way through a fisherman's market, and I rolled up the window quickly as several vendors started making their way to our slow-moving vehicle.

"Keep your head down, Ren."

His reply rumbled through his chest and into my thigh. We drove through the market to the dock, passing pier after pier and several large boats. I asked Mr. Kadam which one was ours.

"None of them, Miss Kelsey. Ours is farther out."

"Oh."

The boats got bigger and bigger the farther we went. *Surely we'd come to ours soon. We were running out of dock.*

Finally, Mr. Kadam slowed near a gated area, so Kishan could flash a card at the security box. The gate swung open, and we drove past a sleek building with uniformed workers tending the extensive grounds.

"What's that?" I asked.

"It's a yacht club. Our boat isn't too far now."

We followed the circular drive around the building toward the ocean and onto a road built on the water. It was designed like a cul-de-sac and branched off into radiating docks, each with its own huge ship.

My mouth dropped. "You own a cruise ship?"

Mr. Kadam laughed. "Technically, it's called a mega yacht."

"You mean it's bigger than the average yacht?"

"Yes. Yachts are classified by size. The general consensus among boaters is that a yacht is defined as any boat needing a crew. Super yachts are roughly seventy-five to one hundred fifty feet, mega yachts are one-fifty to two-fifteen, and giga yachts are two-fifteen to three hundred feet. It's rare for anything bigger to be owned by an individual."

I blinked and teased. "Mr. Kadam! I'm shocked that you don't own a giga yacht."

"I thought about it, but giga yachts are too large for our purposes. This one is close in size to the smallest giga yacht. I feel that this boat will be sufficient."

"You think?"

He nodded soberly and said, "I believe so, yes," missing my sarcasm completely.

Mr. Kadam turned left onto the third dock, and we drove the length of the ship while I gaped out the window. The mega yacht was glossy and gorgeous. The top half was white, full of windows, and looked to be about three decks with a short white tower at the top. The bottom half was black, and had smaller windows. I guessed there were maybe one or two more decks under the waterline.

As we passed the stern, I looked up and saw the boat's name written in Hindi.

"What's she called, Mr. Kadam?"

"She's called the *Deschen*."

Mr. Kadam navigated the Jeep up a sturdy ramp attached to the side of the massive vessel and stopped the car in what was essentially the boat's garage. Ren changed to a man again, winked at me, and we all scrambled out.

Mr. Kadam immediately took charge. "Ren? Kishan? If you two don't mind, would you haul our gear up to our rooms and let the captain know we are on board and will be ready to leave as soon as he gives the word? I'd like to give Miss Kelsey a tour, if she doesn't mind."

I nodded mutely and handed my backpack to Kishan, who squeezed my arm briefly before following Ren up the stairs. Two men had come down to remove the ramp. As they secured the boat's outer doors, I inspected the well-lit garage. Another car could have easily fit inside.

Tarps covered some items along the back wall. Other than that, we could have been standing in a very clean garage in any home. Blinking, I still couldn't quite believe we had driven directly onto the biggest boat I had ever seen.

"Shall we?"

Mr. Kadam indicated I should go first, so I headed up the stairs.

"The only thing I know about boats is that the bow is the front and the stern is the back. I can never remember the other two."

"Starboard and port. Starboard is on your right. A way for you to remember is to think about Peter Pan."

"Peter Pan?"

"Yes. Neverland is the second star to the right—star on the right. Then you'll know port is to your left. The body of the vessel is called the hull, and the upper edge all around is the gunwale, which you can remember easily because in warships that's where the guns are mounted. Through here, Miss Kelsey."

I followed him toward the center of the ship, and we came upon a circular, glass-sided elevator. I spun around. "You have an elevator? On a yacht?"

Mr. Kadam chuckled. "It came with the ship. It's very convenient. Shall we start with the wheelhouse?"

"What's that?"

"The bridge of the ship. You can meet the captain."

We stepped into the *Deschen*'s Willy-Wonka-style elevator. It had a lever like old-fashioned, bellboy-operated hotel elevators. We were apparently on the fifth of six levels. Mr. Kadam pushed the lever all the way to the top, and we began to rise. We passed a lounge area, a library, a gym, and stopped at a sundeck. We stepped out, climbed another set of stairs, and entered the bridge.

Mr. Kadam explained, "The wheelhouse doesn't technically have a

wheel in it anymore, and most call it a bridge now. I'm old-fashioned enough to still use the old name. The captain's cabin is aft of the wheelhouse, and he has a nice office just around the corner."

"How many crewmembers are on board?"

"The captain, his assistant, three crewmen, a chef, two maids, and, eventually, our diving instructor."

"Isn't that, you know, a lot of people around? Can't you drive the boat yourself? We are doing top secret stuff, remember? Why do we need a chef when we have the Golden Fruit?"

"Trust me, Miss Kelsey. These people have been in my employ for quite some time. Nilima has thoroughly checked their backgrounds, and they have proven themselves loyal, trustworthy, and well trained. The only newcomer is the diving instructor, but his background has also been checked, and I believe him to be aboveboard. We need a chef because the staff needs to eat as well, and they might be alarmed if food was produced without us taking on any supplies."

I whispered, "But what if we face *dragons* or something? Won't they freak out? What if they all run away, and we have to drive this giant ship ourselves?"

Mr. Kadam laughed. "If something like that happens and our crew mutinies, then Nilima and I are fully capable of getting our ship back to shore. Don't over-worry, Miss Kelsey. These people will not shirk in the face of danger. Come. Let us meet the captain and put some of your fears to rest."

We stepped onto the bridge, which was a pristine gleaming window box of white and stainless steel, and found a man staring out the window with binoculars.

"Miss Kelsey, allow me to introduce Captain Diondre Dixon."

The man lowered his binoculars, turned, and smiled. "Ah! Kadam, my friend. Is dis de young lady you been tellin' me so much aboot,

den?" He stepped closer and clapped Mr. Kadam on the back. He wore loose white pants and a green Hawaiian shirt. I recognized his accent immediately.

"You're from Jamaica?"

"Dis is true, Miss Kelsey. De lovely island of Jamaica is de place I call home, but de sea, she is my wooman, eh?" He laughed, and I immediately liked him. I guessed he was about sixty-five. He was slightly plump, his skin was light brown, and his cheeks and forehead were darkened with freckles. He had a white beard and mustache, and his thick white hair was combed away from a receding hairline.

I shook his hand warmly and said, "It's very nice to meet you." I took a quick peek out the window. "How far up are we?"

Captain Dixon joined me. "I believe we be currently aboot fifty feet aboove de water line. Come. Let me show you de wheelhouse."

Two large leather captain's chairs sat on a dais in the middle of the room, overlooking a long console full of buttons and knobs. On top of that, at an angle, rested a row of monitors showing various readings. One was set to weather, another showed the depth of the water, and another displayed measurements that I couldn't identify. The wall behind us had two large panels of instruments encased in glass.

"This boat is so huge! It's amazing you can maneuver something so large using just a few buttons. It's beautiful up here!"

"Yes. It's a nice view. Hav' you been on de cruise before, Miss Kelsey?"

"No. It's my first one."

"Ah, den I will try ta make your first cruise as comfortable as possible."

Mr. Kadam interrupted, "Come, Miss Kelsey. The captain has many things to do to prepare for our departure, and we have a tour to complete."

Captain Dixon smiled. "It's good ta meet ya. I hope you enjoy de journey. Anytime you want ta visit, please stop by. Maybe we let her drive de boat aways. What you tink, Kadam?" he teased.

"I believe Miss Kelsey can do anything she sets her mind to. I'll be back to visit you again soon, Dixon."

"Wonderful! Until we meet again, Miss Kelsey." He dipped his head and turned back to the window.

We left Captain Dixon behind, as Mr. Kadam took me back down the steps to show me the rest of the deck. As we walked, he told me more about the ship.

"Her length is 210 feet, 3 inches, with a beam, or width, of 41 feet, 10 inches, and a draft of 12 feet, 5 inches. She can hold approximately 30,500 gallons of fuel and 7,500 gallons of water and she has two 3,516 horsepower diesel inboard engines. She can make twenty knots, but usually cruises at sixteen."

I was just about to tell Mr. Kadam all those figures were lost on me when he said something I finally did understand.

"This is called the sundeck," he said and guided me to the even more impressive front of the ship where I spotted an exterior observation seating area and a sunken lounge.

The lounge was extraordinary. It looked like a fancy living room sitting right on top of a boat. A sofa and two love seats were set back against the wall. A hatch opened on either side leading back into the interior of the boat, while across from the sofa, there was a semicircle of cushioned seating in cream and black with a small oval dining table in the center. It was the perfect setting for a romantic dinner under the stars.

We entered the hatch and moved on. The sundeck had an interior lounge as well, where we could watch movies. Mr. Kadam said we also had a satellite dish that could get any channel in the world. The sundeck aft featured al fresco dining for up to twelve people and had a bar and buffet. Mr. Kadam told me we'd most likely breakfast there.

The next level down was called the observation deck. A stunning lounge with floor-to-ceiling windows showcased the ocean. In the stern was an enormous onyx-and-marble pool complete with a fountain. A spacious, professionally equipped gym and exercise area, a changing room with showers and restroom, and a juice bar completed the deck. We skipped the next deck and headed to the lower deck.

"This is where the crew cabins are located," Mr. Kadam explained. "All of them stay here except the captain. No one is allowed on the Main Deck where our rooms are without Nilima's permission. We can't have them catching a glimpse of our tigers, now, can we?"

The crew quarters were set around a central lobby. Each cabin had a bathroom, which Mr. Kadam called a head, including a shower.

"There are a few nice guest rooms down here as well. Our diving instructor will be staying in one of them. The laundry room and kitchen, or galley, are also located here."

Mr. Kadam guided me toward the fully stocked galley. There was enough food to feed a small army for a month. It had a huge walk-in pantry, two dining tables for the staff, and a serving counter.

He showed me one of the service walkways that ran throughout the ship, and we went down to the next level. "This is the well deck where we'll find the dry garage. The Jeep is through that door, and over here," he stepped through a hatch, "is our wet garage."

"Why is it called a well deck?"

"In some ships this area can be flooded like a well filling with water to allow other craft to dock inside. We don't really flood this area, but we do use it for similar purposes."

I ducked my head and found myself in a nautical wonderland. One wall held fishing equipment, towing rings, and windsurfers. The other

wall held a variety of sizes of mounted water skis. Four wave runners sat against one wall covered with tarps, and two fast-looking watercraft rested on what looked like a ramp.

"You have boats in the boat?"

"They're Boston Whalers. One's a twenty-two footer and the other one's an eighteen footer."

Mr. Kadam was practically giddy with glee as he pointed out the sleek water toys. I hadn't realized the businessman's affinity for expensive vehicles included watercraft, but it was clear this boat and everything in it brought as much pleasure to him as his McLaren.

Continuing the tour, Mr. Kadam showed me a wooden bench area with lockers. "This is our diving prep area. We've got snorkeling gear, scuba tanks, wet suits, BCs, and regulators. I have no idea how all the equipment is used, as I've never been diving before. I plan to learn rudimentary skills with the rest of you."

I groaned. "That's not something I'm looking forward to."

"As for me, I am extremely enthusiastic about exploring the ruins of the City of the Seven Pagodas, and the only way to do that is underwater."

I nodded. "If it was just going to be ruins, I might like it too, but so far my experience with hunting magical objects is that big bad things like to chase me."

"Then we'd better make sure you can use your lightning power underwater. Shall we finish with the Main Deck? I think you'll like your room."

We took the elevator, and Mr. Kadam led me into a beautiful lounge area in forest green and burgundy with deep soft chairs and a polished cherrywood library stacked high with books. Large curtained windows overlooked the sea, and the carpet was so thick I couldn't hear our footsteps. We stopped at the first room, which was Kishan's. He emerged and showed me around briefly. He had his own private bath and a large bed.

"Can you show Miss Kelsey the rest of this deck, Kishan? I'd like to get us under way."

"Sure. So what do you think of our floating home?"

"The ship is amazing! You've been here before?"

"Once. Kadam, Ren, and I came out to see the boat a couple of weeks after you left. We didn't head out to sea, but we did sleep here overnight." Pointing the way, Kishan continued, "I'm here, and this is Kadam's room. Nilima's is here. Then Ren's. Yours is down here."

Kishan opened the door to my cabin which was so big I could have easily fit Li's entire wushu studio inside.

I gasped. "It's much bigger than all of yours."

"We gave you the master suite." He wrapped his arms around me from behind, hugged me, and said softly, "Our girl deserves the best."

I thought briefly about Ren's wish. *I want to give her the best of everything.* I squeezed Kishan's hand. "I already have the best. I have all of you."

Kishan let me go, and we stepped into my room—which was palatial. A familiar tune was quietly playing overhead. The huge bed resting against one wall was covered with a cream-and-gold bedspread and pillows, and faced a panoramic floor-to-ceiling set of windows. My grandma's old quilt lay folded at its foot.

"This is the stern, right?"

He nodded and headed for the bathroom. I passed under a vent and felt a cool brush from the air conditioner. I had my own personal giant screen plasma television and a walk-in closet already full of my clothes. The impressive bathroom had a sunken Jacuzzi tub and a shower. Stacks of cream-colored towels rested in polished cherrywood cabinets. We moved back into the bedroom, and I found my laptop sitting on the desk, a new iPad, and a few of my research books.

"Do we get the Internet here?"

"Yes. Internet, e-mail, fax, you name it."

"Is it hard to get that?"

"Not when you own a satellite."

"You own a satellite? A space one?"

"Yes. You hungry?"

My stomach growled when he said the word.

"Apparently you are. Want to raid the kitchen?"

I laughed at the cavalier attitude Kishan displayed regarding his wealth, and said, "Won't that bother the staff?"

"Nah. I'm sure we can scrounge something up. Let's go."

goa

We got under way soon after our snack. Kishan and I went up to the sundeck to watch the boat leave the dock and head to open water. The ship rumbled briefly as the engines cut on. The breeze hit my face as the ship started to move, and I peered down into the sea as we carved through the blue-green water. Eventually, Ren joined us. He gave me one of his special smiles and squeezed my shoulder before he too leaned over to look at the churning water below.

"Kadam says we should be in Goa by tomorrow morning," Ren commented. "It's only around three hundred and fifty miles from here. The diving instructor will come on board in the late afternoon. We can show Kelsey the town and maybe do some shopping."

Kishan replied, "Sounds fun."

"What kind of shopping?" I asked.

Ren shrugged. "Window shopping if you want, though most of the markets are open air."

"I *would* like to send something to Mike, Sarah, and the kids, and also to Jennifer from wushu class," I said, feeling a twinge of guilt for not being able to keep in better touch.

"We can arrange that. Nilima will make sure that whatever you choose gets routed to them and can't be traced back to us. She sends our mail to contacts in other countries. They mail it to other destinations in America. Then it gets boxed and shipped again. It's a complex system."

"Lokesh sure has complicated our lives, hasn't he?"

"This time we'll beat him. We'll be more prepared," Kishan declared.

I shuddered, and both men took a step closer to me. Trying to lighten the mood, I asked, "Want to watch a movie? I think it's time I introduced you tigers to *Jaws*. You both need a healthy dose of the ocean jitters, so I'm not the only one afraid to go in the water."

Jaws was followed by *Jaws 2*. Both Ren and Kishan agreed that the first one was better, despite the old-time special effects. Unfortunately, they still scoffed at my fears. I guess being predators themselves made them less afraid of other predators.

We joined Mr. Kadam and Nilima at the outdoor dining area where a seafood buffet awaited: candied teriyaki salmon drizzled with scallion butter, honey-orange scallops, crunchy shrimp with spicy cocktail dip, lobster-stuffed mushrooms, crab cakes with lemon cream sauce, salad, rolls, and virgin mango berry daiquiris. I took a seat at the lovely polished table. The sun was hot, and I appreciated the shady canopy that had been rolled out to cover us.

I was full after one plate, but the brothers went back several times. After teasing them about leaving some for the staff, I headed back to my room and soaked in the Jacuzzi until my fingers wrinkled. When I got out, I wrapped my body in the robe Kishan had given me for my birthday and brushed my hair. On my pillow, I found a poem.

The Sea Hath Its Pearls
Heinrich Heine
(English translation by
Henry Wadsworth Longfellow)

The sea hath its pearls,
The heaven hath its stars;
But my heart, my heart,
My heart hath its love.

Great are the sea, and the heaven;
Yet greater is my heart,
And fairer than pearls or stars
Flashes and beams my love.

Thou little, youthful maiden,
Come unto my great heart;
My heart, and the sea and the heaven
Are melting away with love!

A noise startled me during my second read of the poem. I jumped off the bed, spun around, and found Ren grinning and leaning against the frame of a door I hadn't opened yet.

"How long have you been standing there?"

"Long enough to appreciate the view." He stepped closer and took the poem from my hand. "Do you like it?"

"Yes."

He put his arm around my waist and dragged me closer. He kissed my robe-clad shoulder and inhaled. "You smell delicious."

"Thank you. You don't smell bad yourself. What's through there? Where did you come from?"

"My room. Want to see?"

I nodded, and he steered me toward his room with a hand at the small of my back. The room looked similar to Kishan's.

"We have a connecting door?"

He grinned. "Yes."

"Did Kishan know about this before you made the room assignments?"

"Yes."

"Huh. I'm surprised he let you take it."

Ren frowned. "We originally thought Nilima or Mr. Kadam should have it, but we both felt it would be better if you had a tiger close by. We fought over who would take it, but I won out in the end." He scowled and mumbled, "Mostly because Kishan knows I can't touch you anyway."

I stifled a laugh and said, "I would have liked to have been a fly on the wall for that conversation."

"My room is nice, but I was kind of hoping I wouldn't have to use it."

"What do you mean?"

"I was thinking that maybe I could sleep with you. As a tiger, I mean."

I quirked an eyebrow and laughed. "Can't get enough of my snoring, huh?"

"You don't snore, and I like being near you. Plus, you're nice to wake up to in the morning—not that you aren't nice to have around now." Ren pulled me against him. "Have I told you lately that you're beautiful?"

I smiled, stretched out my hand, and brushed the hair away from

his eyes, letting the silky strands twine between my fingers. He dipped his forehead to touch mine, but after several seconds, he moved away. Ren's face had paled and his eyes were closed. I squeezed his arm before stepping back.

"I'm alright, just give me a minute."

"You recover, while I change," I said and pushed him back into his room, closing the door behind me. I put on my silky Indian pajamas and then reopened our adjoining door.

Ren let his gaze trail lazily down my body and grunted in appreciation. "Those pajamas are very nice, but I like the robe better."

"You should have seen the original robe in Shangri-la. I'm not surprised you like the pajamas. You gave them to me, you know."

"I did? When?"

"Before we went to the cave to get the prophecy."

"Hmm. I obviously had designs on you already at that point."

"You told me you started having feelings for me even back at the circus." I walked to the bed, pulled back the covers, and turned around. Ren was right behind me.

"Aren't you feeling sick?"

"Mildly. But being close to you, especially when you're wrapped in silk, is worth it."

I grinned lopsidedly, and he opened his arms. After a brief hesitation, I stepped into his embrace and pressed my cheek against his shirt. He hugged me tightly as he ran his hands up and down my back.

"This is nice," he said.

"It is. It's just way too brief."

"Come on. I'll tuck you in."

As I slid between the sheets, he pulled the comforter lower and covered me with my quilt instead. "How did you know that's the way I like to sleep?" I asked.

"I pay attention. You love this old quilt."

"Yes, I do."

"Goodnight, *iadala*."

"Goodnight, Ren."

He turned off the light and settled himself somewhere in the room. I had a hard time falling asleep because of the movement of the ship and being in a new environment. I couldn't consciously feel it move. It wasn't like being on a jet boat, but it still threw off my equilibrium. Half an hour later, I leaned over the side of my bed and stretched out my hand.

"Ren? Where are you?"

A nose pressed against my palm.

"I can't sleep. The boat's moving too much."

He moved away. I listened for him, but he moved too quietly over the thick carpet. Suddenly, the bed dipped heavily behind me as Ren's furry tiger form settled on it. I rolled over to face him and sighed happily. He started to purr.

"Thanks."

Scooting closer I buried my face in his soft neck fur. I stroked his side until I fell asleep with my arm draped over his chest.

When I woke the next morning, my head was resting on Ren's white shirt, and my arm was draped over his stomach. His arm was wrapped around me, and he was playing with my hair. I tried to move away, but he pulled me back.

"It's okay. I've been a man for only a minute. The pain isn't bad yet. I haven't touched your skin."

"Oh. Hey, the boat's not moving."

"We docked several hours ago."

"What time is it?"

"I'm not sure. Maybe 6:30. It's dawn. Look."

I peered out the window at the pink sky. We were docked near a large city. Tall palm trees thickly lined the golden sandy beaches that were empty of even the most dedicated sunbathers. Nestled among the trees were large, curved, white hotels, and behind those, the tops of other buildings were just visible through the trees. The early-morning quiet was peaceful. It looked like paradise.

"That's Goa?"

"Mmm-hmm." Ren's fingers stroked through my hair, and I relished the touch.

"You used to do that all the time."

Ren laughed. "I imagine I did. I love your hair."

"Really? It's just plain old boring brown. Nothing special. Nilima's got beautiful hair. Ebony. Very exotic."

"I like yours. Curled, straight, wavy, up, down, braided."

"You like it braided?"

"I like playing with the ribbons, and every time you wear braids I'm tempted to undo them."

I laughed. "Ah, now that makes sense. On several occasions, you tugged the ribbons out of my hair and pulled out my braids. Now I know why. You have a braid fetish."

Ren smiled and kissed my forehead. "Maybe I do. Are you ready to go shopping?"

I sighed against his chest. "I'd rather stay here and snuggle with you."

"I knew there was a reason I liked you." He pressed me close and hugged me. "Unfortunately, I'm starting to feel the effects of snuggling."

"Okay."

Ren slid out of bed, walked to his room, and turned. Leaning against the doorjamb, he sighed. "I think the universe is conspiring against me."

"How so?" I stretched and rolled over to look at him while bunching my pillow under my cheek.

"Because I can enjoy your warm, beautiful self, all sleepy and cuddly in silky pajamas only from a distance. Do you have any idea how extremely tempting you are? I am very, very glad that Kishan's door is not connected to yours."

I laughed. "You are one dangerous, smooth-talking man, my friend. But I've known that for a while, and I like that about you. Now go get dressed. I'll meet you at breakfast."

He grinned and shut the door behind him.

After breakfast, Ren and Kishan led me down to the dry garage. Automatically, I opened the door to the Jeep.

Kishan stopped me. "We're not going in the Jeep."

"We're not? Then how are we getting to town? Walking?"

"No," Ren said. "We're taking these." He lifted a tarp to uncover two powerful racing motorcycles.

I backed away a step. "And, uh, do you guys know how to ride those? They look . . . dangerous."

Kishan laughed. "They are. The motorcycle, and this one in particular, is one of the best things about this century, Kells. We bought these six months ago, shortly after you left for Oregon and we do know how to ride them."

Ren pushed his bike out of the boat's garage. It was sleek and tricked out like something from a James Bond film. I saw the brand name Ducati on the side. Ren's was cobalt blue, and Kishan's was bright red.

"I've never heard of Ducati."

"Ducati motorcycles?" Ren responded. "They're Italian. They came with the jackets."

I snorted. "I bet they did. They're probably the most expensive motorcycles in the world. A Ducati is probably to a motorcycle as a Ferrari is to a sedan."

"You're exaggerating, Kells."

"I don't think so. Have you guys even heard of the word *budget?*"

Kishan shrugged. "We lived with nothing for centuries. Time to make up for it."

He had a point, so I let it go. A pair of black leather jackets with racing stripes in red and blue were lifted from a cabinet. Kishan tossed me yet another jacket. "Here. Kadam had this one made especially for you. It should fit."

I shrugged into the jacket, but protested, "There's no room for me on the bike anyway, so maybe you guys better go by yourselves."

"Sure there is," Ren replied as he zipped up his jacket.

Wow. I didn't think it was possible for him to look any more intoxicating than he already did. But a leather-clad Ren, helmet in hand, standing next to the gorgeous racing motorcycle made my brain go numb. It was a this-is-your-brain-on-drugs moment. Well, a this-is-your-brain-on-seeing-Ren-in-tight-leather moment anyway. If the Ducati Company was smart, they would have used him in a commercial and given him the bikes for free.

Ren popped the back cover off his bike to reveal a hidden seat. "See?" He handed me a black helmet while I stared at him.

Kishan cleared his throat. "I think Kelsey needs to ride with me."

Ren stiffened. "I don't think so."

"Be reasonable. You'll get sick, have an accident, and she'll get hurt."

Ren clenched his jaw. "It will be fine. I can control it."

"I won't let you take that risk with her, and if you would stop being jealous for a minute, you'd agree with me."

"He's right, Ren," I interjected and touched his leather sleeve regretfully. "I'm scared enough of these machines without worrying if you're going to get sick. I'll go with Kishan."

Ren sighed with frustration. "Fine." He touched my cheek briefly, smiled wistfully, and then helped me put on my helmet, whispering, "Hold on tight. Kishan likes to take curves at deep angles."

Kishan popped the back piece off his bike and helped me to straddle the bike. Then he swung on and pulled on his helmet. "Are you ready?"

"I guess."

"Hold on to me and lean when I do."

I wrapped my arms around Kishan, clutching him for dear life while he balanced us and kick-started the bike. It roared to life, followed by Ren's. He rolled up to us, frowned at Kishan, and then looked at me. I could tell he was smiling from the crinkling around his eyes.

Ren took off first, heading down the ramp and skidding into a sharp ninety-degree turn before accelerating down the dock at breakneck speed. Kishan followed at a reasonable speed.

Once we had a straight shot down the dock, he sped up and chased Ren toward the town. I was nervous at first, mentally ticking off a list of all the possible ways I could die while joyriding on a motorcycle, but then I relaxed and started to have fun. Kishan was very skilled and was obviously holding back to make me feel more comfortable. Ren slowed down to keep pace with us, and we rode through town slowly enough that I could get a good feel for its layout.

By the time we'd been through most of the town, I was itching for more speed. *Huh. Apparently, I'm a motorcycle junkie.* It made me feel powerful and free, and I wanted to go faster. We stopped at the edge of town, and I asked Kishan if there was a place we could race. Ren pulled up near us so the brothers could confer. They agreed to race, but both insisted that we not do anything too dangerous. Thanks to the curse, they could heal quickly, but I couldn't, and neither wanted to risk hurting me.

We rode out of town to an area with miles of deserted dirt roads. Ren scoped out the path ahead and came back to warn us that there

were a few small jumps and turns. The brothers lined up their bikes, revved their engines, and Ren gave the signal to go.

Ren got ahead of us quickly, probably because Kishan was being more cautious with me, and the extra weight of two people was slowing him down.

I yelled, "Faster!" and heard Kishan laugh as he twisted the accelerator for more speed. We came upon the first hill that shot us into the air for a few seconds. We landed hard just before a turn appeared. Kishan leaned into it. I leaned too and edged closer to him, linking my hands around his waist. He accelerated again, and we drew closer to Ren who took a jump so fast he almost lost control of the bike and wiped out—but he somehow righted himself and kept going.

As Kishan and I came to the same jump, he sped up at the last second. We flew on some good air and touched down, back wheel before the front. I laughed out loud. We immediately dipped into a right turn before accelerating again. When we got to the end of the road, we rolled to a stop next to Ren, who was leaning against his bike, looking quite nonchalant.

Kishan and I got off the bike too and removed our helmets. I grabbed Kishan in a hug and blurted out all at once, "That was so fun! You're really good! I wasn't scared at all. Thank you!"

He hugged me back. "Anytime, Kells."

Ren scowled. "I'm hungry. Let's get lunch and shop in the market."

We sped quickly back to town and parked the bikes outside a large market. Several people stopped to watch us. I would have stopped too if I saw two gorgeous, leather-clad men with beautiful motorcycles. They looked like movie stars.

We went to an outdoor stand where we bought barbeque wraps. Mine was spicy chicken tikka wrapped in an Indian flat bread called *paratha*. Even though Kishan asked them to make mine less spicy, it was still really hot. My mouth was on fire. We sipped on fruited lemonades to cut the heat. After that, we walked the markets.

I bought dangly golden earrings for Jennifer, a box of assorted incense and a marble incense stand for Mike and Sarah. It was shaped like a dragon. An incense stick poked through its nose so it looked like it breathed fire. For Sammy and Rebecca, we picked out a hand-carved wooden toy collection with soldiers, battle elephants, camels, horse-drawn chariots, and a royal family all painted in bright vivid colors. Kishan insisted we add a second prince. Ren rolled his eyes, but I laughed and let him pick another one. Ren spoke with the salesperson about having our purchases sent to the ship.

Next, we visited a store with beach toys and attire. I stopped short in front of several racks of women's swimsuits.

"I forgot to pack my bathing suit. It's hanging over the shower back at the house."

Ren walked over to the rack. "Let's get you a new one, then."

I leaned in to whisper, "Can't we just have the Scarf make one?"

"We could, but whenever a material has synthetic elements like spandex, for example, the Scarf substitutes natural materials. Your swimsuit might end up being made of thin cotton, which I am totally willing to let happen." Ren winked and grinned rakishly.

I punched him in the arm and laughed. "No thanks. I guess we'll buy one here."

All three of us started thumbing through the racks. Ren selected bikinis with varying levels of nakedness.

Kishan stuck them back on the rack, saying, "Don't you know Kelsey at all? She's not a bikini kind of girl. What about this one, Kells?"

He held up a one piece metallic foil print with a twisted bodice.

"It's okay," I responded.

"Not her color." Ren grabbed it and put it back on the rack.

Kishan countered, "And I suppose you want blue."

Ren pushed more hangers to the side. "Actually, no. I want her in something bright, so we don't lose her in the water."

They rejected my own preference for a basic black suit, saying my choices were boring.

We all finally agreed on a twist-front halter in a Santorini red-and-ginger print with solid red hipster bikini bottoms. It revealed a little of my waistline but not enough to make me feel naked, and it was comfortable and bright.

Ren picked out deck shoes to go with it, a sun hat, and sunglasses, and we gathered up our purchases and headed to the bikes. The weather had warmed quite a bit. A swim in the pool would be nice when we got back to the boat. Kishan stowed both of our jackets as we got on the bike.

When I wrapped my arms around Kishan for the return trip, he was wearing only a thin T-shirt. I became overly aware of his warm, muscular body and held on only lightly. As he drove off and leaned into a curve, I almost fell. He grabbed my hand and yanked me closer, pressing my hands tightly against his middle.

I repeated the mantra I'd used with Ren in Kishkindha when I was trying to ignore his attractive qualities. I reminded myself that it was okay to appreciate the merchandise as long as I only window-shopped. *Kishan's just a very nice male specimen. So what if I wrap my arms around his muscular torso on the ride back? I don't really have any other options at the present time.* I sighed and enjoyed my ride home.

As Kishan helped me off the bike, I suddenly felt awkward and shied away from him, avoiding his eyes.

"What's wrong?"

"Nothing."

He grunted and took a step closer just as Ren drove up the ramp. The three of us agreed to meet at the swimming pool in ten minutes, so I could show off my new suit while we all cooled off.

I arrived at the pool first and found someone already swimming laps.

When the man reached the edge, he tossed his head, flicked his blond hair back, and then climbed the ladder and grabbed a towel. He scrubbed his face, arms, and legs dry and grinned at me. "You must be Kelsey."

"Yes." I smiled back tentatively and asked, "Who are you?"

He laughed in a way that made me think he did that a lot. "Do you want the whole name?"

"Sure."

"Wesley Alan Alexander the third, at your service. But you can call me Wes."

"It's nice to meet you, Wes."

"Nice to meet you too. This is some boat you've got here."

"Oh, it's not mine. I'm just along for the ride."

"Ah." He smiled easily. "Daughter, niece, granddaughter, cousin, or girlfriend? And please don't say girlfriend." He laughed.

I laughed with him. "I guess I'm probably a little bit of all of those."

"I was afraid of that. I never get the gigs where the beautiful girl is available. But only a little bit of a girlfriend gives me some room to maneuver." He took a seat and stretched out. "In case you were wondering and were just too darn polite to ask, I'm your diving instructor."

"Yeah, I figured that out on my own."

He raised his eyebrows. "Oh, look out! This girl's got a sense of humor. I like that. Most of the beautiful girls I meet don't have much going on in the brain department."

Wes seemed to be the kind of guy who was perpetually happy and always laughing at a joke. He swept back his blond hair and grinned at me. He was cute, had blue eyes, a very nice tan, a nicer body, and he was an American.

"Where are you from?" I asked.

"Texas."

"How does a guy from Texas end up in India giving diving lessons?"

"It's a long story. Sure you want to hear it?"

"Yes."

"Well, I'd much rather talk about you than myself, so I'll give you the short version. I'm supposed to be at Harvard, but I like diving better, and I had to go all the way to India to get beyond the reach of my parents. Now, how did a pretty young American girl from—"

"Oregon."

"*Oregon?*" He raised an eyebrow. "Oregon . . . find her way to India?"

"It's an even longer story than yours."

"I'm dying to hear all about it . . . but it would appear we have company." He stood and in an exaggerated whisper said, "You didn't mention you had *two* boyfriends. Two big, *angry* boyfriends," Wes teased, not showing any signs of discomfort at all.

I giggled and turned around to see Ren and Kishan approaching, wearing identical scowls on their faces. I rolled my eyes at both of them. "Ren, Kishan, meet Wes, our diving instructor."

"Howdy! How're y'all doin' today, sirs?"

Wes shook their hands energetically. I stifled a laugh as the boys halted mid-stride, unsure what to make of Wes and his newly affected Southern charm.

"I was just gettin' acquainted with yur pretty little filly here. I sure thank ya for the opportunity to hitch a ride. I'll jus mosey on off to my bunk and let y'all enjoy yur swim. We'll start the lessons at the crack o'dawn if that'll be alright with all y'all. Well, I'd better get to gett'n." Wes rubbed his stomach. "I hope we're fixin' ta eat soon. I'm startin' to feel all catawampus in the bread basket—I like to eat a whole hog—if you know what I mean." He grinned at both boys then turned to me. "Why it sure was nice making your acquaintance, ma'am. I hope ta see ya again *real* soon."

I dipped in a slight curtsey. "It was nice chatting with you, Wes. See you at dinner."

The teasing Texan winked, picked up his things, and left.

Ren walked up to me and threw his towel on the deck chair. "I have no idea what that man was talking about, but I don't like him."

"That makes two of us," Kishan added.

"I don't know what your problem is. Wes is perfectly likeable, and he's fun."

"I don't like the way he was looking at you," Ren said.

I sighed. "You never like the way any guy looks at me."

"I agree with Ren. He's up to something."

"Will you two relax? Come on, let's swim."

Ren looked me up and down. "I don't like that swimsuit anymore. I think we should go back and get one that covers more of you."

I poked his chest. "I like this one. Stop being jealous. Both of you."

The brothers folded their arms across their chests in identical stances and stared me down.

"Fine. Suit yourselves. I'm going to swim."

I dove into the pool and swam to the other end. I didn't need to look back to know that Kishan and Ren had followed.

At dinner, we were joined by our new diving instructor, who made himself comfortable next to me despite the threatening looks Ren and Kishan sent him. Wes continued his Southern drawl and told lots of cowboy and Texas jokes that went completely over Ren's and Kishan's heads. Mr. Kadam excused himself, saying he needed to speak with the captain about getting under way, but the boys sat stubbornly watching Wes talk to me, while contributing nothing. We talked about Texas and Oregon and what kinds of food we missed and what we liked to eat in India. I asked for another joke.

"Alrighty. What do a Texas tornado and an Alabama divorce have in common?"

"I don't know. What do they have in common?" I asked.

"Either way . . . somebody's gonna lose a trailer."

I laughed, and Wes snuck an arm around my shoulder. I heard a soft growl. I couldn't tell which tiger was responsible, but it meant if I wanted Wes to live until tomorrow, I'd better move away.

"Thanks for all the jokes, Wes. I'd better *hit the hay* if I'm going to get up early in the morning."

"Right you are. And I'm expectin' ta see ya bright-eyed and bushy-tailed come dawn."

I laughed and quipped, "How about I'll be bright-eyed and the boys will be bushy-tailed?"

Ren narrowed his eyes at me.

"Goodnight, everyone." I stood to leave.

"Wait, Kelsey." Kishan jumped to his feet. "Let me walk you back."

"*I'll* walk her back," Ren said.

I rolled my eyes and heard Wes give a long whistle. "I'd say there's a few too many bulls in the pasture. Best see to it a pretty little heifer like yourself doesn't get trampled."

"The heifer can take care of herself. And I'll see *myself* back. Good-night, pardners."

Ren and Kishan both frowned unhappily while Wes laughed and took off in a different direction.

diving lessons

There was a hollow in the pillow next to me when I awoke. I rolled over and inhaled the scent of sandalwood and waterfalls. When I grabbed the pillow to hug it, my hand touched a piece of paper.

Moon And Sea
By Ella Wheeler Wilcox

You are the moon, dear love, and I the sea:
The tide of hope swells high within my breast,
And hides the rough dark rocks of life's unrest
When your fond eyes smile near in perigee.
But when that loving face is turned from me,
Low falls the tide, and the grim rocks appear,
And earth's dim coast-line seems a thing to fear.
You are the moon, dear one, and I the sea.

I smiled and reread the poem a few times. Maybe it was a sign. I'd told Phet I was like the moon. Maybe the universe was trying to tell me that I belonged with Ren. It was an accurate comparison. The moon and the sea were destined to affect one another but were never able to touch. I sighed and saw it was past dawn. I put on my swimsuit, shorts, and a T-shirt, skipped breakfast, and ran to meet Wes at the pool.

I was the first student there. He was busy setting out diving equipment.

"Good morning. Need some help?" I asked.

"Hey!" He smiled. "Good morning, yourself. Thanks for asking but I'm all done. Are you ready for your first lesson?"

"Yes. Did you lose your accent overnight?"

"Nah. It comes in handy when I'm trying to put overprotective fathers or jealous boyfriends at ease. It's also gotten me a lot of dates and better grades in college. Unfortunately, you have both overprotective *and* jealous boyfriends. I'm surprised they haven't killed each other."

I laughed. "Believe me, they've tried, and now you've given them someone new to focus their angst on, I'm afraid."

Wes shrugged and grinned, revealing a cute dimple in his right cheek. "That's okay. Keeps things interesting. In fact, here comes trouble. Stand back and watch the show." He turned to Ren and Kishan. "Well, good mornin', fellers. Looks like Kelsey wins the award for early riser. And doesn't she look purtier than a pat of butter meltin' all over a stack of griddle cakes?"

Ren ignored Wes and leaned over to kiss my cheek. "Did you eat?"

"No. No time."

He opened his bag. "Brought you an apple." Ren winked and sat down on the other side of Kishan.

"Alrighty now. Let's get started, shall we? First things, first. There are two barriers that prevent humans from diving. The first is we don't have gills. And if you ever do find a man with gills you can fry me up, call me a catfish, and serve me with hushpuppies. The second problem

is that water puts a great amount of pressure on your chest and lungs and would eventually cause your lungs to collapse. Sure as shootin', they'd pop like a smoked sausage left too long on the barbeque."

As he got down to business, his accent gradually dropped off.

"Without your gear, your lungs wouldn't have the power to inflate even if you had a way to get air, so your tank provides not only oxygen but also measures the psi, or pounds per square inch of pressure, and equalizes it so your lungs will work. SCUBA is an acronym for self-contained underwater breathing apparatus. We're going to be working with both open-circuit sets and rebreathers."

Mr. Kadam walked in and took a seat. Wes nodded and continued. "As I was saying, Mr. Kadam felt you should learn to use both as he is as yet undetermined which one will suit your diving purposes. We'll start with the open-circuit and work our way to the rebreather.

"In our training today, we'll learn the name and functions of all the diving equipment. We'll start with the easy ones first." He began passing different pieces of equipment around so we could examine them. "Booties, underwater compass, depth gauge, dive knife, and BCD, or buoyancy control device. You wear it like a jacket. I'll show you how to use it later. Right now I want you to focus on the names and the uses for things."

Wes winked at me, and I giggled. Kishan snapped the depth gauge in half, and Ren squeezed the compass too hard. The glass popped and cracked, and the compass fell apart.

"Sorry," they both mumbled tightly while I glared.

They didn't sound apologetic, but Wes just let it roll right off his back.

"No problem. They belong to you anyway." He went on, "We've got fins or flippers, a hood for cold-water diving, and a slate. There are two types, one with common fish pictures you can point to, and the other is

blank with a special pencil. They're normally attached to the BCD, and which one is the BCD, Kishan?"

"The jacket."

"And what does it stand for, Ren?"

"Buoyancy control device."

"Good. We've got about five more to go. This is your primary regulator that provides your oxygen. This is the octopus or alternate air source—it's your backup second-stage regulator. If your primary fails, or if you need to share air, you use this. It's usually a neon color, and you'll find it on your right side between your chin and rib cage. We've got a snorkel for breathing if you're swimming on the surface, an SPG, or submersible pressure gauge, to tell you how much air is in your tank, and then there's the cylinder, which is your air tank. Most contain about twelve liters of oxygen."

"How long does that last?" I asked.

"It depends. Nervous, inexperienced divers can use twice as much air as experienced ones. Smaller framed people use less than larger." He quickly glanced at Kishan and Ren. "And the deeper you go, the more air you use. The average is about an hour dive at sixty feet. More experienced divers could stay under as long as two hours."

As I nodded in response, Kishan handed me a bottle of water. I smiled at him, mouthed, "Thanks," and opened the bottle.

"The other two things you need to learn about are the weight system and the wet suit. Wet suits keep you warm underwater. We'll be doing some dives with the wet suit and some without."

"Is the wet suit, uh . . . bite resistant?" I smiled shakily at Mr. Kadam, who smiled back.

"The wet suit does protect your skin from cuts and scrapes though it still can be torn. So in answer to your question, no, it's not bite resistant unless the fish are very small."

I grimaced while Kishan added, "She's afraid of sharks."

"Shark attacks on divers are not unheard of but are also not as common as people might think. I've been on dives and fed sharks, and I thought it was exhilarating. We might see some sharks, but I doubt they'll bother us or give us any trouble. We can spend some extra time drilling on what to do if you are attacked by a shark, if you like."

"That would be a good idea. Thanks," I added.

"The other thing we're going to be working on today is the weight system. Most people need weights to help them sink into the water. We'll be practicing today with both weight belts and integrated weights."

Wes went over every piece of equipment in detail and then asked us all to get into the deep end of the pool. Mr. Kadam and I were first in. I cleared the water out of my eyes just in time to see Ren, Kishan, and Wes peel off their shirts. *Sheesh, it's like being at a GQ beach photo shoot.* I could easily picture Jennifer hyperventilating at the sight. I snorted. *She'd likely faint and drown if she was in my position.* I was already used to seeing muscular bronzed chests, but even I had a hard time paying attention. If I ever intended to walk down the beach with any of them, I'd have to warn them to prepare for swooning girls falling at their feet. *Hmm, good thing we're taking CPR later.*

Wes had us practice using different weights and getting a feel for how they pulled us down. The biggest one was too heavy for me. I couldn't resurface carrying it, so I left it on the bottom for Kishan to retrieve. When Wes was satisfied, he had us all swim laps for the next half hour. He said we'd reconvene in the afternoon in the media room to get certified in first aid and CPR.

I was starving by the time we had lunch and ate a huge sandwich. Then I showered, changed, and met our group in the media room. I'd taken first aid and CPR classes before, but this was all new to Ren and Kishan. They both listened attentively and learned quickly. I partnered with Mr. Kadam to keep peace between the brothers. He wrapped a sling around my arm, and I practiced the Heimlich maneuver on him.

Ren wasn't happy having to sit so far away, but he'd spent most of the day near me, and the effect it was having on him showed. I asked during a break how he was doing. He just smiled and said, "Headache." I moved even farther away at that point, although Wes kept trying to get me back into the circle.

Ren left after class and either skipped dinner or ate in his room. Kishan purposefully sat next to me, leaving no option for Wes except to take the seat across from us.

Wes and I chatted again, but it didn't annoy Kishan as much as it had before. Instead, Kishan seemed surprisingly content to sit and listen to our conversation.

Wes mentioned that the thing he missed most about Texas was the barbeque. "There just isn't anything in this world like slow-cooked beef brisket and pulled pork with slaw and beans. That's my little version of heaven. I'm sure the angels would all have sticky fingers and sweet, spicy sauce on their cherubic faces if they were able to sample it."

I laughed. "I feel that way about cheeseburgers."

"It's been, oh, about three years since I've had a good barbeque. Three long years of rice and curry."

"I'm not much of a curry fan myself. Maybe we can ask the chef to arrange something special for you."

"Why, aren't you just about as sweet as syrup on a sundae? I sure would appreciate that, ma'am." He winked. "How'd you like ta stroll the deck of this fine ship with me and watch the sunset? I need a purty girl to put her arm around me and steady this wandering cowboy as he finds his sea legs."

I raised an eyebrow and affected a Southern accent. "Why, I think you're a-pullin' my leg there, Texas. You've had your sea legs a lot longer than I have."

Wes rubbed the stubble on his face. "You might be right at that. Well then, how about you taggin' along to keep me warm?"

"It's about eighty degrees."

"Shoot, you're a smart one, you are. Then how 'bout I jes say that a feller can get pretty lonesome by hisself in a strange country, and he'd like to keep comp'ny with you fer a while longer."

Wes offered his arm with a charming grin. I was just about to take it when Kishan stood up between us and stared Wes down.

"If Kelsey wants to stroll the deck, *I* will take her. Why don't you . . . mosey back to your buckhouse?"

"That's *bunk*house." Wes grinned and crossed his arms over his chest. "And tellin' a man to git lost and makin' him do it are two entirely different propositions."

"I'm happy to *tell* you and would be even happier to *make* you. Your choice."

"Kishan, cut it out. I'll walk with you tomorrow night. Wes is our guest, and he won't be here very long. You're not planning to make any fresh moves are you?" I asked Wes.

"No, ma'am. I consider myself a perfect Southern gentleman. I ain't never laid a finger on a gal that didn't want me to, not that any of them ever turned me down before." He grinned mischievously.

That statement made Kishan glower even more fiercely.

"There, you see, Kishan? Wes will be a perfect gentleman, and you know darn well that I'm fully capable of protecting myself." I raised my eyebrows, so he'd get my meaning. I turned to Wes and said, "I'd love to see the sunset with you."

Wes gave me a brilliant dimpled smile and held out his elbow. I took his arm, shooting a meaningful glance at Kishan over my shoulder as we turned the corner. We walked to the railing at the front of the boat and I sighed.

"Those two sure are keeping you hopping," Wes said.

"You have no idea. Have you met the captain yet? Would you like to?"

"Maybe later. I'd rather enjoy the sunset with a pretty girl first."

I smiled, sat on the deck, and rested my arms on the railing, letting my feet dangle over the side. Putting my chin on my arms, I looked out at the beautiful Arabian Sea. *The ocean is so beautiful . . . and dangerous,* I thought. *Just like tigers.*

He soon joined me. "How long are you planning on juggling those two?"

"I don't know." I flashed a smile. "You're incredibly astute for a dumb hick, you know."

"Hick I am, but dumb I ain't," he said with a dimpled smile. "But seriously, you look about as trapped as a piglet at a baby-back-ribs cook-off. Wanna talk about it?"

"They fought over a girl a long time ago, and she died accidentally. They both blamed each other until they finally got over that. They've come to terms and forgiven each other."

"And now they're doing it again . . . but with you."

"Yes."

"How do you feel about it?"

"I love both of them. I don't want to hurt either one. Ren has always been the one I wanted, but there's a good chance we can't be together."

"Why not?"

"It's, umm . . . complicated. Our relationship has been bumpy. Kishan adds another major bump."

"There never was a horse that couldn't be rode; never was a cowboy who couldn't be throwed."

I laughed. "What does that mean?"

"It's cowboy wisdom. It means that there's no such thing as an insurmountable object. If you want to, for lack of a better term, 'ride

that horse,' you do it. You might get thrown, but at least you've tried. It's worth the bruised posterior if that's what you want. And if you let that opportunity pass you by, you'll always wonder 'what if.'"

"Right, but what if I can't fit the pieces of our relationship back together? What if there are too many parts broken or even lost?"

Wes considered for a moment. "My momma always said, 'You can't tell how good a man or a watermelon is 'til it gets thumped.' If he's not willing to help you find the pieces or rediscover the lost ones, then he's not worth keeping."

"Being willing and being capable are different things."

"Not even the most willing mule with the biggest heart will ever win the Kentucky Derby, honey. Sometimes we don't get a choice. We want something out of our reach, and no amount of wishing will make it happen. If he's not capable of being the man you need, then you need to move on. Find a strapping stallion, such as myself, for example." He laughed but stopped when he saw I wasn't. "I'm sorry. I've made you droopier than a corsage the morning after the prom."

I laughed and wiped away a tear.

He sighed. "When the girl *loves* the mule, he wins her heart, even if he can't win the Derby," the charming Texan remarked.

I nodded and stayed with Wes until the moon came up. It wasn't long after I climbed into bed that I heard a soft scratch on the connecting door. I opened it and wrapped my arms around my white tiger's neck.

I mumbled, "I do love my mule," and resettled in the bed. He gave me a questioning look, jumped up next to me, and snuggled against my back.

The next day, Wes had us watch diving videos all morning. We learned about diving safety, techniques, equipment maintenance, how to plan a dive, and how diving affects the body. He also told us about common dangers and mistakes novice divers make.

"Decompression sickness, or the bends, happens when you ascend too quickly. Tiny gas bubbles form in your body when you're deep diving, and they need a chance to dissipate. Following the rules of ascent will greatly diminish your risk.

"Narcosis, or the rapture of the deep, is much more common, and it's hard to tell at what depth it will affect you. The key is to watch for the signs and ascend to shallower depth if you feel the symptoms. The signs are similar to that of alcohol intoxication. In early stages it's a feeling of tranquility or mild euphoria. Later you will start to have delayed response time, you become altered, confused, dizzy, and will hallucinate. It's been compared to altitude sickness."

"Wes? I get altitude sickness. Does that mean I'm more susceptible to narcosis?" I asked.

"Hmm, maybe. We'll watch you carefully your first couple of dives to figure out your tolerance levels. Some people get it worse than others. I heard stories about divers who go too deep, get narcosis, and take off their regulator to give it to a passing fish, presumably because the fish needs air too. That's one reason we always dive with a partner."

The rest of the morning he had us practice how to assemble and disassemble our equipment. After lunch, we were in the pool again, but this time we worked with our equipment. Ren wanted me to partner with Kishan while he worked with Mr. Kadam. Kishan was happy to oblige.

"This is your confined-water training," Wes said. "We'll practice all the basic skills here before we go into deeper water."

First we did pre-dive safety checks to make sure all our equipment was functioning. We learned how to clear our regulators and how to recover them if they were knocked out. We practiced clearing our masks, removing and replacing them, and breathing without them. Then we actually dove in the deep end of the pool to practice standard hand signals, how to secure air from an alternate source, and did buoyancy checks.

Wes told us to take a breath from our regulator, hold it, and see if we remained steady floating at near eye level. If we sank, then we needed to lighten the weight. Mr. Kadam and Kishan sank a little, so they lightened their belts. Then we were supposed to exhale. If we sank, we were fine. If we floated, we needed to add more weight. Kishan, Ren, and Mr. Kadam all sank fine, but I floated. Wes added more units of weight to my belt until I sank like the others. He told us we needed to go through this process on every dive.

When we were done, Wes had us swim laps for half an hour again. Ren and Kishan decided to work out after that while Mr. Kadam and I both agreed we were done for the day. We retired to the library to research.

The *Deschen* docked at a place called Betul Beach that afternoon, and Mr. Kadam gave the crew the night off. We told the chef that we would be bringing in a catered meal that night. When no one was around, we used the Golden Fruit to create a Texas barbeque buffet.

When the three men came up to dinner that night, Mr. Kadam and I smiled as we opened the buffet servers with a flourish. A look of rapture crossed Wes's face as the aroma of Texas barbecue hit him. He grabbed me, kissed me hard on the lips, and spun me around.

Ren threatened, "Put . . . her . . . down."

"Gosh, I sure am sorry to be kiss'n on yur gal, but this is the nicest thing anyone's done fur me since Miss Louellen Leighton, the runner-up for the Miss Austin, Texas, beauty pageant, paid a thousand dollars to win a date with me at our high school annual football fundraising auction."

I laughed. "That must've been some date."

"A Southern gentleman never kisses and tells," the cowboy said soberly.

Wes piled his plate full of fried okra, pulled pork, baby back ribs, barbeque chicken, beef brisket, garlic bread, and corn on the cob. Then he got a second plate for his barbeque beans, fresh coleslaw, hot biscuits, salad, and buttered green beans with onions and bacon. Mr. Kadam stuck with chicken and vegetables while Ren and Kishan ate almost everything.

"Whoo-eee! This is a little taste of home right here."

As Ren and Kishan filled their second plates, Wes paused to watch them. "You two fellers are a little bit different, then, aren't you?"

Everyone at the table froze. I nervously took a sip of lemon water in the sudden tense silence. "What do you mean, Wes?"

Wes speared the air with his fork. "What I mean is that most men from India wouldn't come closer to eating barbeque than they would a rattlesnake. They'd be eating more like Mr. Kadam over here. Sticking with the chicken and the veggies."

Ren and Kishan looked at each other briefly. Kishan answered slowly while pulling apart some ribs.

"I've hunted boar and buffalo. They taste almost the same as pork. Though this is a little bit more *well done*."

Wes leaned forward. "A hunter? What kind of rifle do you own?"

"I don't."

"How did you hunt without a rifle?"

"Ren and I hunt more . . . primitively."

Wes nodded as if understanding. "Ah, a bow hunter. I've been meaning to try that. My cousins hunt deer and javelina that way. It's much more dangerous and requires more skill."

Kishan nodded and kept eating.

Wes added, "Well, whoda thunk it? That I'd be teachin' two carnivores in India how to dive?"

I coughed and choked on my water over that remark. Kishan tried to help me by thumping my back.

"Maybe if we have time I can give you a few lessons in sea hunting," Wes offered.

"Sea hunting?" I asked.

"Yeah. Spearing fish. Dart harpoons. That sort of thing."

"We would both be interested in spear fishing," Ren said quickly, making eye contact with Kishan.

"Yeah. I wouldn't mind learning that myself," I added.

"Really? Well, ain't you as full of surprises as a lady's tea party!"

I laughed, and the boys finally began communicating with Wes. They spent a couple of hours talking about spear fishing, asking what types of weapons were used and how they worked underwater.

We spent the next day by the pool again preparing for our open water training, which Wes hoped to start the following day. We practiced entering the water four ways: giant stride, controlled seated, backward roll, and belly flop. He taught us that how we entered the water depended on the diving conditions. We worked on changing back and forth from snorkel to regulator, removing our scuba units underwater and replacing them, and hovering. We practiced doing a tired-diver tow back and forth across the pool. Kishan had it easier than I did. A few quick strokes took him across, dragging me along behind him, but I had to work three times as hard to pull him along.

Then Wes had us practice massaging out cramps. Kishan spent an extra-long time massaging an imaginary cramp from my leg. When I protested, he pushed my head underwater and laughed. I threatened to trade partners and he apologized profusely and promised he'd never push me underwater again. Then he picked up my other calf and started massaging my leg with a great big grin on his face. I rolled my eyes and asked if we could move on to the next subject.

As we were drying off and stowing our gear, Wes announced that we were ready to skin dive the next morning from the beach. If all went well, we'd dive deeper the next day. I immediately panicked. Learning how to dive in the safety of a swimming pool is one thing; entering the ocean is something entirely different.

"Wait a minute, Wes. Are we ready for that? I mean, have we learned enough? I think I need a few more lessons."

"You'll be getting more lessons, just out on the water."

"Right. But I think I might need a few more in the pool."

"Sorry, darlin', there's only so much I can teach you in a pool. It's time to face the briny deep."

I was going to be sick.

While Ren looked on, Kishan said, "We'll be with you, Kells. Nothing will get through us."

Wes added, "If anyone can overcome a fear of the ocean, you can, little lady. Courage is being scared to death and saddlin' up anyway."

I nodded and thought of nothing else for the rest of the day. Nerves were wearing a hole in my stomach, so I skipped dinner. The next morning, I put on my swimsuit and followed Mr. Kadam glumly down to the wet garage to load our gear in the twenty-two-foot boat. He pushed several buttons and the side hatch opened while hydraulic cables lowered the ship into the water. Kishan leapt into the boat first, followed by Mr. Kadam and Wes. Then Ren took my arms, pressed a kiss on the top of my head, and lowered me down to Kishan, who caught me around the waist.

Ren jumped into the boat after me, sighed, and sat as far away as possible. Mr. Kadam drove the boat close to a point on the beach where Wes wanted us to practice. He asked us to team up, and I went with Kishan again. We slipped into the water, equalized our ears and masks, and put on our fins.

We practiced vertical dives, swimming underwater, and clearing our snorkels. After a while, I started to relax and enjoy myself. The water was crystal clear and placid. I could see about five to ten meters all

around me. Wes ran us through navigation drills, in which we had to swim following a straight line, using our compass. After that, we just enjoyed ourselves.

We discovered beautiful shells and pretty coral fields. I saw hundreds of fish. I couldn't even begin to identify most of them, but I did recognize angelfish and groupers. Thankfully, I didn't see one shark, but a sea turtle and some kind of a ray swam lazily past us. I looked down to find Ren looking up at me. His eyes crinkled just as a school of colorful fish swam past him, and I suddenly realized this was one of my dreams from Shangri-la.

I'd dreamed of swimming with Ren in the ocean—and there he was. He gave the thumbs-up sign to mean we should head to the surface. I emerged near him and began treading water.

"What do you think?" he asked.

"I really like it. As long as I don't see any sharks, I'm fine."

"Good."

"Did you want to ask me something?"

"No. I just wanted to tell you you're beautiful." He winked at me, grinned, and ducked underwater again.

After we'd returned to the boat and had finished lunch, we all agreed that we were ready for our next lesson that afternoon. We put on our wet suits and our tanks. This time we dove right from the yacht. I followed Kishan's example and took a giant step right off the boat ramp. We swam a little away from the ship and ran through CESA drills—controlled emergency swimming ascent drills—which Wes said are used when a diver runs out of air and has to ascend on one breath while exhaling slowly.

Then we went through five-point ascents and descents. For ascents, we signaled the dive was over, ascended to fifteen feet, did a safety stop and checked the surface for ski boats or Jet Skis, signaled our buddy,

then extended the deflator and released air slowly from the BCD. I carefully watched my gauge and my air bubbles. Wes had told us never to ascend faster than our slowest air bubbles. Once we were up and had established buoyancy, we circled looking for hazards and signaled the boat.

Wes felt we'd done well enough to go on a short dive together. He asked Ren and Kishan to partner and said he would work with Mr. Kadam and me. We were to all stay together and practice being buddies. This time I saw a barracuda and a lion fish. I touched some brain coral, a starfish, and a huge conch. A large crab scuttled into view, so I followed its path across the rocky seabed for a while.

The sea was full of color, movement, and even sound. Seaweed swayed. Fish darted, swam, and drifted, and I could hear the hiss of bubbles and feel the vibrations of the currents pulling me as I moved. Getting lost in my environment for too long, I noticed that Wes was ahead of me, so I hurried to catch up.

He swam around an outcropping covered with seaweed and swarming with fish. I followed and descended to swim between a rocky mound and a jutting ridge. Just at that moment, an eel of some kind darted out from the rock, passing right over my arm. I kicked backward as hard as I could, screamed, and lost my regulator. Panicking, I reached for my octopus backup regulator and slammed into the ridge behind me. I got the backup on okay but forgot all my training and tried to rise immediately away from the rocks without taking stock of my environment.

I ascended a few feet quickly and slammed the top of my head into the ridge above me. I could just make out the others swimming toward me before I blacked out.

10

durga's temple

I came to lying on a hard surface. The first thing I realized was that I couldn't breathe. I choked and gagged and was quickly rolled to my side. After hacking up about a gallon of seawater, my lungs burned, but I could at least take in oxygen again. I took a couple of raspy breaths, was rolled onto my back again, and found myself staring up into Kishan's worried face. He was still wearing his wet suit, and his hair was dripping.

I coughed out, "What . . . happened?"

Kishan responded, "Shh. Just relax and take deep breaths."

I finally figured out where I was—on the floor of the wet garage. Wes and Mr. Kadam stood over Kishan's bent figure, and all three of them were studying me closely. I coughed again and looked around. "Where's Ren?"

"I'm here."

He was standing against the wall far away from me.

"Can you sit up, Kells?" Kishan asked.

"Yes. I think so."

I sat up but swayed dizzily, and Kishan shifted to support my weight against his chest. Wes crouched down to feel around my head. He began asking me questions like my age and my birthplace to gauge my alertness.

Satisfied, he said, "You sure gave us a scare. What happened down there?"

"An eel touched me, and I freaked. I didn't look where I was going and slammed my head into a rock. Thanks for pulling me out of the water, Wes. You're a good partner."

"Wasn't me. It was Ren over there."

I smiled weakly at Ren. "Looks like you saved my life. How many times is it now?"

He returned my gaze with a tight expression. "I just pulled you from the water. Kishan did CPR." After he said that, he abruptly left the garage.

Kishan helped me to stand. "Let's get you back to your room, Kells. Kadam? Can you call for Nilima to meet us there and help Kelsey?"

"Of course."

As I walked back to my room, I found leaning on Kishan was no longer necessary. My head hurt where I hit the rock, but it wasn't terrible. Nothing some Tylenol wouldn't fix. Kishan insisted that Nilima stay with me for the next hour or so, and she helped me out of my wet suit so I could shower. Kishan brought dinner to my room even though I told him I felt fine and was looking forward to diving again. They all seemed to think I should rest for a day or so. Wes said he wanted to do more drills.

I kept telling them that I made a stupid mistake and just happened to hit my head hard enough to black out. It was a fluke. It wouldn't happen again. I'd learned my lesson. But they outvoted me, and even Mr. Kadam made excuses, saying he was too busy to dive the next day. Finally, to put their minds at ease, I told them I'd go to bed early. I went to my room hoping I could find Ren. He'd disappeared for the rest of the day, and I wanted to ask him more about what happened. Everyone was acting very strange. I just couldn't figure out why.

Ren wasn't in his room. I waited hours for him to come to my room and even left the connecting door open, but he never appeared.

Ren didn't join us in any of Wes's drills the next day. Wes partnered with Mr. Kadam and Kishan with me. When I asked Mr. Kadam or Kishan where Ren was, they admitted Ren was on the ship and was safe—and that he did not want to be found.

I became angry with Kishan and used every persuasive method at my disposal to get him to tell me why Ren was hiding, but Kishan wouldn't budge. He said that when Ren wanted to talk with me, he would. I paced back and forth in my room, hour after hour wondering what was wrong and feeling frustrated that I couldn't help. I begged Mr. Kadam and Nilima to assist me, but they also politely refused, saying that Ren would speak with me when he was ready.

Soon, the *Deschen* was under way again and moving on to our next port city. I skipped dinner and went to bed early. Repeating the same pattern as other nights, I stood in our connecting doorway, staring dully into Ren's dark room.

Where could he be? Is he angry with me? Is he hurt? Is something wrong? Is he stuck as a tiger somewhere? Did something happen between him and Wes? Between him and Kishan?

Questions filled my mind, and my heart ached with worry. I'd promised not to use the cell phone tracker, but I still physically searched the ship, repeatedly looking in every nook and cranny. There was absolutely no sign of him.

On the third night without Ren, I went to bed but couldn't sleep. Around midnight, I decided the cool ocean breeze might help me clear my head.

Taking the outside stairs to the sundeck, I stood at the railing near our dining area for a while. The wind was blowing hard, and when I brushed back my hair, I could hear the soft murmur of male voices that it carried. I wondered if the speakers were the captain and a crew-member and thought I might say hello. Following the sound of the voices, I walked around the outside breezeway only to freeze when I saw Ren and Kishan. They had their backs to me. I was upwind, and the weather was a bit stormy, so they didn't hear or smell me.

As I walked toward them, I heard Kishan say, "I don't think she'll do what you expect."

"She's already halfway there. Out of sight, out of mind," Ren replied.

"I think you underestimate her feelings."

"It doesn't matter. I've made my decision."

"You aren't the only person involved."

"I know that. But it's for the best. Surely *you* see that."

Kishan paused. "It doesn't matter what I see, what I think, or what I want, for that matter."

"This is the way it has to be, Kishan. I won't let this happen again."

"It wasn't your fault."

"Yes, it was. *I* did this. *I* have to accept the consequences."

"It will hurt her."

"You'll be there to help."

"It won't matter."

"It will." Ren put his hand on Kishan's shoulder. "Over time . . . it will."

"You have to tell her. If you're going to break up with Kelsey, she deserves to hear it from you."

Break up?

I hurried the last few steps, stormed up to the brothers, and shouted, "What on earth do you two think you're talking about? I certainly hope I am sleepwalking and that I did *not* overhear this conversation!"

Both of them turned around. Kishan looked guilty, but Ren hardened his expression as if ready for a fight.

I poked Ren in the chest. "Where have you been for the past few days? You have some explaining to do, mister! And you!" I turned to Kishan. "How dare the two of you conspire and make plans about me without my input! You both know better!"

Kishan grimaced. "I'm sorry, Kells. You and Ren need to talk. I'll find you again later and let you yell at me more then."

"Fine."

Kishan exited quickly while Ren leaned back against the railing with a determined expression on his face.

"Well? Are you going to explain yourself, or do I have to zap you?"

"You overheard what I wanted to say. I want us to break up."

My jaw dropped. "You what?"

"I don't want us to be together anymore."

I couldn't think of anything to say except, "Why?"

"I can't . . . it won't . . . we shouldn't . . . look, I have my reasons, okay?"

"No. Just saying you have reasons isn't good enough."

Something flickered in his eyes. Pain. But it disappeared quickly and was replaced by gritty fortitude. "I don't love you anymore."

"I don't believe you. You'll have to do better than that. I read your wishes at the Star Festival. Remember?"

He grimaced. "I forgot about that. But you should believe me anyway. It'll be easier for both of us that way. Kishan has feelings for you, and it would be better if you were with him."

"You can't tell me who to love and who not to love."

"You already love him."

"I love *you*, you big idiot."

"Then stop."

"I can't just turn my feelings on and off like a water spigot."

"That's why I won't be around anymore. I'll avoid being near you. You'll never see me."

"Oh, I see. You think just not seeing you will fix everything?"

"Probably not. But it will help."

I folded my arms and looked at him with utter incredulity. "I can't believe you are telling me to be with your brother. It's really not like you. Please tell me what I did to cause this."

"You didn't do anything."

Ren spun around, leaned over, and placed his elbows on the railing. He didn't say anything for a minute so I walked over near him and leaned over too. Eventually, he said quietly, "I couldn't save you."

"What do you mean?"

"I couldn't. I tried to do CPR, but I became violently ill. I couldn't save you. Kishan had to intervene, and in my jealousy and frustration I pushed him away. I almost let you die because I didn't want him to touch you. That's when I realized I had to let you go."

"But, Ren—"

I reached out to touch his arm. Ren looked down at my hand and stepped away.

I stiffened and said, "I'm sure you're exaggerating."

"No, I'm not." He turned away from me as if he was going to leave.

"Alagan Dhiren Rajaram, you stay right here, and you listen to me!"

He spun back to me, angry. "No. Kelsey. No! I can't *be* with you! I can't *touch* you! And I *can't* save you." He gripped the railing so hard his knuckles turned white. "You need a man who can do those things. That man isn't me. It's been months, Kelsey. I haven't found the trigger. I probably never will, and you'll waste your entire *life* waiting for me! Kishan needs you. Kishan wants you. Be with him."

"I don't want to. I choose *you*, and I don't care about those other things. I'm sure we'll figure out something. *Please* don't push me away because of this."

"It's for the best, Kelsey. We know what's best for you."

"No, you don't! *You're* what's best for me."

"I'm *not*. And I'm *not* discussing this with you anymore. I've made my decision."

"Oh! You've made your decision, have you? Well, this may come as a shock to you, but you don't make decisions for me! The two of you can plan and scheme all you want, but you can't force me to feel differently about you than I do!"

Ren's shoulders fell and he said resignedly, "It won't be force. Your feelings for him will come naturally, and at the same time, your feelings for me will diminish."

"*Not bloody likely!*" I started panicking. Ren was serious. He had never backed off when he set his mind to something before, and I wasn't making any headway at talking him out of this. I began hyperventilating. Tears trickled down my face. "Nothing about this feels natural. I can't believe you're willing to give me away."

"Don't be stubborn about this, Kelsey."

I laughed wetly with sardonic humor. "I don't think I'm the one being stubborn here."

He sighed. "We need to face the fact that our relationship is dysfunctional. Why put us both through the pain when it's not necessary? You can be happy with Kishan and . . . I'm sure I can find someone else too."

I'm sure he could. All he'd have to do is walk down any street in the world, and there would be hundreds of "someone elses" lined up for blocks.

I inhaled shakily. "But there isn't anyone else I want. I don't want us to break up."

Ren laughed cynically. "I knew you wouldn't listen to reason." He sighed. "Fine. Then let's do this the hard way." He squared his shoulders, and his mouth turned up cruelly. "People break up all the time, Kelsey. Just accept it. The fact of the matter is, it was nice for a while, but it's time I moved on. No forgotten memories could possibly be worth all this . . . pain. All this drama."

"I still don't believe you. I know you still care about me."

"How can I care about a girl when my gut twists in agony every time I touch her?"

"You never complained before."

"You're the only girl I've ever kissed, and a kiss that can only last a few seconds just isn't worth it."

"You know what I think? I think you are feeling extremely guilty about the CPR thing, and you're trying to protect me. You've always been overprotective, so now you think breaking up with me will save me. You've got some kind of hyperactive Superman complex, and your favorite pastime is to sacrifice our being together for my safety."

He grunted and ran a hand through his hair. "Apparently I'm not making myself clear. I . . . don't . . . *want* . . . you. Not anymore. I'm not even sure I want a girlfriend right now. Maybe I'll just play the field for a while, break a few hearts. I think I'll try a redhead or a blonde next time."

"I'll believe it when I see it."

"Is that what it will take? You have to see me with another woman before you believe I'm serious?"

I folded my arms. "Yes."

"Fine. I'll be happy to accommodate you."

"Oh . . . no . . . you . . . won't! If I see you with another woman, I will personally strangle you, Tarzan!"

"I don't want to hurt you, Kelsey, but you're forcing me. I'm serious about this. We don't belong together, and until you come to accept that, you won't see me." Ren turned to leave.

"You coward. Hiding from a girl half your size."

He spun back around. "I'm no coward, Kelsey. You once left me saying we didn't belong together. That we didn't . . . match. I've come to believe you're right. *You* are not for *me*. I'll find someone else. Someone," he worked his jaw, "prettier. And a little less mouthy would be good too."

I gasped softly as fat, wet teardrops fell to my cheeks.

Seeing me falter, Ren moved in for the kill. "I'm sure we'll both be able to move on quickly. Maybe even within the week."

I turned around to hide my emotional turmoil, still speechless.

"The good news for you is, you already have a backup boyfriend or two. You have it easy. Men seem to flock to you like bears to honey, so count your blessings."

I wrapped my hands across my stomach trying to contain the pain. Sucking in a shaky breath, I asked quietly, "So is that it? This is good-bye? We won't mean anything to each other anymore? You won't even be my friend?"

"That's right. I'll help on the tasks to break the curse, but other than that, don't expect to see me. And when Durga's tasks are complete, I'll just disappear. You'll never see me again."

He took a few steps away but stopped when I softly said, "Ren?"

He sighed. "Yes?"

I turned and took a few steps so I could face him. I looked at his handsome face, searching for a sign that he would end this foolishness. His visage was set as hard as stone. There would be no changing his mind, no relenting. I tried another tack and threatened, "If you do this . . . if you leave me again . . . there won't be another chance."

Another fat tear plopped onto my cheek. He took a step closer, reaching out his finger to the teardrop. Our eyes met, and my heart thumped horribly in my chest. I loved him so much it hurt. *How could he do this to us?* It felt wrong. These words he was saying were false. I knew it in my mind, but my heart was in pain regardless. *My* Ren would never say these things to me, but was he still *my* Ren? Had he really changed that much?

Ren studied the teardrop as he rubbed it between his finger and thumb. He looked up, his blue eyes hardened sapphires. "I won't need another chance. I won't be seeking you out again."

Maybe he wasn't really my Ren anymore. Maybe I've been fooling myself all along, wishing and hoping for something I'll never get back. Angrily, I said, "You'd better be sure. Because if I commit myself to Kishan, I won't leave him for you. It wouldn't be fair to him."

Ren laughed wryly. "I consider myself duly warned."

He walked off as I whispered, "But I'll still love *you*."

If he heard me, he didn't stop. I stood at the rail for a long time trying to figure out how to swallow again. Emotion clogged my throat, and I could only inhale in shallow breaths.

Ren was true to his word. I didn't see him that whole week. The rest of us went diving as scheduled. Everyone kept their eyes trained on me, but I was much more composed and did fine. I even saw a nurse shark swimming on the seabed and didn't freak out. I had lost my appetite though, and Kishan kept trying to shove food in my face.

One morning, I'd skipped breakfast. Wes found me sitting on top of the wheelhouse in a little spot I thought nobody else knew about. He took a seat next to me.

"Whoo-wee! This looks like about the top of the world. Why, I think I can even see the curve of Earth from up here."

I nodded.

"So your feller called it quits, I hear."

I didn't respond, so he went on. "A good feller's as scarce as teeth on a chicken. I sure am sorry about that, honey. A guy that would dump a pretty, sweet little gal like you . . . well, it just don't make no sense. The boy likely figures the sun comes up just to hear him crow."

"Have you ever broken up with anyone?"

"Once. I still regret it."

"What happened?"

"She was my high school sweetheart. Everyone figured we'd graduate, and I'd go off to college. She'd go to the local community college until

I was a junior, and then I'd come back and slap an engagement ring on her finger. My whole life was planned out for me. It wasn't a bad life, but I wanted to have some say in it. When I started getting itchy feet, I quit her before I even quit the college. I loved her. Still do. She might've even come with me. I suspect she waited for me awhile, but when I didn't call or write, she gave up and married another."

"Maybe you should call her now."

"Nah. She's got young 'uns now. And once you let that cat out of the bag . . . well, let's say it's easier to let it out than it is puttin' it back in."

"I understand. Regret is a hard thing to live with."

"She probably happily hates me now. I imagine it's better that way."

"I can't imagine she'd hate you. I could never hate Ren."

He rubbed his jaw. "You couldn't, huh? Well . . . maybe someday I'll write her a letter."

"You should."

"Your Mr. Kadam says y'all are goin' to town tonight. He said you have some business near Mangalore. He'd like to talk with you about it. Want to head down with me?"

"I suppose."

Wes escorted me to Mr. Kadam, who was busy researching. He indicated a chair nearby.

"Thank you, Wes. I would have sent Kishan, but he seems to be missing at the moment."

"He's probably running errands for the invisible man," I commented.

"Yes. Perhaps." Mr. Kadam patted my hand sympathetically, and Wes left with a nod.

Getting straight to business, Mr. Kadam turned his laptop around to show me a picture of a temple. "This is the Sri Mangaladevi Temple near Mangalore. We will be going there around midnight to try to awaken the goddess Durga once again. I believe that tonight's offerings should

be related to the pillar representing water. Here is a picture of it. It's slightly damaged, but you can still make out the carvings."

The picture showed the goddess Durga at the top of a stone pillar ornately carved with starfish, shells, and fish. The images showed fishermen gathering their nets from the sea, a river sprouting from a conch shell, and farms with rain clouds above them. Villagers offered basins of water along with the bounty of the sea.

Mr. Kadam continued, "I thought you and I could go shopping today to gather some items we may need while I secure access to the temple after hours."

I shrugged, not caring what we did.

At the appointed time, I waited for Mr. Kadam by the Jeep and dully watching the dockworkers lower the ramp so we could drive off the boat.

Ren is infuriating. What is he thinking? Does he really believe he can just shove Kishan and me together, and that everything will be fine? Get a man for Kelsey. Any man and she'll be happy. Phet said I'd make a choice. This isn't a choice; this is a setup. Well, I don't need to be set up. I know it's not easy having a girlfriend you can't touch, but I was willing to put up with that. That particular problem goes both ways. It affects me as much as it does him.

Kishan told Ren that the CPR thing wasn't his fault. I'm okay. No harm done. How does he expect me to put up with his 180-degree mood swings? Seriously! I should keep a daisy around so I can pluck off the petals to figure out if he loves me or loves me not. If he doesn't want to be with me, then fine, but he can't make me love Kishan or anyone else. Why does my life have to be so complicated?

I stood there gnawing my lip and thinking while I waited for Mr. Kadam. He finally showed up, apologizing for being late. Apparently, he'd had a problem locating Ren too.

Fine. Let him play hide-and-seek. I have other things to do.

Mr. Kadam and I spent the afternoon in town purchasing a bag full of items related to the ocean or water. We ate lunch at a little café while he talked of mundane things. He didn't have any advice to give except to try to be happy. He didn't have any ideas about how I *could* be happy but said he felt confident that I could do it.

As soon as we got back to the boat, I pulled out my cell phone tracker. Now that we had broken up, all bets were off, and I turned on the small screen with a vengeance. Ren's blip showed that he'd moved down to the guest quarters a deck below us, but he never stayed put for long. I followed his blip on my GPS for a while that afternoon. I let him stay out of sight while keeping an eye on his whereabouts, but I started to feel like a stalker-girlfriend—the kind that circles parking lots looking for her ex-boyfriend's car. So I closed my phone and stopped looking for him.

That evening, I pulled out the bag of purchases and placed all the items in a backpack. We'd bought sunglasses, flip-flops, shells, starfish, a small sealed copper pot of Ganges river water, sunscreen, a live goldfish, coral, a package of dried seaweed, a bottle of drinking water, a CD of ocean sounds, and I added the feather of an ocean bird I'd found on the beach.

I'd taken a nap when we got back and was reading a book in the lounge area when Nilima came in.

"Hi, Miss Kelsey. How are you?"

"As good as can be expected, I suppose. And you?"

"Very well. I hope you don't mind, but I wanted to do something for you."

"What's that?"

She handed me a piece of beautiful silk cloth. "Will you take this with you tonight and offer it to Durga as well?"

"Okay, but why?"

"At the temple you are visiting, maidens participate in a fast called Mangala Parvati Vrata, or the fast of the Durga Mangalore Temple. Women go without food every Tuesday in the summer for many weeks and then offer silk to the goddess."

"Why do they do that?"

"Because they believe the goddess Durga will find them a charming and handsome groom who will be good to them."

"Oh, I see."

"Yes. When I heard that Grandfather wanted to come to this temple, I began to fast, not for myself, but for you."

"So you fasted yesterday? On Tuesday?"

She tossed her beautiful black hair over her shoulder. "No. I have been fasting much longer than that. You may recall I have not been at dinner or breakfast much since we got on the boat."

I leaned forward and took Nilima's hand. "Do you mean you haven't eaten for more than two weeks?"

"I have had water and milk, but I have not eaten solid food for that time. I have hoped that even though I have not fasted every Tuesday that my many days of fasting will show my dedication. My wish is that Durga will help you find happiness."

"Nilima, I don't know what to say." I hugged her. "No one's ever done anything like this for me before. I would be happy to accept the silk, and I'll give it to Durga tonight."

She smiled and squeezed my hand. "Just in case, I'll wait until you return to break my fast. Good luck to you tonight, Miss Kelsey."

"Thank you for being such a good friend. I never had a sister, but I can't imagine a better one than you."

"And you are my good friend and sister as well. Goodnight."

"Goodnight."

Nilima went off to bed, and I returned to my chair. I fingered the

beautiful cloth she'd brought and thought about her offering until Mr. Kadam came to retrieve me. I picked up the backpack, slung it over my shoulders, and slid Fanindra onto my arm. We went down to the garage and met Kishan, who had a bag with the Golden Fruit, the Scarf, and the weapons, just in case.

Kishan opened the passenger door for me and got in the back. Suddenly, the door behind me opened and Ren climbed into the Jeep. He looked at me only briefly and then closed the door and put on his seatbelt. The ride into town was awkward and silent.

At the temple, we parked around the back. The building was lit up brightly, so bright, in fact, that it looked like a Disneyland attraction. The structure was conical in shape, like the other temples we'd visited, and had two square buildings attached at each side. The side buildings had glass windows that reminded me of fast-food take-out restaurants except golden statuettes were placed in the windows.

With the lights on, the temple seemed an orange or golden color, but in reality it was white with gold trim. When I expressed concern about the lights, Mr. Kadam assured me that he'd arranged for us to be alone and that it was normal for the temple to remain lit this time of year.

We walked through the unlocked door, entered the temple, and passed several doorways. Mr. Kadam led us down the hall until we entered a spacious open area. On the far end of the room, lit up from every possible angle, was a golden statue of Durga seated on a golden throne.

Her eyes were closed, and she was dressed in red silk cloth. Precious jewels were wrapped around her neck along with garlands of flowers. When I asked Mr. Kadam if she was made of real gold, he said that actually she was bronze and that all statues of Durga were either made of stone or bronze. He did acknowledge, though, that it was possible for her to have been painted gold or to have a golden overlay.

Durga's tall, pointed hat was jeweled and garlands of flowers hung from the curved top, which made it look like a feminine version of a Native American chief's headdress. I could see only four of her arms and only two of her weapons: an axe and a staff. Two of her hands had symbols carved on the palms. Her lips were painted red. She looked so different from the other stone statues that I wondered if she would awaken.

Mr. Kadam hoped to stay this time, but he was prepared to leave at a moment's notice. I unzipped the backpack, removed our offerings, and placing them at Durga's feet. I took out the piece of silk last and gently laid it across her lap. No one asked any questions, which was a relief. It wasn't until we all took a few steps back that I looked around the room. There weren't any pillars to hold onto.

"Things could get a little bumpy, so be forewarned."

Kishan nodded at me, and I brushed the bell anklet with my finger. I choked on the sweet memory of the anklet but quickly shoved the thought to the back of my mind. Touching my fingertips to the amulet around my neck for courage, I held out my hand to Kishan. He stepped forward and took it. I held out a hand to Ren also, but he moved to the other side of Mr. Kadam, who took my hand instead. I gritted my teeth, waited for Ren to take Mr. Kadam's hand, and then spoke.

"Goddess Durga, we've returned again to ask your help as we begin this third quest. Help us break the curse that has fallen upon these men and defeat the evil one who set it upon them."

I squeezed Kishan's hand, and he stepped forward. "Beautiful goddess, please appear to us once again and grant us the tools necessary to overcome those who would prevent us from finding your prize."

I looked pointedly down the line at Ren, who said, "We come seeking your wisdom and strength. Please aid us in our time of need."

"Mr. Kadam? Would you like to say something?" I asked.

"What do I say?"

"Say whatever it is you'd like Durga's help with."

He pondered for a few seconds. "Help me come to the aid of my . . . princes and bring an end to their suffering."

"Okay, now if you two would change to tigers."

They did, but nothing happened.

Mr. Kadam asked, "What usually happens next?"

"Hmm, the second the tigers switch, some kind of shaking or earthquake or terrible wind starts."

"Perhaps my being here is detrimental."

"I don't think so."

"What is different about this other than my being here?"

"The statue is golden, not stone. Both Ren and Kishan are here. Before it was just one or the other."

"Did you always hold hands like that before?"

"Yes."

"Let's try that before we abandon this temple. Kishan and Ren, if the two of you will hold Miss Kelsey's hand, I will stand back this time."

Ren reluctantly took my hand. He grunted softly, and I imagined I could feel the burn too. The three of us quickly went through our requests once more before the brothers changed into tigers. Suddenly, the room rocked. Ren changed back into a man just before I slammed into his chest. He put his arms around me to hold me steady. Wind swept through the temple, and the floor pitched again. We both crashed into Kishan, and all three of us fell in a tangle to the floor.

Water began dripping down the statue. It started as a trickle. Then something seemed to burst and a flood poured down and pooled across the floor. A river of water rushed into the temple from every door. Waves of water beat against my legs like surf, and a whipping wind pummeled us. Just as the lights went out, drops of rain hit our faces. Soon our feet

no longer touched the floor. We had no choice but to swim in the dark water as the waves grew bigger.

Ren yelled, "Kelsey! Grab onto my shirt! Don't let go!"

I screamed when something grabbed my leg.

"It's me!"

"Kishan? We have to find Mr. Kadam!"

The three of us bobbed, riding impossibly high waves as we called out to Mr. Kadam. Finally, we heard him. "I'm here."

Ren left me with Kishan and used the tired-swimmer tow Wes had taught us to bring Mr. Kadam closer. Soon the wind quieted, and the waves stilled. I heard a sucking, draining sound. After a few minutes, Ren said he could stand again. It wasn't long before I could stand too, and the four of us huddled together in the darkness, wet and uncomfortable.

"I should have asked more questions before I decided to tag along," Mr. Kadam said as he chuckled. "I might have decided to let you three do this on your own."

The water was almost gone, and Kishan wandered across the room to retrieve our backpacks. He pulled out a glow stick from his and used the light to examine the statue. The beautiful gold and silk were now sodden and filthy. Mud and seaweed covered it, the floor, and us.

"Uh . . . you might not be getting your deposit back, Mr. Kadam," I said drolly.

"Indeed."

"Kelsey! Here!" Kishan gestured me closer.

A handprint had emerged on the throne where none was before.

"Okay. Stand back."

Kishan retreated only a little as I pressed my hand onto the print and released my lightning power. My hand turned blue and then translucent, and Phet's marks surfaced once again. I felt something shift in the statue before Kishan pulled me back. A soft rain fell from above.

The sodden headdress and golden crown melted away. The golden throne melted too and became a seat of coral encrusted with shells, starfish, and jewels. Durga's arms dripped rainwater, and two of them began moving.

The goddess brushed water droplets from her arms, and where she wiped, her iridescent glowing skin brightened the room enough for us to see her clearly. Her skin had a pearly luster of alabaster that shifted as she moved, shimmering with blues, greens, and purples. She turned slightly, and a spectacular gleam of light caused me to close my eyes. When I opened them I thought the swirling patterns on her skin reminded me of a pearlescent nail polish, or maybe it was more like the scales of a fish. Whatever it was, it was lovely.

Durga pushed away the remaining piece of her headdress and brushed back her hair in the rain as if she was showering. I watched in fascination as all the gold washed away to reveal the beautiful goddess's long, dark hair. She wore a simple sea-green dress and a lei of lotus flowers. Her feet were bare. When the shower stopped, she squeezed the water out of her hair and pulled the dripping mass over one shoulder.

With a voice like a tinkling mermaid, Durga laughed. "Ah, Kelsey, my daughter. Your offerings are accepted."

From the corner of my eye, I saw objects shimmering from all over the room where the water had deposited them.

Durga clucked her tongue. "Oh, but you are all uncomfortable. Let me help." She clapped a pair of her hands together, and when she drew them apart, a rainbow appeared. She nudged it, and it wound toward us like a snake, encircling all of us. Within moments, we were clean and dry. The rainbow circled around Durga as well before dissipating, leaving her dry, with coral-red lips and rosy cheeks.

With a crooked finger, the goddess beckoned me closer. Fanindra came alive and slid from my arm to Durga's lap, then coiled around her wrist.

Durga spoke as she patted the snake's head. "I miss you too." She picked up Nilima's piece of silk and pressed it to her cheek.

Indicating the cloth, she said, "We will talk of this soon. But first, I must meet someone."

"Yes. This is Mr. Kadam," I said gesturing to him.

Mr. Kadam came closer and knelt on the ground.

"Please rise and speak with me."

He stood, pressed his hands together, and bowed.

"I am glad that you have come to see me. You have sacrificed much and will be asked to sacrifice more. Are you willing to do that?"

"I would sacrifice anything for my children."

The goddess smiled at him. "Well said. If only there were more men, more fathers such as you. I sense your great pride and joy in them. This is the greatest blessing and fulfillment a father can have: to spend your years developing and nurturing your children and then to see the glorious results—strong, noble sons who remember your lessons and who will pass them on to their own. This is what all good fathers wish for. Your name will be remembered with much respect and love."

A tear dripped down Mr. Kadam's cheek, and I squeezed his hand. Durga turned her attention to Kishan.

"My ebony one, come closer."

Kishan approached the goddess with a wide grin. She held out a hand for him to kiss. She smiled at him in return, and, for a second, I thought it was more than just a goddess-to-subject kind of smile. "This is for you," Durga said. She took a thin necklace I hadn't seen from her neck and placed it around Kishan's. A nautilus shell was strung on the end.

"What is it?" he asked.

"It's a *kamandal*. Once dipped into the Ocean of Milk, it will never empty."

Kishan bowed. "Thank you, my Lady."

"White tiger, come to me."

As Ren approached, I moved to the other side of Kishan.

"I have something for you as well." Another arm materialized from behind her back to hand Ren a golden weapon that looked like one of the Sai knives hanging in Mr. Kadam's sword collection at home. I heard a click as she turned the knife and separated its wicked blades. After joining them again, Durga twisted the handle until the points rolled and the head rotated.

The staff lengthened and became a trident. She pointed it away and pushed on the end. A long, thin spear shot out of the center tip and buried itself into the stone wall. A replacement spear materialized. She twisted the handle again, and it shrank back to its smaller form. Ren took it from her palm, marveling at the golden weapon.

"This is called a *trishula*, or 'trident.'"

"Thank you, goddess." Ren backed away, saying nothing else.

She studied him thoughtfully for a moment, and then turned to me with a smile. "I would like to speak with my daughter alone now."

The men all nodded. "We'll wait for you in the car, Miss Kelsey. We have plenty of time before we need to head back to the boat."

Ren was the last to leave. Briefly, he looked at the goddess and me, before disappearing down the hall with the others. When I turned back to Durga, she was petting Fanindra and cooing at the snake. I let them visit for a minute, wondering what I would say about the silk offering.

She finally turned her attention back to me and reached out a finger to lift my chin. "Why are you still so sad, dear one? Did I not keep my promise to watch over your tiger?"

"You did. He's back and safe, but he doesn't remember me. He's blocked me out, and he says we aren't meant to be together."

"What is meant to be is meant to be. All things in this universe are known, and yet mortals must still seek to discover their own purpose,

their own destiny, and they must make choices that take them on a path of their own choosing. Yes. Your white tiger has made the decision to remove you from his memory."

"But why?"

"Because he loves you."

"That doesn't make any sense."

"Things often don't when you have your nose pressed against them. Take a step back and try to see the whole picture." She rubbed the silk cloth between her fingers. "Much sacrifice has been made on your behalf. Many maidens come to this shrine seeking my blessing. They wish for a virtuous husband, and they want to have a good life. Is that what you seek also, Kelsey? Do you wish for an honest, noble young man to be your life's companion?"

"I . . . I haven't really been thinking of marriage, to be honest with you. But yes, I would like my life's companion to be honest and noble and my friend. I want to love him without regrets."

She smiled at me. "To have regret is to be disappointed with yourself and your choices. Those who are wise see their lives like stepping stones across a great river. Everyone misses a stone from time to time. No one can cross the river without getting wet. Success is measured by your arrival on the other side, not on how muddy your shoes are. Regrets are felt by those who do not understand life's purpose. They become so disillusioned that they stand still in the river and do not take the next leap."

I nodded.

Durga leaned over to stroke my hair. "Do not fear. He *will* be your friend, your mate in every way. And you will love him more fiercely than you have loved before. You will love him as much as he loves you. You will be happy."

"But which brother is it?"

She smiled and ignored my question. "I will also consider your sister Nilima. A woman of such devotion needs love too, I should think. Take this." She handed me her lei of lotus flowers. "It has no special power except that the blooms will not fade, but it will serve a purpose on your voyage. I want you to learn the lesson of the lotus. This flower springs forth from muddy waters. It raises its delicate petals to the sun and perfumes the world while, at the same time, its roots cling to the elemental muck, the very essence of the mortal experience. Without that soil, the flower would wither and die."

She placed the lei over my neck. "Dig down and grow strong roots, my daughter, for you will stretch forth, break out of the waters, and find peace on the calm surface at last. You will discover that if you hadn't stretched, you would have drowned in the deep, never to blossom or share your gifts with others."

I nodded and wiped a tear from my eye. Durga's limbs started moving and tightening, taking on a golden hue once again. "It's time to leave me, precious one. Take Fanindra."

The snake flicked her tongue out a few times and then, leaving Durga's wrist, wound onto my arm. Liquid gold began rising up the sides of the throne, covering the coral and shells.

"When you get to the City of the Seven Pagodas, seek out the Shore Temple. A woman waits there for you. She will give you guidance on your voyage."

"Thank you. For everything."

Durga's coral-red lips smiled again and hardened. Liquid gold swept over her body and face, and she was soon a statue. The piece of silk was still clutched in her hand as if someone had tucked it into her fist.

"Good-bye." I turned away from the statue and patted Fanindra's head. The lights flickered on, and the hall looked as if it had never been disturbed. I inhaled the sweet scent of the lotus flowers as I made my

way back to the Jeep. The flowers smelled like citrus, grapefruit, maybe. The scent was light and floral and feminine, a little bit like jasmine and gardenia. I was thinking so hard about what Durga had said that when a warm hand took my elbow, it startled me.

"Are you alright?"

"I'm fine. You didn't have to wait for me, Kishan."

He kissed my forehead. "Sure, I did. Come on. The others are in the car. Let's get back to the boat."

When we got back to the ship, Ren gave the trident to Kishan before disappearing again.

beach party

By the time I woke up the next morning, the *Deschen* was under way again. I met Wes, Kishan, and a reluctant Ren in the media room that afternoon for some shark training. We watched DVDs of sharks in their native environment. Wes didn't believe in watching shark-attack videos. He felt they only created panic.

"The less panicked you are, the better chance you have of surviving," Wes said. "The first thing you should learn about sharks is how to avoid drawing their attention. Sharks like to hang out between sandbars, near steep drop-offs, and anywhere the fishing is good. If you see a lot of birds in an area, that means lunch, and lunch means sharks. Don't dive during feeding hours—that would be dawn, dusk, and night. But if the grub is good, sharks will eat any time of the day. Don't wear shiny, flashy clothes. Muted shades are better, like your wet suit. A flash looks like fish scales in the water."

Ren raised his head to look at me. "We'll get you a black swimsuit at the next port."

"I believe you were the one who insisted I buy a colorful suit."

"I'm glad you won't be wearing that one anymore anyway. It's too . . . enticing."

I glared at him across the room. "You don't get to choose what I do with my life anymore, remember? And if I want to *entice* someone, I will."

Ren replied in a dangerous tone. "Fine. Entice every shark in the ocean then. Is that what you're trying to accomplish?"

"You'd probably like that. It sure would be a lot easier on you if some giant shark made off with me. That would solve *all* your problems now, wouldn't it?"

Kishan interrupted after shoving Ren on the arm. "Nobody wants you to get eaten by a giant shark, Kells. Not even Ren."

Ren and I were staring angrily at each other across the room when Wes howled with laughter. "Whew! You two are blowin' hotter air than a tornado circlin' a volcano in Hades. It's likely ta melt all the bolts holdin' this boat together."

"Sorry, Wes, but he started it," I said huffily.

"And I'll be more than happy to finish it."

"I'd like to see you try, you hardheaded—"

Ren smiled coldly and countered, "*Unbending*."

"Mulish!"

"Unreasonable!"

"Bullheaded, pigheaded, *tiger*headed—"

"*Tiger*headed?" Wes asked in puzzlement.

Kishan just shrugged his shoulders.

I went on, now that I was on a roll. "Cold-blooded, insensitive, inflexible . . . *heartless* man!"

Ren yelled, "Fine! Wear what you want. Swim naked for all I care! Any shark that eats you will probably get a stomachache anyway and spit you right back out."

"Ha! You'd have a lot in common then, wouldn't you?"

Wes threw his hands in the air. "Alrighty, then. Let's take a break and simmer down. Nilima left us some fruity drinks at the bar so why don't you two go get one, work this thing out, and be back in five?"

I stormed off to the juice bar with Ren trailing silently behind me. When I reached the tray, I seriously thought about throwing the tall glass of juice into Ren's face. I took a few deep breaths, all the while feeling him staring at my back. The warmth of him seeped into my skin, prickling my nerves. He reached around me, deliberately brushing my arm when he picked up his drink.

"Why do you have to make everything so hard, Kelsey?"

"Why do you?"

"Believe it or not, I'm *trying* to make things easier."

"Why are you here anyway? I thought you were avoiding me."

"I *am*. But I need to learn about sharks."

I sipped my juice and then said, "Doesn't a predator already know all about other predators and how they think? Maybe if I pay extra special attention, I'll finally figure you out."

"I'm easy to figure out. A tiger only needs three things to be comfortable. Lots of food, sleep, and . . . actually, no, it's just those two things."

I snorted. "Somehow I don't think Kishan would limit himself to only those two."

"I'm sure he wouldn't," Ren responded tightly. "He'd probably add you to his list."

"Now why would he need me? An unreasonable, unattractive female?"

"I never said you were unattractive. I said I'd look for someone prettier. I didn't say I'd *find* someone prettier, just that I'd look."

"Well, what's keeping you, then? Go look already and leave me alone."

"That's my plan. Now stop goading me in class so I can learn something."

I fumed as he walked off. When I entered the room, Ren was sipping his juice as calmly as if we'd never fought. Kishan waved me over to sit next to him. I was still extremely angry and had a hard time paying attention. I handed Kishan a glass of juice while I stared at Wes, who had already begun teaching, but all my thoughts were focused on Ren, picking apart every little thing he said. Finally, something Wes said brought me back to him.

"Sharks can smell blood a mile away, so don't enter the water if you have a cut. Don't splash around a lot. If you're diving and a shark approaches, descend to the ocean floor and hide. It limits the angles it can get at you. And don't play dead; it doesn't work on sharks. Really, it doesn't work on any major predator. They'll eat you anyway—bears, wolves, tigers. They don't really discriminate."

"Exactly," I mumbled. "They'll chew up and spit out any helpless girl who comes along."

Puzzled, Wes looked at me. "Right."

Ren ignored me, and Kishan sighed.

Wes continued. "Okay, now suppose you *are* attacked by a shark. Poke him in his gills or his eyes. Hit him. Aggressively. Use whatever weapon you have at your disposal and beat him like a granny beats her rug. Try to remain vertical because it's harder for him to get a bite. If you are bitten, stop the bleeding even if you're underwater. Don't wait until you get ashore."

He handed us a small gadget and said, "This is called a shark shield. It's a device that's starting to become commonplace among divers and surfers."

"What does it do?" I asked.

"Sharks have gel-filled sacs on their snouts that they use as sensors when they're looking for a snack. The shield sends out an electric wave that tickles their noses. They don't like it too much and leave. Attach

one part to your ankle and the other part to the front of your BCD. There's some debate on its effectiveness, but I've worn them, and I've never been attacked."

"Okay. What else?"

"That's about all you can do. If the shark is smaller you might get away, but you have about as much chance of escaping a big shark as you would a T. rex. They're fast and powerful. Most of the time, the reason divers and surfers get away is because they don't taste good. Humans are too bony. Sharks much prefer fat, blubbery seals.

"You see, the way sharks hunt is to come at you fast and hard and hit before you even know they're there. They circle under you, gather speed, and shoot up like a torpedo, disabling you in one hit, mostly by slamming into you with such force it breaks bones. The great whites can swim around thirty miles per hour in short bursts, but they generally don't attack humans like that. That's a real attack—the way they hunt seals.

"Most of the time when a shark attacks humans, they're just looking for a taste. If you taste good, they make more of an effort. Sometimes they leave you alone. They're curious. Their teeth are like a cat's whiskers. It's how they experience their world.

"One surfer told me he was sitting on his board resting when a seventeen-foot great white popped up out of the water and started nibbling on his board as gently as a mouse. It didn't like the taste and dropped under the water again like a submarine."

When our lesson was over, Wes invited me to go spear fishing with him and the guys that afternoon, but I declined. He promised to catch some fresh seafood for me. I nodded weakly because I didn't have the heart to tell him that I couldn't eat meat if I was thinking about how it was killed.

Instead, I met Mr. Kadam that afternoon, and we did a little

underwater shooting of our own. He wanted me to try out my lightning power in water. We started in the wet garage at the open ramp where Ren and Kishan had set up a group of floating buoys. The buoys were weighted enough to rest just below the surface of the water. I aimed at the closest one and missed. When I tried again, it exploded like an underwater mine.

"Good, Miss Kelsey," Mr. Kadam said. "You should practice your aim above water as well as below. With the refraction of the water, your aim will be different than it is on land."

After I'd finished blowing up the buoys, Mr. Kadam took me to the pool where there were several more underwater targets. Just as I was about to slip into the water, he stopped me.

"We're going to try this with a dummy first. If we're successful here, we'll move to salt water later. Now don't fire full blast. We're going to try this in increments. Let the power build gradually."

"Isn't this going to electrocute me or blow up the pool?" I questioned dubiously. "Like dropping a hair dryer into the bathtub?"

"I don't believe so. First of all, I don't think your power is electric. I have a theory that it's heat—a fire that burns so hot it turns white. Even if I'm wrong and it is electric, water in its perfect form is not really a conductor. The impurities in water such as dust, salt, and other trace elements are what conduct the electricity.

"I had all the water removed from this pool while we were dockside. The tiles have been scrubbed and cleaned, and I've had it filled with low-conductivity water. It was expensive, but I think it will be worth it. Now let's get started. Would you like to name our test dummy?"

I grinned evilly. "Sure. Let's call him Al, shall we?"

Mr. Kadam nodded, took "Al" by the waist, and put him into the water. We both stood to the side of the pool as I aimed at the first target with the lowest level of power. Nothing much happened. I increased the

power level until I burned a hole through the piece of weighted wood. Al floated on the surface undamaged and oblivious.

"Good. Now turn up your power until the stream turns white, but try not to burn a hole through the pool. Our rooms are directly under it."

I focused very carefully and started out low, letting the power flow through me until it turned white. The water started boiling where the stream of light entered, and the wood turned black. I stopped just before it formed a hole. Our dummy was still floating happily on the boiling water.

Mr. Kadam and I moved to another target for further practice. After he was satisfied with the inanimate tests, he picked up a cage and took out a small white duck. Letting it go on the pool's surface, he asked me to try to hit the target wood again. I apologized briefly to the duck and used my power on the next target. The duck kept away from the area but swam around the pool without discomfort. After a few more trials, Mr. Kadam decided that it was time to test it with a human. He jumped into the pool.

"No. I don't want to risk you. I'll do it myself."

"I'm already in the pool, Miss Kelsey. I will not get out either, and it's not smart to risk both of us. You're much more crucial to this quest than I am."

"That's highly debatable."

"Even so. Here I am. If Daffy's alright, I'll be fine too."

"Daffy?"

"Yes. Daffy Duck. I'm rather fond of *Looney Tunes*."

"I absolutely did not know that about you, Mr. Kadam! I would have never guessed. My father loved Coyote and Roadrunner. Okay, well, here's to hoping it's wabbit season and not duck season."

I used my lowest level and built the power burst up again. Mr. Kadam reported that he was fine and even moved closer to the target.

"Interesting. The water is warmer here. I believe it's time for you to join me, Miss Kelsey. Let's practice some underwater aiming."

I hopped in with a mask and snorkel and tried again, this time with my hand underwater. I watched Daffy's feet paddle as I tucked my head underwater and focused on the task. Mr. Kadam gave me the thumbs-up sign every time I blasted each target. We spent the rest of the afternoon practicing under the pool water and then moved to the ocean to test it out in salt water. We went through the same careful process on the ocean as we did in the pool, first testing with Al, then with Daffy, then Mr. Kadam, and me last.

"I definitely believe your power is more like fire than lightning," Mr. Kadam concluded when we had finished our session. "It reminds me of a blowtorch. Did you find you had to exert more energy than you do on land?"

"Yes. In the ocean, especially."

"I thought so. The ocean is a lower temperature than the pool. It takes more energy to maintain a hotter flame in the ocean than on land or in the pool. This was very productive, Miss Kelsey. I believe you are well prepared for any underwater situation. And now, I will, as they say, hit the showers."

As Mr. Kadam walked away carrying Daffy, once again snug in his cage, I leaned against the back of the wooden bench and sighed. *Well prepared? Not by a long shot.*

Dinner consisted of a bass that Wes and Kishan had speared. It looked very nice, but I couldn't touch it. Kishan held out a forkful asking me to at least try it, but I pushed his arm away. I filled up on salad and bread instead, noticing that Ren was missing from the table.

Changing the subject, Wes mentioned that we'd be docking in Trivandrum in a couple of days. "Every year Trivandrum has a giant

beach party," he explained. "All the surfers, divers, and the townspeople go. It's a great time. There's music, food, dancing, girls in bikinis . . . in fact, why don't you come with me? You all should. Everyone's invited."

Mr. Kadam chuckled, "I think I will be staying on the boat, but you all go and enjoy yourselves."

"Girls in bikinis? No wonder you want to go," I teased. "But I'm not sure I'm up for a bikini babe kind of party."

Wes shot me a dimpled smile. "Ah, now if I'd a had a pretty sweet young thing like you on my arm, I wouldna even notice them other gals."

"I'm sure," I giggled.

"How about it, Kelsey? Will you go to the party with me?"

"I'll think about it and let you know tomorrow."

Wes grabbed my hand as I rose and kissed it while Kishan growled softly. "Don't make a feller wait too long. A feller waitin' on a gal can get ornery'er than a huntin' dog that's treed its squirrel."

"I'll definitely keep that in mind. I think I'll walk the deck for a while. Goodnight, Wes."

"'Nite."

Kishan quickly rose behind me, taking my hand. "I'll walk with you."

Hand-in-hand, we walked around to the other side of the boat and stood at the railing. I pointed out some dolphins that were swimming near our ship as if they were racing us. We watched them until they swam off.

Kishan leaned forward on the railing, looked at me, then took a deep breath and stared at the water again. "I was wondering something. Are you seriously considering going to that party with Wes? Because I don't think it's a good idea."

"Why on earth not?"

"I don't trust him."

I laughed. "Didn't you just go spear fishing with him? He could have shish kebabbed you, and he didn't, so obviously you do trust him."

"I trust him with diving, just not with you. He's too . . . slippery. Too free with his compliments. Too flippant. Those kinds of men take advantage of vulnerable women. He's not for you."

"And how would you know what kind of man he is and, even more importantly, what makes you think I'm vulnerable?"

"*Kelsey*. Ren just broke up with you, and you're still hurting from that. You *are* vulnerable, believe it or not."

"Well, vulnerable or not, I still get to make my own choices. You tigers can't plan every aspect of my life. If I want to go with Wes, I will."

"I know that. I . . . just didn't think you were ready to move on yet."

"Apparently, moving on is what I have to do."

"That doesn't mean you're ready, Kelsey."

I sighed. "Durga said I had to keep leaping. She said the point in life is to get across the river. She doesn't want me to stagnate in the mud. So I guess I might as well get a move on."

Kishan was quiet for several seconds, then said, "Are you sure you're ready to take that leap?"

"As ready as I'll ever be."

He turned to look at me and took my hands. "Then . . . I want you to consider going with me instead."

I squirmed inside. "Go with you?"

A jumble of thoughts raced through my mind. *Going with Wes to a party was one thing. I could have fun with Wes and feel comfortable knowing he didn't expect anything from me. Going with Kishan was an entirely different matter. With him it would be like a real date. Was I ready to take that step*

with Kishan? No matter how much Ren or Durga pushed me to, the answer was . . . no. Okay, let him down gently.

"I can't go with *you*," I said flatly. *Not really very gentle, Kells.*

"Why not?"

Why not? "Because . . . well . . . Wes asked me first. It would be rude to accept your invitation after he asked me."

Kishan thought about that and nodded in understanding. I mentally sighed in relief.

He said, "But I'll be there regardless. I won't interfere, but I'll feel better if I can keep my eye on you. Like I said, Wes is slippery. Lots of men are, and I'm sure the place will be packed with men—and half of them will be trying to get their hands on you."

"I think you're exaggerating."

"Don't you remember the Star Festival? There was a line of men around the block waiting to dance with you."

"Now I know you're exaggerating. You danced with me four times."

"I cut in line."

He was so serious, I laughed. "Come on, Kishan. You can walk me to my room."

The next morning, I heard movement in the adjoining bedroom. Thinking it was Ren, I knocked briefly and opened the door to find Kishan standing at the dresser in jeans searching for a shirt.

"Kishan?"

"Good morning, Kells."

He turned and thankfully pulled a shirt over his head so I could stop staring at his bronze-muscled chest.

"Are you sleeping in this room now?" I asked.

Kishan shrugged. "You need a tiger around, Kelsey. Are you feeling alright? You look a little flushed. Did you sleep well?"

"I'm fine, just embarrassed about catching you half dressed." *And enjoying the view.*

I looked around the room. "I thought Ren didn't want you in here."

"He's changed his mind."

"Yeah," I said sadly, "he does that a lot."

"Kelsey—"

I raised my hand. "Never mind. I don't really want to go there."

Dropping the matter entirely, Kishan and I spent the day together, relaxing and playing water sports. He quickly became adept at the Jet Ski, and I found it as exhilarating as the motorcycle ride.

At least I did when I wasn't overly conscious of my arms wrapped around Kishan, or my cheek pressed against his sun-warmed back. Now that I knew it was a serious possibility that we'd end up dating, I felt different around him, more awkward.

When Durga was talking about my life mate, she said I'd love him more fiercely than I'd loved before. Phet had said either brother would be a good choice, but I had been so determined to pursue a relationship with Ren and so resolute about keeping Kishan at a distance that it felt wrong for me to openly consider crossing that line. We had fun together, and Kishan didn't pressure me, so I left it at that.

When we docked at Trivandrum, Wes disembarked but said he'd be back to pick me up at six. I spent most of the afternoon with Mr. Kadam researching our new weapons. Kishan stopped by from time to time to check on our progress.

We discovered that the trident, also called a *trishula* or *trishul*, was a weapon rich in symbols. Mr. Kadam showed me a picture.

"Look here, Miss Kelsey. Each of the three prongs represents a variety of ideas. When wielded by Shiva, it reflects his three roles— creator, preserver, and destroyer. It also symbolizes the three *shaktis*, or powers—will, action, and wisdom. Sometimes it is a reflection of

the past, the present, and the future. With Durga it is said to represent states of being—inactivity, activity, and nonactivity."

"What's the difference between inactivity and nonactivity?"

"In this instance, I believe inactivity means 'doing nothing, resting, or perhaps stagnation.'"

"Uh-huh." I winced thinking about Durga's encouragements to leap forward.

"The word *tamas* is used for the third prong, which is the same prong as nonactivity. *Tamas* also means 'darkness, ignorance, or sin.' Perhaps in this case, the nonactivity is worse than the inactivity."

"Maybe it's the difference between doing good, doing bad, and doing nothing."

"Hmm . . . I could certainly see that view being applied. Another book I read indicates that the three prongs represent the three types of human suffering—physical, mental, and spiritual. The *trishula* is to remind us that Durga can help stop that suffering."

I took careful notes while Mr. Kadam buried his head back in the book.

Later while I was getting dressed for the party, I thought about the symbols of the trident. Some people believed that making a mistake was better than doing nothing. Maybe Durga was trying to tell me that if I just did *something* then my pain would diminish. I could only hope so.

The idea of living without Ren was like a tight vise wrapping thick bands around my throat. I felt like I'd been dragged onto an emotional roller coaster against my will, and all I could do was suffer through it with my head between my knees and try not to throw up. Screaming "I want off" wouldn't do any good. There was no getting off the ride at this point. I had to see it through to the end and hope the safety bar was secure enough.

I was supposed to meet Wes on the dock, so I hurried through my primping. Nilima had the Divine Scarf make me an outfit like one she saw in a magazine. I'd just finished straightening my hair when she brought it into the room. She was all dressed up.

"Are you going to the party too, Nilima?"

She patted her hair. "Oh, I thought I might stop by. I'll see you there."

As she left, I picked up the hanger. The champagne-and-black sleeveless dress was pretty. It was ruched at the empire waist and had a sheer outer layer decorated with beautiful black bead accents. Examining the beads more closely, I discovered they weren't beads at all, but some kind of tightly woven shiny threads that looked like beads. Ren had been right about the Scarf making substitutions.

I slipped into the dress and strapped on a pair of black sandals I discovered in my closet. Wes was waiting for me on the dock. He whistled in happy appreciation and made a fuss about how nice I looked. I felt out of place because he wore a casual pair of board shorts and a white unbuttoned shirt that showed off his nicely tanned chest.

"Oh, I'm overdressed," I muttered awkwardly. "Ren and Kishan are always wearing over-the-top fancy things and I didn't realize this might be less formal. Just wait a sec and I'll change." I turned to head back to the boat.

Wes ran a couple of steps and blocked my path. "No way, darlin'. I plan on showin' you off."

I laughed as we began to walk. "It's not like I'm wearing a French bikini. I doubt anyone's going to pay attention."

"There's a big difference between crass and class, sweetheart. And you are 100 percent class. Any feller with any sense would see I got a gem on my arm."

"You're kinda sweet for a Texas cowboy."

"And you're gettin' a nice tan for an Oregon gal."

Wes entertained me with wild stories about his family, each one more unbelievable than the last. We walked toward the pulsing throb of loud party music.

The beach was full of people. There must have been at least a thousand party goers. Wes paid an entrance fee for both of us, and we headed into the throng toward a giant bonfire where people were dancing. The weather was cooler now because we were in the middle of the monsoon season, and the bonfire's heat would be welcome as the evening temperature dropped.

Wes shouted, already moving his body to the beat, "Do you want to eat first? Or dance first?"

"Dance first."

He grinned and pulled me along until he found a spot among the other weaving bodies. The pulsating rhythm of the Indian live band was impossible to resist. No one cared if they were good dancers or not. Everyone just moved happily, jumping, nodding, waving their arms, and clapping. It was a communal experience unlike dancing in America. The mood was jubilant as the crowd moved together as one.

The music almost made me feel like I was an Indian goddess sinuously moving my many limbs or a gypsy girl wearing a tinkling costume. I didn't move to the music, the music moved me until I felt like I was a part of it. I was thrumming, pulsing, and alive. Wes was thoroughly enjoying himself too.

I didn't compare the experience with my Valentine's dance with Ren. *Well . . . I almost didn't.* I slipped off my sandals and let my toes sink into the sand as Wes wrapped an arm around my waist and spun me dizzily around, effectively twirling away any negative thoughts.

After several songs, Wes said he was thirsty and hungry, so we went to the buffet tables under a canopy strung with paper lanterns. We picked up our plates and perused the choices. Wes promised he'd steer me clear of curry.

They offered roasted, buttered corn on the cob; fresh coconut; sliced tropical fruits; lamb kebabs; idli, which were savory steamed cakes dipped in chutney; cheese-filled dosas similar to crepes; daigi roast (sort of like spicy hot wings); and dabeli pao, which looked like miniature hamburgers, but the butter-toasted bun was filled with potatoes, onions, and spices and was served with tamarind chutney. Not exactly a cheeseburger, but they were good.

Wes got us tall glasses of water filled with fruit. It was extremely refreshing, and I finished one quickly and returned for another. A DJ took over when the live band quit. He incited the crowd to more frenzied dancing, and Wes was soon itching to get back out there. We passed a vendor selling roasted peanuts and another one selling ice cream.

"Come here. I want to show you something."

Wes said something to the vendor in Hindi, and the man opened his cart so we could see inside. His little freezer was full of long cylinders of precut ice cream lying across the bottom like Yule log cakes. Each cylinder was a different flavor: tropical, tutti-frutti, chai, pistachio, fig, mango, coconut, ginger, saffron, orange, cardamom, jasmine, and rose.

"No chocolate?" I asked Wes.

He laughed, told the man we'd be back later, and pulled me toward the dance floor. As we wove through the crowd, something caught my attention, and I looked up to find Kishan standing off to the side. He smiled at me briefly before heading to the food. I felt at ease knowing he was there. I could relax. Not that I was on edge with Wes, but there was something comforting about having one of my tigers nearby. I knew I was absolutely safe, like I had my own personal superhero watching over me. Kishan's presence steadied me and calmed me in a way that

bothered me to think about, so I stopped thinking and turned my attention back to Wes.

Throughout the evening, I'd spotted Kishan only one more time, but I felt his eyes on me often. It wasn't until Wes and I were dancing by the bonfire that I saw Ren.

I froze and didn't hear a thing Wes said. Ren was surrounded by beautiful, laughing women. Most of them were scantily clad and were flirting with him outrageously. He wore black slacks and a sea-green shirt with the top few buttons undone, which was somehow more appealing than all the other bare-chested men around him. His silky black hair fell over one eye, and he pushed it back as he danced. He paid attention to one girl and leaned over to whisper something to her. Then, when another girl pouted and touched his arm, he gave her his attention and touched her cheek with his fingertip.

There was a blonde, a brunette, a redhead. Tall girls, petite girls, long haired, short haired. I couldn't stop staring as girls gyrated around him, jockeying for his attention while trying to snuff out the competition. A tall, tan blonde leaned closer to say something to him; he wrapped an arm around her waist and laughed, his white smile dazzling. She reached up to brush the hair out of his eyes, and my pulse slammed. Blood pounded through me. The air became thick. I couldn't breathe. I took deep gulps trying to prevent myself from throwing up.

Wes had been watching the scene too. "Come on, Kelsey. Let's go. You don't need to see that."

I let Wes pull me away, and the sick feeling turned into a deep burning rage. I trembled with it. I wanted to heat up my hand and blast the head off of every single girl who'd touched him. I wanted to pummel him with electric shocks. Better yet, I wanted lightning to strike me dead, so I could stop feeling this terrible vibrating rage, this bitter hurt. I felt like everything good and happy had been drained out of me and

had been replaced with burning lava. I wouldn't have been surprised if steam was shooting out of my ears.

I spied Kishan at the edge of the crowd, which calmed me. My mom would have said, "Kells, now that's a young man you can rely on," and she would have been right. He'd been a constant at my side since Oregon. Never pushing, never asking more of me than I was willing to give. He was good to me.

Kishan and I looked at each other for a brief moment. In that look, I knew he was asking if I needed him. I shook my head slightly and closed my eyes. When I opened them, he was gone. The lava cooled and cracked. My insides turned black and crumbled into dust. No amount of water could wash away the thick dust choking me. My limbs were heavy weights. I sagged under the pressure and felt like collapsing to the ground.

Wes touched my hand, and I snapped out of it.

"Sorry, Wes. I'm just . . ."

"You're in shock. I understand. He shouldn't have come out here and paraded himself around like that."

I stated dully, "He can do whatever he wants to. It doesn't matter anymore."

"Let me get you a fruit drink. Some sugar will do you good."

Wes brought me back something tall and red and delicious. I sipped it slowly to humor him. I felt the sweet drink slide down my throat before dropping into a never-ending pit in my middle. I imagined it hit the black char inside me, hissed, and disappeared along with everything else.

Wes wanted to dance some more, and I told him I'd stay but only for a few more songs. We stayed far away from where I'd seen Ren. I danced, but my heart wasn't in it anymore. I just wanted to go to the ship. Wes agreed to take me back, and somewhere in my mind I felt sorry for ruining the big party that he'd looked forward to all year, but the regret was quickly overwhelmed with my own personal list of "sorry fors."

We started back up the beach. The music had changed to a slow song. I spied a flash of green out of the corner of my eye and couldn't help it. I turned to look.

Ren was dancing with a pretty Indian girl in a yellow sari. Her long dark hair reached almost to her waist. His hand was splayed out on the bare skin of her back. Laughing, he ducked his head to listen to something she was saying. When he raised his head and spun the woman toward me, I gasped. The beautiful woman was *Nilima*.

I tore my eyes from the couple and stared straight ahead. Wes was talking about something, but his words couldn't penetrate the mental fog in my brain. Eventually, he stopped talking and just held my hand as we walked back to the ship. He dropped me at my door, kissed my cheek in sympathy, and then I was alone.

I tore off my dress and fell on my bed staring wide-eyed at the dark ceiling. I heard the unmistakable sounds of fireworks and the cheering of the crowd out on the beach. Something burst inside me, a wall or a shield, maybe. It cracked and broke and silent tears slipped down my cheeks. Once they started, they wouldn't stop. It was the first time I'd cried since Ren broke up with me, and as I wiped away the tears I vowed it would be the last.

I had nightmares, but someone came into my room, a man. He touched my forehead while I slept. I was aware of it, but I was too exhausted to open my eyes. He whispered comforting words in his native language. The inner turmoil calmed, and I dropped into a restful sleep. Perhaps it was real; perhaps it was a dream. Either way, I knew I was loved.

The next morning, I rose, washed my face, dressed, and headed up to the gym. I found Kishan there getting ready to do his morning workout.

"Hey, Kells. Want to work out with me?"

"Maybe later. I came here to ask you a question."

He set down a towel and turned to me. "Okay. Go ahead."

I wrung my hands and looked at the floor as I mumbled, "Will you have dinner with me tonight?"

12

something new

"Don't I eat dinner with you every night?" Kishan laughed.

"I'm . . . I'm trying to ask you out on a *date*," I mumbled quietly.

Kishan stood silently staring at me until I began to fidget.

How do guys do this? It's so nerve-racking. "Well?" I asked impatiently. "Would you like to go out with me or not?"

Kishan took a step closer and touched my cheek. "Yes, I would like to have dinner with you tonight. Would you like to go into town?"

I considered the idea. "Yes. That would probably be the easiest thing to do."

"And we'll be alone."

I nodded. Kishan grinned and told me the name of the restaurant we would meet at. I gave him a shaky smile back and fled the gym. I felt a strong need to escape, to get off the boat, and to be on my own for a while. *Maybe a little retail therapy would help*, I hoped.

Mr. Kadam agreed to let me borrow the Jeep and head into town on my own as long as I checked in with him every two hours. He gave me some credit cards that read K. H. Khan, the same name as my passport, and reminded me to sign the slips properly. I parked in town, checked my cell phone for a good signal, and started walking.

I went into a clothing store and found a mauve blouse with crystal

beads and matching silver sequins. The long sleeves were tight at the top and flowed at the wrist. I bought some silver sandals and hoop earrings to match and found a pair of dark jeans to go with them at the next store. It would be nice to have something new for my date later that night.

I had an enjoyable, mindless afternoon strolling through the markets and shops. Most of the vendors spoke at least a little English. I checked in with Mr. Kadam often so he didn't send the cavalry out after me and bought myself an iced fruit drink to sip as I walked.

I passed a store that sold beads, a bookstore, a shop with candles and incense, and then strolled a vegetable market and browsed in what looked like a pharmacy. I passed a hair salon and heard the feminine chatter of several women talking and laughing. On a whim, I turned around and headed in the door. A pretty middle-aged woman approached me.

"Hello, miss. Would you like a cut, then?"

"A cut?"

"Or a wash and a style maybe?"

I involuntarily tugged on the tail of my braid where it hung over my shoulder.

"A cut? Yes. Why not?"

She smiled at me and guided me to a chair. I hadn't cut my hair since high school graduation. Honestly, I didn't usually give my hair much thought, but suddenly it seemed to be the right thing to do. It was time for a change. The hairdresser brought over a book of hairstyles to look at, but I waved the book away and asked for her opinion instead. She turned my head to several angles and studied the shape of my face very seriously.

"I think I know just the thing. Trust me, and I will make you gorgeous."

"Okay."

After she washed my hair, she handed me a pop-culture magazine. It had only snippets of English, but I liked looking at the pictures of all the Bollywood actors and actresses. Another girl approached with a cart of nail polishes and asked if I'd like my nails done.

"Sure, why not. I have a date tonight so I'll splurge."

They asked many questions about the man I would see, and I was able to describe Kishan in great detail. They chattered excitedly and wondered if he had a brother. I snorted and said nothing. Apparently, they were single and still looking for a good match, but so far they'd been unsuccessful. They moaned and said all the good men in the city were already taken. They even remarked that the women outnumbered the men at least two to one and told me I was lucky to find such a nice man for myself.

I nodded and bit my lip. *Huh. That explains the flock around Ren, I suppose. Not that it would really matter. He'd have a flock of women no matter where he went. For all I knew, he was already engaged or, at the very least, proposed to by a dozen women.*

We chatted most of the afternoon. I selected a mauve-colored nail polish to match my blouse and watched as the manicurist carefully painted my toenails.

I gasped when I first saw several inches of wet hair fall to the floor, but I quickly recovered, reminding myself that it was time for a new me. The stylist blew out my hair and spent forty-five minutes curling and pinning it up. When she turned me to the mirror, I was shocked. She explained that my hair was now just past shoulder level and layered. A mass of curls framed my face and brushed the back of my neck, tickling it as I moved. My hair felt light and bouncy. They let me change into my new clothes behind a curtain and even offered to refresh my makeup. I took them up on it and emerged from the salon with a new style, a new hairdo, and a new outlook on life. After generously tipping the women, I made my way over to The Seven Seas seafood restaurant that Kishan had picked.

I arrived before Kishan. The waiter sat me at a table and brought me an ice-cold lemon water. I watched the passersby and heard the motorcycle before I saw it.

Kishan pulled up, took off his helmet, and searched the street for me. He wore a pair of dark blue jeans, faded along the thighs, and a long-sleeved gray shirt with embroidery details across the chest and the back. His hair was wet and longer than Ren's.

He was a very handsome man, but better than that, he was a good man, and someone I considered a friend. Surely it wouldn't take me long to love him. He walked into the restaurant and perused the room. His eyes flitted past me and then shot back and widened as he took in my appearance. He smiled and approached the table.

He dipped his head over my hand and kissed it warmly. "You look beautiful. I almost didn't recognize you."

"Thank you, I think."

He pulled out a chair, then stopped and winced. "That's not exactly what I meant. I meant to say that you look even more beautiful than you usually do. I like that color," he said indicating my blouse. "It makes your skin look like cream."

"Thank you."

He studied my appearance carefully. "You cut your hair."

"Yes. Do you like it?"

"That depends. How long is it?"

I pulled a curl down and showed him it ended just past my shoulder.

He grunted. "That's still long enough, so I like it."

"Long enough for what?"

"Long enough for a man to run his hands through."

I blushed as he smiled warmly, his golden eyes twinkling mischievously.

Kishan picked up a menu and glanced at me over the top. "Can I ask you something? Why did you ask me to dinner?"

The waiter arrived just before I had to answer, buying me time to organize my thoughts. Kishan ordered an appetizer to share and a soda for himself and then turned his attention back to me, waiting patiently for my reply.

I picked up my napkin and twisted it in my hands. "I asked you on a date because . . . it was the right time."

"Are you sure it's not just because of Ren?"

I winced. "Honestly? That's part of it. I was very angry last night. I don't like that feeling. I'd rather make an effort to be happy, and dwelling on him isn't making me happy."

He leaned across the table and captured one of my hands. "Being with me is not something you have to do, Kells. Just because I have feelings for you doesn't mean you are obligated to act on them. I'll be here for you when you need me, no matter what."

"I know that. I don't feel obligated. I'm not saying it will be easy for me to forget him, especially when he's on the ship with us, but I'd like to try."

Kishan's golden eyes probed mine thoughtfully. Then he nodded and changed the subject as our appetizer was brought the table. We chatted through dinner, and he shared some funny stories about growing up a prince and about hunting in the jungle.

When we were finished eating, he asked me to go riding with him. The motorcycle was as thrilling the second time as it had been the first. We stopped at the top of a hill to watch the sun go down. He balanced the bike with his long legs and pulled me in front of him, drawing me back into his arms so I could rest against his chest.

He said nothing, and I relaxed, enjoying the security I felt being near him. Kishan was a quiet man, a peaceful man. A life with him would be pleasant. This time, when we rode back on the dark streets, I felt comfortable with my arms wrapped around his waist and moved a little closer. It wasn't until we were back on the ship that I realized the Jeep was still in town. He helped me off the bike and assured me a crewmember would get it in the morning.

We strolled the deck for a while holding hands. Later, when Kishan walked me to my room, he stopped me at my door, and raised my hand to his lips. "We can do this as slowly as you need to. I don't want to pressure you."

I nodded and to prove something to the both of us, I wrapped my arms around his neck, and we held each other tightly as I kissed his cheek. "Goodnight, Kishan."

He smiled and wrapped a curl around his finger. "Goodnight, *bilauta*."

Wes was leaving the ship the next day, and I was really sorry to see him go. Our diving lessons were over. We had all passed with flying colors.

Kishan knocked on our adjoining door and asked if I was ready. When I emerged, Kishan studied my hair again. I'd taken out all the pins the night before, so it fell loosely to my shoulders. He brushed his hand through the curls, smiled, and kissed my forehead.

When Wes finally showed up in the dry garage, he whistled at my haircut and shot me a dimpled grin. I apologized for ruining his party, to which he gallantly said I was the best part of it. Kishan shook hands with Wes, and then I took a step forward and hugged him.

Wes whispered in my ear. "Good luck with everything, Kelsey. I sure will be thinkin' on ya from time to time."

"I'll miss you, too."

Wes backed up, pulled the imaginary brim of a cowboy hat in salute, picked up his bag, and secured the strap over his shoulder. He winked at me and said, "Don't forget now, if you start feelin' tired of them mules and decide it's time to find yerself a nice prize stallion, look me up."

"I will." I laughed.

As we watched Wes walk down the ramp, we heard someone else fast approaching with the clickety-clack of stiletto heels.

Kishan tugged my arm impatiently.

"Let's go, Kells."

"What's the rush?" I teased.

He stiffened, and I heard a simpering female voice say, "Why, aren't you the sweetest thing? Inviting me to spend a few days here with you!"

I peeked over Kishan's large bicep and locked eyes for a split second with Ren, who had suddenly appeared arm in arm with a woman. His eyes widened briefly when he saw me and then tightened as he glared. I glared right back, but he quickly looked away and smiled at the curvy piece of insubstantial cotton candy that had attached herself like a leech to Ren's arm. She pushed past Kishan and me and boldly made her way up the ramp.

"Oh! Isn't the garage so huge! Is that a motorcycle under that cover? I just *love* motorcycles. Especially when they belong to *big, strong* men," the voice purred.

"The garage is not very exciting," Ren said. "Come on, Randi. Let's check out the pool instead."

The Barbie-shaped blonde turned to look at us. Her gaze flitted up and down my frame and, after quickly dismissing me, she turned her attention to Kishan. Her collagen-injected lips widened to something resembling a smile. "Wait a minute, gorgeous. You haven't introduced me yet."

Ren edged forward stiffly and said, "This is my brother, Kishan, and this is Kelsey."

"Why, I'm charmed to meet you." She brazenly sauntered over and put her hand on Kishan's bicep. "My, my, they sure grow them big in India, don't they?"

"This is Randi," Ren finished.

Randi turned her attention to me when I asked if she was from America.

She blinked prettily. "America? Oh, yes. I'm from Beverly Hills. And where are you from?"

"Oregon."

She wrinkled her nose. "I could never live in Oregon. I need to have the sun. Oregon's much too cold. If I lived there, I'd never be able to lay out on the beach. But I can see laying out isn't something you like to do, so Oregon's probably the ideal place for you, then, isn't it? I think everyone should know their place in the world and stay in it. We'd all be so much more comfortable then, wouldn't we? It's been so nice to meet you."

Randi smiled at me evilly, the way the winner in a beauty pageant would smile at the runner-up. On the surface she was polite, but beneath the white smile was a layer of something very unpleasant.

"Shall we go then, handsome?" She winked at Kishan before following along after Ren. Randi didn't walk up the stairs—she wiggled her way up them. As they left, she trailed a finger down Ren's arm, pouting, "Are we going to swim? All I have is my one bikini, and I really shouldn't be getting it wet."

"I'm sure we can arrange to get you another one," he said.

"Oh, aren't you just the sweetest thing." She leaned over and pressed a slobbery wet kiss on Ren's mouth as the two of them disappeared around the corner.

Kishan and I stood there quietly for a moment, and then he said, "You might want to close your mouth, Kells."

"What? Who? How? *Why* is she here?"

He sighed. "She's a girl Ren met last night. In fact, I was planning to talk with you about it right after Wes left."

"You knew about her and that she was like . . . *that*?"

"Yes and no. I hadn't met her yet. Ren just told me about her." Kishan frowned. "Her parents also have a boat and are staying in Trivandrum. The good news is that the *Deschen* sets sail again in a few days so she won't be here long."

"Well, I don't like her."

"Hmm. We'll do our best to avoid them both. How does that sound?"

"Sounds good to me."

But avoiding Ren when he didn't want to be avoided was impossible. Later that afternoon, I was sitting in an outdoor lounge chair reading. A shadow fell across my legs. I finished my paragraph and leaned over to pick up my bookmark.

"Back already?" I asked, assuming it was Kishan.

"*No.*"

I shaded my eyes and looked up. Ren was glaring at me, livid. His fists were clenched at his sides. I set down my book and asked, "Is something wrong? What happened?"

"What happened? What *happened*? You cut your hair!"

"Yes. I did. So what?"

"So *what*?" he asked incredulously. "It's so short now you can't even braid it!"

I ran my fingers through my hair and pulled a lock forward to study. "Hmm . . . that's probably true. I could do small, thin braids I suppose, but it doesn't matter. I like it this way."

"Well, *I* don't!"

I frowned at him. "What exactly are you upset about?"

"I can't believe you just went off and cut your hair without telling . . . anyone."

"Women do that all the time. Besides, it's none of your business what I do with my hair, and Kishan likes it even if you don't."

"Kishan—"

He worked his jaw and was about to say something else when I interjected. "If you need to see a girl in braids why don't you just ask your new girlfriend to braid her hair? I'm sure Miss Beverly Hills would love to do it. She can play Helga to your Thor. Where is she now anyway? Better keep your eye on her, or she'll sneak off to cozy up to someone else. Now, if you don't mind, I'd like to get back to my book."

I saw Ren clench and unclench his fists several times in my peripheral vision, as I pretended to read a paragraph. Finally, he spun around and stormed off through the hatch.

I didn't see Ren or his new girlfriend again until dinner. Kishan and I had just filled our plates and sat down when they showed up. Nilima and Mr. Kadam were sitting at the end of the table talking with each other quietly.

"Oh, how wonderful! I'm so famished," Randi said and approached the buffet table, warning Ren not to eat the chicken or the shrimp that was being served.

She took a seat across from us and explained, "I'm very careful about what I eat. I only eat vegetables, and occasionally some fruit. It helps me maintain my figure."

Her plate had two forkfuls of salad and a wedge of mango. Carefully, she pushed the croutons away with a butter knife. I looked at Ren. He was staring at his plate of vegetables like a man who'd just been sentenced to prison.

Randi continued, "I've never eaten meat in any form. Not even eggs or milk. I just think animals are so filthy. I can't imagine ingesting them. I don't even like house pets. Especially cats. Their fur is so dirty. They lick themselves all over. And their little paws touch you everywhere." She shuddered. "I think animals should be kept in zoos, don't you agree? That's all they're good for, after all."

I sniggered *loudly*, took a bite of chicken, and sipped my papaya juice.

She leaned over and, in a stage whisper, said to me, "You *do* know that papaya juice makes you fat. My personal trainer says you should never eat sugar in *any* form." Her gaze dropped deliberately to my waist. "But I can see that maintaining your figure is not a priority for you." She smiled sweetly at Kishan, who was frowning. "A girl should always try to look her best, shouldn't she?"

Ren looked up, smiled at her, and said, "Yes and your figure is . . . exquisite."

She pecked him on the cheek, and Ren went back to picking at his plate.

Kishan set down his fork, stared at Ren incredulously, and said, "There is absolutely nothing wrong with Kelsey's figure." Then he stood and picked up his empty plate, heading back to the buffet again.

Randi quickly backpedaled. "Oh, of course *you* wouldn't think so because you're such a gentleman, but you are biased after all." She pushed aside her plate. "Oh dear, I've eaten too much. Now I'll have to work out for an hour." Half of her salad was still on her plate. She pouted prettily at Ren, who consoled her by telling her that she looked beautiful.

I poked my stomach covertly. It still seemed pretty lean to me. Obviously, I wasn't built like a supermodel, but all the swimming and workouts were keeping me trim enough. Kishan took my hand, squeezed it, and brushed a kiss on my fingers before setting it back onto my lap. I

smiled at him in gratitude. He smiled back and began eating his second helping. Ren scowled at his half-eaten dinner plate. Barbie said she wanted to take a nice romantic stroll around the deck. Ren rose quickly, taking her with him, and we all were finally able to relax and enjoy the rest of our meal.

Kishan purposely made a giant ice cream sundae for us to share, and we had a great time feeding each other spoonfuls. I "accidentally" missed his mouth and smeared ice cream on his nose and he "accidentally" dropped a spoonful down my shirt. After that, it was a free-for-all. He grabbed the canister of whipped cream, and I grabbed the bottle of chocolate syrup. Nilima and Mr. Kadam quickly exited, leaving us to our food fight.

Several minutes later, our arsenal had run out. We stood there laughing at each other. A big glob of whipped cream slid from my hair to my cheek, and Kishan was coated in chocolate syrup. I ran a finger down his arm and put it in my mouth.

"Mmm, you taste pretty good."

He scooped up a glob of whipped cream and smeared it across my cheek. "Hmm . . . you're not quite done yet." He picked up a bottle of confetti sprinkles and shook them dramatically over my head while I stood still with a small smile waiting for him to finish.

"There. All done."

Kishan wrapped his arms around my waist and tugged me closer. I looked up into his handsome face and felt an immense wave of appreciation and love overwhelm me.

"Thanks," I said softly.

He laughed. "Thanks for what? The sprinkles?"

I shook my head. "Thanks for making me happy."

"Anytime." Kishan hugged me, and we stood there in the wind long enough that we started sticking together. "Want to go for a swim in the ocean and get all this stuff off?"

"You're on."

As we strolled down to the dock, taking the back stairs so we wouldn't muss the carpet, he said, "That woman is crazy. How could anyone live without sugar?"

I grinned and twined my fingers through his as he draped his arm across my shoulder. "I don't know. What's life without something sweet?"

He nodded in agreement.

Kishan and I managed to avoid Ren and Randi the next day by having picnic meals using the Golden Fruit. For breakfast we ate egg sandwiches while our feet dangled over the railing, and for lunch we climbed on top of the wheelhouse. Kishan had the Scarf make comfortable cushions and surrounded them with silk flowers.

He placed a heavy linen napkin on my lap and used another napkin to blindfold me. He then hand-fed me a variety of scrumptious foods, making me guess what they were. Some were easy, especially the fruits. Dips were hard. He included a pear torte from Shangri-la that I hadn't yet tasted. I did the same for him and I giggled mischievously choosing weird dishes like tuna surprise. He just smacked his lips saying each one was better than the last. After we were full, we sipped sparkling grape juice and leaned back against the cushions to watch the clouds.

We'd planned to swim during the afternoon, but I found Randi sunning herself at the pool in a tiny red bikini held together with thin gold chains. I mentally groaned in disgust. Kishan and I would have to swim later. I turned to exit, but she'd spotted me.

"Oh, there you are! I'm so glad you're here. Can you be a dear and ask that serving girl, Nilima, to come here?"

"Nilima is not a serving girl."

Randi waved her hand in the air and flipped over onto her back, talking in great detail about a certain kind of lotion she *must* have. Her top barely covered her heaving bosom.

They looked too perfect to be real and I briefly wondered how much something like that cost. *Wow. What if one pops?* I giggled.

"It's not funny," she languished. "If you cared about your skin at *all*, you would understand why I need to have that lotion. It would be so much easier to have blotchy, uneven skin like yours. Why, no one even *expects* you to look pretty. You don't have the same pressure that I do. Wrinkles might not matter to you, but they do to me."

Kishan strolled to the pool area and kissed my cheek.

"Kelsey would look beautiful in wrinkles."

Randi's expression changed immediately. "Isn't that just *sweet* of you to say something like that, but the truth is women don't age as gracefully as men do. In the blink of an eye, men move on from their forty-year-old wife to a twenty-year-old."

Kishan frowned. "I would never do that."

She gushed, "Oh, I know *you* wouldn't. But so many men do. A girl just has to do the best she can with what she has."

"Can't you ask Ren for what you need?" Kishan asked. "We're busy."

She sniffed, "He was here, but he disappeared."

"We'll find him for you and make sure he gets your lotion."

She smiled coquettishly. "Thank you so much. Such considerate men in one family. Your mother must be so pleased."

"She was," Kishan said abruptly and turned me around. "How about a workout and a massage instead of a swim?"

"Sounds good." We left and started walking toward the gym. "Aren't you going to go find Ren and tell him she needs him?" I asked Kishan.

"Nah. I'm sure he already knows. If I were Ren, I'd be avoiding her too."

On the way, I ran into Nilima, who was furious with Randi.

"She's so demanding! She's insulted every member of the crew. The chef, who I had to beg to come here, has been demeaned in front of his staff. The captain has taken to locking the wheelhouse, and Grandfather refuses to come out of his room until she's gone. If she's not infuriating them, she's flirting with them. She uses every trick at her disposal to get what she wants. I don't care why Ren invited her here. I want her *off the ship!*"

I'd never seen Nilima so upset. I was glad, though, that I wasn't the only one who disliked Randi. I'd been concerned that I was responding with jealousy, which might have been true at first, but now the situation seemed kind of funny to me. I actually felt a little bad for Ren.

The next morning, Kishan burst into my room. I sat up and rubbed my eyes sleepily. "What's wrong?"

He was wet and had a towel wrapped around his waist. "She's gone too far."

"What is it?" I tried to keep my eyes locked on his face and ignore the very nice bronze torso barely hidden under the skimpy white towel.

"Randi came unbidden into my room and interrupted my shower!"

I frowned. "Why would she do that?"

"She claimed that she was desperate to find Ren."

I shrugged. "There might have been some truth to that. She probably kept him up for most of the night, and he still has to be a tiger for twelve hours a day. I'm sure he's just hiding out somewhere."

"Even so, she had no right to barge in on my shower! I'm going to finish in yours. You keep an eye out."

I giggled. "Okay, I'll watch out for any dangerous women. Don't worry. I'll protect you from their crafty wiles. You can go shower in peace."

He ducked his head through the door and grinned. "Just so you know, *you* are welcome to barge in on my shower *anytime.*"

I laughed. "Good to know."

After Kishan was safely ensconced behind his suite door, locked against intruders, I headed off to breakfast. On my way, Randi accosted me and demanded my help in locating Ren.

"He's really being a terrible host. In fact, I think *you* should help me find him, *and* you convince him that he's in love with me."

I folded my arms across my chest. "And *why* would I do that?"

She smiled. "Because if you don't, I'll just move on to the next rich eligible man, his brother, and I don't think you'll be too happy about that."

"Kishan wouldn't touch you with a ten-foot pole, and honestly I never would have suspected Ren would either. Besides, it's time for you to go. There's no time for more of your games."

"You'd be surprised at the things I can get men to do in no time at all." She adjusted her skimpy tank top to show off her cleavage. "I don't mind switching to Kishan. He's handsome, and the brothers are obviously wealthy and well connected. Daddy would be pleased either way. I'm sure I could win over Kishan just as quickly."

I put my hands on my hips and stared her down. "I don't love them because they're rich. I love them because they're sweet, good, and honest men. And neither of them deserves to be saddled with a witch like you."

Randi tittered mockingly. "Oh, you are naive, aren't you?" She patted my cheek condescendingly. "You need to learn there's no such thing as a good man, honey. Men are stupid and only think of one thing."

She swished her hips and was out the door before I could think of a response so I just shook my head and sighed. Obviously she didn't really care about Ren at all. *Someone should tell him so he can deal with her and get her out of all of our lives.*

Ren's new room was empty. The bed was made and the clothes were all put away. His dog-eared book of Shakespeare quotes was lying open. I flipped it over and found a line highlighted: "But O, how bitter a thing it is to look into happiness through another man's eyes."

Turning the book over, I set it down gently where it rested before and reached into my pocket for my phone. Flipping it open, I located

Ren on the GPS tracker and found him hiding out in the back of a
storage room in the garage. I didn't see him at first. Boxes were stacked
everywhere, as well as cleaning buckets, mops, brooms, and shelves full
of parts and supplies. In the very back, on a mat, lay my white tiger.

I squatted down next to him. He kept his head on his paws. His
chest rumbled softly.

"Your new girlfriend is making trouble for everyone, you know." I
couldn't help myself; I reached over and petted his head. "I don't know
what you were thinking. She doesn't even like cats." I grinned lopsidedly,
then sighed. "Kishan and I will try to keep her occupied for a couple of
hours so you can be a tiger. But you owe us a big favor. She's trouble.
The 'double, double toil and trouble' kind."

Ren started purring when I scratched behind his ear. Then the
sound cut off abruptly, and he shifted away from my hand.

I stood up. "Well . . . see you later," I said, as I headed off to breakfast.

When I found Kishan, he was so happy to see me I laughed.

"Ren needs to be a tiger a while longer, and I promised him we'd
keep her busy," I whispered.

"Because *you* asked," he kissed my forehead, "I will help you
entertain her and try to tolerate her ceaseless talking and flirtation."

I smiled. "I knew there was a reason I liked you."

He put an arm around me. "The feeling is mutual."

Kishan suggested we all watch a movie. Randi agreed and sat on the
couch patting the seat next to her when he strolled over. He deliberately
sat in a recliner instead, snagged my wrist, and dragged me over to sit
with him.

No one paid any attention to Randi, who sulked from the couch,
and claimed she was bored after the first half hour. We gave up and
decided to swim instead.

Kishan and I dove in and swam laps. Randi came over and sat on the edge of the pool, leaning back in the sunshine, presumably to soak up rays, but I believed it was actually a ploy to show off her artificial bosom.

At a break, I stopped near her and turned to watch Kishan stroke smoothly through the water.

"I'll still get him, you know. Either him or the other one. I've never met a boy I couldn't have. You really shouldn't swim without a cap. The chlorine ruins your hair."

I smiled falsely, nodded, and began swimming laps again until I felt a hand grab my ankle and yank me underwater. Big arms wrapped around me and pulled me to the surface.

Kishan grinned. "We're done babysitting. Ren came to retrieve her on the last lap."

I looked over his shoulder and sure enough, Randi was gone.

"Now . . . how would you like to change and finish snuggling in the media room?"

"I thought you'd never ask." I yelped as he carried me quickly up the pool steps and sent me off to the showers to change.

That evening, as the *Deschen* drew anchor, Kishan, the crew, and I made sure that Ren escorted Randi off the ship.

Ren smiled and bent to kiss her cheek. He murmured something quietly and pressed her close in farewell. Kishan smiled secretively.

"What? What is it?" I asked.

He whispered, "Ren called her a *sukhada motha*. 'A delightful weed.'"

I laughed. "He does have a knack for nicknames."

Randi headed our way and grasped Kishan's arm. In a stage whisper, she said, "I hope your little girlfriend didn't mind me watching you shower. I'm *sure* she'll understand. Please contact me *anytime*." She slipped a pink card into his hand and pressed her ample bosom to his

chest as she went to peck him on the cheek but purposely hit the corner of his mouth instead. She winked at him meaningfully and sashayed down the ramp, swiveling her hips like a church bell.

As soon as Randi's stilettos were out of sight, there were murmurs from the staff of locking the ramp to the side of the boat just in case she decided to come back.

Kishan wiped his mouth with the back of his hand and grunted. "My mother would have eaten her for breakfast."

"Really?" That made me smile.

"Yes." He grinned. "You, on the other hand, she would have loved."

He draped his arm around my shoulders and as we headed back upstairs, I looked for Ren but he was gone.

When the *Deschen* finally lifted anchor, everyone on the ship breathed a collective deep sigh of relief.

13

lady silkworm

After we were under way again, I headed up to the wheelhouse to visit with the captain.

"Ah, hallo, Miss Kelsey. And how are we feelin' ta'nite, eh?"

"Hey, Captain Dixon."

"Jus' call me Dix."

I laughed. "Okay, Dix, Mr. Kadam had me bring up dinner because you didn't get a chance to eat tonight."

He smiled and glanced at me briefly, then returned his gaze to the window. "Jus' set it down right dere if ya would, den, miss."

I set down his tray, leaned my hip against the console, and quietly watched him work.

He peered at me out of the corner of his eye. "You're lookin' more at ease dan I've seen you in a while, if I may say so."

I nodded. "I've been doing better. Kishan takes good care of me, and we finally got rid of the sea hag."

"And happy was de hour she stepped off of me boat too."

I laughed. "I heard you locked her out of the wheelhouse."

"She was coming to bodder me all times of de day and night. She be complaining dat she was seasick and all manner of rubbish." He set a few instruments and picked up his dinner tray. "Would ja be keepin' an old sea dog comp'ny while he eats his dinner, den?"

"Sure."

He sank into the captain's chair and sighed. "Every time I settle me old bones in a chair it gets a little harder to coax meself out of it."

I sat in the chair next to him. "A good chair is worth its weight in gold, my mom always used to say."

He laughed heartily. "Dat's right. Many an old man would radder sink himself into a comfy old chair dan be rich."

"So how long until our next stop?"

He chewed and swallowed. "I'm hopin' we won' be makin' any more stops. At least not ta pick up any passengers. My plan is ta head straight to de Shore Temple. We should be on de ocean for a week or so."

We chatted casually until he set down his dinner tray. He checked the instruments and said, "Would ja be wantin' another yarn of de sea today, Miss Kelsey?"

"Have you another one ready?"

"De day dis captain run outta stories is de day I turn in ma cap."

I grinned and crossed my legs, getting comfortable. "Go on, then. I'm ready."

He pushed back his hat and scratched his forehead. "Do ya ever watch de seabirds as dey fly out over de ocean?"

"Sometimes."

"If yer watchin' real close, ya can see dem carryin' twigs and branches and sometimes stones. Dey drop 'em in de water."

"Why do they do that?"

"Listen, and ye will learn. Once der was a beautiful maiden named Jingwei who loved de ocean. She 'ad a little boat, and she spent many hours on de water. She'd row out in de morning and would'n return 'til dusk. For many years de sea accepted her, but dere was a charming sea captain, a good lookin' man, almost as handsome as meself."

He waggled his eyebrows, making me giggle.

"Jingwei fell in love wid de captain and wanted ta ride de waves wid him. But he wanted her ta stay home and raise a family. 'De water is no place for a wooman,' he said."

"What did she do?" I asked.

"She told him dat if she can't be on de water, den neither could he. Dey settled down near de beach, but both of dem longed for de sea. One day Jingwei tell him dat she gonna have a child. Dey were both happy for a while. But when neither of dem was lookin', dey both stared at de water. De captain, he tink his wife bein' with child will keep her home. So he go fishin' early one mornin'. But de ocean, she been waiting for dis. You see, de sea, she's a jealous mistress and was very angry wit dem.

"De ocean rise up and swallowed de ship. Jingwei, heavy with child waited for her man all day, but he never return. Later she heard he drowned. She took her little boat and rowed offshore. Den she shook her fist at de sea and ask why did she take her man?"

"Then what happened?"

"De sea, she laughed and told Jingwei all de handsome captains belong ta her. She can't steal dem away."

"Huh . . . sounds like Randi."

Dixon laughed out loud. "Ah, dis much is true. Jingwei argued and treatened de ocean but de ocean sent de laughing bubbles ta the shore. When she tired of listenin', she sent de big wave ta drown Jingwei, but Jingwei is part magic and changed her body ta a seabird. Dat is why de seabirds screech so noisy at de shore. Dey are still yellin' at de ocean. Dey drop rocks and sticks into de water ta fill it up so no other men will drown. But de sea? She's still laughin', eh? If you listen you can hear dem bubbles. Dis is de story of Jingwei and de boundin' main."

"What does *the bounding main* refer to?"

"De boundin' main is de waters of de earth. De waters abound over de planet, and dey are de main resource. Much more abundan' dan de lands."

"There you are." Kishan leaned against the doorjamb and smiled.

"Hi!" I stood and put my arm around his waist. "Just getting another story."

"Good. You can share it with me later." He looked up. "Mind if I steal Kelsey for the rest of the evening, Captain?"

Captain Dixon chuckled. "Sure ting. Jus' make sure ya keep her away from de waters tonight. De sea, she listens. Lookin' ta drown young lovers."

I laughed. "Goodnight, Dix."

"Ga'nite, Miss Kelsey."

Kishan pulled me into a hug after we went down the stairs, and I tucked my head under his chin. "I missed you. Let's go for a walk."

It was a very romantic setting. The full moon had just risen, and the black water was as smooth as silk. It lapped softly against the ship and gently whispered secrets as the boat pressed on, slipping into her cold embrace. Thousands of glittering stars hung in the night sky which seemed to go on forever. I imagined they were lanterns left to guide handsome sea captains home to the women who loved them. Some grew dim over the years, but some burned fiercely, demanding to be seen.

There was no land in sight, just endless moonlit water as far as the eye could see. We stood at the railing, looking out. When I shivered, Kishan pulled me against his chest and wrapped his arms around me. Comfortable in his embrace, I found myself relaxing drowsily.

"This is nice," I murmured.

He ducked his head near mine and said, "Mmm . . . it is." He rubbed my bare arms until they warmed and then began lightly massaging my shoulders. I sighed in pleasure and stared vacantly at the moon as my thoughts drifted. In fact, I became so detached from my surroundings that I hadn't even noticed when Kishan started kissing my neck.

One of his hands stroked my arm and the other was wrapped around the curve of my waist. He pressed soft kisses along my shoulder, then his lips traveled up the arch of my neck. He made slow progress, leaving a tingling trail behind. When he touched my hairline, he reached across my body, took my hand, and gently turned me to face him.

My heart started pounding. He ran his hands up my arms again, cupped my face, and slid his hands into my hair. He smiled, his golden eyes twinkling in the starlight.

"There. You see? Still plenty of hair for a man to bury his hands in."

I smiled nervously as I fidgeted slightly. He tilted my head, stepped closer, and pressed silky, light kisses against my neck. "Do you know how long I've wanted to touch you like this?" he murmured softly. I shook my head and felt him smile as his lips grazed my collarbone. "It seems like years. Mmm . . . it's better than I imagined. You smell *so* good. You *feel* so good."

He trailed slow kisses from my neck to my forehead. I wrapped my arms around his waist and closed my eyes. His chest rumbled against mine. He kissed my eyelids, my nose, my cheeks with warm, soft lips. He made me feel cherished and treasured, and I enjoyed his touch.

My skin tingled where he grazed it with his fingertips. My heart beat faster when he whispered my name, and I responded to him, involuntarily moving closer. I waited for him to touch his lips to mine but he patiently, slowly kissed every other part of my face and trailed his fingertips over its planes, seeming to delight in each sweet caress. His kisses were tender and loving and gentle and . . . *wrong*.

Unbidden thoughts sprang up that I couldn't push aside, no matter how I tried. Despite my best efforts to staunch my internal struggle— keep it hidden—it surfaced. Kishan paused and lifted his head. I saw his expression change from sweet adoration and happiness, to surprise, and ultimately to resignation and disappointment. Cupping my face, he wiped tears away from my cheeks with his thumbs and asked sadly, "Am I that hard to love, Kelsey?"

I lowered my head and closed my eyes.

He stepped away from me to lean over the railing again while I angrily dashed away the tears from my face. I was very annoyed with myself for ruining this sweet moment between us and especially for hurting him. Regret filled me. I turned to him, ran my hand up his back, and then slid my arm through his. I leaned my head on his shoulder. "I'm *sorry*. And, no . . . you're not hard to love at all."

"No, *I'm* sorry. I moved too fast."

I shook my head. "No, it's okay. I don't know what I was crying about."

He turned toward me, captured my hand, and played with my fingers. "*I* do. And I don't want our first kiss to make you cry."

I smiled lopsidedly, trying to tease. "This wasn't our first kiss. Remember?"

"I mean the first kiss I didn't steal."

"That's true." I laughed softly. "You *are* the world's best kissing bandit." I bumped him with my shoulder and squeezed his arm in apology, but sadness still showed on his face.

He clasped his hands on the railing. "Are you still sure about this? About me?"

I nodded against his shoulder. "You make me happy. Yes, I'm sure about this. Will you try again?" I tried to snuggle closer.

He wrapped his arms around me and kissed my forehead. "Another night. Come on. I'm in the mood for a story."

We headed downstairs, hand in hand.

We didn't see Ren all week. According to the GPS tracker, he hid in one place or another in the lower decks of the ship.

Kishan didn't try to kiss me again, at least not like before. He stroked my hair and held me, rubbed my shoulders and spent whole days with me, but when I stepped close to hug him goodnight in the evenings, he would hold me for a few moments before kissing my forehead. He was giving me more time, which made me feel both relieved and stressed.

We finally docked in Mahabalipuram, or the City of the Seven Pagodas, a week later. We were now on the opposite side of India, the eastern side, floating on the Bay of Bengal on the edge of the Indian Ocean.

It was time to start our third quest, and the idea of dealing with dragons both excited and frightened me. I was also itching to go ashore again. Kishan obliged by taking me sightseeing on his motorcycle. We spent the day strolling shops. He bought me a beautiful bracelet decorated with diamonds clustered like lotus flowers. Slipping it onto my arm, he said, "I had a dream of you wearing a lotus blossom in your hair. This bracelet reminds me of you."

I laughed. "You probably dreamed of lotus because you sleep right next to the table where I put Durga's lotus garland."

"Maybe," he said with a smile, "but a good dream's a good dream. Please wear it."

"Okay. But only if you let me buy you something."

Kishan grinned. "It's a deal."

I made him sit at an outdoor table while I went into a shop. Several minutes later, I nervously sat down. He leaned forward to snatch my bag, but I pulled it away.

"Now wait a minute. Before I give this to you, you have to promise to let me explain what it's for and try not to be offended."

Kishan laughed and held out his hand for the bag. "It's very difficult to offend me."

Eagerly pulling my present from the bag, he held it in the air, stared at it in confusion, and then looked at me with a raised eyebrow. "What is this supposed to be?"

"It's a collar for a very small dog."

He dangled the black leather collar between his thumb and forefinger. "It says *Kishan* on the side in gold letters." He laughed. "Did you think this would fit me?"

I took the collar from his hand and walked around the table. "Hold out your arm please." He watched me curiously as I wrapped the collar around his wrist and buckled it. He didn't seem upset, only puzzled.

I explained, "When Ren changed to a man for the first time, he had been wearing a collar. He held it out to me to prove that he was the tiger I'd been traveling with. He was quick to discard it. To him, it was a physical reminder of his captivity."

Kishan frowned. "You are giving me a gift and talking about Ren?"

"Wait, let me finish. When I first met you, you were wild, a true creature of the jungle. You had ignored your human side for many years. I thought a collar would be a different symbol, a symbol of becoming reclaimed, a symbol of rejoining the world, a symbol of belonging. It means you've come home. That you have a home . . . with me."

I dropped his hand and shifted to my other foot, waiting for his reply. I couldn't read his expression. Kishan stared at me thoughtfully for a few seconds. Suddenly, he took my hand, yanked me onto his lap, and brought my hand to his lips.

"It is a gift I will treasure always. Every time I look at it, I will remember that I am yours."

I pressed my forehead to his and sighed in relief. "Good. I was worried you'd hate it. Now that that's settled, shall we head back to the boat? Mr. Kadam wants us all to meet an hour before sundown so we can go to the Shore Temple together. Unless you think I'd better go back to buy a leash. You might wander off," I joked lightly.

Somberly, he took my hand, "Leash or no leash, I will never leave your side. Lead on, my proprietress." He smiled contentedly as he draped his arm across my shoulders.

At the ship, we found Mr. Kadam waiting on the dock. Ren soon came down the ramp from his most-recent hiding place. After Kishan stowed the motorcycle, the four of us climbed aboard the motorboat.

The snap of the wind blew my hair back from my face, and I beamed happily at Kishan when he looked back to check on me. My gaze drifted, and I suddenly found myself staring into Ren's blue eyes.

"New bracelet?" he asked.

I looked down at the twinkling diamonds and smiled. "Yes."

"It's . . . pretty. It suits you."

"Thank you."

"I—" he hesitated and shifted in his seat.

"What is it?" I prodded gently.

"I'm happy for you. You seem . . . content."

"Oh. I guess I am."

Despite the happiness I felt in being with Kishan, I realized there was a leak somewhere in my heart, a hole that wouldn't close over. It seeped a bitter disappointment that trickled into my limbs, and being near Ren like this was like drizzling lemon juice into the hole. It stung.

I nodded noncommittally and let my eyes drift to the water. Holding out my hand, I let it splash against my fingers. I felt Ren watching me still. Something tangible sparked between us but only for an instant. A tug that was there one second and gone the next.

The sun had gone down by the time we reached shore. The brothers leapt out of the boat, dragged the prow onto the sand, and using a long rope, tied it to a sturdy tree limb.

I studied the temple as we walked toward it. It was cone-shaped but had two structures instead of one. Mr. Kadam fell back to walk with me as Kishan and Ren strode boldly forward. They both carried weapons, just in case—Kishan the *chakram*, and Ren his new trident.

"Mr. Kadam, why does this temple have two buildings?"

"Each one is a shrine. This particular temple has three, but you

can't see the third from here. It's nestled between the other two. The taller one is roughly five stories."

"Who is worshipped here?"

"Shiva mostly, but historically, others would have been worshipped here as well. The Shore Temple is the last of the seven still above water." He pointed to the wall. "Do you see those large statues there?"

"The cows?"

"Actually, they're bulls. They represent Nandi, the servant of Shiva."

"I thought Nandi took the form of a shark."

"He did, but he is also known for taking the form of a bull. Come over this way. There's something I want to show you."

We walked across the stone porch and approached a statue that looked like a large tiger with a doll clinging to his paw.

"What is it?" I asked.

"It's Durga with her tiger."

"Why is Durga so small?"

He leaned forward and traced the carving with his finger. "I'm not sure. Just the design, I suppose. Do you see this cavity in the tiger's chest?"

I nodded.

"It was probably used as a shrine as well."

"Should we make an offering here?"

"I'm not sure. Let's explore the temple first and see what else we can find."

We entered the temple through an arched vault. Mr. Kadam told me it was called a *gopuram*, an ornate temple entrance designed to awe and impress. Its function was similar to the Japanese spirit gates. People entering the temple would feel they were stepping away from worldly things to enter a place considered sacred.

We caught up with Ren and Kishan and walked into the dark temple together. Its inky gloom was made even denser by the overhanging eaves blocking the moonlight. Kishan turned on his flashlight so we could navigate.

"This way," Mr. Kadam said. "The inner sanctum would rest directly under the central dome." We explored the smaller of the two structures first and found nothing out of the ordinary. Mr. Kadam pointed to an uncarved rock set in the middle of the room. "This is the *murti*—the idol, or icon, of the shrine."

"But it isn't carved to symbolize anything."

"An uncarved icon can represent something just as much as a carved one. This room is the *garbhagriha*, or the womb of the temple."

"I can see why they call it a womb. It's dark in here," I said.

We all stepped to the walls to study the carvings. We'd only been at it a few minutes when I caught a flash of white at the door. I turned my head, but nothing was there. Mr. Kadam said it was time to move to the next shrine. As we passed an arch that opened to the outside, I looked down at the ocean. A beautiful woman, dressed in white with a gossamer veil over her hair, was standing on the shore. She pressed a finger to her lips as she gazed up at me before melting into a nearby mulberry tree.

"Kishan? Mr. Kadam?"

"What is it?" Kishan asked.

"I saw something. A woman, she was standing there. She was dressed all in white, and she looked Indian or maybe Asian. She sort of disappeared by actually walking inside that mulberry tree."

Kishan leaned out and scanned the grounds. "I don't see anything now, but let's stick together."

"Okay."

He took my hand as we walked into the next shrine. We passed Ren, who I hadn't noticed standing in the darkness behind us. His arms were crossed over his chest in one of his classic "watching me" poses. In the next shrine, I stayed close to Kishan while we scanned the carvings on the wall together. I found a carving of a woman weaving at a loom and traced the outline with my finger. At her foot rested her thread basket, and one of the threads had become unraveled. Curious, I followed its thin line through several more carvings.

The thread was wrapped around the ankle of a farmer, and then a cat toyed with it. The thread trailed on through a wheat field, where I lost it and had to search several carvings before finding it again. It joined a scarf wrapped around a woman's neck, and then wove itself into a thick rope that blazed with fire. It became a fishing net, it wrapped around a large tree, it tripped a monkey, it was held in a bird's talon, and then . . . it stopped. It ended at the corner of the room, and, though I searched the adjoining wall, I couldn't find a place where it continued.

I pressed my thumb against the carved line to feel its texture. It was so thin, my thumb could barely sense it. When I hit the corner at the end of the trail something strange happened. My thumb glowed red—only my thumb—and when I stepped back from the wall, I saw a butterfly crawl out of a crack. It began flapping its wings rapidly, but it didn't fly. I peered at it closely and realized it wasn't a butterfly but a large white moth.

It was hairy, almost furry, with large black eyes and some kind of brown feathery antennae that reminded me of the teeth on a baleen whale. When it flapped its wings, something happened to the wall. This small section of wall had been smooth, which was odd because the rest of the wall was covered in detailed carvings.

Thin white lines appeared, and they all radiated from the carved thread I'd been following. They glowed with a light so intense, I had to squint to watch them. When I reached to touch one, the light jumped from the wall to my hand. At the same time, the white lines burst with all the colors of the rainbow. They outlined Phet's henna design on my hand with white light that quickly began shifting color.

I turned to look back at Kishan, but behind me was only blackness. I couldn't speak. There was nothing I could do except watch the wall as the lines stretched faster and faster. They were drawing something—a woman, sitting by a window, embroidering. One second I was standing next to the wall, looking at the drawing, and in the next second, the woman breathed and blinked, and I was inside the drawing with her. She was the same woman I'd seen standing on the beach. She was dressed in a white silk gown and wore a gossamer veil over her hair.

She smiled and pointed to the chair across from hers. When I sat, she handed me a circular embroidery frame that had the most lovely stitched version of Durga. The stitches were so small and delicate, that it looked like a painting. She'd created flowers that looked real, and Durga's hair flowed from her golden cap in waves that looked so soft that I had to touch it. The woman passed across a needle and a small box full of tiny seed pearls.

"What do you want me to do?"

"Durga needs her Necklace."

"I've never sewn with beads before."

"Look here . . . they have tiny holes. I will show you the first two, and then you can finish it."

Deftly, she threaded the needle, made the tiniest stitch, slipped a seed pearl onto the needle, tied the thread around it, and inserted the needle back through the fabric. I watched her go through the same process again before she handed the needle to me and placed the box of pearls on the windowsill.

She picked up her frame, selected some blue thread, and continued working. After I'd affixed two beads and was satisfied with my effort, I asked, "Who are you?"

She kept her eyes on her work and answered, "I am called by many names, but the one most commonly used is Lady Silkworm."

"Durga sent me to you. She said you would help to guide us on our

journey." I blinked. "Oh! You're from the prophecy. You're the lady who weaves the silk."

She smiled while looking at her needle. "Yes. I weave and embroider silk. Once it was all I lived for, but now it is my penance."

"Your penance?"

"Yes. For betraying the man I loved."

I dropped the frame to my lap and stared at her. She looked up and shooed at me with her hand until I picked up the frame and continued.

"Shall I tell you what happened?" she asked. "I haven't shared the story with anyone in many years, and something tells me you will understand."

I nodded mutely, so she began. "Many, many years ago, women were admired for their skill in needlework. Girls were trained at a very young age, and those most highly skilled were taken to sew for the emperor. Some, a very few, even became wives for noblemen, and because of their skill, their families were well provided for.

"At the celebration of every New Year, young girls were chosen to learn this skill. They gather around a bowl of water and dip their fingers in at the edges. A needle is then placed on the surface of the water and spun. When it stops, the girl who the needle points to is taken away for special training in embroidery.

"Baby girls born with slender, long fingers were watched carefully in the hope that they might bring the family fame and fortune through the art. I was such a child. I was praised as being the most talented worker of the needle in the entire empire, and the designs I created were highly sought after by the wealthiest of men. My father received fifty offers of marriage for me before I turned sixteen, but he rejected them all. He was a proud man and thought I might get even better offers as I grew into my skill."

"Then how did you meet the one you came to love?"

She clucked her tongue. "Patience, young one. To create something beautiful takes practice and much patience."

"I'm sorry. Please continue."

She leaned over to peruse my work. "You have some skill with the thread, but you need to take out the last two and do them again. They are spaced just a bit too far apart."

I peered closely at the fabric. They looked exactly even to me, but it was her project, so I obediently took them out and started again.

"A few years later, at age twenty, I met someone, a handsome young man who worked with silk. His family formed the worms, spun, and dyed the threads, and they were very good, the best in the country. Once I felt the fine thread and had seen the perfection in the coloring, I made a point of only ordering from them.

"I'd been commissioned to make a wardrobe for the future bride of the emperor. He'd planned a fantastic ceremony though he still hadn't selected the lucky woman. My father was paid handsomely to bring me to the palace. I was to live there for a year and sew marvelous clothing and a bridal veil for the emperor's new wife. The prospect was exciting to such a young girl. I was given generous living arrangements near the emperor himself, and I wanted for nothing. When my family was allowed to visit from time to time, I could see the joy my being there brought to them.

"There were only two problems. The first was that the emperor was very selective and his tastes changed every day. He visited me every week to check on my progress. I would only just begin a design, and then he would change his mind. He'd want birds one week, flowers the next, gold one week, then silver and blue, red, the lightest lavender, the richest purple, and so on. The man changed his mind more often than he changed his bathwater. Perhaps that was why he took so long to select a bride."

I laughed quietly.

She frowned. "The second problem was that he soon began to make romantic overtures on his visits. When I would mention his fiancée, he would laugh and say, 'I'm sure she won't mind. I haven't even decided which woman to choose, but I should marry by the end of the year. An emperor needs heirs, don't you think? We have plenty of time to get to know one another in the meanwhile, eh, my sweet?' I'd nod and tell him I was busy and usually he left me alone.

"Because of the emperor's eclectic and varied tastes, I became very familiar with the young man who delivered the silk fabrics. He was kept very busy bringing new thread and material. Sometimes he'd sit and talk with me as I sewed. Soon I began to look forward to his visits, and it wasn't much later that I started to invent new reasons to have him come. I often found myself daydreaming of him, and my work began to suffer.

"Though I loved sewing, I lost enthusiasm for the emperor's projects and attentions. I stared out the window one day when I saw my young man walk across the courtyard. Inspiration struck, and I became excited about starting a new project, one that *I* wanted to do. I'd never made anything uncommissioned before. I'd been working for others since I was a young girl and never had any extra time. I envisioned in my head exactly what I wanted to create—a gift for my young silkmaker. I couldn't sleep, so enthralled was I by my task.

"Day and night I worked, knowing my young man would visit me again at the end of the next week. At last, he knocked on the door. I hid my creation behind my back as I asked him to enter. He greeted me with a warm smile and set down his package. 'I have something for you,' I said.

"'What is it?'

"'A gift. Something I made for you.'

"His eyes lit up with surprise and happiness as I handed him the

present I'd wrapped in brown paper. He carefully opened it and picked up the scarf. Mulberry trees ran down the length of the golden fabric, and silkworm cocoons hung from the branches. White silkworm moths sat on some of the leaves, and silken threads of every hue were wound around a shuttle on either end of the scarf. He held it gently in his hands and touched an embroidered leaf. 'It's lovely,' he said. 'I've never been given anything so fine.'

"'It was nothing,' I stammered.

"'No. I know how long this must have taken you. You have given me something very valuable.'

"I lowered my eyes and hesitantly said, 'I would give you more . . . if you asked.' That was when he touched me. He simply took a step forward and brushed the back of his fingers across my cheek. 'I cannot . . . be with you,' he said.

"'Oh,' I said, disappointed, and stepped away.

"He pressed on, 'Ah, you misunderstand. If there was anything I could do to make you mine, I would not hesitate. But I am not a rich man. Surely not rich enough for one such as you. But I *would* choose you if I could.' He cupped my cheek with his palm. 'Please believe this,' he said.

"I nodded, and as he left, I tried to accept that we could not be together. Still, I watched for him week after week and as the year passed, we fell deeply in love. Though it would bring shame and disappointment to my family, I told him that my love for him was too strong to deny. We made plans to secretly elope and marry as soon as I was finished with the emperor's commission. We would give all the riches to my family and leave. He would take some silkworms, and I would bring my skill, and together we could start anew in a province far away.

"Finally, the year was up, and the emperor let me finish the veil. It was fine work. Not my finest, for that belonged to the one I loved, but it was pretty. The veil was light pink with dark pink roses embroidered around the edges. When I presented it to the emperor, he lifted it over my head and pronounced that he was now ready to marry his bride. Then he suggested that I should prepare myself.

"'Prepare myself for what?' I asked.

"'For the wedding, of course.'

"'Am I to assist your fiancée with the veil?'

"'No, my dear. You *are* my fiancée.'

"Women came into the room to help prepare me. I panicked and begged the emperor for another day. I told him I needed to speak with my father. He responded that my father had happily agreed to the marriage and was waiting to escort me. Thinking frantically, I stammered that I wanted to make him a rose kerchief to match my veil. He patted my cheek and said that he was feeling generous and would indulge me. He would give me one more day.

"I sent word immediately to my young man, demanding that rose thread be delivered at once. When he arrived, I wrapped my arms around him and held him close. He hugged me back and asked me what was wrong. I explained that the emperor had made plans to marry me and that my father had accepted. I begged him to take me away, quickly, that evening. He said he didn't think we could escape with the guards watching the palace, but he knew someone, a wizard, who he thought could be bribed to help us. He told me to wait for him, that someone would come for me that night and would wear the scarf I'd made for him. He asked me to trust him."

"What happened?" I asked. "Did someone come?"

"Yes. An ordinary brown plow horse came."

"A plow horse?"

"Yes. He trotted slowly to my window and neighed softly. He wore the scarf wrapped around his neck."

"The horse wore the scarf? Where was your young man?"

"I didn't know. I was frightened. The horse stamped his feet and neighed louder, but I stood at the window, wringing my hands. I didn't know what to do. Should I climb out the window and onto the horse's back? Where would I go then? The horse became more agitated, alerting an annoyed guard, who tried to shoo him away. Men were sent to take the horse to the stables, but he kicked and bit and neighed loudly. Finally, one of the head guards came out and told them to shut the horse up before it woke the emperor.

"Nothing they tried to do would settle the animal. The scarf slipped from around its neck and fell into the mud. The soldiers tromped on it and ruined the lovely gift. I cried and wondered where my young man was. I despaired thinking he'd been shot or killed on the road. They finally managed to take the horse away, so everyone could settle down for the night. My young man never came. I watched for him at the window all that night.

"The next morning the emperor came to me and had me escorted to a bathing chamber. Women bathed and dressed me in the beautiful clothes I had made, and just before I was led into the great hall, the emperor came into my chamber, sent out the servants, and closed the door behind him. 'I have a wedding present for you, my dear.' He handed me the scarf I'd given to my young man. It had been cleaned and pressed but many of the delicate stitches were torn. Tears fell down my face.

"'An interesting incident occurred last night. It seems a plow horse entered the palace grounds wearing this very scarf. He made enough noise that the guards took him away and locked him in the stables. The next morning, to our surprise, we found not a horse but the silkmaker in the stall. We asked him what magic he used and why he'd come. He won't speak. He refuses to share his reason for infiltrating my palace in the middle of the night.'

"He touched the scarf lightly to my face and said, 'I can only assume that he came to assassinate me. How fortunate you are that your husband-to-be is safe.'

"Before I could guard my words, I exclaimed, 'He *didn't* come to assassinate you!'

"The emperor tilted his head thoughtfully. 'Didn't he? Are you sure? You do know him better than anyone else here. Perhaps he came here for a completely different reason. Why do you think he came, my dear?'

"'I . . . I'm sure he was only bringing me more thread. Perhaps he was set upon by a warlock, and he needed some help.'

"'Hmm . . . what an interesting suggestion. But why would he come to you and not go to his family? Or perhaps to one of the guards?'

"'I . . . don't know.'

"'Come with me,' he said.

"He made me stand at the window overlooking a courtyard. My dear love was tied to a post, while a man stood nearby with a whip. The emperor raised and lowered his hand abruptly. I heard the whip snap in the air and whimpered as if I too could feel the burn of the lash as it tore the back of my love. The emperor whispered coldly, 'Did you think I wouldn't recognize your handiwork, my dear? You have bestowed your favor on this man.' I cringed as I heard the whip crack again.

"'Please don't hurt him,' I begged.

"'You can stop his torture whenever you wish. Just tell me that I'm mistaken and that this young man did not come for you. That all of this is just a simple misunderstanding. And . . . say it loudly so that all may hear.'

"I heard the groan of the one I loved and turned to the emperor. 'This young man—'

"'Louder, please. And make sure everyone outside can hear you as well.'

"'This young man did not come for me, and I do not love him! I have no wish to see him harmed! He is just a simple and poor silkmaker. I would never pledge myself to someone so common and impoverished. Please let him go!'

"My love looked up at me; his eyes burning with my betrayal. I longed to shout out that it was a *lie*. That I *did* love him. That I only wanted to be with *him*, but I kept silent, hoping to save his life.

"'That is all I needed to hear,' said the emperor. He shouted down to the men, 'Put him out of his misery.'

"The emperor raised his hand and made another slashing movement in the air. The man with the whip scrambled out of the way for a line of soldiers with bows. They raised their bows and filled my love's chest full of arrows. He died believing that I didn't care for him, that I loved him no longer. I fell to the floor in despair while the emperor threatened, 'Remember this lesson, little bird. I will *not* be made a cuckold. Now . . . compose yourself for our wedding.'

"When he left, I prostrated myself on the floor and wept bitterly. If only I had trusted what I did not understand. If I had not been such a coward, my love and I might have escaped and lived a happy life together. He had been the horse all along. He had been with me, near me, the whole time, and I refused to see it. Because I was shortsighted, I lost everything.

"Later, a kind woman rested her hand on my shoulder and dried my tears with her silken handkerchief. She said she loved my work and that my gifts could still be used to benefit others. That woman was Durga. She offered to take me away, to help me escape from the emperor, but said that I could never return to a mortal life. She picked up his golden scarf from where I'd dropped it and told me that my silkmaker would always be near, for I had sewn love into each stitch.

"So here I sit. I am Lady Silkworm. Still wrapped in my cocoon of

sorrow. Stitching, always stitching. I sew to bind others, but I remain alone. I tie threads together to give my existence meaning, to have a purpose. It does give me some happiness to help others weave their lives together." She leaned forward. "But I will tell you now, young one, without your love—life is nothing. Without your mate, you are utterly alone." She dropped her frame and grasped my hands. "Above all else, I beg you to trust the one you love."

She picked up my finished work from my lap. "There, now. You see? You did an excellent job." She smiled. "It's time for you to return. Take this with you."

She slipped the fabric she'd been embroidering from its frame, carefully folded it, and pressed it into my arms. "But I—"

She shushed me with a look and guided me to the wall. Lifting a delicate hand, she traced her finger across a carved thread. "I cannot speak of this anymore today. The sadness is too great. It is time for you to leave. Follow the silkworm, young one."

She cupped her hand against the wall, and when she removed it, a white silkworm clung to the carved thread. As it began advancing along the line, I turned to say good-bye, but Lady Silkworm had disappeared. The worm made slow progress to a crack in the wall and then slipped inside. I tentatively touched the same crack. First my fingers and then my whole hand disappeared into the wall. Taking a deep breath, I stepped forward to find myself encompassed by blackness.

# of dragons and lost continents

I held out my hand in front of me, groping blindly, and gasped when I felt warm fingers touch mine. I followed the gentle pull of the hand, letting it guide me forward until I hit a barrier. Tracing its surface, I searched for an opening. The hand holding mine tugged harder and pulled me from the blackness with a pop. I slammed against a very well-developed, masculine chest, as arms cradled me close. I'd returned to the slightly brighter main room of the Shore Temple.

I blinked and looked up into the face of my liberator. "Ren."

"Are you alright?"

"Yes. Thank you."

He let out a relieved sigh and briefly touched a strand of my hair.

I was about to ask him a question when I heard a voice shout out, "Kells? Mr. Kadam! I heard her!"

Mr. Kadam and Kishan approached quickly from another room.

Kishan pulled me from Ren's embrace and wrapped me in his own. "Where were you?" He turned to Ren. "How did you find her?"

Ren replied. "I don't know. A carving of a horse with a scarf wrapped around its neck appeared on this wall, and it hadn't been there before. The horse transformed into a man who pointed to another carving that suddenly appeared. It was of Kelsey sitting in a chair by a window, sewing. When I touched it, my hand disappeared into the wall. Then

the carving of Kelsey stood and moved toward me. I stretched out my hand, touched her fingers, and pulled her closer. The next thing I knew, she was standing in front of me."

Kishan grunted. "Are you okay, *bilauta*? Are you hurt?"

"No, I'm fine. How long was I gone?"

Mr. Kadam stepped forward. "You've been missing for the last hour. Everyone was becoming . . . *worried*."

I could see by his expression that it had been worse than that. I hugged Kishan and patted Ren's arm briefly to comfort my tigers. "I was visiting with Lady Silkworm." I looked down at the folded silk nestled in my arm. "Come on. Let's get back to the ship. I have a lot to tell you."

We quickly made our way out of the Shore Temple and back to the boat.

Kishan wrapped an arm around me. "I was worried, Kells."

"It's okay. Everything worked out, and we got what we came for."

"I don't like you disappearing like that. We couldn't even track you on GPS. You just vanished. Your dot was gone."

"I'm sorry." I kissed his cheek and squeezed his arm. "Until the curse is broken, unexpected things are likely to happen to all of us. You know that."

"I know." He kissed my forehead. "I just wish I could always be there to protect you. It's frustrating when there's nothing I can do."

I nodded and leaned my head on his shoulder. Ren was watching us. He looked at me thoughtfully for a brief moment and then turned to look out across the open sea. When we pulled up near the yacht, Ren leapt out first and quickly disappeared into the bowels of the ship. Kishan jumped up and helped Mr. Kadam and then held out his hand to me. We went to the lounge near our rooms while Mr. Kadam questioned Nilima about the staff.

We took our seats, Mr. Kadam in the chair and Kishan and I on the sofa. I asked, "Doesn't Ren want to know what happened? I thought he would help us with this."

Mr. Kadam replied, "I will tell him everything later. He . . . only wants to be present when we absolutely need him."

"I see." I held my tongue and sighed in resignation, before taking Kishan's hand and then shared the story of Lady Silkworm, starting with the line of thread I'd followed on the wall and ending with emerging from it. Mr. Kadam and Kishan kept silent throughout the whole story. When I was finished, I held out the silky gift to Mr. Kadam. He carefully unfolded it.

It was a black silk kimono. The back featured five hand-embroidered dragons in exquisite detail. They looked more like Chinese serpents than dragons. Their long sinuous bodies curved and coiled. They were bearded, had long tongues, and four short limbs with taloned feet. On the top left of the robe's front was a map with seven dots and symbols. Mr. Kadam studied the front carefully, while Kishan and I looked at the back.

"Red, white, gold, green, and blue. Yep, those are our dragons alright." I traced a symbol. "Kishan . . . look at this." I pointed to the red dragon. It looked as if it was walking in the stars. A different symbol surrounded each of the five dragons: stars, clouds, lightning, waves, and snowflakes. "I wonder what this means."

Mr. Kadam set down the kimono and went to his writing desk to unlock a file drawer and gather some papers. "I believe what we're looking at is a map with instructions. It's telling us where to go and which dragon to seek first."

"How do you know that?" I asked.

"The seven dots are the seven pagodas. This one is the Shore Temple. There are corresponding numbers written in Chinese next to each temple. See here? The Shore Temple has the number one next to it."

He traced a pattern starting at the symbol that looked like a hyphen and moved from dot to dot following Chinese numerical order.

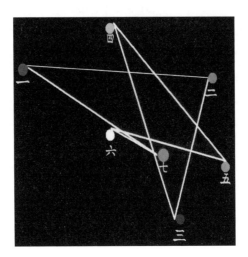

"It's a star!" I pronounced.

"Yes, I believe it is."

"So, Mr. Kadam, you're saying we should find the first dragon at the number two temple or pagoda?"

"Yes."

"There's a slight problem with your theory."

"Yes, I know."

Together we said, "There are only five dragons."

Kishan leaned forward. "What do you think awaits at the last pagoda then?"

Mr. Kadam pressed his hands together and sat back, tapping his lip while thinking. Finally, he said, "I think the danger is not necessarily going to come from the dragons but from what you find at the last pagoda. In Chinese mythology, dragons are revered for being helpful, especially water dragons."

"Then why do we have to go in order? If we know Durga's Necklace is hidden in the last pagoda, why not just go there and be done with it?" I asked.

Mr. Kadam shook his head. "No. The directions were given to us for a purpose. Perhaps the dragons will guide you or help you get to the next temple. You couldn't have skipped the four houses in Shangri-la. You had to be tested at each one before proving yourselves worthy of continuing on. I suspect meeting the dragons will be a similar test."

I groaned. Mr. Kadam began telling us some stories about dragons, and before I knew it, I'd fallen asleep on Kishan's shoulder.

I awoke when Mr. Kadam chuckled. "Why don't you two head off to bed while I study this a bit further. Tomorrow I will teach you what I've learned of the seven pagodas. Meet me here after breakfast."

Kishan squeezed my hand as I nodded sleepily. We said goodnight to Mr. Kadam, and Kishan walked me back to my room.

After brushing my teeth and changing into pajamas in the bathroom, I found Kishan reclining on my bed wearing only a pair of lounge pants that hung dangerously low on his hips.

"Uh . . . what's up?" I stammered nervously.

He blinked open his golden eyes and looked at me. "I thought we could spend some time together if you aren't too tired."

"Oh."

He patted the space on the bed next to him, and I approached hesitantly.

What is wrong with me? He is my boyfriend, isn't he? If it was Ren on the bed I wouldn't have paused. Why am I so nervous with Kishan?

He watched me with a mixture of curiosity and a twinge of sadness, so I wiped the errant thoughts from my mind and lay down next to him. He put his arm around me, cuddled me against his rather expansive warm chest, and rubbed my back. I eventually relaxed as sleepiness overtook me again.

"What's wrong?" he asked quietly.

"Nothing, really. I guess I'm just nervous at the idea of being close to you physically."

I heard a rumble in his chest. "You don't need to be nervous with me, Kells. I'd never hurt you."

My mind snapped back to a green-tinged fire. I'd been wrapped in Ren's arms as he said those exact same words. *I hope you know I'd never hurt you, Kells.* My heart beat lopsidedly. For a second, it felt like my heart would rip in half.

I put my arm across Kishan's chest and hugged him. "I know you'd never hurt me. It's normal for two people who are getting to know one another to feel . . . hesitant and a little awkward. Don't take it personally. I like being near you like this."

"Good," he grunted, "because I'm not moving." He took my hand and pressed it against his chest, holding it captive there. "Are you tired?"

I nodded. "Aren't you?"

"Not yet. Go ahead and sleep."

I made myself comfortable against his shoulder and slept, not even noticing when he changed to a tiger.

The next morning after breakfast, we met with Mr. Kadam who had pulled out all his research on the City of the Seven Pagodas.

"The first documented accounts of the city are records written by Mr. John Goldingham in 1798. He wrote of seven pagodas built near the sea. Either he was writing on hearsay, or they were not underwater at the time.

"As I told you before, it is rumored that Marco Polo visited the city as it is listed on one of his Catalan maps of 1275, but there is no record of this. What interests me most about this city are the ties I've found to Shangri-la."

"How exactly is it tied to Shangri-la?" I asked.

"Do you remember the utopian societies we've researched and about how the story of the flood has common ties in every culture?"

"Yes."

"In Shangri-la, you found objects that crossed mythical boundaries between many peoples. The ravens Hugin and Munin from the Norse, the sirens of the Greek, the Ocean Teacher of Tibet, the Spirit Gates of Japan, even the Kappa of the Chinese in Kishkindha . . . all of these things go beyond the borders of India and, as a result, I have begun to explore sunken cities of other cultures. The most famous of which is—"

"Atlantis."

Mr. Kadam smiled at me. "Correct. Atlantis."

"What's Atlantis?" Kishan asked.

Mr. Kadam turned to him. "Atlantis is thought to be a fictional creation of Plato, though there are scholars who believe the story to be based in fact. As the story goes, the isle of Atlantis was a beautiful land that belonged to Poseidon. The king of the island was Poseidon's son, Atlas, which is where the name came from. The island was said to be larger than Australia, located on the Atlantic Ocean, which was also named for Atlas, by the way, and was located several miles outside the Pillars of Hercules, or the Straits of Gibraltar.

"Poseidon was proud of his son and of the strong and brave people who lived on his isle. Although the paradise offered the people everything they could wish for, they became greedy and wanted more. They knew wealthy lands were not far away, so the Atlanteans created a military and began conquering territory inside the Pillars of Hercules. This in and of itself was tolerated by the gods, but the Atlanteans also forced those conquered into slavery.

"The gods met to discuss what was happening, and steps were taken

to intervene. Earthquakes, fires, and floods were sent to humble the Atlanteans, but the lust for power and wealth was so heavy, they refused to change their ways. Finally, the gods forced Poseidon to destroy Atlantis. He raised the seas and caused great earthquakes to rip the land apart. In his wrath, he flung pieces of the broken isle across the ocean, where it sank into oblivion. Atlas, who had been a wise mathematician and astronomer, was punished by the gods and was forced to bear the weight of the heavens."

"Wait a minute, I thought Atlas held the Earth on his back," I said.

"No. Actually, he held up the sky. Homer said that Atlas was 'one who knows the depths of the whole sea, who keeps the tall pillars, and who holds heaven and earth asunder.' It has been said that when Atlantis was destroyed and the pieces torn apart, Atlas felt great despair and agony over his people. The gods were disappointed in him, and, what was worse, he'd lost the respect of his father. As each piece was ripped away, Atlas felt as if it had been torn from his own chest. He grieves as he bears the weight of his lost city. This is why many pictures of Atlas show him bowed down in despair as he does his duty."

"I had no idea. Now you said there are other sunken cities. I haven't heard of any others."

"There are many sunken cities. More than I can name. Each tale I research leads me to five others. There is Meropis, as told by Theopompus; the lost continent of Mu that was sunk in the Pacific between Polynesia and Japan; and Lemuria, a lost land that sank either in the Indian Ocean or the Pacific Ocean. Then there's Kumari Kandam, a sunken kingdom nicknamed the Land of Purity at the southern tip of India, and Ys or Ker-Is of Brittany. The Danes have Vineta, Egypt has Menouthis and Herakleion, Jamaica has Port Royal, and Argentina has Santa Fe la Vieja.

"Some of these cities have been found, and some remain only in stories shared among different cultures. The common thread is that the people angered the gods and were punished by the sea. Many of the legends say to seek these cities is to seek the curse that condemned them in the first place."

"Does such a curse exist for the City of the Seven Pagodas?" I asked.

"I don't know. I hope not. Perhaps by following Lady Silkworm's pattern, we will avoid falling victim to the same fate. Perhaps the sea will spare us."

Mr. Kadam set out drawings he had found of the five dragons. "In Chinese culture, the dragons are each assigned a territory, one for each compass point: north, south, east, and west. That leaves the fifth dragon."

"Maybe he's homeless or the center point of the compass," I offered.

"Yes. In fact, there is a mention of a homeless dragon, but I suspect the center point of the compass may be more accurate in this case. They are also called the dragons of the five oceans."

"What are the five oceans?"

"The ocean of the North is the Arctic, the Pacific is the East, the Atlantic is the West, the Indian Ocean is the middle, and the Southern Ocean is the South."

"So we have an ocean for each dragon. Do you think we have to go to each ocean?"

"No. I believe we will find what we seek here. Perhaps they will be summoned."

"Maybe they commute to work."

Mr. Kadam laughed dryly. "Yes. Perhaps."

I picked up a paper with a picture of a Chinese dragon dance. "I saw one of these dances at the wedding I went to with Li."

I handed the picture to Kishan as Mr. Kadam nodded and explained, "The dragon dance is typically seen during the Chinese New Year. It honors the dragon and asks it to bestow good things for the coming

year. Dragons bring the rain, watch over waterways, guard treasure, and bestow strength, wealth, good fortune, and fertility. In centuries past, the Chinese people have even called themselves the Children of the Dragon.

"At a wedding, the newlywed couple asks the dragons to bless their marriage; at New Years, those requests would be applied to all of the citizens. Incidentally, I've also been doing some research on colors. It appears that every color has different powers and characteristics. The red and black dragons are fierce and destructive. They can cause violent storms; they battle in the clouds and are said to be the source of lightning and thunder.

"Black dragons are considered evil and deceptive. Reds are associated with all the symbols of red: blood, temper, anger, love, fire, passion, volcanoes. Blues are more peaceful. They like ice and cold waters. Golds are the kings and queens of dragons; they hoard wealth. Greens can heal and promote wellness but also cause earthquakes, spew acid, and eat humans. Whites are reflective and wise; they are seen only rarely, tell half-truths, are omens of death, and their scales shine like mirrors."

"Sounds great."

Kishan put his arm around me and squeezed my shoulder.

"Remember, Miss Kelsey, that this is all research. Your dragons could be similar to these or completely different."

"I know."

"Half of my research on gourds was never applicable, remember?"

"Yes. I remember. But still it's nice to be prepared."

Kishan suggested, "Perhaps you'd better go over the ways to kill them, just in case."

Mr. Kadam agreed and went on for another two hours describing different types of dragons and their tendencies. He spoke of the Indian serpent kings, of crystal palaces beneath the ocean where dragons dined on opals and pearls and were served by crabs and fish.

He talked about weather patterns caused by dragons such as waterspouts, typhoons, and hurricanes. He spoke of bearded dragons, hairy dragons, long tailed, short tailed, five clawed, four clawed, some that could fly, some that lived in caves, some that breathed fire, and he named them: Ao Guang, Ao Qin, Ao Run, and Ao Shun, the Chinese dragons of the four compass points. He didn't know what the fifth dragon would be called.

When Mr. Kadam was satisfied that we knew everything there was to know about dragons, he suggested heading up to the wheelhouse to peruse some of the captain's maps. When I mentioned having lunch on the upper deck, he said we'd be relying on the Golden Fruit because he'd sent all the staff ashore for a day off, including the captain and his first mate.

I retrieved the Golden Fruit as Mr. Kadam carefully gathered his notes and locked them away again in the desk drawer. Then the three of us went up to the wheelhouse. He brought the kimono with him so he could compare maps. When we arrived, he pulled out a large laminated map of the Bay of Bengal. The Fruit made sandwiches and a tray of sliced melon, which I offered to Mr. Kadam but he waved it away, so intent was he in his studies of the map. Kishan and I ate without him.

When I was finished, I picked up the kimono and traced the red dragon before laying it out, dragon-side down, on the shelf above the row of monitors. I put my finger on the Shore Temple and followed the line of stitching over to the red dot, the first of the seven pagodas. The red dot grew, and my hand began to glow. Its threads came undone and started restitching themselves with an invisible needle. They disappeared around the side of the kimono.

I nervously called for Kishan and Mr. Kadam, who were both leaning over the map, as I flipped over the kimono. The red stitches were still moving until they reached the red dragon. The dragon blinked and roared before settling into the fabric again.

Panicked, I exclaimed, "What did I do? What's happened?"

Mr. Kadam hurried over and put his hand on my arm but then froze. "Can you feel that, Kishan?"

"Yes."

"What? What is it?" I asked. They both turned to the window and looked out at the ocean.

"Somebody tell me. What's going on?"

Kishan put his hands on my shoulders. "It's the ship, Kells. We're moving."

the red dragon's star

"We're moving? How is that possible?"

"I'm not certain." Mr. Kadam quickly checked the ship's instruments. "Everything's off. We should still be at anchor."

I picked up the kimono and flipped it around again. "Mr. Kadam. Look at this."

A tiny stitched boat had appeared on the front of the kimono and, as we watched, it crept forward one stitch. It was aimed for the red dot.

Mr. Kadam quickly turned around. "Kishan? Would you mind climbing to the top of the wheelhouse and taking a look around? Take note of our direction and the location of the city."

Kishan returned a moment later, his face incredulous. "Based on the sun, we're heading east but there *is* no city. There's no coastline. Nothing but water surrounds us for miles."

Mr. Kadam nodded as if he expected this. "Please locate Ren and Nilima for me and ask them to come to the wheelhouse."

Kishan made eye contact with me and smiled briefly, then turned and left.

Mr. Kadam played with the instruments a moment longer, and then frowned.

"What's wrong?" I asked.

"Nothing's turning on. We shouldn't be moving. The engines aren't on. The anchor is still down according to this. Nothing is working—satellite, radio, everything's off."

When Kishan returned with the others, Nilima and Mr. Kadam began charting our progress on a large map as best they could. Mr. Kadam sent Ren and Kishan to check on the anchor. He asked me to keep my eye on the compass and shout out directions but the compass just spun in circles. It would point east for a few seconds then swing south, then west, then back to the east again. Eventually, Mr. Kadam had me watch the horizon instead. We couldn't steer the ship, but I was to watch for possible obstacles while he and Nilima tried to figure out what to do.

Ren and Kishan returned and reported that the anchor had actually been trailing in our wake, like a raft floating along behind the ship. They'd had to reel it in manually. We tried our cell phones but found no signal. The five of us spent a quiet afternoon in the wheelhouse, talking only when necessary. Without saying it, we all knew we'd entered another world—a world without the rules and boundaries we were used to. A world where dragons ruled the seas, and all we had to protect ourselves were our weapons and Mr. Kadam's research.

I could feel the change in the air. The warmth and heat of the India summer was gone, and the air felt heavy and wet and cold, more like the air near the sea in Oregon. Kishan readied our scuba gear just in case. The temperature had dropped from the nineties to the sixties. Ren retrieved our weapons and a sweater and Fanindra for me. I didn't put on the sweater but thanked him and slid Fanindra onto my arm.

It was time for all of us to suit up. Ren helped me strap the bow and quiver of golden arrows over my back with a fabric strap from the Divine Scarf. He helped me practice taking the bow out a few times. He asked the Divine Scarf to shrink down to a hair ribbon and, after a pointed look at my sheared hair, knotted it securely around my wrist.

The Golden Fruit was placed in a bag and slid into the quiver with the arrows.

Ren had made himself a belt with the Divine Scarf also, creating fabric hip holsters for the *gada* and the trident. When Kishan returned, Ren handed him a similar belt with a loop for the *chakram*. Kishan hung the *kamandal* shell around his neck, and we stood quietly facing the window for a time—me between my two warriors. We were ready for battle.

Mr. Kadam and Nilima called us over to the kimono to tell us that they had given up trying to figure out where we were. Ren, Kishan, and I nodded in understanding. The three of us knew that once we began the hunt, there were no maps; there was no rational path to take. We depended on fortune and destiny to lead us to the place we needed to go.

Afternoon quickly turned into evening. We were more than halfway to the red dot now. Based on the speed we were moving across the kimono, Mr. Kadam figured we would arrive around midnight. We didn't feel like going below deck so the three of us—Kishan, Ren, and I—climbed to the top of the wheelhouse. I used the Scarf to make cushions. Despite my nerves, the discomfort of Fanindra on my arm, and the bow and arrows on my back, I fell asleep leaning against Kishan's chest.

Several hours later, Kishan gently shook me awake. I blinked open sleepy eyes to stare at his long jean-clad leg stretched out in front of me. In my sleep, I'd moved to using his thigh as a pillow.

I groaned and rubbed my aching neck. "What is it?"

Kishan's warm hands began kneading my sore muscles. "It's nothing. My leg was just falling asleep."

I laughed then winced as he hit a tender spot. "Well, it's probably safe to say I hurt me more than I hurt you."

"You're probably right."

I looked up and saw the silent form of Ren standing as far away as possible. He watched the horizon, ever vigilant. "Ren? Why don't you take a break and let me or Kishan take watch for a while?"

Ren turned his head so I could see his profile. "I'm fine. You sleep, Kells."

Once he turned back, I stared at him in confusion. "Hey. Have you two gone more than twelve hours as men now?"

Ren nodded briefly and Kishan said, "For me, it's been fourteen. We're in the no-need-to-be-a-tiger zone, it seems."

I sat up further. "I'm hungry. What time is it?"

Ren answered, "About 11:45. I could use something to eat too."

Kishan stood and stretched. "I'll stand watch. You eat something with Kelsey."

Ren hesitated but stepped aside and sat down a good five feet away from me.

"What would you like?" I asked him kindly.

He shrugged. "It doesn't matter. You choose."

I wished up some kettle corn and root beer in frosty bottles. I gave a giant bowl to Ren and took one to Kishan, who kissed my forehead and turned to watch the dark horizon again.

After I settled myself and started munching on the warm, buttery snack in my own bowl, I looked at Ren who was staring hard at the popcorn. "Is something wrong?" I asked.

"No. It's good. It just . . . tastes different."

"What do you mean? You've had popcorn before."

"This is sweet."

"Oh. It's kettle corn. You used to eat it all the time in Oregon."

He picked up a popped kernel and studied it. He mumbled quietly to himself, "A blue dress. I dropped the bowl."

"What did you say?" I asked.

"Hmm?" He looked up suddenly. "Oh. Nothing. It's good."

We ate quietly. I tipped back my bottle of root beer and looked up at the sky. "Look at that." I pointed. "The stars are so bright!"

Ren pushed his empty bowl and root beer away and lay back on the cushions with his hands behind his head. "You're right. They're very bright. More than usual. Do you see that constellation up there?"

"The one to the right?"

"No."

He slid closer so his head was resting against mine and gently took my wrist. He moved my arm until my finger was pointing at a very bright star. My heart started beating harder, and my face flushed. A light scent of sandalwood mixed with the sea was coming from his hair that was tickling my cheek. He moved my arm to point out a path from star to star. "Can you see it now?"

I sucked in a breath. "Yes. It's like a serpent."

He nodded and let go of my wrist. Sliding away, he put his arms under his head again. "It's called Draco. As in the dragon."

"That makes sense."

"He guards the golden apples of Hera, the Greeks say. Others say he is the serpent who tempted Eve."

"Huh. That's interesting. What do you think about the . . . Ren! Did you see that?"

"See what?"

"There! Look at the Draco constellation. Something's moving."

He peered up into the night sky but nothing happened for a moment. I was just about suggest it must have been a figment of my imagination when I saw several stars winking on and off. They started shifting and writhing, becoming bigger and distorted.

Ren stood up. "I see it. Kishan? Protect Kelsey. I'll be right back."

Ren disappeared over the side of the wheelhouse while I instructed

the Divine Scarf to clear away the cushions and the Golden Fruit to take away the bowls and bottles. Kishan and I stood in the battle stance he'd taught me. I was ready to use my lightning power if I needed to. Kishan pulled free the *chakram*.

A black undulating shape made its way toward us. It distorted the night as if the sky was the underside of a blanket and something big was rolling across the top of it. The stars bulged and trembled as it moved.

I felt a hand touch my arm. Ren had taken a ready stance with the trident on my other side. We turned as the shape circled above us, keeping it in our line of sight. Suddenly the sky seemed to balloon out and rip, and a dark shape slipped through the tear.

A head emerged, followed by a sinuous long body. It dipped and twisted in the air like a twirling stunt kite. It circled the boat at a slow, leisurely pace, moving lower and lower until we could clearly see what it was—a dragon. But this was not a type of dragon I'd ever seen in the movies. It looked more like a snake. There were no wings; instead it slithered through the air like a sidewinder on the sand. This was definitely not the dragon of St. George; it looked more like the drawings of Chinese dragons Mr. Kadam had shown us.

Moist pockets of air whipped against us, and a thick silence spread around us as if our ears were stopped up. The sea had stilled; its blackness reflected the starlight so it looked as if we were standing in the middle of space. The dragon came closer. Its underbelly was black, but the top was streaked with vermillion, and it seemed to glow with a red light that reflected dimly on the black water below.

Its head was the size of a Volkswagen Beetle. Long black-and-red tendrils trailed from its black-bearded cheeks. As it moved through the sky, its four short, taloned legs pawed the air. The body moved toward us, and the air pockets left in its wake crashed against the ship like waves. The dragon flew around the boat again. This time it was near enough that its entire body circled the ship. Shiny scales about the size of dinner plates ran down the length of its body and gleamed in the starlight. Its head came closer and stopped near us. We faced the red dragon as its head rose up and down in the air, as if bobbing on a current.

Huge nostrils puffed cold air on us as one great, long-lashed eye blinked and stared. One red iris with a black pupil considered us thoughtfully. I took a step closer and peered into that bright eye. It shone in the middle as if a star were captured inside.

"Step back, Kelsey," Kishan warned softly.

I moved back as both he and Ren took a step forward and angled their bodies slightly toward me, ready to defend me from attack. The dragon shook its head, and its mighty black beard swayed and settled. Its great jaw opened, and a long red tongue rolled out as if tasting the air and then retreated back, curling into its gaping, toothy mouth.

The boat suddenly listed to one side and then the other. Kishan and Ren stood their ground and steadied me as the boat settled. I turned briefly and saw that the dragon had draped its long body on the outside of the yacht. Ren and Kishan never took their eyes off the dragon. The creature shuddered delicately, and its pointed, black-tufted ears turned toward the stars as if listening to a message only he could hear.

Its jaws opened slightly almost as if smiling at me, and I heard a voice in my head echo like tinkling bells, "*Měnghǔ, wǒ jiào Lóngjūn.*"

I blinked and looked up at Ren, who whispered, "It said, 'Fierce tigers, my name is Lóngjūn, the Dragon of the West.'"

Kishan took a step forward and spoke several words in Mandarin. Ren softly translated, "He asked if the great dragon could also speak English."

I heard the tinkling voice in my head again, and the dragon opened its mouth and bobbed its head up and down as if it was laughing.

Yes. I can speak in this tongue as well, though it's not as pretty as my own.

The eye blinked, and I watched the fluttering lashes in fascination.

You come to ask a favor of me. Do you not?

"We do," I voiced tremulously.

Name your favor, and I will name my price.

We shifted uncomfortably. Ren asked, "If the price is too high, can we negotiate?"

Yes. The long forked tongue rolled out to taste the air near Ren. Ren stood his ground, and the tongue retreated.

"Fine," Kishan said. "We seek Durga's Black Pearl Necklace."

Ah, then you must visit my brothers. I can show you how to find them, in exchange—

"In exchange for what?" I asked hesitantly.

The dragon shifted its body while thinking, and the ship lurched to one side. I fell heavily against Ren, but he easily caught and righted me.

The item you need to find my brothers is in my sky palace. One of you would have to accompany me there to retrieve it.

Kishan responded, "That's fine. I'll go."

But wait, the dragon said. *If you wish to take it with you, you must give me something in exchange. A moment while I consider. Ah, yes. One of my stars has dimmed. You may repair it.*

"You want us to repair a star? How do we do that?" I asked.

How is something you must decide.

"Okay, then how do we get up there?"

This time, when the head turned, its long tongue curled out to taste the air near me.

Are you brave, young lady?

Ren murmured quietly, "She's the bravest woman I know."

I turned to stare at him, but he was still looking at the dragon. The great beast made a sound in our minds, the equivalent of a dragon grunt, I suppose.

If the three of you have the courage, you may ride the stars on my back.

I nodded and had taken several steps forward before both Ren and Kishan put an arm out to stop me. Kishan said, "We'll go, Kelsey. You stay here."

"You know you'll need me. I'll have both of you with me. It will be okay."

I approached the dragon's eye and bowed my head respectfully. "Lóngjūn, may I climb onto your back?"

The dragon opened its mouth and tinkling laughter sounded in my head. *So polite. Yes, my dear. You and your tigers may climb upon my back. But I warn you now. If you fall, I will not catch you. Make sure you are secure. You may hold onto the spikes on the back of my head if you wish.*

When the red dragon lowered its head, I stepped forward and touched a reddish-black spike that had been hiding in the coarse hairy tendrils trailing from the dragon's cheeks and head. The spike was actually more like a horn. There were two—both protruding from the back of the head. They were soft and rounded at the tips and covered in a black velvety coat that reminded me of new antlers growing on a young deer.

Ren stepped forward and climbed onto the dragon's back. Kishan sat behind him but left enough space to pull me up between them.

Ren examined the horns until he found a good place to hold. With a sudden jolt, the dragon lifted its head and body from the ship. We rose several hundred feet into the air in just a few seconds and then plummeted toward the ocean just as quickly. I locked my arms as tightly as I could around Ren's waist and pressed my cheek against his back, but I still felt my weight lift into the air as we dropped.

I had an epiphany during our downfall and mentally asked the Divine Scarf to tie our bodies to the dragon. I couldn't hear the whispering of the threads over the shrieking of the wind, but I felt the fabric circle my waist and press down on my thighs as it strapped me

to the dragon. It was just in time too, because after the dragon had freed its body from the ship, it dipped and swirled in the air at frightening speeds.

My stomach lurched as we soared up into the sky then flipped upside down and hung there several moments before turning in spiral freefall. It was like riding the scariest roller coaster in the world, and the only thing keeping me from sure death was the strong grip of the men holding me and the threads of the Divine Scarf.

The air became colder the higher we went, and soon I could no longer tell where we were. My breath frosted and hung in the air. I pressed myself closer against Ren's back, grateful for the warmth of both my tigers. The ocean was so black and clear that it looked like the sky. We were riding the winds of the universe, dragonback, surrounded by winking stars.

As we went higher, the stomach-wrenching maneuvers of the dragon slowed, and it stayed right-side up as it wound back and forth through space. I thought it must look like a giant anaconda weaving its lazy way through a black river. I began to shiver, and my breathing became shallower. Kishan scooted closer and pressed his warm cheek against mine. Because we were moving slowly now, he let go and ran his hands up and down my bare arms.

"I wish I would've brought that sweater."

Tinkling laughter rippled through my mind.

The stars are bright but cold. While I am with you, you will not freeze. Look there. That is my palace, it voiced with pride.

I looked up and saw that the red dragon was heading for a bright cluster of stars. It surged ahead with increased speed, and Kishan leaned forward again, grabbing onto Ren's waist, crushing me between them. The head of the dragon angled upward, and I slid back into Kishan's chest as the dragon flew straight up in the air. The Divine Scarf's ties pulled against us, threatening to tear. Ren's arms strained as he held the weight of all three of us, and I felt Kishan's legs tighten as he gripped the dragon between his thighs. I could do nothing but lie against Kishan's chest and hope the two of them had enough strength to keep us from falling.

Finally, the dragon evened out again, and Ren leaned forward heavily, panting. He was probably also sick now from my close proximity. He briefly looked back at me over his shoulder. His face was pale and clammy. His arms, slick with sweat, shook with tremors.

I felt a kind of weightlessness. *This must be what zero gravity is like*, I thought. My hair began to rise, and my arms were light as if the buoyancy of the ocean was holding my body afloat. I became very aware of the movements of the dragon. I could feel its smooth muscles roll under us. Its tail seemed to be propelling it forward now. It twisted back and forth like a shark and rolled the rest of its body from side to side.

The star cluster was much closer and brighter now, brighter than anything I'd ever seen before. It radiated energy and pulsed softly like a beacon. As we neared, my mouth fell open in awe. The dragon's palace was like a diamond mansion hung in the sky. It gleamed and reflected light from its many facets. When the dragon neared, a door opened to a room big enough to house a couple of airplanes. The dragon slid along the clear diamond floor on its belly, circling back so its sinuous body was folded in half, and came to a stop.

At Kishan's whispered request, the Divine Scarf undid our bands, and he jumped off the beast. I slid down into Kishan's arms, and then he turned to Ren, who staggered off the dragon and stooped over, clutching Kishan's arm for support. I moved away several steps, and after a moment, Ren nodded to Kishan and stood.

The dragon shivered, and its body began to convulse. It started shrinking; its long shape diminished and twisted. Then with a snap, it

disappeared, and a man stood in its place. He was black skinned and beautiful with red eyes and red robes. His white teeth were brilliant against his skin. He bowed briefly.

"Welcome to my sky palace. Perhaps I could interest you in a game? Refreshments?"

Kishan shook his head. "We'd like to get what we came for."

"Ah, yes. Forgive me. It's been so long since I've had visitors." The dragon man smiled toothily. "Come. I will show you the item you will need."

He guided us through his diamond mansion. Everything sparkled and reflected back our images. I felt like I was in a hall of mirrors. I would have quickly become lost if not for our guide. He led us to a pedestal, on the top of which rested a diamond object. I squinted in the light, trying to recognize the shape.

Kishan hefted it in his hands and said, "A sextant."

Inching closer to inspect the heavy apparatus, I saw a sparkling telescope mounted onto a pie-wedged diamond frame. Numbers were etched into the arc along the edge. What parts would normally be made of glass and metal were instead made of priceless polished gemstone.

"Yes, a sextant," said the red dragon. "It will guide you to my brother. Now for the agreed upon price."

He led us to a door that opened to a balcony—and beyond that, space. He pointed up at a pair of stars. One was dim and the other bright. "You agreed to fix my star."

The four of us stared at the stars for a while, and then the dragon went inside while we quietly brainstormed on how to repair the star. I tried to use my lightning power, but it couldn't cross the distance. Kishan wanted to throw the *chakram*, but I was worried about losing it in space. Not coming up with any other ideas, Kishan disappeared inside to talk with the dragon about other options and shortly returned.

"Lóngjūn has agreed to play a game of chess with one of us instead. If we win, we get the sextant. If we lose, one of us must remain behind."

"That's no good," I said. "I'm terrible at chess."

Ren and Kishan stared at each other for a second, and then Ren said, "You're the better chess player. Kadam only wins most of the time with you."

Kishan nodded and disappeared inside. Ren and I followed him and watched the game. The dragon took the black diamond pieces while Kishan took the clear ones. Kishan began. After several moves, I began to fear that Kishan was going to lose. The dragon sat back smiling and patiently waited for Kishan's next move. I panicked and elbowed Ren.

He followed me outside, and I told him I wanted to try one more thing. I asked for his trident. He handed it over, and I used the Divine Scarf to make hundreds of meters of stiff rope and tied one end to the balcony. I also asked it to weave the other end tightly around the trident.

Next, I handed Ren the trident.

He looked at me, puzzled. "What do you want me to do with it?"

"I want you to shoot the trident into the star and pull it toward us."

"You think it will go that far?"

"I'm hoping the momentum of space will help carry it. The Scarf can create more rope as it travels and if we miss we can pull it back. I'd do it myself, but you have more power in your arm."

Ren nodded and stepped forward. Aiming carefully, he shot the trident into space like a giant arrow. It soon became obvious that he'd missed.

I had the Divine Scarf pull the trident and rope back, and he was soon ready to try again. We heard the dragon yell "Check" gleefully from the other room and knew we were running out of time.

"Aim higher this time. The light from the star is reflecting off the palace. Maybe it's throwing off your aim."

This time his aim was true, and when the trident shot into space with a twang, it continued on a direct path toward the star. It impacted with a distant boom. Now came the hard part. I picked up the silky rope the Divine Scarf had made and asked it to retreat while Ren and I pulled. We strained for a minute and then were gratified to feel the rope coming back. We pulled until the star came loose and quickly began gravitating toward the palace. When it neared, Ren stood on the balcony and braced against the wall to catch it.

I knew everything that had just happened was physically impossible. First of all, stars don't move, and even if they did, they would have burned up anything that came close. I decided it would be better if I didn't try to make sense of what just occurred.

Ren wrenched the trident from the star and told the Divine Scarf to take back all the rope, and then turned to me. "Now what?"

"Now we use fire."

I lifted my hand toward the star as the familiar feeling of hot molten lava burned in my middle and shot up my arm. My hand glowed and my white light shot into the star. I pumped all my energy into it and though the star flickered more brightly, it soon dimmed again.

Ren stepped forward. "What's wrong?"

"I don't know."

"Try again."

I lifted my hand and white light burst from my palm again, brightening the star. I stayed there for several minutes but soon felt exhausted. My energy waned. Ren put his hand on my arm to stop me, and during that brief touch, golden fiery hot light shot out from my hand. The star brightened threefold. I stopped and looked at Ren.

"Stand behind me and touch my arms."

He looked at me for a brief moment, but I lowered my gaze and focused ahead. I was acutely aware of him as he slowly moved behind me. I raised my hand to fire again. White light surged forward. Ren pressed his cheek against mine and slid his hands down my arms. It burned. He twined his fingers through mine and the light turned gold and then white again. It blazed with an intensity ten times more fierce than it had been before. The star pulsed, then expanded and brightened with a golden inner core that turned white hot.

I held the blaze for several minutes. Ren started shaking with the effort. His fingers tightened, and his arms trembled. I felt like I was burning with him. My limbs quaked, and it was all I could do to remain standing. I heard him groan with pain. The heat coming off of our entwined limbs was terrible and brilliant.

Soon I couldn't stand upright anymore. I collapsed back against Ren's chest, and the fire died. My blood pumped through my body in time with the pulsing star, quickening down my arms where Ren's skin still touched mine. Despite the agony I was sure he was feeling, he held me gently and then led me to the wall. We rested against it for a few moments.

Ren moved several feet away and leaned over, clutching his stomach and panting. The skin of his cheek where he'd pressed it against mine and the inside of his arms were glowing with the same golden color as the star. Surprised, I looked down at my own arms and found them shining in the same way. I lifted a tired limb and watched the radiance slowly fade and then disappear altogether.

Leaning my head back against the wall, I watched Ren, though I could barely keep my eyes open. He climbed the balcony rail, braced his feet, and pressed his palms against the pulsing star. With a Herculean shove, he launched the star back into space. Eventually it settled itself into its former position.

Ren climbed down and collapsed to a sitting position against the railing. He leaned his head back and closed his eyes. I closed mine too,

and we both sat there for several minutes, exhausted. A voice whispered my name. I knew that voice. I'd heard it in my dreams. I kept my eyes shut tight. If I opened them, he would be gone.

"Kelsey."

I shook my head in silent denial and groaned softly.

"Kelsey."

I twisted uncomfortably and realized I was sitting up. *Why would I sleep sitting up?* He called me again.

"Kelsey."

I blinked open my eyes and stared at the diamond palace in confusion. "Where are you?"

"Over here."

I saw Ren still sitting in the same spot, his head against the railing and his long legs stretched out in front of him, his feet crossed at the ankles.

His eyes locked onto me, and I blushed, remembering his fingers entwined with mine. His look was hot, sultry, and tangible.

"Are you alright?" he asked.

My throat closed, and my tongue felt thick. I licked my lips so I could speak and saw his eyes tighten. I sucked in a breath and just nodded.

"Good." He smiled, then closed his eyes, and at that moment we heard the dragon, Lóngjūn, shout out, "Checkmate!"

A crestfallen Kishan appeared on the balcony followed by the beaming dragon. Lóngjūn clapped his hands together and said, "Now then. Which one of you would like to be my companion here among the stars?"

Kishan immediately knelt at my side and pushed a strand of hair from my face. "Are you alright? What happened?"

I nodded weakly and pointed toward Ren, who was seated on the floor, his head resting in his hands. Kishan spoke quietly with Ren and then returned to me. He sat next to me and pulled my body into his arms. I snuggled against his chest, but when I opened my eyes, Ren's blue eyes captured mine again. I felt like I was staring into a shiny blue reflecting pool. On the surface the water was calm, but I felt that if I could have looked farther into the depths, I'd find the water churning, roiling, full of thoughts and memories I couldn't access. I couldn't see through the surface of those eyes though. I couldn't pull the man I knew from the depths of his mind. He was hidden from me.

The dragon laughed. "None of you will choose? Fine. I will choose myself."

I looked up. "You don't get to choose. We fixed your star."

"Zěnme?" the dragon asked incredulously.

"Look for yourself."

He walked to the balcony and peered up at the sky. "How did you do that?"

"As you pointed out earlier, our job was to figure out how, not to explain it to you."

The dragon frowned and rubbed a cheek. "Still . . . a game was lost. I must have some kind of compensation as the winner."

I groaned and stood up. Kishan rose immediately to help me. "Would you be satisfied with this?"

I put my hands on the dragon's shoulders and pecked his cheek. It felt very warm and leathery. He pressed his hand against his cheek, shocked. "What was that?"

"A kiss," Ren said as he rose silently next to us. "Men have been known to fight over the favor."

I lowered my eyes and felt Kishan take my hand and squeeze it. The dragon's eyes twinkled. "A kiss. Yes. I am satisfied. You may take the sextant and go."

He turned to leave, and I said, "Lóngjūn? Would you consider giving us a ride back to our boat?"

The dragon man stopped to weigh his answer. "Yes. If you give me another . . . *kiss*. But this time in my true form."

I nodded as we followed the dragon back through his house of diamonds. Kishan picked up the sextant, and we asked the Divine Scarf to make a bag to carry it in.

As Kishan strapped it across his back, Lóngjūn warned, "You may only use it while in my realm and only to find my brother. Once you leave our oceans, it will return to me."

Kishan adjusted the weight and bowed briefly. "Our thanks, great dragon."

His body quivered and erupted in an explosion of scaly flesh that quickly spread across the room. As Ren moved toward the dragon, I put my hand on his arm then quickly let it drop. He turned to me.

"Will you be okay?" I asked. "Do you need to rest longer?"

He took a deep breath and let it out slowly. "I'll be fine. Just make sure the ropes are tight."

I nodded and Ren and Kishan climbed onto the dragon's back while I approached its reddish head and pressed a warm kiss onto its black-bearded cheek.

While the dragon shook its mighty head, I heard tinkling laughter in my mind.

What a pleasant gift. Climb on quickly, my dear. The stars are waning.

Kishan pulled me up, and in the instant I had commanded the Divine Scarf to create ropes to wrap around our legs and secure us, the red dragon dove over the floor of its sky palace and spilled into space like a hapless pebble over a waterfall.

16

the blue dragon's pet

If I thought going up on dragonback was bad, going down was much worse. Lóngjūn plummeted hundreds of lengths straight down, and then spun and wove through the sky like a great snake. Kishan's arms locked around me, holding me tight. I fell against Ren's back and closed my eyes as I desperately tried not to throw up. I breathed a sigh of relief when we finally reached the water.

When the red dragon met the sea, it didn't submerge but glided on top of it. The ocean was still quiet, fortunately, and the dragon raced quickly across the water. As we reached the boat, Lóngjūn raised its upper body to the top of the wheelhouse to let us off and impatiently shook its head to further motivate us to disembark as soon as possible.

Kishan and Ren leapt off quickly, but I wasn't fast enough, so the dragon gave a final quick thrust of its body that shot me straight up into the air. I rose up, screaming to the accompaniment of tinkling laughter. Just as I started falling over the side of the wheelhouse, both Ren and Kishan leaned over to grab an arm. I was unceremoniously yanked up and landed with a thud on the deck between the brothers.

After I could suck in a breath again, I said, "Thanks . . . I think," and spun around to stare over the edge with the guys. They were watching the dragon's retreat. It bounced across the water, then gathered its body

and sprang into the air. As it climbed higher, the three of us watched it fly up into the stars and vanish. In the blink of an eye, it was gone.

With a heavy thump, Ren grabbed the sextant from Kishan and disappeared over the side of the wheelhouse, presumably to confer with Mr. Kadam.

Kishan rolled toward me and gently pushed the hair away from my face. "Are you alright?" he asked. "Do you hurt anywhere?"

I laughed then groaned. "I hurt just about everywhere, and I could sleep for a week."

Kishan raised himself up on an elbow. "Come on, then. Let's get you to bed."

He helped me down the ladder of the wheelhouse and briefly ducked his head inside. "I'm putting Kelsey to bed."

Mr. Kadam nodded and dismissed us with a wave, being already absorbed in his new toy, but Ren looked up and studied me briefly before bending over to look at something Mr. Kadam was showing him. Kishan walked me down to my room, stripped me of my gear and shoes and asked, "Clothes or pajamas?"

"That depends."

"On what?"

"On if you plan on staying to help."

He grinned and rubbed his jaw. "That's an intriguing question. What would you *like* me to do?"

I poked him in the chest. "Why don't you wait here while I change in the bathroom."

His face fell in disappointment, and I couldn't help but laugh.

I changed into my pajamas with my eyes closed because I was so tired, washed my face, brushed my teeth, and groped my way back toward the bed. My hand bumped into Kishan's broad chest, and I was quickly scooped up off my feet and placed between the cool sheets. Kishan turned the light to its lowest setting and knelt beside the bed.

My weary head immediately sank into the pillow. I shifted slightly and whimpered.

"Where does it hurt, Kells?"

"My elbow."

He examined my bruised elbow and pressed a soft kiss against it. "Anywhere else?"

"My knee."

He pulled down the sheet and slid my silky pajamas to above my kneecap. He squeezed my knee gently. "You've skinned it, but I think it will heal." His lips touched my knee as he kissed me sweetly there as well. "Next?"

Drowsily, I pointed to my cheek. He pushed my hair back and kissed me a dozen times across my forehead and cheeks. His lips trailed down to my ear as he stroked my hair. He whispered, "I love you, Kelsey."

I was just about to answer him when I fell asleep.

I slept for a long, long time. Kishan was gone when I awoke. The hot water of the shower hurt as it hit my bumped and bruised skin. I briefly wondered why I wasn't healing as fast here as I did in the other realms. I suspected that powering up that star drained me so completely that it was difficult for my body to catch up. I made a mental note to ask Mr. Kadam about it later.

Starving, I entered the wheelhouse, and a kind Nilima made me breakfast even though it was way past dinnertime. I sipped apple juice and carried my plate to the desk where everyone was working. The boys looked well-rested, but Mr. Kadam didn't.

I had the Golden Fruit make Mr. Kadam a cup of his favorite orange blossom tea before I sat in a chair to eat my cream-cheese-and-strawberry-stuffed french toast. He winked at me gratefully and sipped from the cup before stretching out his bent back.

I accused, "You've been working all night, er, day, haven't you?"

Mr. Kadam nodded and picked up his tea.

"When did you last eat?"

He shrugged, so I asked the Golden Fruit to make a hot blueberry scone with butter and honey to go with his tea. He smiled appreciatively and took a seat next to me. Ren and Kishan moved closer to the chart they'd been staring at, bumped heads, and growled at each other. I smiled and turned to Mr. Kadam.

"So what have you discovered? We're moving again, aren't we?"

"Yes."

"How is that possible? Are we moving under our own power?"

"The satellite and some of our other instruments are still not functional but the engine has come back on, though that doesn't help us much if we don't know where we are. That's where this comes in."

He reached over and handed me a small book from the table. I flipped through the pages and saw columns of Chinese writing. "What's this?"

"It's, for lack of a better term, a dragon almanac."

"Where did you get it?"

"I found it in a hidden compartment under the sextant. I've been translating it."

Kishan moved to the wheel and made some adjustments.

"We now know the latitude and longitude of the next dragon. This very unusual sextant allows me to plot our course. All I have to do is look through the eyepiece and find the star of the next dragon. Our next scaly friend is the blue one. Once the star is in view, the sextant whirs and clicks, almost like a compass. It shifts and gives a longitude and latitude. It also tells how many hours it will take us to arrive, depending on our speed."

"Then what do you use the almanac for?"

"The almanac tells where to find the star."

"I see. So when do you expect to arrive at the blue dragon's lair?"

"At our present speed and if the weather holds . . . around 8:00 a.m."

Mr. Kadam picked up a notebook and a pen, and we spent an hour talking about the red dragon and its diamond palace. He'd already gleaned the details from Kishan and Ren but he wanted my version too. He asked me dozens of questions, including an awkward one about the golden light I'd used to rekindle the star. I hesitated and said, "Didn't Ren tell you?"

"He only told me about pulling the star close using the trident and the Scarf. He said it was up to you to tell me the rest."

"Oh."

I bit my bottom lip and turned to see Ren had raised his head. He looked at me with an unfathomable expression, and then bent over the chart again, but I could tell he was still listening to the conversation. Kishan finished whatever he was doing at the wheel, sneaked his arm behind my shoulders, and kissed me on the top of my head.

I cleared my throat. "I, umm . . . must have hit a deep lava tube or something. I don't know why the golden light came. Maybe it's from being in this realm," I lied.

Mr. Kadam nodded and scribbled some notes on a pad. Kishan squeezed my shoulders and began massaging them. I risked sneaking a peek at Ren, but he had quietly disappeared. I sighed guiltily. I wasn't sure why I felt the need to keep what happened between Ren and me a secret. I knew it would likely hurt Kishan, but that's not why I didn't share. I just couldn't. The experience was very . . . *intimate* between the two of us, and it seemed wrong to talk about it.

Kishan, Mr. Kadam, and I spent several hours together in the wheelhouse while a tired Nilima napped. They showed me all they'd discovered while I was sleeping. Mr. Kadam began to teach me the fundamentals of the boat's instruments, but I could tell he was exhausted.

Kishan noticed my look of concern and told Mr. Kadam he'd take over and finish instructing me. After some denial and protesting, we finally convinced him to go take a long nap. We told him we'd wake him if something went wrong.

Kishan spent the next few hours patiently teaching me how the ship worked. He didn't have as much experience as Mr. Kadam or Nilima, but he seemed to have learned quickly. To pass the time, we played a couple of games of Parcheesi and shared another meal. While he played captain, I wrote in my journal and read for a while.

During a break, I joined Kishan at the helm. He seemed quiet as he stood watching the water. I bumped him with my hip. "Penny for your thoughts."

Kishan turned and smiled, and then pulled me to stand in front of him. He wrapped his arms around my waist and rested his chin on the top of my head. "I'm not thinking of anything much except that I'm content. For the first time in . . . centuries, I feel happy."

I laughed. "So you have a thing for fighting demons and monsters, then?"

"No. I have a thing for you. You make me happy."

"Oh." I turned in his arms to face him. "You make me happy too."

He smiled and trailed his fingers down my cheek. His eyes drifted to my lips as he leaned closer. I thought he was going to kiss my mouth, but he seemed to change his mind at the last second and kissed my cheek instead. He trailed kisses over to my ear and whispered, "Soon." He held me close and as I pressed my cheek to his chest I wondered why he'd stopped.

Maybe it was something I did. I was pretty sure I wanted him to kiss me and that I wouldn't cry this time. I care for him. No . . . I love him. I want to make him happy. I bit my lip. Maybe he knows I lied about Ren. Maybe he notices we are acting strangely. No. He would say something, wouldn't he?

I smothered the guilt as we separated and walked over to look at the kimono. The first stitched line of the star, the one going from the Shore Temple to the Star Temple, was complete. I turned the fabric over to take a good look at the blue dragon. I thought I heard a tinkling bell, and I could have sworn the red dragon winked at me. I frowned at him and folded the sleeve over to hide him from view.

The blue dragon was resting on gray clouds and had steam coming from his nostrils. I traced a cloud and heard a snort. A wispy puff rolled across my knuckles. I blew it away and looked up.

We were heading south into the starry night. The sun would be coming up soon. Ahead I noticed thick fog rolling out across the water. The stars began to disappear, captured and snuffed out by cloudy puffs. I leaned out an open door and felt wind whip across my face. The ship bounced on a wave.

I looked at my watch. Only seven hours had passed. "Kishan? I think it's time to wake up Mr. Kadam."

He left and returned with a sleepy Mr. Kadam, who joined me at the window.

"I'm here. What is it, Miss Kelsey?"

"I think the blue dragon's a fog maker. Can we sail through that?"

Mr. Kadam sent Kishan to wake Nilima, and then replied, "We should be fairly safe. There are not likely to be other boats around here to crash into and most of our instruments appear to be operating. Though our satellite feed can't seem to gauge our position, our depth equipment is functioning, so if we suddenly come upon an island, we will be alerted. The water is too warm for icebergs, so we don't need to worry about hitting one of those. If it will make you feel better, I could have Ren or Kishan stand watch. They have excellent vision, even in the fog."

"No," I said with a sigh, "I don't think that's necessary."

Mr. Kadam must have seen my worried expression because he sought to distract me. As he checked some instruments, he asked, "Did

you know the Vikings used special sunstones to navigate in the fog so they could better surprise their enemies?"

It worked. My lip twitched up in a grin. "No, I did not know that."

"The height of the time of the Vikings was in the eighth century. As you likely know, they were famous for pillaging, and in that part of the world they'd frequently encounter fog on raids. They'd board their ships, called *drakkars*, and invade and plunder villages from Iceland to Greenland, Europe to the British Isles, and even North America."

"How did they use the sunstones?"

"Sunstones have an unusual property. They have embedded birefringent crystals that can polarize and show the position of the sun. Any Viking worth his salt could navigate by the sun, and the sunstone worked well for them in all but the worst of storms. Researchers believe the sunstone was likely a member of the feldspar family, though there is some debate about that. We have other means now of ascertaining our location but still, I think we'll slow our speed a bit."

I nodded. When Kishan and Nilima appeared, Mr. Kadam sent Kishan and me to our rooms to sleep. He wanted us to get some rest before we reached the next dragon. I went to my room and quickly fell asleep.

It turned out our reprieve was a brief one. I'd been asleep for only a couple of hours when I sat up in bed with a start. I woke confused as if from a nightmare. Ren was standing at my open door, and he stared at the bed with a stunned expression.

He quickly averted his gaze and said stiffly, "You're needed in the wheelhouse." With that, he turned and left, closing the door softly behind him.

I was just wondering what his problem was when I felt a hand rub my back. I jumped out of the bed as if it was on fire. A bare-chested Kishan leaned up on an elbow. "Are you alright?"

"I'm . . . *fine*," I stammered.

"Why'd you jump up like that?"

"I was . . . confused. Usually, I only sleep next to a tiger."

"Oh."

"Umm . . . you're not . . . that is . . . you *are* . . . wearing something under there . . . right?"

Kishan grinned and threw off the covers. I squeaked and then breathed a sigh of relief. "You could have just answered the question instead of being all dramatic."

"That's not nearly as much fun. But yes, I'm dressed."

"Huh, barely."

All Kishan had on was a pair of shorts. *Ren must have thought . . . it doesn't really matter what Ren thinks now, does it?*

"Well, get dressed. Ren said—"

"I heard what Ren said." Kishan hugged me briefly and kissed my forehead. "I'll wait for you outside."

In no time at all, we were headed to the wheelhouse. I thought about what had happened that morning. Even though it was technically only a nap, and I'd slept near or next to either Ren or Kishan as tigers many times before, I felt . . . uncomfortable sleeping with Kishan as a man. Ren had never pushed me in that area, and was, in fact, adamant about us *not* being physical.

I'd assumed Kishan wouldn't either, but despite the similarities between them, they were very different men, and I had to remember that. I'd need to speak with him about it soon. *Would I feel the same way if it had been Ren and not Kishan?* I shoved that thought aside and refused to consider the answer.

The *Deschen* was anchored in a dense cloud cover. Mr. Kadam pulled us aside as we entered the wheelhouse.

"The island came up out of nowhere," he said. "I guess the depth

perceptor isn't working. The only reason I was able to stop the ship in time is because Ren had been on the lookout."

Kishan and I stared out the window into the cold nothingness.

"How are we supposed to know what to do?" I mumbled out loud. Nobody answered me—not that I'd expect anyone would have an answer.

Mr. Kadam stood next to us. "According to my notes, we *are* in the right place."

Ren peered into the sky. "Then where's our scaly friend?"

He and Kishan began debating the idea of taking a small boat to get closer to the island when I got an idea. I put my hand on Mr. Kadam's arm.

"What is it, Miss Kelsey?"

"Let's use the winds."

"The winds?"

"I mean the Scarf. Fūjin's bag."

He stroked his short beard. "Yes. That just might work. Let's give it a try." He opened a cupboard and took out the Scarf. It shifted to orange and green in his hand, but when he passed it to me the Scarf turned a solid cobalt blue. I blushed, hid the Scarf behind my back, and asked all of them to climb to the top of the wheelhouse to try an experiment.

After the others climbed the ladder, I chastised the Scarf, "Can't you turn red or black or something? Just ignore my thoughts, okay? I'm trying to focus, but it's hard." The Scarf shifted colors but stubbornly remained cobalt blue in the center. I sighed. "That'll have to be good enough." With a final warning to the silky object, I headed up the ladder.

When everyone was assembled on top, I said, "Fūjin's bag, please." The Scarf twisted in my hands and doubled over on itself, creating long finely stitched seams down its sides. "Now everyone grab on."

We all took a section of the wide opening, and I shouted, "Divine Scarf, gather the winds!"

I was immediately hit in the face with a strong gust of wind that blew my hair back and whipped it so fiercely that it stung my neck. The bag quickly filled and expanded. The winds bucked inside as the bag grew like a hot air balloon. It tore at my arms. I twisted the edge around my wrists to keep hold. Even Ren and Kishan were straining.

Finally we held a very full bag and could feel not the slightest wisp of a breeze against our faces.

"Get ready," I shouted. "Aim it toward the island."

I let Kishan and Ren take the lead in aiming because they could see the island and the rest of us couldn't.

Kishan hollered over the shrieking bag, "One! Two! *Three!*"

We opened the bag and held on for dear life. It bounced and howled as the wind screamed through the opening like a cyclone. The noise level was incredible. It was worse than skydiving, worse than riding dragonback. It was concentrated, pummeling every nerve ending, and pounding in my eardrums. Ren and Kishan were squinting. If the sound was bad for my ears, I imagined it would be much worse for the tigers. As the fog blew away from us, we turned as a unit to drive the mists and vapors as far away from the island as possible.

By the time the bag had completely exhausted itself, the fog had been driven far enough away that it was just a vague haze on the horizon. I combed my fingers through my hair and transformed the Scarf back to its normal appearance. Kishan stared over my head. He put his hands on my shoulders and twisted me around to look at the island. It was really more of a large jutting rock than an island. It rose straight up out of the water and there were no beaches. Apparently, the only way to access the top would be by rock climbing.

I bit my lip, imagining climbing that sheer face. Then I heard the noise—a deep rhythmic whoosh. In . . . out. In . . . out. The sun was

just over the island, and it was too bright for me to see the peak. In . . .
out. In . . . out. I shaded my eyes and blinked several times. "Is . . . is
that a—"

Kishan answered, "Yeah. It's a tail."

Our blue dragon was wrapped around a castle ruin on top of the
island, snoring. Puffs of fog streamed out of its nostrils as it slept. We all
stood there in silence, staring at the snuffling blue dragon.

"What are we supposed to do?" I asked.

Kishan shrugged. "I don't know. Should we wake it?"

"I guess we have to. Otherwise, who knows how long it'll sleep."

I shouted up at the creature, "Great dragon! Please awake!"

Nothing happened. Ren shouted, "Wake, dragon!"

Kishan cupped his hands and hollered, bellowing in a deep voice.
He switched to a tiger and roared so loudly, I pressed my hands to
my ears. We tried shouting together. We tried both Ren and Kishan
roaring. Finally, Mr. Kadam went below and rang the ship's foghorn.
The blast of noise was loud enough that rocks tumbled from the top of
the mountain.

A great, rumbling bass voice echoed the foghorn as it reverberated
in our heads.

What . . . do you want? it said grumpily. *Can't you see you're disturbing
my res-s-st?*

The mountain vibrated, causing the water at the bottom to ripple.

Ren shouted, "Your brother, Lóngjūn, has sent us. He said we must
seek your aid in retrieving Durga's Necklace."

I don't care what you seek. I'm tired. Go away, and bother me no more.

Kishan stepped forward. "We cannot turn back. We need your help,
dragon."

*Yes. You do. But I don't need you. Leave me now, or suffer the wrath of
Qīnglóng.*

I answered, "Then we must risk your wrath, Qīnglóng, for we can't leave. But perhaps, there is something we can do for you, something to make helping us worth your time."

And what could you do for me, little girl?

The mountain rumbled as the blue dragon unwound its upper body from the tower and dropped down closer to us. Though similar in size to its brother, this blue dragon looked different. Its head was longer, narrowing more at the nose. Instead of a black beard, its cheeks and brow were covered with feathers that swept away from its face and shimmered like fish scales in brilliant blues and purples.

Similar feathers flowed down the spine of its back and fanned out at its tail and limbs like the hair around a Clydesdale horse's hoof. Sharp golden talons gripped the air, opening and closing while it swayed back and forth above us like the tail of a kite caught in a tree. Its scaly skin was brilliant blue, and as it hissed in vexation, the feathers along its back and the top of its head stood up like a crested cockatoo's.

Yellow eyes peered at me and a purple tongue pressed against long white teeth as it spoke again in my mind.

Well? Are you just going to stand there like a fish with its mouth opening and closing, or are you going to answer me? It suddenly jerked closer and bit the air near us. Its jaws snapped together like a bear trap, and I heard its laughter. *That's as I thought. You're too weak to do anything for me.*

Ren and Kishan immediately responded by leaping in front of me and changing to tigers. They both roared and swiped claws angrily near the dragon's nose.

It wasn't enough to frighten the dragon, but it was enough to catch its interest. It leaned closer and puffed foggy air over us. Cold dew settled over my skin, and I shivered. Ren and Kishan changed back to men but continued to stand in front of me. I stepped between them.

"Give us a task to prove ourselves," I suggested bravely.

The dragon clicked its tongue and twisted its head. *What could you possibly accomplish, young woman?*

"You'd be surprised."

The dragon grunted and yawned. *Very well. Your challenge will be to make the journey up to my mountain temple. If you can do that, I will help you. If you can't . . . well . . . let's just say you won't be worrying too much about the Necklace anymore.*

It rose in the air and began to coil around the temple again.

"Wait!" I shouted. "How do we get up there?"

There is an underwater tunnel with steps leading up, but you must get past my guardian first, and it's not as . . . accommodating as I am.

Desperate, I questioned, "Who guards you?"

Yāo guài yóu yú.

I whispered to Ren, "What does that mean?"

"Uh . . . it's something like a devil squid."

Qīnglóng snorted. *Bah! It's called the kraken. Now, be off with you.*

The dragon's soft laugh soon turned into a snore. I watched for a moment as fog drifted lightly from his nostrils and dissipated into the blue sky.

Kishan and Ren began heading toward the ladder.

I leaned over the side and asked, "Where are you two going?"

Kishan looked up. "To suit up. Looks like we're diving."

"Oh . . . no . . . you . . . don't! Didn't you hear what it just said?"

"Yes."

"I don't think you did. The dragon said there's a kraken down there."

Kishan shrugged his shoulders. "And?"

"And . . . the kraken is huge! There's no way we can fight it!"

"Kelsey, calm down. Just come down here, and we'll talk about it. There's no need to get hysterical."

"Hysterical? This isn't even close to being hysterical. Have you ever seen a kraken in the movies? No, you haven't, but I have. They destroy whole ships! A couple of tigers would be like kibble! I insist we plan with Mr. Kadam before you two jump into the water."

Ren was standing on the deck, and Kishan landed next to him with a quiet thump. They both looked up and gestured for me to come down.

"Promise me you know what you're doing."

Kishan said, "What we're doing is getting the Necklace, Kells. Now come down so we can talk to Kadam."

"I don't know if I can be of assistance, Miss Kelsey," Mr. Kadam said, rubbing his temple dubiously.

"What! What do you mean you don't know? You know *everything*!"

"All I know about the kraken is what I've seen in movies and the little bits and pieces I've already told you. Nothing can kill it. It's immortal. It's originally from a Norse myth, described as a giant tentacled beast that attacks ships. It's likely based on the giant squid. They were considered fantasy until recent years when a couple of them washed onto beaches."

"That's it? There's nothing else? How do we fight it?"

Mr. Kadam sighed. "I only know a few middling facts. In the myth, when the kraken opens its mouth, water boils. When it raises its head above water, the stink of it is more terrible than any living creature can endure. Its eyes have great illuminating power; when they shine it's like looking into the sun. The only things I've ever heard it's afraid of are kilbits."

"What are kilbits?"

"Mythological creatures resembling giant worms that latch onto the gills of large fishes, similar to marine leeches, though marine leeches are small enough that they're unlikely to frighten a kraken."

"That's it? You want us to fight a kraken with worms?"

"Sorry, Miss Kelsey. There is a poem about a sea creature called Leviathan that some also call the kraken . . ."

Mr. Kadam picked up a book, turned a page, and began to read:

From THE MARRIAGE OF HEAVEN AND HELL
by William Blake

But now, from between the black & white spiders,
a cloud and fire burst and rolled thro' the deep black'ning all beneath,
so that the nether deep grew black as a sea, & rolled with a terrible noise;
beneath us was nothing now to be seen but a black tempest,
till looking east between the clouds & the waves,
we saw a cataract of blood mixed with fire,
and not many stones' throw from us appear'd and sunk again
the scaly fold of a monstrous serpent;
at last, to the east, distant about three degrees
appear'd a fiery crest above the waves;
slowly it reared like a ridge of golden rocks,
till we discover'd two globes of crimson fire,
from which the sea fled away in clouds of smoke;
and now we saw, it was the head of Leviathan;
his forehead was divided into streaks of green & purple
like those on a tyger's forehead:
soon we saw his mouth & red gills
hang just above the raging foam
tinging the black deep with beams of blood,
advancing toward us
with all the fury of a spiritual existence.

I sat back in my chair and reached for Kishan's hand. "Well, that's just great. Monstrously vague. Terrifically amorphous."

When Mr. Kadam began describing theories and comparisons between the creature known as Leviathan and the monster called the kraken, I noticed Ren running his fingers over another book that he had set discreetly on the floor.

I turned to him and asked, "What is it, Ren? If you've found something else, you might as well share it."

"It's nothing. Just a poem that I'd found."

Despite my love of his reading voice, the passage gave me chills.

THE KRAKEN
By Alfred, Lord Tennyson

Below the thunders of the upper deep;
Far, far beneath in the abysmal sea,
His ancient, dreamless, uninvaded sleep
The Kraken sleepeth: faintest sunlights flee
About his shadowy sides; above him swell
Huge sponges of millennial growth and height;
And far away into the sickly light,
From many a wondrous grot and secret cell
Unnumbered and enormous polypi
Winnow with giant arms the slumbering green.
There hath he lain for ages and will lie
Battening open huge sea worms in his sleep,
Until the latter fire shall heat the deep;
Then once by man and angels to be seen,
In roaring he shall rise and on the surface die.

Mr. Kadam pressed his fingers together and tapped his mouth in deep thought. "That final part references the end of the world. Supposedly the kraken, or the Leviathan, will rise from the deep in the last days. Then it will finally be destroyed, and the world will be forever at rest. There are biblical references to the Leviathan being the mouth of hell or even Satan himself."

"Alright. Stop right there. That's enough for me. It's bad enough thinking of fighting demons without dragging the devil into it. I'd rather be surprised. The more I learn, the scarier it gets, so let's just get this over with."

I took the Golden Fruit, my weapons, and the Divine Scarf and rushed down the stairs with everyone chasing after me.

"Kelsey! Wait up!"

Kishan quickly caught up, and Ren was right on his tail. Mr. Kadam puffed down the stairs behind us, but we soon outpaced him. I slammed into the wet garage like a hurricane and picked up my wet suit. Ren and Kishan were resigned to my actions at this point, and picked up their wet suits without protest and headed to the changing rooms. When I emerged, they were ready. Kishan had tied his *chakram* at his waist and the *kamandal* hung from a thong around his neck.

Ren left the *gada* but took the trident. I decided to leave my bow and arrows behind because they wouldn't work underwater anyway and felt pretty naked with no weapon except my lightning power. Kishan pushed the button that opened the ship's garage door. The fog was appearing again. Apparently, our resident dragon's snoring was creating the miasma that seemed to seep into my bones. The normally blue-green warm water seemed gray and cold. Bubbles hissed and popped on the surface, and I allowed my mind to create the terrifying monster below.

I imagined the kraken waiting just beneath the water, gaping, toothy mouth open, patiently waiting for me to step off the boat and into his terrible maw. I shuddered. Just then, Mr. Kadam hurried in to hand Fanindra to me. I slid her up my arm and felt better knowing she would be with me. Ren approached and strapped the diving knife to my leg while Kishan handed me my mask and snorkel.

"Do you think she can breathe underwater?" I asked Mr. Kadam.

"She was twisted up, ready to go when I went to get her. I'm sure she'll be fine."

Ren and Kishan didn't want to be hindered by the tanks just yet. This was to be an exploratory dive. We were just going to scope out the island and look for the underwater opening. If we needed the tanks we'd come back. I sat on the edge looking up at the jutting, rocky island and put on my fins. Ren went first, followed by Kishan. They looked around and gave me the thumbs-up sign. I pushed off with my hands and slipped into the cold, gray water.

After clearing my mask, I started off toward the island following Ren. Kishan stayed behind me. The water was calm if not clear. The island looked like a giant mountainous column just sitting in the middle of the ocean. There was no sandbar, no gentle slope of land. It just went on below the water as far as I could see. It wasn't very big either, maybe the size of a football field. It took only an hour or so to swim all the way around the outside.

We studied the surface above as much as below, and it wasn't until we were ready to return to the ship that we found the underwater entrance. After Ren did a short exploration, he confirmed that we would need diving gear. The only good news was there was no sign of the creature.

I'd exited the ship in a rush of reckless bravado, but now that I'd been in the water for a while, I felt my bluster diminish, washed away by the lapping ocean tide. I accepted the fact that I was afraid. Deathly

afraid. I nervously stammered in an attempt at humor. "He's probably just waiting for all three of us. He'd rather get the combo special. A chicken, a cheese, *and* a beef enchilada. I'm the chicken, by the way."

Kishan laughed. "I'm definitely the beef, which means Ren must be the cheese."

Ren grinned malevolently at Kishan and punched his arm.

Kishan smiled good-naturedly. "That reminds me. I'm hungry. Let's head back."

After we ate lunch, enchiladas being the main dish, we strapped on our tanks and headed straight for the cave. This time I went slowly, cautiously, and let Ren and Kishan call the shots. I listened to the hiss of my bubbles as I descended. When we neared the cave, I felt a twitching on my arm. Fanindra became animated and unwound herself, moving away from my limb. Her golden body sparkled, gleaming in the water. Her mouth opened and closed several times, and she twisted, as if in pain.

Her hood collapsed against her body while her head elongated. Her tail stretched and flattened into a thin paddle and her body became thinner, laterally compressing, as if someone was squishing her between their hands. Her jeweled eyes shrunk to small beady buttons but kept their emerald brilliance, and her nostrils moved closer together.

The tip of her forked tongue shot out, and Fanindra swam around my body. Her paddle-shaped tail swung back and forth, propelling her forward quickly. As I paused, she floated lazily nearby. Her winding movements reminded me of the dragons. She'd become something new. She was a sea snake.

We began swimming toward the cave again. Ren kicked his fins and entered first, disappearing into the blackness beyond the opening, and was followed by Kishan. Fanindra and I took up the rear. Sunlight streamed into the opening, casting turquoise rays across the pebbled floor. My hand scraped against the bumpy rock wall, which was covered with green algae. Tiny fish swam in and out of dark holes. The cave floor was covered with basaltic rock, the only color coming from phosphorescent plants that grew between them in patchy clumps.

Bubbles hissed from Kishan's regulator, and his fin hit the bottom, kicking up sand that momentarily obscured my vision. I swam carefully, trying not to disturb the area. We needed to see as far as possible. As we passed a rocky grotto, a strand of seaweed touched my hand. I jerked back but then, seeing no danger, tried to force myself to relax. The cave became darker. I worried that if it was too dark we wouldn't be able to see where we were going. We turned a corner around a bumpy outcropping, and the light was cut off completely.

Fanindra's body began to glow brighter, and she lit up the area around us like a powerful beacon. Pale stalactites hung down from the ceiling ready to impale us. I swam a little closer to the cave bottom. We approached another opening. This one was much smaller. Ren stopped and turned to signal us. He asked if we should go on or turn back. Kishan said go on. Ren swam through first while we waited.

He came back and gave us the thumbs-up sign, and we continued through. I kicked quickly to catch up. The opening was a tight squeeze for me, so it must've been claustrophobic for the two of them. We came to a wider area and floated, scanning the water around us. It was as black as the inside of a covered well. Fanindra swam out of the hole and lit the area. More stalactites hung from the ceiling. The gritty floor angled down and disappeared in the murky water below. Fanindra shot ahead of us, and we followed.

We'd used one quarter of our air. When we approached the halfway mark we'd have to turn around. The cave was wide enough to swim side by side now. In fact, we couldn't make out the sides of the cave at all

anymore. Ren and Kishan dropped back to flank me on each side. I had the creepy feeling that we were being watched. I scanned the water below, expecting a giant shark to attack, jaws open, but then I also had goose bumps across the back of my neck and wondered if an attack might come from above.

I looked up, but the water was so dark even Fanindra could light up only the area directly around us. I realized that we were very visible to any creature that happened to be looking when suddenly the entire cave lit up. We stopped swimming and hovered. The bright light was coming from the overhead stalactites. I could now see the sides of the grotto and the floor that dropped down into a deep chasm.

I could also see we were about halfway across to our destination. On the far wall, carved rocky steps led up through the ceiling. One light turned off, and another turned on. There seemed to be two lights about ten feet apart, and they were moving. One would hide behind a stalactite while the other one shone down on us. Then the lights both shut off and turned on again. I felt the water move me, shoving me against Kishan. The cavern shook, and the lights blinked again.

They . . . blinked? I panicked. *Those aren't lights. Those are eyes!*

A stalactite started moving toward us.

No! It's not a stalactite. It is a tentacle!

I grabbed Kishan's arm and pointed up. He quickly unhooked his *chakram.* I pounded Ren's back, but he'd already seen it. The purplish-brown tentacle that shot toward us was thicker than a tree trunk.

Hundreds of pale white, subspherical suction cups trembled, ready to grab anything the tentacle contacted. The arm shot between Kishan and me, and I got an up-close-and-personal view of the cups. The round discs were ringed with sharp, jagged rows of chitin and ranged in size from a teacup to dinner plate. On its way back, the tentacle touched Kishan, probing his shoulder as if testing his freshness.

The eyes blinked again, and I felt another rush of water as the giant creature moved closer. It shot out two more tentacles, and this time one smacked against Ren. The meaty arm slapped his chest and pushed him several feet back. The suction cups caught onto his wet suit and yanked him forward at an incredible speed before Ren could push it off, ripping the front of his wet suit in the process. He turned to check on me, and I saw three large circular wounds on his chest ooze blood into the water.

Ren started healing quickly, and Kishan swam over to check Ren's gear. His tank and straps were all still secure; he'd been lucky. Another tentacle snuck out while we were distracted and wrapped around my leg. I barely stopped myself from screaming. Kishan swam over quickly, sliced cleanly through the tentacle with the *chakram*, and gently removed it from my leg. The detached arm quivered and pulsed as if still alive. It oozed black blood as it spun in a circle, falling to the rocky cave bottom below. My leg was bleeding, but I couldn't tell how badly. I mentally asked the Divine Scarf to make a bandage to wrap around it. I felt it wrap tightly and hoped it was enough to stop the bleeding.

Another arm shot toward me, and I fired on it with lightning power. A black hole appeared in the tentacle, and we all heard the scream. It vibrated in the water all around us. The giant eyes moved quickly toward us, flashing revenge.

In a flurry of brownish-purple waving tentacles, the creature approached. Arms clung to the long stalactites as it moved like a monkey descending a tree limb. It paused when it reached the end and dangled in the black water above us. We finally got a good look at what we'd been fighting.

The kraken hung from one tentacle; its soft bulbous mantle was pressed between stalactites, but it slowly slipped through like a blob of Jell-O, reforming itself to fit between the small spaces. Its skin pulled, and its eyes seemed to stretch. It oozed toward us—a dark, pulsing, fleshy monster. *It looked hungry.*

It got stuck briefly, and we heard a scream of frustration. Goose bumps rippled across my skin, and I began kicking backward. The kraken saw me move and suddenly thrust toward us violently, using its tentacles to propel itself closer. It ripped its flesh in several places on the rough stone but didn't seem to care. It was determined to reach us. Its body shifted, and I stared, fascinated as its beaky mouth snapped violently several times, ready to carve us up and scoop our bloody chunks into its mouth.

Then it was free of the stalactites and its massive head ballooned into its normal shape. It blinked again and hung free in the water for a moment. *Probably calculating which of us would taste the best.* It was enormous. The elongated oval mantle was as big as a bus, and its tentacles were easily twice as long. It centered its attention on me, and my heart stopped beating.

The creature shifted, angling its head down as if lying back, and began shooting arms out toward me. Then it suddenly stopped. Ren has raised his trident and was trying to get the monster's attention. The colossal black orbs turned to him. Its eyes had the reflective sheen that only animals that live in the dark possess. As it turned, I noticed that the bright light seemed to come not from its eyes but from the paddled tips of its longest tentacles.

As a tentacle moved past its head, I saw its posterior surface change color. Its purplish-brown skin briefly turned pale with black spots. I saw the funnel above its eyes shoot out a stream of bubbles as it moved again, thrusting out powerful tentacles. The water surged around us.

Ren twisted the staff of his trident and shot three spear darts in quick succession toward the beast. One glanced off a moving limb, one speared a tentacle to the stalactite, and one grazed the mantle. Black blood clouded the area where the creature hung. With a quick move, it yanked its pinned tentacle away from the stalactite. Others shot out in every direction. I blasted one that wrapped around Kishan's throat, but it hung on tenaciously. He began sawing at it and was successful in getting it off, but it tore away his breathing tube. Kishan reached for his backup and gave me the thumbs-up sign.

Ren and I pummeled the monster with lightning power and darts. The mantle expanded, and in a flash of light and a rush of water, the creature was gone. I swam in circles trying to see where it went, but with the lights off, it could have been anywhere. I kicked my legs and moved closer to Ren, figuring it might help if we fought back to back. Kishan had just started moving closer to us when the lights came back on. The kraken was right behind Kishan.

Two fleshy limbs wrapped around his body and shook him in the water. One of his fins came off and dropped slowly into the chasm below us. Ren swam powerfully forward and thrust the trident into the largest tentacle. The creature squealed but held on. Kishan slashed with the *chakram* and, at the same time, I raised my hand to blast through it. That's when I felt a tug. The beast had wrapped a limb around my waist and yanked me toward it at a frightening speed. Attacking Kishan had been a diversion. The creature pulled me aside and shut off the lights.

Fanindra shot away from me like an arrow and disappeared. Suddenly, I was far apart from Ren and Kishan, who probably hadn't even noticed I'd been taken. Suction cups gripped me hard, digging bony little pinchers into my skin, like acupuncture needles. I blasted fire-power into the limb, but the only result was that the pressure increased. It had me around the ribs, and when it squeezed, I thought my lungs would collapse. The turbulence of the water increased the closer I was to the creature. Kishan and Ren turned on flashlights. I could see them, but they couldn't see me. They had finally detached themselves and were searching for me, but I knew they'd never get to me in time. The monster curled its arm, and my perspective changed. I was now facing the mouth of hell.

A part of my brain shut off, and I was able to analyze the creature from what seemed a safe distance. I could coldly calculate the manner in which I would meet my end. The mouth snapped open and closed. It opened and closed similar to a fish. The similarity stopped there. The orifice that I was rapidly nearing reminded me of the Sarlacc pit in *Star Wars*, a round black hole filled with several rows of sharp teeth. Three long green tubules shot out from the gaping mouth and began slathering my face and wet suit with an oily substance that I could only assume would help me to slide down its gullet easier.

I used my power to blast the kraken's mouth. The beast shook angrily in response and clacked its razor beak several times. The long green tubules wrapped around my throat, waist, and arms, pinning them to my sides and drawing me closer. I was trapped. I couldn't use my lightning power anymore. I was going to be eaten by the kraken. The tentacles squeezed me roughly a final time, shook me, and let me go, trusting that I was sufficiently incapacitated by the green tongues.

I writhed back and forth, desperately trying to free my hand, but I was beaten. I couldn't move. I tried to turn my head to see if Ren or Kishan were near, but I couldn't twist enough. My mask was torn off as the creature shifted me. It was apparently going to eat me feet-first. I squinted in the murky water, trying to see without my mask. I thought I saw a golden blur near me, but I wasn't sure it if was the trident or Fanindra.

Something brushed my arm, a long sinuous shape. *Probably another tentacle to give me a final tenderizing.* My feet were in its open mouth. I kicked a leg, but my calf hit a serrated tooth. My leg burned. I had the Scarf wrap a bandage around this new wound, which was probably moot as the kraken was going to eat me any second. I waited for my leg bones to crunch, but the creature didn't bite down. *Maybe it was going to swallow me whole?* An idea surfaced, and I asked the Scarf to tie both ends of its beak open. The threads raced up, wrapped around the creature's body above and below, and then wrapped several times around the top and bottom of the monster's beak to hold it open.

The kraken thrashed and moved, shaking violently like a shark trying to rip the flesh from a whale. When its razor beak started ripping through the threads, I asked the Scarf to reinforce it, but I knew it was just a matter of time. The kraken would eventually get angry enough to bite through the thread all the way and cleave me in half.

As my body was whipped back and forth in the water, I briefly wondered what my parents would have thought about the way I was going to die. I thought about the afterlife and wondered if people shared death stories. If so, I'd have the coolest story ever. *You died in your sleep? Drunk driver? Cancer, huh? World War II? Well . . . yeah, those deaths are great and all, but wait till I tell you what happened to me. Yeah . . . that's right . . . I said a kraken.*

I should have panicked. I should have drowned. But I just drifted in the wake of the surging limbs and calmly waited for the creature to swallow me. *What was taking so long? Sheesh. Get on with it already.*

The kraken's body gave off a strange sort of glowing light as if it had tiny winking bulbs under its skin. I could see its black outline in the water, barely.

I felt like someone had thrown me into a giant washing machine. I could feel the smooth flesh of tentacles, the rubbery discs of suction cups, and the sharp sting of teeth as they whirled past me in the wash. I heard the screeches and felt the surging of the agitated water and the pulpy slick probing of the tongues as they continued to slather me in oil. I hung like a fish caught on a line, waiting to be reeled in—but something was distracting the fisherman. I cracked open my eyes and saw black whirling tendrils of blood.

Wriggling shapes shot past me, one golden. *Fanindra*. She lit the area, although I decided I'd rather be in darkness. The monster loomed over me like a fleshy purple cloud in the water, ready to destroy me with the violence of a hurricane. I watched her as she swam over to a tentacle and bit. The creature shivered.

More long shapes swam toward me—yellow-and-black striped, black-and-white striped, gray, green, long, thin, thick—sea snakes. The cave was full of them. They attacked the beast, swarming over it like needles in a pincushion. In fact, I watched as several snakes followed Fanindra's example. Some of them bit savagely into the purple flesh and wriggled their way inside. They moved under the squid's skin like worms, biting and tearing as they went.

The creature screamed and filled its mantle. Black ink jetted out from the funnel and coated me in warm waves. It stung my eyes. I quickly shut them and almost threw up as the funnel pushed water again. Suddenly, the kraken moved dozens of body lengths away from where it had been, dragging me violently along with it.

In the confusion, the kraken loosened its grip on me. I had shifted out of its mouth, but it still held me paralyzed in the grip of its tongues. It was just in time too, because the monster's movements snapped the threads clean through. *It would have sheared me in half.* As I pondered my lucky state, I watched the snakes that were still attached to its skin. I saw Fanindra bite the skin next to the giant, black eye, and the beast shook itself. Tentacles flailed back and forth in the water, desperately trying to dislodge the snakes.

Something touched me, and I flinched but then felt a hand squeeze my arm. Ren grabbed a green tongue and removed it from around my neck. The powerful muscle began to wind itself around his arm, but he tugged hard and got it off. Kishan swam up to us and sawed through the green tubes. Slick, oily liquid gushed over us as he severed the tongues from the creature's body. He freed my legs while Ren freed my arms. Kishan wrapped an arm around me in the distressed swimmer grip and started swimming away, tugging me along with him.

Bent on violence, Ren swam up to the beast. He thrust the trident deeply into the creature's maw over and over again. Black blood rushed out in a cloud, and soon I couldn't see him anymore. Kishan pulled me closer to the rock steps. After we reached them, we turned and watched as the creature jetted murky ink again. The last we saw of it was the blinking lights on the tentacle pads as the kraken descended into the dark chasm below. We waited anxiously another few moments until we first saw the gleam of the trident and then Ren making his way toward us from the black cloudy water.

Sea snakes shot out of the chasm by the hundreds and hovered in a wriggling cloud nearby, Fanindra at the head. A small light high above us indicated a way out. We swam up. Kishan led with me gripping his hand. He broke the surface in a white tiled pool and reached down to pull me up. Ren shot out next to me and removed his breathing apparatus. We all sucked in several deep breaths. Kishan tugged me to the side of the pool. He carefully removed the tank and my flippers and began checking me over.

"Are you okay?"

The question made me laugh hysterically until finally I could shake my head. "No."

"Where are you hurt?"

"Everywhere. My leg especially. But I'll survive."

He took his diving knife and cut off the leg of my wet suit to inspect the damage. I'd used the Scarf to create a bandage. Wes had taught us to leave the bandage on and keep putting more bandages on until the

blood stopped. It wasn't bleeding through, so I had hopes that it wasn't that severe of an injury. I had the Scarf wrap another layer, and Kishan squeezed my arm.

"How bad is it?"

"It could be worse. I think it will be okay."

He nodded and stood, looking around.

We were in an underground room, completely enclosed except for a set of stairs. I grunted in pain, and then padded on bare feet to the stairs, limping, and looked up. The stairs were too small for a dragon. *It must be able to change into a man like Lóngjūn.* Motivated to hurry while the kraken was licking its wounds, I started up slowly, favoring my strong leg and the brothers followed.

At first, I leaned heavily on Kishan and bit my lip trying to control the pain. After one flight, he growled and picked me up, carrying me up the rest. We climbed. Ten floors. Twenty steps per floor, but Kishan wasn't even breathing hard. When we finally reached the end of the stairs, we stepped out onto the stony roof on top of the ruined castle. Kishan carefully set me down on a rocky bench, and he and Ren approached the head of the sleeping blue dragon.

"Wake up!" Ren roared.

The dragon shifted and snored. A cloud of fog descended on the brothers.

Kishan shouted, "Get up. Now!"

The dragon huffed and cracked a lazy eye. *What do you want?*

Ren worked his jaw angrily. "You will wake and speak with us, or I will ram this trident into your fleshy throat!"

That got the dragon's attention. The fog turned black, and the dragon whipped its head around and bit the air. It narrowed its eyes.

You may not speak to me in that manner.

Ren threatened. "I'll speak to you in any manner I wish. You almost killed her."

Killed who? Oh. The little girl? I never touched her.

"Your filthy beast did. If she had died, I would have come up here and killed you."

She obviously didn't die, so you should be happy. I warned you that the task was hard.

Kishan stepped forward. "Give us what you promised."

The dragon moved a heavy limb and bared its neck. *Take it then.*

A large disk hung from the dragon's neck by a thick leather cord. Kishan stepped forward and, using the *chakram*, freed the disk. The brothers turned and headed back to me.

The blue dragon shifted its bulk noisily. *Don't I get a thank you?* Qīnglóng said. *After all, the sky disk is no trifle.*

Ren picked me up and turned his head slightly toward the dragon. "*Neither* is she."

I looked up into Ren's blue eyes. His livid expression calmed somewhat, and he pressed his forehead against mine for a brief moment. Then he passed me to Kishan, said, "Help her," picked up the disk, and started down the stairs.

remembering

I protested that I could try to walk, but Kishan ignored me and carried me down the stairs. My leg had started bleeding through the bandage, and I asked the Scarf to wrap it several more times until the bleeding stopped.

When we finally got to the pool, Ren was already waiting for us. I didn't relish the thought of getting back into the water with the kraken again, but I gamely slipped on my tank.

Kishan had just offered me his goggles when Ren interrupted. "Her goggles are here. So is your other flipper. Fanindra brought them up."

A golden head popped out of the water. I leaned over to pat her head, and she slid over my arm. Kishan checked the gauges on my tank as Ren slid into the water.

"Her tank's low."

"We'll share," Ren replied.

I watched him drop all his weights, but he still couldn't achieve buoyancy with the sky disk. It was too heavy. When I expressed concern, he turned away and said, "I'll manage."

Ren took the bag I'd made with the Scarf and positioned the strap across his chest while I equalized the pressure in my ears.

"We'll have to be quick," Kishan warned. "We'll just swim across and get out of here as fast as we can. If we run into the kraken again, just turn around and swim back here. We'll figure out a different way to get back to the yacht. Okay?"

"Okay."

He smiled and kissed my nose before lowering his goggles. I took an experimental breath on the regulator and dove through the hole in the pool, following Ren. Fanindra stayed close to me as we descended. The sea snakes swarmed to welcome her back and surrounded us as we swam.

It was dark again without the light of the kraken, but Fanindra seemed to know the way. She gave off just enough light that we could see ourselves cocooned in our sea snake bubble. I kept my eyes peeled for the kraken, but there was no sign of it. Still, it seemed like giant eyes were watching our progress and I expected a quivering tentacle to snatch me away to oblivion.

My nerves stood on end. I felt like I was one of those dumb high school girls in a scary movie that opens doors she shouldn't, putting herself in harm's way, deliberately taunting the monster chasing her. The only difference was, I wasn't making out with a boyfriend in a haunted house or wearing a miniskirt.

We crossed the black cavern without incident and made it back to the small passageway. Ren entered first, surrounded by wriggling snakes. I steeled myself to follow.

By the time we'd made it through the other side, my air tank was empty. I gave Ren a signal, and he nodded, handing his regulator to me. I sucked a deep breath and passed it back. We did this a couple of times until Kishan emerged from the passageway. He touched my arm and nodded, indicating that he would share with me now so Ren could lead on.

Being underwater without my own air was frightening. It was all

I could do to stop myself from swimming wildly up. I knew there was nothing above me but rock, but the intense survival instinct to head for the surface was compelling. The only thing that kept me grounded was Kishan's solid presence at my side.

I kicked and followed Ren. The light was getting brighter. The murky water changed from midnight black to dark indigo and then, thankfully, to the clear turquoise blue of the open ocean. Finally, we turned a corner and I saw the cave opening ahead and the late afternoon sunlight slanting into the water.

Kishan passed me the regulator, and I took a breath. The air hissed and stopped flowing. His tank was empty too. He gave me a signal to wait and smiled in reassurance. He swam after Ren, who returned and pressed his regulator into my hands. I took a breath and handed it to Kishan.

The three of us moved slowly out of the cave toward the surface, sharing one tank of oxygen among us. The sea snakes, released from escort duty, darted quickly away for the open ocean. Many of them twined their bodies with Fanindra's as they passed her. A moment later, they were gone.

Kishan took a small breath. Ren's tank was almost empty. He signaled this, and we looked up. We'd have to make a break for it. Kishan handed me the regulator so I could take the last of the air. I shook my head, but he insisted, and I took a final breath and started swimming for the surface. I let my breath out slowly as the water became brighter and brighter. I needed air. I wasn't going to make it.

Death by drowning was much less exotic than death by kraken. It was almost an embarrassing way to go, as if your death was somehow your own fault. I'd fully expect the other dead people to say, "Drowned? Well, what did you go and do a thing like that for? Couldn't ya find the valve? It says *A-I-R* on the side. Did you forget that apparatus under your eyeballs? It's called your nose. You breathe through it." Oh sure, I'd try to explain what happened, but I'd go through eternity being the butt of dead people's jokes. My mother would think it was hilarious.

Fanindra swam in front of me, leading the way, but it didn't matter. I started to see black spots in my vision. The surface was close, maybe only twenty feet away. I kicked harder and tried to suck another breath from my own tank, but it was no good. My lungs felt like they were being branded by a hot iron. The burning was intense as my body screamed at me to take a breath.

I would have liked to have thought my brain was dominant, that I could face the inevitable drowning serenely, calmly. But when facing death, the body reigns. A raging, wild need to survive took over, and I started clawing at my mask and gear like a berserker. A hand grabbed mine. It was Kishan. He was kicking hard and tugged me along with him.

We broke to the surface, and he held me close as I choked and gasped. Air rushed into my burning lungs, and I became a being wholly focused on respiration. For the next few seconds, nothing existed except the hurried rhythm of inhale and exhale. Ren surfaced a few seconds later and panted.

The weight of the disk must have made it doubly hard for him to reach and stay at the surface. When his head ducked underwater, Kishan swam to help, and I whispered for the Divine Scarf to make a double strap so Kishan could take half the disk's weight.

The ocean was covered with fog again. The cold water had numbed my throbbing leg, but I could tell the injury was bad. It pounded like the thrum of distant cannons, muffled but dangerous. Kishan and Ren swam next to me as I turned in a circle looking for the *Deschen*.

Ren said, "Stay close. We shouldn't be too far from where we anchored. We'll follow Fanindra. Will you be okay?"

I nodded. He blew the water out of his snorkel and led me to the ship.

Finally at the yacht, Kishan threw his fins into the wet garage and scrambled up the ladder. Ren handed him the sky disk and then threw his own fins over. My limbs were shaking. I couldn't put any weight on my injured leg. I threw an arm around Ren's shoulder and slowly hopped up the ladder into the safety of our boat.

Grabbing a net, Kishan scooped Fanindra out of the water. She wriggled and gyrated on the deck. Her wide mouth opened and closed several times as if gasping for air. I sympathized, watching her body expand and shake violently. The skin around her head rippled and tore, creating a hood. Her jeweled eyes grew bigger, and the shape of her face changed. Soon the erratic fish-out-of-water movements ceased, and she was a golden cobra once more.

Nilima wrapped a large towel around me. Carefully, I leaned my head back against the wall and groaned. Ren helped her take off my equipment and set it aside. I gasped in pain when she touched my leg.

"What happened?" she asked.

"Kraken bite," Ren replied. "I'm not sure how bad it is. She's had it well wrapped since it happened."

Nurse Nilima sent Ren for a first aid kit and Kishan to bring me a change of clothes.

While they were gone, she helped me out of my wet suit and wrapped me in a robe. She carefully undid the bandages to check my wounds.

"Your leg is the worst one. You'll need stitches. What happened here?" She indicated the band around my waist.

"The kraken grabbed me with its tentacle."

"Hmm . . . your wet suit probably protected you here. It's mostly bruised, but there are circular cuts too, fairly shallow."

"Suction cups."

She shuddered.

A glob of green goo dripped from my nose onto my arm where I'd been cut, and I screeched in pain. It stung. She washed it off quickly, and the burn lessened. The boys returned. A blob of green slime oozed slowly down Kishan's arm and plopped onto the deck. It didn't burn him like it did me, probably due to his super-speed tiger healing.

Nilima stared at it. She said, "Both of you go shower now. The green stuff seems toxic. Probably some kind of acid. Get it off as quickly as possible. I can't have you near Kelsey or touching her with it. It may not affect you, but it hurts her."

The boys hesitated.

"Don't worry," Nilima assured. "She'll be fine. The bleeding is under control. She's safe."

Nilima picked up the showerhead and cleaned the slime off of me quickly and thoroughly. She gently cleaned my wounds. When I was sufficiently scrubbed, she put antibacterial ointment over the cuts circling my ribs, had the Scarf wrap me in fabric bandages, and then helped me dress.

Next, she turned her attention to my leg. The skin was puckered and swollen, irritated from the salt water. I bit off a cry of pain. My leg throbbed sickeningly. It started bleeding again after Nilima cleaned it. I swallowed thickly when I saw my gaping flesh.

"Don't look at it. I think it will heal fine but, like I said, it will need stitches. I need to get Grandfather for that." She had the Scarf bandage me again. "Will you be alright for a minute?"

I nodded and leaned back on the wooden bench, closing my eyes. I imagined I could feel the venom of the kraken in my veins. My nerves prickled like I had little fire ants under my skin. I was tired. I nodded off then jerked awake at a noise. Fanindra approached me.

"Are you going to bite me? If so, I'm closing my eyes. Make it fast."

I didn't hear anything and cracked open one eye. Fanindra had curled up and rested near my foot.

"I must not be dying then, eh? Thanks for keeping me company. Still, what's a bite of healing between friends? Don't want to waste your golden venom, I see. Fine. Wake me if I die."

Kishan returned a moment later, freshly showered, and sat next to me, taking my hand. Soon Ren, Nilima, and Mr. Kadam joined us. Mr. Kadam unzipped a bag and shook a pill into his palm, offering it to me with a bottle of water.

"What is it?"

"An antibiotic." Mr. Kadam handed the bottle to Kishan. "Make sure she takes one in the morning and one at night for the next ten days."

Kishan nodded.

"Now let's see this wound." Mr. Kadam told the Divine Scarf to remove the bandage and took a look at the cut. I kept my eyes closed this time. "You're right, Nilima. She'll need stitches. I didn't think to bring sutures with us. All we can do at this point is keep it carefully wrapped, clean, keep her on antibiotics, and hope the kraken isn't poisonous. Kishan, if you would carry her to her bed? She needs her rest."

"Wait." Ren stepped forward. "I have an idea."

He explained what he wanted to do and Mr. Kadam looked at me. "Are you willing to try it, Miss Kelsey?"

I nodded, closed my eyes, and squeezed Kishan's hand in a death grip as Ren commanded the Divine Scarf to stitch up my wound.

Everyone watched my leg curiously as the Scarf began to work. I gasped at first, feeling the strange pulling sensation on my skin. Kaleidoscope threads sharpened to a tiny point and slipped through the layers of my skin with barely a pinch, then pulled the edges of my skin together and tightened. In less than a minute, it was done. Tiny stitches ran down the side of my leg, making it look as if I was wearing a gothic pair of back-seam pantyhose slightly askew.

Nilima smeared antibiotic cream over the wound and asked the Scarf to bandage me up again. I gave Ren a smile, which probably looked more like a grimace, before Kishan picked me up, carried me to my room, and tucked me into bed. He brought me some aspirin and a glass of water. Obediently, I took my medicine and fell asleep.

Twelve hours later, I woke achy, bruised, and ravenous. Nobody was around, which was nice for a change. I sat up in bed and asked the Divine Scarf to remove my bandages. A ring of greenish-yellow bruises circled my torso and went down one hip, but the cuts had all nicely scabbed over. *Hmm . . . the bruises should still be purple and the cuts more painful.* It hurt but not like it had yesterday. *My leg actually looks pretty good too, all things considered.* It looked like I'd done a week's worth of healing in one night. It wasn't as fast as the boys healed, but it was still impressive.

I decided the first order of business was a shower. Clean, hair washed and conditioned, bandaged, and dressed, I emerged from the bathroom to find Kishan waiting for me. He carefully pulled me into his arms.

"How are you feeling?" he asked as he massaged my neck.

"Better. I think my wounds heal quickly here, just not as fast as yours do."

Kishan brought me a tray with eggs, strawberries, a cinnamon roll, orange juice, aspirin, and an antibiotic. After handing me a fork he sat down next to me and waited for me to finish. Something was bothering him.

"Are *you* okay, Kishan?"

He looked at me and gave me a half smile. "Yes. I'm just—"

"Just what?" I scooped up a forkful of fluffy eggs and chewed, knowing he would take his time to answer.

"I'm just . . . worried."

"Don't worry about me. I'll recover. In fact, I'm feeling pretty good now." I smiled.

"No. *Worried* is perhaps the wrong word. Sometimes I think . . ." Kishan sighed and ran a hand through his hair. "It's not important now. You need to heal. You don't need to hear about my petty jealousies."

"What petty jealousies?" I set the tray to the side and took his hand. "You can tell me."

He leaned forward and studied my hands. "I think that maybe," he said with a sigh, "that maybe you're having regrets. About *us*, I mean."

"Regrets?"

"I see how you and Ren look at each other sometimes, and it makes me feel like I'm an outsider. I feel like no matter what I do, I won't be able to bridge the chasm between us or fix the rift in your heart and find a way to be with you."

"Oh, I see." I flashed back to when Ren and I fixed the star in the red dragon's lair and bit my lip guiltily.

He continued, "I want you to feel the same way about me that I feel about you. But more than that, I want you to be whole and happy again, like you were in Oregon." He leaned forward and brushed my cheek with his fingers. "I *love* you, Kelsey. I'm just not sure if you feel the same or if it's even possible for us to be together."

I quashed my guilty thoughts, brought his hand up to my mouth, and kissed his palm. "You know what the problem is? We've had very little alone time together on this ship and being in this realm of the Seven Pagodas doesn't really give us much opportunity for romance. Why don't we have a candlelight dinner tonight, just the two of us? You wear a tie, and I'll wear a dress. What do you say?"

"What if we reach the third dragon by then?"

I shrugged. "We'll improvise. We'll play it by ear. Has Mr. Kadam figured out the sky disk thing yet?"

"No. He and Ren are working on it. We're away from the fog of the blue dragon, but we're at anchor until they figure out what to do next."

"Okay. Then let's tell Mr. Kadam we need the night off. It'll give my leg a chance to heal more too."

Kishan nodded. "If you're sure."

"I'm sure. If a girl can't take a sick day after fighting a kraken, when can she?"

He laughed. "Truer words were never spoken."

I was left on my own for the rest of the day, except for Nilima's constant pillow fluffing. After a couple of hours of boredom, I did some research on the sky disk, which was similar in design to the German Nebra Sky Disk dated 1600 BCE that I'd read about in my art history class. The Nebra Sky Disk was a record of the stars and the summer and winter solstices, so farmers would know the right time to plant certain crops.

The blue dragon's sky disk was obviously not used for farming. It had markings of stars and seven suns instead of the Nebra's moon design. A path wound between the stars leading from one of the suns on the bottom to one of the suns at the top.

I flipped open a book to other famous disks and found the Aztec calendar showing the five ages of the world. Each day-sign of the calendar was assigned to a different deity. I thumbed through the pages but didn't really find anything else that might apply to our situation.

Frustrated, I sighed and set the books and paperwork aside. My mind drifted to something I definitely didn't want to think about.

It's time. It's time to really let Ren go and move on with Kishan. It's not like I don't love Kishan. I do. But I still love Ren too. I think a part of me always will. Kishan deserves my full attention. He's probably sensing my inner wavering. I don't want him to feel like that. I want him to know that I'm committed to him.

I had told Ren that once I committed to Kishan I'd stick by him, and I wasn't the kind of person to play games with people's feelings. I *would* stick by him. If I couldn't forget Ren, then at least I could hide my feelings. I'd lock them away in a tiny part of my heart and never let them out. Drown them in the depths of the sea. Weight my heartache and drop it overboard, letting it sink into the dark abyss.

I wanted things to work out with Kishan, but I knew there was a part of me I'd been holding back. I hadn't given him my full heart. I hadn't loved him the way I loved Ren. *He deserves more. He deserves better. It's time for me to let myself love again.*

I got out of bed and tested my leg. It seemed much better, and the cuts and bruises around my torso were virtually gone. After consulting with Nilima, we both agreed it was time for the stitches to come out.

She asked the Scarf to remove my stitches, and the threads gently pulled out of my skin. There was still a scar line running down my leg, but it was completely closed and I could walk on it comfortably now. I asked Nilima to help the Scarf make me a dress, and she whipped up a satin cocktail dress with capped sleeves and a scooped court neckline. It was gathered at the right side of the waist, shirred, and pinned with a black jeweled appliqué. The tight knee-length skirt was embellished by a ruffled length of material that curved over my right hip and draped dramatically to the hem.

My original thought was to make it blue, but I quickly realized that would send Kishan the wrong message. We decided to make it antique bronze instead, and the color turned out to be very flattering on me. It brought out my eyes and made my skin look nice. I had the Scarf make me some flat satin slippers to match, which featured the same appliqué as the dress. Thanking Nilima, I began to brush out my hair, and my thoughts turned to the evening ahead.

What could I do? How could I make Kishan realize he wasn't an outsider?

That I really did want this? Want him? I tried to tune in to the little voice in my head and ask my mom for advice. I expected *something*. She'd always been there before when I needed relationship help. Instead, I got nothing.

Thanks a lot, Mom. What? I'm trying my best here. It's not like you're around to help me with this stuff. Sometimes a girl needs her mother, you know. I paused in mid-thought and sent a mental reproof. *You should be here.*

I stared in the mirror while mechanically brushing my hair and then finally set the brush down. I looked thin. Pale. I had shadows under my eyes. *Not exactly looking my best for a date, though I can blame my appearance on the kraken.* I felt prickly . . . nervous. I had a knot in my stomach. Numbly, I applied my makeup.

Seeking inspiration from my now shoulder-length hair, I curled it and plucked one of the lotus blooms from Durga's lei. I studied the flower and expressed a silent hope that she would guide me, that she'd help me get past my stubbornly strong feelings for Ren and give Kishan the love he needed. She *was* the one encouraging me to take the leap after all.

I swept back one side of my hair with a comb and pinned the white flower over my right ear. Its perfume did give me a sense of comfort. A feeling of peace washed over me, and I felt as if a soft arm had briefly draped across my shoulders, squeezing me in reassurance. Whether Durga or my mother, that feeling gave me a sense of conviction, a belief that everything would be alright. I slipped into my dress and had just put on my slippers when there was a knock on my door.

I was relieved Kishan hadn't wasted any time. I'd been alone with my thoughts for too long. I slapped a determined smile on my face and opened the door. It turned into a genuine one when I saw how happy he was. He openly admired my dress and handed me a bouquet of silk flowers.

"Sorry they aren't real. There aren't any flower shops in the dragon realm it seems."

"That's okay. I don't mind."

"You look beautiful."

"So do you."

He did. Kishan was wearing a tie, though I didn't really expect him to. He wore black slacks and a copper silk shirt with a striped black, copper, and gold tie to match. I stepped forward and smoothed his tie. He captured my hand, kissed it and smiled. His golden eyes twinkled, and he offered me an arm.

"How's your leg?" he asked.

"Good. It's almost healed. Another day and I should be ready to tackle another kraken."

He frowned. "I hope we don't have to."

I nodded, and we made our way to the sundeck. The moon was out, and the sea was calm. It was beautiful. The dark sky was clear, and the stars were vivid. It was the perfect setting for a romantic dinner.

Instead of taking me to the dining area in the stern, Kishan guided me toward the bow of the ship.

"Aren't we going to eat?"

"Yes. I set up a table over here. And don't worry about us being observed from the wheelhouse. Mr. Kadam and Nilima are taking the night off. Everyone is below deck."

"Doesn't someone have to be ready to jump into the wheelhouse just in case of emergency dragons or something?"

"That's going to be my job for the next few hours. If something comes up, we'll be the first to know."

I squeezed his arm. "That sounds nice. Oh, Kishan! It's lovely!"

I let go and moved ahead of him to the beautifully set table. Kishan had used the Scarf to create a shimmering silver tablecloth and napkins.

A set of china and gleaming heavy silverware with mermaids etched into the handles graced the table. Delicate goblets with tiny starfish attached to the stems were filled with golden, sparkling juice. He'd set up conch shells in clusters on the deck. Their candles flickered in the miniscule breeze, dazzling despite the simplicity. Lantern lights overhead added to the effect, and soft music played somewhere in the background.

I stretched out a finger to touch a conch shell. "This must have taken you a long time."

He shrugged. "Not too long. I wanted it to look special."

"It does."

Kishan pulled out my chair. He sat across from me and grinned at my expression. "You like it."

"To say 'I like it' would be something of an understatement."

He laughed. "Good. Are you ready to eat, then?"

"Yes. How does this work exactly? I imagine you're using the Fruit."

He nodded. "I came up with a menu. Do you trust me?"

"Of course."

He closed his eyes and a scrumptious dinner appeared before us. We dug in and talked about what we might find with the third dragon. At first we were being serious; then we started wildly guessing crazy dragon scenarios such as, "What if he is toothless? What if he is the size of a house cat? What if he is a scaredy dragon who tells jokes like the Eddie Murphy dragon in *Mulan*?"

Kishan had never seen that movie, so we made plans to watch it later. I sang him the "Puff, the Magic Dragon" song, at least as much as I could remember, and he told me a crazy Chinese story about a dragon that lost his tail.

For dessert, Kishan created an eight-layer chocolate raspberry cake with hot fudge sauce and fresh raspberries with chocolate whipped cream.

I closed my eyes and groaned. "You really know me well. Chocolate is my weakness."

He leaned forward. "I sincerely hope so."

I laughed. "The problem is . . . I'm too full now to eat it."

"We have time. It can wait." He stood and held out his hand. "Would you dance with me, Kelsey?"

"I'd love to." I took his hand, and he pulled me close.

The music was soft, and the night was cool. I cuddled against him, enjoying his warmth.

"You know, this is the first time I've been able to dance with you without worrying that someone's going to come along and rip you away from me."

"Hmm . . . that's true."

He took my hand and twirled me in an awkward spin. I giggled as our arms tangled.

"Sorry. I know I'm not the best dancer. It's just that—"

I lifted my head. "What is it?"

"You just seem to like the fancy kind of dancing. Like the way you danced with Ren. I'll probably never learn to do that."

"Kishan, you don't need to compare yourself to him. I like you for who you are, not because I want a carbon copy."

"What's a carbon copy?"

"It's a . . . it doesn't matter. The point is just be yourself. I don't expect you to change. If you don't like dancing, that's fine."

"Oh, I *like* dancing; I'm just not very good."

"That's okay. I'm not that great at it either."

"Really?"

"Really." I put my head back on his shoulder and closed my eyes, letting him lead me, guiding my footsteps. I trusted him. I knew he wouldn't hurt me, and I wanted to offer him the same sense of peace he'd given so freely to me. I wanted desperately to not just love him but to be *in love* with him. Little thoughts of being in another man's arms crept into my mind. I viciously ripped them up and tamped them down. I wanted my only thoughts to be about Kishan. About *this* good man who loved me unconditionally.

Thankfully, he interrupted my thoughts. "Do you know when I first fell for you?"

"No."

"It was when I watched you tend Ren's wounds after we fought in the jungle. It was before you knew we were fast healers, and you cried."

"I remember."

"It broke my heart that you could cry over animals, over men, as wild and vicious and cursed as we were. You showed such tenderness and concern. I wanted to comfort you. I wanted to make you happy. To stop your tears."

"You do."

He grunted. "Do you remember when I came out of the jungle the first time and surprised you?"

"Yes."

"I'd been watching you. You fascinated me. It was almost like I could tell what you were thinking just based on your expressions."

"I didn't think I was that easy to read."

"You have an open face, a kind one."

"Thank you."

A small breeze blew my hair onto my cheek, and Kishan tucked it behind my ear and lightly caressed my neck. "Did you know that you were the first person I'd talked to in more than a hundred years?"

I blinked. "I didn't know that. You must have been so lonely."

He looked at me with his deep golden eyes, and I found myself absorbed in the copper flecks. He put his other arm around my waist.

"I was. I'd been alone for so long, I felt like I was the last man on Earth. Then when I saw you, it was like a dream. You were an angel who'd come at last to rescue me from my miserable existence. I didn't even care if I was alive or dead as long as it would bring an end to my isolation. Then, when you left, I thought I could go back to the way I was before. I didn't really have any hope that you could someday be mine. It was obvious Ren had claimed you for himself. So I ignored the pull. I ignored my feelings. But it didn't matter. I was drawn to you.

"I returned to the land of the living. I learned to walk on my own two legs again. I learned what it meant to be a man. Then you went away and a secret part of me was happy. My intention was to give you some time and then seek you out. But it didn't work out that way."

I nodded but said nothing. I couldn't help but reflect on that time in Oregon, but I quickly shut the door on those thoughts and snapped back to the present. I smiled at Kishan.

He went on, "When I saw you again, happy in America, I decided I would have to content myself with being your friend and protector. I tried to keep my feelings in check. To do what I must to help you be happy. But when we were alone in Shangri-la, I fell even harder for you. I wanted you, and I didn't care who I hurt or how it made you feel. I was angry when you asked me to back off. I wanted you to want me in the same way, and you didn't. I wanted you to feel the same way about me that you felt about Ren, but you couldn't."

"But, Kishan—"

"Wait . . . let me finish."

I nodded.

"Maybe it's what that idiot bird did to me in Shangri-la, but I've been able to see more clearly since then—not only about my past and about Yesubai, but also about you, about my future. I knew that I wouldn't be alone forever. I saw that in the Grove of Dreams. And after that, I could see that you loved *me* too. But I rushed it. I pushed you. Then *he* came home and despite everything, you still wanted him. Maybe that won't go away. Maybe you'll always feel that connection with him."

I made a sound, and he touched a finger to my lips.

"No. It's okay. I understand it now. I wasn't really ready to be in a relationship then. I didn't have anything to give, anything to offer. Not to a woman of this time. But Shangri-la gave me something more valuable than six more hours a day as a man. It gave me hope. A reason to believe. So I waited. I learned how to be patient. I learned how to live in this century. And now . . . most importantly, I think I've finally learned what it means to love someone."

Kishan lifted a finger and trailed it from my forehead to my chin, tilting my face to look into his eyes. "So I suppose the only question remaining, Kelsey, is . . . are my feelings echoed in your heart? Do you feel even a small part of what I feel for you? Is there a piece of you that you can reserve for me? That I can name mine? That I can lay claim to and keep forever? I promise you that I will cherish it. And I will guard it jealously all of my days."

Kishan's hands squeezed my waist, and he dropped his forehead to touch it to mine. "Does your heart beat for me at all, love?"

I pressed my hands against his face as a tear slipped down my cheek. After only a tiny pause, I assured him, "Of course it does. I won't let you be alone ever again. I love you too, Kishan."

I leaned forward and pressed my lips to his. He shifted to hold me against him and kissed me back. It was gentle and soft and sweet. I draped my arms around his neck and pressed closer. He tugged me up against his chest and wrapped his arms more tightly around me. At first, it just felt nice. It was pleasant and enjoyable. But then, something happened.

I felt a crack, a splinter, a pull. My heart jerked wildly, and a fire burned suddenly within me. It consumed me, and I blazed inside with

a heat I hadn't felt in a long time. I kissed Kishan with a disoriented vehement passion, and he returned my ardor tenfold. The flaming inferno burned on, sizzling, cleansing, purifying. I wanted to bask in the warmth of the heat being created between us. It was consuming and powerful. My heart opened. My connection was back. My frame shook from the intensity of it. I was whole again. Time seemed to stop.

Something huge hit the deck behind me, and several candles extinguished in a sudden warm wind. I heard wood splinter and crack. My body vibrated from the impact, and the shock of it made me topple. But Kishan held me upright easily though our lips parted. I thought, *What is it? A dragon? A meteor?*

I blinked unbelieving as a deck chair flew past with a whoosh and landed in the ocean with a splash, taking the china, goblets, cake, and candlelit shells on the table with it. Kishan looked at me in confusion and then froze as we heard an enraged, intractable voice in the dark somewhere above us threaten, *"Let. Her. Go."*

making up is hard to do

Kishan and I scanned the deck but couldn't see anything.

The voice in the night repeated, "I *said. Let. Her. Go.*" A dark shadow stepped into the light and stood on the decking above us.

I gasped and whispered, "Ren?"

Kishan took a step back and pulled me against him. Ren growled fiercely and stepped off the edge of the upper deck and into the air. He descended from above dressed in white, barefoot, his blue eyes blazing, and landed in a crouch. He stood slowly and stalked toward us like a dark angel full of the fury of God.

Cold, calculated, and merciless, he said, "*Don't* . . . make me *repeat* myself."

His eyes never left Kishan's. His severe expression was frightening. He was like a violent storm gathering speed. I put my hand on Kishan's arm, and Ren's infuriated eyes fixed on my touch. His eyes lifted to meet Kishan's with the intensity of a lightning blast.

Kishan spoke. "Ren? What's wrong? Calm down. You're not yourself." Without looking away, Kishan took a step back, shifted slightly, and said, "Kells? Move behind me. Slowly."

I swallowed dryly and took a step back. I lifted my hand from Kishan's arm. Ren watched us like a cat watches a cornered mouse.

He blinked and tilted his head, studying our movements calculatingly. Kishan began talking to him in low, quiet tones while moving the two of us gradually backward.

Kishan quietly directed, "If Ren springs, run. I'll keep him occupied while you get Kadam."

I nodded against his back.

Ren took a step forward. "Move *away* from her, Kishan. Now!"

Kishan shook his head. "I'm not going to let you hurt her."

"*Hurt* her? I'm not going to harm her. You, on the other hand, I'm going to destroy."

Kishan held up a hand. "Ren, I don't know what's gotten into you. Maybe it's kraken poison. Just calm down and back off."

"*Vishshva!*" Ren spat.

Then he began yelling at Kishan in Hindi, speaking so fast I couldn't pick out anything. I don't know what he said, but Kishan bristled and clenched his jaw. I heard a rumble of warning from Kishan's chest.

Through clenched teeth Kishan quietly said, "Kelsey? It's time to go. Run."

Whatever was going on with Ren was getting worse. Kishan said some things back to him that were obviously not helping. In fact, they appeared to be spurring Ren on, making him even angrier than he already was.

Kishan reached back and squeezed my hand. "Go. I'll hold him off."

I had just turned to leave when I heard a terrible groan of pain and the sound of someone dropping heavily to the deck. I whipped around and saw Kishan standing over a prostrate Ren.

"What did you do?"

"Nothing. He clutched his head and fell."

Ren was on his knees, bent over so his head touched the deck. His hands were pressed into his hair, and he twisted and pulled the strands as he moaned in agony. Suddenly he flung back his head and threw out his chest. Fists clenched at his sides, he screamed out in pain—the kind of mortal cry that reverberates through anyone who hears it. It was a cry of utter agony. In it, I could hear the echoes of Lokesh's laughter as he hurt him, the physical suffering of months of torture, the emotional turmoil of having nothing left to live for.

I had to go to him. He needed me. His anguish seeped into my body until it became a living entity. I had to vanquish it. I couldn't let him suffer like this, couldn't allow him to feel this pain. I knew somehow that I could destroy this blackness, this darkness that overshadowed his mind, his soul.

That's when I felt it. Under the hurt, under the layers of torment, there was something solid, something strong, something unbreakable. It was back. The bridge between Ren and me had been rebuilt. It was hidden under waves of pain. It was flooded over, but it was there, and it was rock-hard and firm. I took several steps toward him, but Kishan held me back.

Ren slumped forward again and braced himself on shaky arms, panting. My heart beat heavily as if in rhythm with his. I could feel my limbs trembling, echoing his shaky movements. The three of us stayed locked in that position for several minutes. Kishan finally took a step forward and held out his hand. Ren took several deep breaths and then clasped his brother's hand. He stood and lifted his head, but he didn't look at Kishan. He looked at me.

I froze in place. My skin tingled all over. My pulse hammered thickly through my veins.

Kishan spoke, "Are you . . . alright?"

Ren replied without taking his eyes off me. "I am *now*."

"What happened to you?" Kishan continued.

Ren sighed deeply and reluctantly looked at his brother. "The veil of concealment was lifted."

"A veil? What veil?"

"The veil in my mind. The one Durga put there."

"Durga?"

"Yes," he replied softly. "I remember now." His gaze shifted to me again. "I remember . . . *everything*."

I gasped softly. The night air now hung thickly around us, warm and sultry when it had previously been cool and crisp. A vibrating hum in my body warmed my muscles, smoothing, melting away the stress of a few moments before, and I became aware of only one thing: the man looking at me fervently with unspoken words in his brilliant blue eyes. I don't know how long we were locked together like that. I didn't think anything could break that visual connection, but then Kishan stepped in front of me and faced his brother. I blinked several times before his words made sense.

"Stay here," he said to Ren. "We're just going downstairs to get Kadam, and then we'll be back. Are you listening to me? Ren?"

Ren spoke without taking his eyes off me. "Yes. I will stay here and wait."

Kishan grunted. "Good. Come on, Kells." He took my hand and started leading me away. I followed him placidly, letting him guide my footsteps as my mind dwelt on what had happened.

Just after we rounded the corner, I heard Ren's soft voice, no more than a whisper on the night breeze entreat, "Don't go, *iadala*. Stay with me."

I hitched a breath and turned to look, but I couldn't see him anymore. Kishan squeezed my hand and pulled me along after him. When we arrived at Mr. Kadam's door, Kishan knocked softly. The door opened a crack, and then all the way, allowing us to enter.

Mr. Kadam wore a gentleman's dressing robe, the type of sleepwear that men a hundred years ago would have worn before retiring for the evening. Kishan quickly explained the situation. They both wanted me to stay put while they spoke with Ren. They were adamant, and I was in too much shock to protest. I sat in Mr. Kadam's chair, lifting a heavy book onto my lap.

I opened the book, but I couldn't read. My brain was unplugged. My body was entirely focused on feeling; and right now, the only thing I could feel was the strong connection in the center of my body. The hole, the missing link, the broken off gaping piece of me, gone since Shangri-la, was back, and I could feel the other end. I was connected to Ren again. I had been alone. Naked. Exposed to the harsh world. And now . . . I wasn't.

Even as I sat here decks away from him, I could feel the warmth of his presence as if a soft blanket had been wrapped around my soul, around my heart. It held me and protected me. It sheltered me, and I knew I wasn't alone anymore. I'd been like a colander, a bowl that could hold onto the major stuff but the precious liquid drops of emotional connection were constantly draining out of me.

Now those holes were sealed, and I was filling. Bursting with some-thing that left me weepy and shaky. *He remembered.* I repeated those words over and over. They flitted across my conscious mind without penetrating, without processing. I felt light-headed, like I was suffering from heatstroke. I licked my lips but was too weak to get up and look for water.

Kishan and Mr. Kadam returned. Kishan knelt beside me and took my hand. He stroked the back of it, but I couldn't feel his gentle touch.

Mr. Kadam spoke quietly. "It appears Ren has regained his memory, Miss Kelsey. He'd like to see you. Do you feel up to it, or should I tell him to wait until tomorrow?"

I hesitated and didn't reply for a few seconds.

"Miss Kelsey? Are you quite alright?"

I sucked in a breath and mumbled. "I don't know what to do. What should I do?"

Kishan sat by me, caring and constant. "I'll support whatever you decide, Kells," he said.

"Okay." I nodded maniacally. "I should see him, right? You think I should see him, don't you?"

I stood and took a few steps and then turned. "No. Wait. I can't. What do I say to him? How do I explain everything?"

Kishan said, "He knows everything. He still remembers everything since we found him, but now his other memories have surfaced. If you don't want to talk to him, you don't have to."

I bit my lip. "No. It's okay. I'll see him now."

Mr. Kadam nodded. "He's waiting for you in the observation lounge."

I took another shaky step and then stopped. "Will you go with me, Kishan?"

He kissed my forehead. "Of course."

We left a worried Mr. Kadam, who told us he would take over watch in the wheelhouse as we were otherwise occupied. I told Kishan I wanted to change first. I washed the makeup off my face and took off my fancy dress. Slipping on a pair of jeans, I pulled a T-shirt over my head. I removed the flower and brushed out my hair, then tugged on a pair of sneakers. Kishan waited for me outside, still in his silk shirt and tie.

I took his hand, and silently we made our way to the observation lounge. We started toward the couches. The room was dark; only the moonlight coming in through the window lit our way. I saw a shadowy figure rise. His form was silhouetted by the moon. I stopped.

Kishan wrapped me in a hug and whispered, "It'll be alright. You go on, and call out if you need me."

"But—"

"Go ahead."

Kishan's comforting presence was gone before I could issue another protest. I forced myself to take a step forward and then another. I was frightened, but I didn't know what was scaring me. I finally reached Ren. He watched my every move with an awareness that made me nervous. He must have sensed my fear, because he dropped his intense gaze and gestured that I should sit. I perched nervously across from him and clasped my hands in my lap.

After a long quiet moment, I said, "You . . . wanted to talk to me?"

Ren sat back in his chair, studying me silently.

"What did you want to say?" I stammered.

He tilted his head. "You're scared. You don't need to be," he said softly.

I dropped my gaze to my hands.

He went on, "You're acting like you did when I first revealed myself to you at Phet's house."

"I can't seem to help myself."

"I don't ever want you to be frightened of me, *priya*."

My eyes met his, and I took a deep breath. "You said you remember. Is that true?"

"Yes. I was . . . triggered."

Shocked, I asked, "What was the trigger? What brought back your memory of me after all this time?"

He looked away. "It's not important. The important thing is that it's over. I remember you. Us. Kishkindha. Oregon. I remember being taken, handing you to Kishan, the Valentine's dance, fighting Li, *our first kiss* . . . all of it."

I stood and walked to the window. I pressed my hand against the glass and kept my back turned to him.

Ren continued, "Phet was right. I did this to myself."

I clenched my fist and touched my forehead to the cold glass. My breath fogged the window lightly then disappeared between breaths. "Why?" My voice broke. "Why did you do it?"

He rose and stood behind me—close enough that his nearness affected me. It was warm and calming, and yet at the same time, my nerves stood on end, prickling my skin until I was sensitive to everything around me. He touched a strand of my hair and his fingers brushed the back of my neck. I jumped but stayed where I was.

"Durga offered to help me block you out and even planted a subliminal aversion to being near you. The idea being that if somehow I was rescued, even then I would stay as far away from you as possible."

"That included you not being able to touch me? The burning you felt?"

"Yes. That way, I'd avoid you, and Lokesh couldn't use me to find you. He was making me say things that I didn't want him to know. He made me hallucinate with some kind of power. He was obsessed with finding you. Forgetting you was the only way I could really protect you. The only way to save you."

A tear splashed on my cheek. Others followed, and I sniffled softly.

He took a step closer and put a hand against the glass near mine. He leaned in and said quietly, "I'm *so* sorry, *iadala*. I'm sorry I wasn't there when you needed me. I'm sorry for the things I said. I'm sorry about your birthday, and worst of all I'm sorry for making you feel that I didn't want you. That was never the case. Ever. Even when I couldn't remember you."

I laughed wetly. "Even when Randi was here?"

"I detested Randi."

"You sure could have fooled me."

"'If you try to fail, and succeed, which have you done?' I pushed you away on purpose. When Kishan gave you CPR, and I couldn't, I knew you needed someone who could take care of you and be there for you. I couldn't be what you needed.

"Kelsey, I can remember every moment I spent with you. I remember the first time you touched me as a tiger. I remember arguing with you in Kishkindha. I remember the fear I felt after the Kappa bit you. I remember the candlelight shining in your eyes at our Valentine's dinner. I remember the first time you told me you loved me right before you left India, and I remember handing you to Kishan in Oregon and letting you go. I thought that was the hardest thing I'd ever experience, but then Durga offered me the chance to save you. I almost didn't do it.

"There was a void in my heart after she took my memories. I felt them drain out of me, and there was nothing I could do to hold onto them. I desperately grasped at each one as they vanished, faded from my mind. The last thing I forgot was your face. That last image of you was so real, I tried to cup your face with my hands and hold on. I refused to let you go, but that image of you faded too until I held nothing. My heart was broken, and I couldn't remember why. To live like that was horrible. I wanted Lokesh to kill me. I actually began to look forward to the torture. It was a distraction for my mind."

He leaned his head and shoulder against the glass so he could see my face.

"Then one day, the three of you came and saved me. I didn't know who you were. I felt like I should know you, but I couldn't stay around you as a man without great pain. Being around you filled the emptiness though. It was worth the physical pain. I don't think Durga expected that. That the emotional pull of you would override the physical discomforts of being close. So we came together again. But this time I was limited, blocked. As a tiger I could be close, be your companion, feel you near, and I fell for you again.

"Because a part of me sensed we belonged together, I was at peace. I would have been content to be your lapdog for the rest of my life. You asked me at the Star Festival if I would want more than that. The answer was no. There was nowhere else, no *one* else who made me feel like you did.

"Then when I broke up with you, I tried to prove to you and to myself that I didn't need you. I avoided you. I hurt you. I paraded other women around, so you would believe I didn't want you. But it was a lie. I had ten women surrounding me, and all I could think about was that cowboy having his hands on you. All I could see was the hurt I'd caused you. I convinced myself I was doing it for your own good. That you would be happier and would have a normal life without me. I selfishly pushed you toward Kishan knowing that if you were with him, at least I'd get to be near you sometimes."

"And you knew he could protect me."

"Yes."

I turned to the side to face him. "And now?"

"And now?" He laughed sadly and ran a hand through his hair. "And now I'm worse off than I was before. At least before, I didn't have the memory of kissing you in the kitchen between batches of chocolate-peanut-butter cookies. I didn't remember what it felt like dancing with you in Oregon. I didn't remember what you looked like in your blue *sharara* dress. I didn't have the memory of fighting *for* you or fighting *with* you. Of dating you or seeing you for the first time in months on Christmas day and how I finally felt . . . whole again."

He sighed. "I know I caused you pain. I know I hurt you. I know I broke your trust, your faith in me. Just . . . tell me what to do. Tell me how to fix this. How to make it right. How to win you back again. If I could take all the pain I caused you into myself, I would. You are more important to me than all the world, and I would *sacrifice* all of the world to make you happy, to keep you safe. Please believe me when I say that."

I sniffed and moved in front of him. I wrapped my arms around his waist and held him fiercely. "I do believe that."

He pressed me tightly to his chest and stroked my hair, quietly. We stood that way a long time. He seemed content to just hold me close. Finally, emotionally spent, I steeled myself and stepped away.

I patted his arm and said, "We can talk about this more tomorrow, Ren. It's way past midnight now, and I'm exhausted. Goodnight."

"Goodnight?" he asked, puzzled.

"Yes. Goodnight." I took two steps away from him and felt his hand on my arm.

"Wait. I'll walk with you."

I quickly glanced away from his confused face and hesitated briefly before I spoke. "Umm . . . you'd better not. *Kishan* is . . . waiting for me."

His face darkened. "You're . . . still going with *him*?"

I sighed. "Yes."

"But didn't anything I say make a difference to you? *Kelsey*—" He grabbed my hand and cupped it between his. "I can *be* with you again. I can *touch* you." He brought my hand up to his cheek and pressed it there. "I can *hold* you. I can *stay near* you." He pulled my palm down to his lips and closed his eyes as he kissed it.

He opened them slowly, and I gulped. "I *know*, Ren, but . . . it doesn't matter. I'm . . . I'm with *Kishan* now."

He dropped my hand as his blue eyes turned icy. "What do you mean you're *with* Kishan now?"

"Kishan and I are dating now. You remember that, don't you? Look, we'll talk about it more tomorrow, okay?" I turned around.

He stepped around me and with a tightly controlled voice said,

"I don't want to talk about it tomorrow, Kells. I want to talk about this now."

"Ren, I don't have the energy to fight about this right now. I need some time to process all this. I'm going to bed. I'll see you in the morning, okay?"

He snagged my hand and tugged me lightly toward him. He pulled me closer and closer until my nose was an inch from his and my back was bent as I tried to keep some distance from him. He leaned toward me and I couldn't help but stare at his mouth. I panicked thinking he was going to kiss me, but instead, he pressed his lips against my cheek and said, "Fine. Go sleep now, but understand one thing. I will *not* lose you again, *meri aadoo.*"

"What does that mean?"

He smiled and whispered, "It means . . . *my peach.*"

He straightened and let me go. I turned around and headed quickly for the door. Kishan waited for me near the exercise equipment and when I came closer, he held out his hand. I smiled and took it while he stared over my head. I turned and saw Ren was casually leaning against the door. He watched as Kishan led me off.

When we stepped into the elevator, Ren stood rooted in the same spot, watching us thoughtfully as we descended into the darkness.

When we got to my room, I went to the bathroom to change into my pajamas. Kishan was sitting in a chair waiting for me when I came out. I sat on the bed and crossed my legs under me.

"Are you okay?" he asked.

"Yes. I'm fine. I'd like to sleep now and talk about it later, if you don't mind."

"Okay. I'm going to help Mr. Kadam tonight. See you in the morning." He stood and pulled the covers over me, tucking me in, pressed a kiss on my forehead, and gently closed the door behind him.

I turned out the light and twisted and squirmed until I got the heavy covers off and pulled my quilt over me instead. I suddenly realized that Ren knew how to tuck me in and Kishan didn't. Angrily, I tossed Grandma's blanket onto the chair and yanked the heavy coverlet up to my chin, stubbornly determined to fall asleep the way Kishan tucked me in. I fell asleep a long time later but moved restlessly all night.

When I woke up, I found that my feet were at the head of the bed and my arm was dangling over the side. I dragged my tired body to the shower and stared at my droopy, baggy eyes in the mirror afterward.

What am I going to do? Ren just wants to pick up where we left off. Can I do that? Can I hurt Kishan like that? Am I that kind of a person? What do I feel for Kishan? More than friendship, surely. He's steady, reliable, comforting. Sheesh! I sound like I'm describing an old car. So what does that mean? He's the Pinto to Ren's Corvette? No. That's not true either. I guess the real question here is what do I feel for Ren?

My heart thudded heavily in response as I allowed myself to picture him. The way I felt when he held me. The way my heart skipped when he touched my wrist. The way I trembled when he looked at me. I closed my eyes and tried to center myself. Set my mind apart from my feelings and analyze the situation logically.

No. I am not the kind of person to do that to Kishan. I told him I wouldn't let him be alone again. Ren knew what he was doing even though he couldn't remember. He had his chance and he gave me away. Kishan deserves to have his chance too. There. I've made my choice. My choice is to stay with Kishan.

With my decision made, I turned the key to my heart. I locked my feelings for Ren away deep inside me and left only the part of my heart open that belonged to Kishan. I felt cramped and uncomfortable, like I was trying to breathe on only one lung, but I had just enough heart left to function. More than a sliver anyway. So what if the other part of my

heart was pounding like I'd wrapped a tourniquet around it? So what if it was ready to burst and undo me utterly? So what if I felt limited, stifled? I could learn to adapt to it like Chinese girls who learn to walk on bound feet. Sure, it would be painful at first, but eventually I'd get used to it.

Heartstrings fully taut, binding my emotions in place, pinching me like tight stays on a corset, I pulled on some clothes and reluctantly made my way up to the wheelhouse. I stopped at Kishan's door and cracked it open. He was sleeping, the sheets bunched around his waist. I walked over to the bed and smoothed the hair away from his face. He smiled in his sleep and turned over. I left him and headed for the elevator.

When I reached the glass door, I found a blue silk rose with a folded note taped to it. I pulled the paper off and opened the note. Inside was a pair of pearl earrings and a poem.

Know you, perchance, how that poor formless wretch—
The Oyster—gems his shallow moonlit chalice?
Where the shell irks him, or the sea-sand frets,
He sheds this lovely lustre on his grief.
—Sir Edwin Arnold

Let me keep my pearl.
—Ren

I crushed the note and jammed it into my pocket along with the earrings. Then I rode the elevator up and went to the wheelhouse where I found Mr. Kadam working furiously on some notes.

"What are you up to?" I asked.

"Kishan and I hit upon the answer to these markings on the sky disk."

"Oh? What are they?"

"Kishan thinks they're obstacles that lie between us and the other pagodas. And that the path shown is a way to weave around them safely."

"Obstacles, huh? I wonder what made him think that," I said dryly.

Mr. Kadam ignored my comment. "We are testing that theory now. We will be approaching the first marker in an hour or so. That's why I've sent Kishan off to rest."

"I see." I made myself some waffles with the Golden Fruit and sat down next to Mr. Kadam as he worked.

"Are you feeling better, Miss Kelsey?"

"I . . . didn't sleep well. Ren and I talked, and he does seem to remember everything now. But that only makes things more complicated."

"Yes. I spoke with him at great length earlier this morning."

I turned all my attention to my plate, swirling the carefully cut bites of waffle in the syrup. "I . . . don't really want to talk about it right now, if that's alright with you."

"Of course it is. You may speak to me whenever you wish or not at all. I am always at your disposal."

"Thanks for understanding."

"Of course."

An hour later, Kishan appeared with my jacket over his arm. He slipped it over my shoulders and turned to study the charts Mr. Kadam had been working on. Something crackled in my jacket pocket. I reached my hand inside and pulled out a paper. It was a sonnet. In fact, it was sonnet #116, which was usually one of my favorites.

Let me not to the marriage of true minds
Admit impediments. Love is not love
Which alters when it alteration finds,
Or bends with the remover to remove:
O no! it is an ever-fixed mark
That looks on tempests and is never shaken;
It is the star to every wandering bark,
Whose worth's unknown, although his height be taken.
Love's not Time's fool, though rosy lips and cheeks
Within his bending sickle's compass come:
Love alters not with his brief hours and weeks,
But bears it out even to the edge of doom.
If this be error and upon me proved,
I never writ, nor no man ever loved.
—William Shakespeare

"What's wrong?" Kishan asked.

I shoved the note back into my pocket and blushed furiously.

"Nothing. I'll, umm . . . be right back. Okay?"

"Okay. Hurry though. We're almost there."

"I will."

I ran down the steps and slammed into Ren's room as he was pulling a shirt over his head. "What exactly do you think you are doing?" I yelled.

He froze and then smiled disarmingly at me and lowered his shirt over his very nice chest. "Getting dressed. And good morning to you too. Now what's all the yelling about?"

"I don't know how you snuck this into my jacket, but you've got to stop."

"What exactly did I sneak into your jacket?"

I thrust the crumpled paper into his hand. "This!"

He sat on the bed and opened the paper slowly, smoothing it out on his jean-clad thigh. I involuntarily squeaked as I realized I was mesmerized by his movements.

"It looks like a Shakespeare poem, Kells. You like Shakespeare so what's the problem?"

"The *problem* is that I'm no longer entertaining poems from you."

He leaned back and assessed me boldly, grinned, and said, "'Was ever woman in this humour woo'd? Was ever woman in this humour won?'"

"Give it a rest, Shakespeare. I'm not a shrew to be tamed. Like I told you last night, I'm dating Kishan now."

"Really?" He stood and stalked toward me.

All of a sudden I couldn't breathe. I kept backing up until I hit the wall. He pressed his hands against it on either side of my head and leaned in close to me. I stubbornly thrust out my chin, refusing to be intimidated by him.

"Yes. I am. It's a good thing I came here to talk with you about it anyway. I don't want you . . . chasing me around or making things," I swallowed thickly, "difficult."

Ren laughed throatily and leaned closer to nuzzle my ear. "You like me to be . . . *difficult.*"

"*No.*" I groaned when he bit my earlobe. "I want my life to be simple and comfortable. And with Kishan, it will be."

"You don't *really* want something *simple*, do you Kelsey?" His lips pressed against the soft skin behind my ear, and I shivered. "Complication," he began trailing slow, teasing kisses down my neck, "is what makes life," he cupped the back of my neck and slid his hand into my hair, "exciting."

I turned my face away, but he just took the opportunity to explore more of my exposed neck.

"Love *is* complicated, *iadala*. Mmm, you taste delicious. Do you know how good it feels to be able to touch you without pain? To kiss you?" He pressed tingling kisses along the length of my jaw, and whispered, "I want to drown in the pleasure of being close to you."

I groaned and gripped his upper arms. *Speaking of drowning, I was going under, and fast.* Blinking open my eyes, I grabbed his shoulders, faced him, and used all my strength to push him away, but he only backed off a few inches.

"That's it, Ren. I mean it. *Read . . . my . . . lips.* I want *Kishan*. Not *you*."

His eyes tightened, but then shone with a wicked gleam. "I thought you'd never ask." Suddenly, he yanked me into his arms. One of his hands splayed against my back, and the other slipped into my hair. He angled my head and crushed his mouth against mine. Our bodies snapped together like two magnets. A driving wave of heat washed through me. I could have sworn I was drowning, and he was my life preserver. I was so desperate to cling to him, to become a part of him. His touch was familiar yet new. He was like the ocean, so vast, so full of life, so essential to the world. *So essential to* my *world.*

My arms slipped around his neck and held on, while he slid his hands up and down my back, pressing me closer. One arm locked around my waist and the other pressed against my middle back. He kissed me wildly, overwhelming me like a giant wave rushing to shore. I was soon lost in the turbulent grasp of his embrace and yet . . . I knew

I was safe. His kiss drove me, pushed me, asked me questions I was unwilling to consider.

But I was cherished by this dark Poseidon, and though he had the power to crush me utterly, to drown me in the purple depths of his wake, he held me aloft, separate. His passionate kiss changed. It gentled and soothed and entreated. Together we drifted toward a safe harbor. The god of the sea set me down securely on a sandy beach and steadied me as I trembled.

Effervescent tingles shot through my limbs, delighting me with surges of sparkling sensation like sandy toes tickled by bubbly waves. Finally, the waves moved away, and I felt my Poseidon watching me from a distance. We looked at each other, knowing we were forever changed by the experience. We both knew that I would always belong to the sea and that I would never be able to part from it and be whole again.

He brushed my cheek with his thumb, touching me lightly, gently. A part of me screamed that I needed him, that I belonged with him, that I couldn't deny this. But another part of me felt guilty, remembered there was another who loved me, who cared for me, who would be hurt. And I'd made him a promise. I moved back and took a step away from Ren's all-consuming presence so I could shake off my reaction to him. It didn't work, but I sucked in a breath determined to pursue my course.

"Hmm," he trailed his finger from my temple down my cheek to my lips and touched my bottom lip lightly. "That's interesting."

Sighing, I asked, "What's interesting?"

"Despite your protestations, I would say that your *lips* definitely want . . . *me*."

I let out a cry of frustration, more at my own betrayal than with him, pushed him aside, and brushed my lips with the back of my hand.

"Kelsey."

"Don't." I held up a hand. "Just . . . just don't, Ren. I can't *do* this. I'm not this kind of a person. I can't *be* this way with you anymore."

"Kelsey, please—"

"No!" I ran out of his room though he called after me.

At that moment, something shook the ship. Ren barreled out of his room toward me, grabbed my hand and yanked me all the way to the wheelhouse. We entered at the same time and got stuck together in the door. Ren thought that was a wonderful opportunity to put his arms around me while I yelled at him. When I finally got through and headed for Kishan, he was frowning, and Ren was smirking. The ship lurched again and I fell into the bookcase and hit my head.

"Can't you at least make sure she doesn't get hurt?" Ren hollered.

"He protects me just fine!" I yelled back.

Kishan pulled me into his arms and rubbed the bump on my head. "Don't let him egg you on, Kells. He's only trying to get a rise out of you."

"Perhaps you three could continue this conversation when the ship is not under attack?" Mr. Kadam said. "Nilima! Take the helm!"

Ren grabbed his trident and rushed to the stairs that led to the top of the wheelhouse. Kishan grabbed his *chakram* and ran to the front of the boat. I took the rear.

Ren shouted loudly, "I can see it! It's a big fish of some kind."

I stared at the water and gasped as I made out a huge tail. "It's heading toward you, Kishan!"

The giant body shoved the boat until it leaned dangerously to one side. When we straightened and the boat fell with a splash, I took off running to Kishan's side. Because the *chakram* couldn't cut through the water, I hit the creature with lightning, and it circled and dove. Everything was silent for a few forbidding minutes, and then a huge shape rose out of the water behind Ren.

My mouth opened in amazement. It was a giant monster fish. Its lower jaw protruded several feet past the upper jaw. Its mouth gaped. Huge vampire-like teeth stuck out from thick gray lips and a giant yellow eye fixed on Ren. Two long flippers whirred in the air like a hummingbird and long black stripes ran from head to tail. Its jaw suddenly snapped shut like a vise.

"Ren! Behind you!"

He spun and thrust the trident into the belly of the fish several times. Black blood pooled from the circular holes. The fish angled its body, and it fell partway onto the top of the tower. Ren fell overboard and slid down the slick fish's body into the churning water below.

"Ren! Kishan, help him!"

Kishan at once dove into the water after Ren.

I screamed at the men below, "How's that going to help?" and ran to the wheelhouse. The fish was circling the area and trying to snap at the two brothers floating next to the ship. Ren used his trident, but he wasn't making much headway. It helped that the fish's bottom jaw seemed too big to get close enough for a bite; it kept banging against the boat instead. I grabbed the Scarf and ran back to the side. By now, the fish had given up on biting them and was trying to smash them into the boat.

I mumbled, "Trying to make a couple of Indian prince pancakes? Well, not on my watch."

I shot the heaviest bursts of lightning I could through my hand, and hit the fish in several places. It twisted angrily in the water, trying to get out of my reach. At the same time, I had the Scarf make a rope ladder that trailed from the railing, down the side of the yacht, to the sea, and yelled at the brothers to grab it. I kept the fish off them long enough that they could climb up.

When they were aboard, dripping and tired, I yelled at Nilima, "Get us out of here!"

I kept blasting bolts at the fish until we were far enough away that it gave up. When I felt that we were finally out of danger, I glared at both the brothers, and then ignored them and stomped up to the wheelhouse.

I shoved in the door and said, "Well, the barrier theory is a sound one. I suggest we plot a course between all those spots. When the boys show up, tell them I said they're idiots, they're welcome, and to leave me alone for a while."

Nilima and Mr. Kadam said nothing. With that, I huffed out of the wheelhouse and went to my room. I locked both doors and filled the Jacuzzi for a good soak. While I soaked, I thought guiltily about the kiss. *Apparently, I'm going to have to strengthen my resolve if I want to be loyal to Kishan. I can't let Ren get me alone. I just don't have the willpower to resist him. He's too . . . too potent.* Despite my self-chastisement, I ended up thinking about him the entire time. I felt a rumble. The boat was moving, so obviously we were headed for the green dragon's lair. I sighed, opened my eyes, and stepped out of the tub.

After I dressed, I went back to the wheelhouse. Everything was quiet. The sun had gone down, and neither Ren nor Kishan was around. I found Nilima alone steering the boat, carefully following Mr. Kadam's instructions. Grabbing a blanket, I cozied up in a nearby chair. She glanced at me from time to time, but I was totally absorbed in my own thoughts.

"You're wondering what to do now, aren't you?"

I sighed. "Yes. I'm wondering how to make Ren understand we can't be together now."

"Oh?" She shifted to look at me. "Is that what you are wondering? I was thinking you'd be wondering which one of them will make you happy."

"Nope. That's not what I'm wondering at all."

"I see. So you are determined to be with Kishan, then?"

"I made a promise to him. A commitment."

"Did you not also do the same with Ren?"

I winced. "Yes. But that was a long time ago."

"Perhaps not so long to him." Nilima stared ahead at the blackness.

"Perhaps not." I studied my hands in my lap. "What do *you* think I should do?" I asked.

She stretched prettily and then settled back into her former position. "You like to write in your journal, don't you?"

"Yes."

"Then I suggest you write about both of them. Write of their strengths and weaknesses. Record what you love about them. Put down what you wish was different. It may help you to see your thoughts on paper."

"That's a good idea. Thanks, Nilima."

I spent the next few days recording my thoughts about both brothers but found I had lots of things both good and bad to say about Ren, and though my list for Kishan was all good, it was also short. I didn't feel I was doing a good job focusing on him, so I set out to spend time with him. I asked him hundreds of questions and then stubbornly recorded his answers in my journal.

I kissed him several times in a clinical way, trying to gauge my reactions to him. He seemed oblivious to my "tests" and enjoyed the kisses for what they were. Not *once* did kissing him cause the same reaction it did when kissing Ren. Despite my best efforts, I found I couldn't duplicate the feeling from that first night either, that first kiss with Kishan, the one when Ren got his memory back. I started to suspect my reaction had not come because of Kishan at all.

One evening, I was strolling the deck with Kishan and had an idea for another test. "Kishan? I want to try something. Do you mind helping me?"

"Sure. What is it?"

"Stand right here. No, behind me. Good. Now stay there for a second."

I aimed my firepower down at the water. White light shot out of my palm and hit the ocean. A cloud of steam rose up. "Okay, now step up behind me and pull me back against your chest."

"Like this?"

"Yes. Good. Now lean your head on my shoulder and touch my arms. Put yours on top of mine."

He ran his hands up and down my arms. I concentrated and pushed with all my energy, but the light didn't change. There was no intense golden burst of power. I wasn't overwhelmed with a sense of connection. My power fizzled and died out. I stared hard at the water.

"What is it?" Kishan asked. "Is something wrong?"

Plastering a smile on my face, I turned toward him. After pecking him on the lips, I said, "No. Nothing's wrong at all. Just a silly idea I had. No big deal."

I heard a noise above us and saw Ren leaning against a post. He was smirking at me knowingly. I glared at him and kissed Kishan hard. Kishan wrapped an arm around my waist and kissed me back, soundly. When I looked back again, Ren was frowning.

Later that evening, I was lying in a deck chair looking up at the stars while Kishan was working out. I felt a warm tug, a familiar pull on my heart and knew *he* was near.

A deep hypnotic voice asked, "May I sit?"

"No."

"I'd like to talk with you."

"Talk all you like because I'm leaving. I think I've had too much sun."

"The sun's not out. Sit down and stay put."

Ren dragged a lounge chair over next to mine and lay down with his hands behind his head.

"How long are you going to let this go on, Kelsey?"

"I don't know what you're talking about."

"Don't you? I saw you testing Kishan earlier today. You don't feel for him what you feel for me. You don't feel *with* him the way you feel with me."

"You're wrong. Being with Kishan is . . . it's like heaven."

"'The *love of heaven* makes one heavenly.'"

"Exactly, our love is heavenly."

"That's not what I meant."

"It means what *I* interpret it to mean."

"Fine. Then you should have no problem interpreting this one. 'The lady doth protest too much, methinks,' or how about 'O, how this spring of love resembleth the uncertain glory of an April day; which now shows all the beauty of the sun, and by and by a cloud takes all away.'"

"A cloud didn't take our love away, you did. I warned you what the consequences would be, and you said, and I quote, 'I won't need another chance. I won't be seeking you out again.' Are those *not* your *exact* words, Ren?"

He flinched. "They *were*. But—"

"No. There is no 'but.' There's no coming back from this one, Ren."

"But, Kelsey, I did it for you. Not because I wanted to, but because I wanted to save you."

"I understand that, but what's done is done. I'm not going to hurt Kishan because you changed your mind. You're going to have to live with the consequences of your choices just as I do."

He got up and knelt beside my chair. Picking up my hand, he twined his fingers with mine. "You're forgetting something, *iadala*. Love is not a consequence. Love is not a choice. Love is a *thirst*—a need as

vital to the soul as water is to the body. Love is a precious draft that not only soothes a parched throat but also vitalizes a man. It fortifies him enough that he is willing to slay dragons for the woman who offers it. Take that draft of love from me, and I will shrivel to dust. To take it from a man dying of thirst and give it to another while he watches is a cruelty I never thought you capable of."

I snorted and he sighed.

"'Thou art to me a delicious torment,' Kelsey."

"Who said that?"

"The first part? Me. That last line, Emerson."

"I see. Go on. You were speaking of your parts being vitalized?"

He narrowed his eyes. "You're mocking me."

"Well, don't you think you're being overdramatic," I held up my fingers in a pinch, "just a teensy bit?"

"Maybe. Perhaps it's because I'm a coward. Shakespeare wrote, 'Cowards die many times before their deaths, the valiant never taste of death but once.'"

"How does that make you a coward?"

"Because I've died many deaths, mostly over you, and I'm still alive. Trying to have a relationship with you is like trying to rescue someone from Hades. Only a fool would keep going back to get a woman who fights him every step of the way."

"Ah, but that makes you a fool, not a coward."

He frowned and said, "Perhaps I am both." He studied my face and asked quietly, "Was it too much to ask you to wait for me? To believe in me? Don't you know how much I love you?"

I squirmed under his gaze.

Ren pressed on, "I die a little death every time we're separated, Kelsey."

I swallowed the guilt and let pride take over. "Lucky for you, cats have nine lives. I only have one life and one heart, and it's been jerked around so much I'm surprised it still beats."

"It would help if you stop offering your heart to every man you meet," he suggested dryly.

"I don't fall in love with every man I meet despite what you think, Mr. Exaggeration." I poked him in the chest. "At least *I* don't parade scantily clad suitors with artificial bosoms around. Besides, *you* pushed *me* away, not the other way around. It's your own fault."

"Well, I didn't expect that you'd immediately settle down with someone *else* now, did I? It's a small ship, I figured. But *no*, leave Kelsey alone for five minutes, and she suddenly has a line of boyfriends. Every man on board immediately moves in, don't they?"

I glared at him. "You *said* Kishan and I should—"

He angrily ran a hand through his hair. "I *know* what I said. It made sense at the time. But even so, a part of me believed you'd never do it. I didn't think I could actually convince you that I didn't love you anymore. It was a bad decision with obviously negative ramifications. I made a mistake. A huge one. But now we're even. You left me, and I left you. Now we're done with that. We can set it aside and forget about it."

"No, we can't. We're not the only ones involved this time."

"There's *always* someone else involved. I have to repeatedly bring our relationship, bring us, back from the brink, and frankly, I'm becoming an expert on yanking you away from moving on with other men. How many is it now? Ten? Twenty?"

"You're exaggerating again."

Ren was becoming irritated. "Maybe I am. But you know what? That's *okay*. It's *fine*. That's right, *F-I-N-E*, *fine*. You just go ahead and keep on lining up your fan club because I am *always* going to be there to keep knocking them down."

A tear trickled down my face, and after a quiet moment, I said, "Ren, you *gave* me away. You pushed me into another man's arms. Did you really think you could just snap your fingers, and I'd come running back to you? That I could break his heart and not hurt my own in the process?"

"I know what I've done has hurt you, hurt us, and I also know it's hurt Kishan. If I was a braver man, I'd leave things the way they are, but I *can't*. You asked me why I'm a coward. I'm a *coward* because I refuse to be without you. I cannot fathom any kind of a happy existence if you're not in it. I won't even consider it. So you'd better get used to it, because I won't stop trying to win you over. If it's a battle for your heart, *iadala*, then I'm ready. Even if it turns out the one I'm fighting against is *you*."

"Really, Ren. Can't you just abide by my decision?"

"*No!* You're just as in love with me as I am with you, and if I have to beat that into your thick head then so be it."

"So much for the poetry, huh?"

He sighed, cupped my chin with his hand, and then turned my face to his. "I don't need poetry, *prema*. I just need to get near enough to touch you." He trailed his fingers lightly down my neck and over a shoulder.

My pulse pounded, and my lip quivered as I sucked in a breath.

"Your heart knows. Your soul remembers." He leaned over and started kissing my neck, barely skimming the sensitive skin with his lips. "*This* is something you can't deny. You *belong* with me. You're mine." He whispered softly against my throat, "'I am he am born to tame you Kate, and bring you from a wild Kate to a Kate comfortable as other household Kates—'"

I froze and pushed him away. "Don't. Ren, stop! Don't you dare finish those lines!"

"*Kelsey.*"

"No." I got up and walked away quickly, leaving my book on the deck by his feet.

I heard him threaten as I left, "The battle lines are drawn, *priyatama*. The more formidable the foe, the sweeter the victory."

Over my shoulder, I said, "Take your victory and shove it up your muzzle, tiger nose!" I headed back to my room to the sound of his quiet laughter.

The next morning, Kishan knocked on my door. I'd been dreaming about Ren as a white tiger, hunting me. I sat straight up in bed as Kishan opened the door, and then I shouted, "I am *not* a gazelle!"

Kishan laughed. "I know you're not a gazelle. Though your legs are almost as long. Hmm. It *would* be nice to chase you and stare at those legs."

I threw a pillow at his head. "Why did you wake me up?"

"One—it's already nine. Two—we're at the green dragon's island. So get up and get dressed, Kells."

the green dragon's hunt

We were anchored near a big island. Warm sandy beaches stretched as far as the eye could see, but farther away from the shore, the island was thick with trees of all types. Colorful birds flew overhead. It was warm, much warmer than the blue dragon's fog-covered island. This island was full of color and sound. We could clearly hear the screech of monkeys and the call of birds.

Ren soon joined us and set our weapons down on the table. He walked over to stand next to me.

Kishan said, "Listen. Can you hear them?"

"Hear what?" I asked.

Ren touched my arm. "Shh." He cocked his head and closed his eyes. I listened hard but could hear only the cries of various animals.

Ren finally opened his eyes. "Cats. Panthers, do you think? Leopards?"

Kishan shook his head. "No. Lions?"

"I don't think so."

I couldn't hear anything except monkeys. "What does it sound like?" I asked.

"It's more of a scream than a roar," Ren explained. "I've heard it before . . . from the zoo." He closed his eyes and listened again. "Jaguars. They're jaguars."

"What are they like?" Kishan asked.

"They look like spotted leopards, but they're bigger, more aggressive. They're smart. Calculating. They have a strong bite. They don't go for the jugular, they bite through the skull."

"I've never heard one before," Kishan said.

"You wouldn't have," Ren continued. "They're not native to India. They're from South America."

Nilima and Mr. Kadam joined us as we began to strap on our weapons.

Mr. Kadam questioned, "You're thinking about heading through the jungle, then?"

"Yes," Ren replied as he secured my quiver of golden arrows. "We'll take the boat over and head through the jungle entering . . . there." He pointed at a section of trees that looked identical to all the other trees to me but he insisted the terrain would be easier in that spot.

Mr. Kadam followed us as we made our way to the bottom of the ship. "If you need help, have Miss Kelsey send a flare with her power."

"Right," Kishan agreed as he leapt into the boat and held out his hand for me.

Mr. Kadam opened the wet garage and lowered the boat into the water. After it was in, Ren dropped off the side of the ship and landed agilely right next to me. Kishan started the motor, took the wheel, and spun us around to face the beach. I almost fell as the front of the boat rose out of the water. Ren reached out a hand to steady me, but I pushed it away and wrapped an arm around Kishan's waist instead. When I looked back, he was glaring at me.

Ren leapt out when we reached the island and dragged the boat up onto the beach. Just as my feet touched sand, I heard a voice. It was rough, gravelly, and as it rumbled in my mind, the trees shook. It felt like a tiny earthquake.

Who sets foot on my island?

The noisy cacophony of the jungle suddenly stilled. We spun around in circles looking for the source of the voice but couldn't find anything.

Who are you? the voice demanded.

I announced, "We are travelers seeking your aid. We need to find your brothers and the Seventh Pagoda, great dragon. We seek Durga's Necklace."

The dragon laughed with the sound of two large stones rubbing together, sending the birds flying to the far side of the island.

And what would you do to secure my help, young woman?

"What do you ask of us?" I ventured cautiously.

Oh, nothing . . . much. I just ask for entertainment. You see, I am often very lonely here on my island. Perhaps you could provide some . . . diversion for me.

"Entertain you how?"

How about . . . a game?

Kishan questioned, "Where are you, dragon?"

Can you not see me? I am very close.

"We cannot," Kishan replied.

The dragon mockingly snorted. *Then you won't be very good at my game. Perhaps I won't play with you after all.*

"He's there," Ren announced quietly. "Up in that tree."

He pointed up, and my eyes focused on the canopy overhead. The leaves quivered, and when I peered closer I saw a golden eye blink.

Ah, good. You finally found me.

The tree rustled noisily as a large branch broke and drifted down to us. The dragon was perfectly camouflaged. Its head was brown and knobby like old driftwood, and its snout was long like a crocodile with pointed teeth. Two golden eyes blinked at me as it came lower. Large antlers sprung from the back of his head. Moss hung off the horns in sections as if it was being peeled away.

The dragon's long snake-like body was similar to its brothers', but it had golden taloned feet and scales resembling green leaves layered over each other. A brown beard and mane fell away from its head, looking like rich cocoa waves of corn silk. The silky hair grew in a thin patch down its back like a horse's mane and ended at a long bushy tail. It was smaller than its brothers, but as it unwound from the tree its body seemed to grow. If stretched out, the dragon would probably be twice as long as the yacht. The green dragon's voice startled me out of my visual inspection.

We should be formally introduced first. It is the proper way of doing things. I am Lùsèlóng, Dragon of the Earth. I already know you've met two of my brothers, the Dragon of the Stars and the Dragon of the Waves. If I decide to help you, you will meet my other two brothers, but I warn you now, they are not as easy to get along with as I, nor are they as beautiful. It chuckled.

Curious, I took a step closer. "I thought you were the dragons of the five oceans."

A golden eye blinked at me. *How refreshingly bold you are. We were born of the five oceans. I was born in the warm Indian Ocean. Qīnglóng was born in the Southern Ocean, Lóngjūn in the Pacific. You've yet to meet Jīnsèlóng or Yínbáilóng. The first was born in the Atlantic, and the second, in the freezing waters of the Arctic. Though I was born in the ocean, I reign over land, and I oversee all things that happen on land.*

"Then who were your parents?"

The dragon blew a puff of warm air over me. *Perhaps you are becoming too bold, my dear. Now shall we begin our game, or are you having thoughts of turning back?*

"We will play your game," Kishan said.

The dragon smacked its lips. *Excellent. Now in any game there must be a prize for the winner.*

Lùsèlóng lifted its head to peer into Kishan's eyes. It held his gaze steady for a moment, and then moved to Ren and did the same thing.

"What are you doing?" I asked.

Skimming their minds. Don't worry, young lady, I'm just reading their thoughts. The dragon snorted and then raised its head in the air, nose pointed to the sky, and laughed uproariously. *This will be the best game I will have created in millennia! A most magnificent sport!* It continued to chuckle.

"What's so funny?" I asked.

They both seek the same prize, you see.

"The same prize?"

The dragon shifted its body cutting me off from Ren and Kishan. *Yes. Come along then, my dear.*

"What? No!"

Oh, yes. Once the game has begun, it must be played to its conclusion.

It stretched forth a taloned claw and circled my waist. I struggled when it picked me up and prepared to leap into the air.

"Wait! What are you doing? You can't do this! We don't even know the rules of the game!"

Kishan and Ren both moved toward me until the green dragon blew a spurt of fire across the sand, halting their progress. I bucked against its claw, but its sharp talons cut into my waist.

Stop jostling, young lady. We don't want our prize to be damaged after all.

"Prize? What do you mean?"

The dragon sighed and kicked into the air. It blew more fire down on Ren and Kishan, so they were totally encircled by it but remained unburned.

Kishan removed his *chakram* and yelled, "Put her down, dragon, or we will kill you."

Lùsèlóng scoffed. *We dragons cannot be killed.*

Ren pulled out his trident and twisted the handle so the prongs elongated to shoot spear darts. "We cannot be killed either, dragon. And we will hunt you until she is safe."

The dragon bent its head toward Ren and hissed. *That is exactly what I am counting on, tiger.*

Kishan shouted as the dragon circled higher in the air, "Bring her back. Now!"

Ren leapt through the fire, threw down the trident, and switched to his tiger form. He scaled up a tall tree in great bounds and ran along a narrow branch. He was much closer to us now. He roared and swung a paw at the dragon.

Lùsèlóng indulgently lowered its head close enough to face the white tiger but remained far enough away so as not to have its nose batted by a paw. Ren changed back to a man and clung to the branch. He looked at me. I could feel his desperation. I was out of his reach, and there was nothing he could do to save me.

His expression turned dark, dangerous, as he faced the Dragon of the Earth. "If she should be harmed in *any* way, I promise you that I *will* find a way to kill you. Take great *care*, dragon."

The dragon narrowed its eyes and smiled malevolently. *Yes, this game will be most diverting. Because you insist on knowing the rules ahead of time, I will tell you this . . . the game is you. I'm going to go on a safari, you see. I will take the form of a man and hunt you. Both of you. You will take your tiger forms. There will be traps and other creatures lying in wait for you as well. If you can make it to the castle hedge before I shoot or trap you, you will be able to move on to the second round. If not, I will have two very beautiful tiger-skin rugs to place before my fire.*

"And if we make it to the second round?"

If you outwit me, which is highly unlikely, then the game will change. You will have to fight your way to the castle through a maze. Put down your flying disk, or I will eviscerate the girl.

I gasped and looked down at the base of the tree where Kishan had crept, *chakram* raised. He lowered his arm, and the dragon spun in a circle like a weather vane. I reeled dizzily from the movement. It trained its eyes on both men as it continued, *Your weapons will be given back to you before you enter the maze. This part of the game is older than the world. The players will be one white knight, one black knight, a dragon, and a princess. You must go through the maze and climb the castle walls. Then there is the dragon to slay, played by me. The winner gets the girl.*

"I thought you were immortal," Ren said.

Oh, I am, but if you can land what would normally be a killing blow for a dragon without being burned to a crisp, you win.

"And if *you* win?"

Why, of course, if I win, then I will get the girl. The dragon smiled evilly and squeezed me slightly.

I sucked in a breath of pain and heard menacing growls from both Ren and Kishan.

Ren spoke slowly, promise ringing in his voice. "We will play your game, dragon, but remember this, for every hurt you cause her, however minor, I will return that hurt to you a hundredfold."

The dragon bobbed in the air, watching Ren, appraising him. *It's been a long time since I've had such brave opponents. I wish you luck. Let the game begin!*

A rush of wind blew over us, and all the weapons shimmered and disappeared. Both men grunted in pain as they were forced to switch into their tiger forms. The black tiger looked at me, roared, and darted toward the jungle. The white tiger remained in the tree watching me until we could no longer see each other.

The dragon rose higher and entered the forest. It wove between the tall trees at a frightening speed. Occasionally, it'd reach out a claw and push off from a tree that was too close, leaving deep, jagged claw marks in the trunk. I shivered. *It's going to rip Ren and Kishan apart. It'll tear through them like butter.*

"Where are you taking me?"

To the castle, of course.

The green dragon shot higher into the air, and I could barely stop myself from throwing up from the fast rise, let alone ask him more questions. The island was much bigger than I thought it was. Its diameter was maybe five miles. Soon we left the trees, skimmed past the beach, and were over the ocean. Another smaller island came into view. It was also surrounded by trees, and rising up in the middle of it was a tall castle built of grayish seaweed-colored stone.

A huge maze of dark hedges at least twenty feet tall surrounded the outside. The castle rose high above the maze but was surrounded by mist. With dismay, I saw that there were no steps, no doors, no way to access the castle except from the top. The tigers would have to scale the outside, while I would be trapped like Rapunzel, *without the hair.*

A lone tower stood at the top, and this was where the dragon headed. It landed with a scrape of claws on the flat roof before finally setting me down. The air seemed to shift around it. It shimmered and popped, and suddenly, standing before me was the human version of Lùsèlóng. White skinned and brown haired, he was handsome but in a dangerous way. His eyes seemed more hazel now than yellow. He was dressed in old-fashioned khaki hunting clothes, tall black boots that shone with polish, and there was even a pith helmet tucked under his arm.

"But it's not fair," I accused. "The hedge and the castle aren't even on the same island. How are they supposed to know?"

"They will figure it out. *Eventually.*" He took my elbow. With a silky accent, he said, "Come, my dear. Allow me to show you to your accommodations."

"Why do you sound Russian?"

He laughed. "Didn't you know the world's best big-game hunters are Slavic? We dragons can take whatever form we wish, and I choose to hunt in the most sporting manner. I will emulate the style of the great hunters of the past who went on safari, for that was when hunting was a sport. Those very few, very brave men who dared put themselves at as much risk as their prey, who relied more on skill and cleverness than on weapons are now a thing of the past. Today I will pay homage to them."

Obviously arrogance was a weakness in this dragon. Maybe I could use it against him. Demurely, I said, "That's such a big risk for you. It's a *brave* thing to do, *really.*"

Confused, he stopped. "What do you mean?"

"Well, if you're truly going to emulate the great hunters, you will be hunting as a human. I mean, you weren't planning on using your dragon senses were you? Your incredible speed, sight, and hearing would give you such an advantage."

"Oh . . . yes. I suppose I could limit my abilities to hunt as a simple man." He continued to guide me into the castle and down a circular staircase.

"It *would* make the game so much more interesting, wouldn't it?" I asked innocently.

"Yes. Yes! It would. I will do it. I *will* hunt as a normal man."

I put my hand on his arm and tried to sound concerned. "But then you might be in *danger.* The tigers are *very* resourceful."

"Ha! There is no danger for me. I will win in the first hour."

"Still, it would be too tempting to use your special abilities. I wouldn't blame you, after all. All it would take is a tiger leaping at your throat, and you'd be tempted to zap him. I'd understand, of course. It's very difficult not to use power when you have it."

"I do not need my powers. My mind and my skills are enough to win the game."

"Well, you could always fall back on it, so you are guaranteed safety."

"I am not concerned with safety! Fine. To prove it to you, we will add another rule!"

"What rule would that be?"

"The rule is that if I use any abilities in the hunt that a normal man wouldn't possess, then the tigers will win."

"Oh! How very brave of you! It's really too bad I will be trapped here and unable to watch you in action."

"Yes, it is," he said thoughtfully. "Ah, then as a special courtesy to you, you will be allowed to watch the hunt."

"You mean, you're taking me with you?"

"And risk them stealing you back before we finish the game? No, *deti dama*, you will remain here in the tower. I will allow my special mirror to show you the hunt. When you want to watch, just approach the mirror, and tell it what you wish to see. Make yourself at home, my dear. Food and drink will be left on your windowsill every day, but you will remain trapped in here until the game is finished."

He started for the stairs with a flourish, just as the heavy wooden door closed behind him and locked itself. I waited until I couldn't hear him anymore and held my hand up toward the door. Nothing happened. I went to the window to send a flare. Again, my lightning power was useless. I sank down on the small bed with the rough woven cover. There was nothing else for me to do.

"Mirror? Show me the hunt."

The mirror turned black before creating a bird's-eye view of the island. A green flash outlined the dragon as it flew back over the water, landed on the beach, and switched to a man. Entering the jungle, he carried an old-fashioned, long-barreled hunting rifle and a sack of provisions—he even had a canteen. *I sure hope he keeps his end of the deal and hunts as a mortal.*

Even if he did, there was a good chance he would catch one of the

two tigers, if not both. Kishan was used to life in the jungle, but it had been a long time since Ren had had to take care of himself. I thought back to the antelope hunt when Ren couldn't catch one by himself. I bit my lip as I considered that his white fur would make him easy pickings. If they could hide well enough during the day, the tigers might have a good chance of hunting the dragon at night when his human vision would be more limited.

Lùsèlóng began carefully picking his way through the jungle, looking for signs of the tigers. I asked the mirror to show me Ren and Kishan. The mirror backed out of the view of the dragon and zoomed in on a piece of the jungle on the other side of the island. I couldn't see anything at first, and then I saw a flash of white behind a bush. It disappeared, but soon, a flick of a tiger's tail appeared from behind a rock. I asked the mirror to zoom out a bit. It showed Ren standing next to a spiked board, trying to spring the trap by batting it lightly with a paw.

Kishan entered the view with something in his mouth—a dead monkey. In fact, on closer inspection, the area was littered with monkey bodies. Kishan tossed the body into the trap, and the sharp end zoomed up at tiger level and fell away. I watched their slow progress as the tigers cautiously moved on deeper into the jungle.

An hour later, Kishan stepped into a side-closing trap, and two spiked wooden slats slammed together on his leg. He violently jerked his leg free, though the spikes tore his flesh. He limped for about twenty minutes until he healed.

Other traps awaited them. They narrowly avoided being impaled with a spear that shot out from the foliage when one of them tripped a wire. Ren stepped on a rock that set off another trap. A bent bamboo pole whipped across Kishan, who managed to leap out of the way, but it hit Ren full in the side. The whipping pole was studded with five-inch nails that were now buried deeply in Ren's fur. Kishan took the pole in his mouth and held it steady while Ren painfully jerked his body away. Blood dripped to the ground. They went on, slowly.

They traveled in the treetops for a while by leaping from branch to branch, but they soon discovered that many of the branches had been sawed through and didn't hold their weight. They moved back to the ground, and that's when they hit the worst of the snares: a Venus flytrap. I knew what it was from studying different types of warfare with Mr. Kadam.

A huge stone rolled across their path, causing both tigers to move quickly backward. Ren's back legs fell into a rectangular pit that had been hidden beneath leafy camouflage. Long metal spikes overlapped each other on the sides of the pit. They pointed downward, which scraped his legs as he slid toward the bottom of the pit. They were so devilishly set that if he tried to pull himself up, they would rip into his body like "wrong way" tire spikes. Once caught in the Venus flytrap snare it was almost impossible to get the victim out without killing him.

Kishan paced around the pit looking for a way to free Ren. He tried pushing the spikes down with a paw, but he slid on their smooth finish and almost joined Ren in the trap. After ten minutes of Kishan's fruitless efforts, Ren roared softly and started dragging his body out. The spikes sank deeply into his haunches and legs. He dug his claws into the dirt, and pulled himself forward inch by painful inch. Kishan sat and watched his progress.

Finally, Ren lay on the dirt panting. The entire back end of his body was a bloody mess. Long jagged furrows ran across his lower back and all the way down his legs. The tigers rested for an hour, which allowed Ren to heal at least partially, and then started moving again. At sunset, they found a place to rest, lying down side by side. One of them always remained awake. I could see their sleepy eyes blinking.

There was no candle or lamp in my room, but food had somehow appeared on the windowsill. I broke off a piece of the bread and sipped from the flagon of water. Saving the apple for later, I bit into the cheese and sank back onto the bed to watch my tigers. After checking the whereabouts of the dragon and finding him still tracking on the other side of the island, I relaxed and eventually nodded off in exhaustion.

I woke to the sound of a gunshot and panting and movement in the trees. I sat up startled and was confused for a moment, before remembering where I was.

"Mirror, zoom out. Find the dragon."

Lùsèlóng had found the blood trail in the night and was standing in the very spot where Ren and Kishan had been sleeping. Turning in a circle, he fingered a broken leaf. He took a few steps and crouched down to touch the depression of a tiger track. Then he picked up some dirt and smelled it, dusted off his fingers, smiled, and started through the trees. He stopped to touch a fern. There was fresh blood on it.

Panicked, I shouted, "Mirror, show me my tigers."

The image retreated and sped ahead a half mile and zoomed in on a running Ren and Kishan. There was a bleeding gash along Kishan's side where a bullet had grazed. They ran for a half an hour, putting a great distance between themselves and the hunter. Slowing to a walk, they panted and rested on the ground.

As the morning passed into the afternoon, I wrung my hands and said, "Please be alright. Please be careful. I'm over here across the water. I'm on another island."

Ren lifted his head as if he could hear me and flicked his ears back and forth. I leaned closer and spoke again, but he suddenly darted up and attacked something I couldn't see. I heard the sound of an alarmed squeal suddenly cut off, and he soon emerged from the brush carrying an animal in his jaws. He dropped a small adolescent boar on the ground, and he and Kishan began to eat.

I estimated their meal to be about fifty pounds—a mere snack considering the amount of energy they were using up. I was sure they were still starving. A few hours later, I was proved right. They'd found another trap, this one with a large haunch of deer hanging over it.

Both tigers circled the obvious pit and stared up at the meat, licking their chops. Kishan leapt completely over the pit, swatting the meat with his paw on the way, which caused it to swing wildly back and forth. Ren, meanwhile, began gnawing on the rope where it was tied to the tree. He used his claws to try to break it. Kishan joined him and added his teeth and claws until the rope frayed, and the heavy haunch of meat fell into the pit with a thunk.

The tigers peered over the edge, and Kishan crouched down to dip a paw experimentally down the side, feeling for a hold. He stretched a little farther and dropped down into the pit with the meat. Getting a good grip on it with his jaws, he stood on his hind legs and stretched his neck out so Ren could grab it. Ren batted with his paw until his claw snagged the rope. He yanked until he could catch it in his jaws with a snap. Dropping the prize onto the ground, he leaned over the edge of the pit to peer down at Kishan.

Kishan backed up as far as he could, then ran, and leapt up the side of the pit. His claws grabbed the edge, but he slipped back down. After three more unsuccessful tries, Ren nudged a nearby log into the pit with his head, and Kishan carefully made his way up. At the top his leg slipped, and he almost fell again, but Ren stretched out and bit into the ruff of Kishan's neck to hold him steady until he was safely out.

After they ate, they kept moving until it was dark again. They soon reached the beach on the western side of the island and ran along the wet sand for a time. Frantically, they searched for the hedge, but I knew they wouldn't find it.

When they bedded down for the night, Ren stood guard first. I had the mirror zoom in close to his face. His blue eyes stared straight ahead as if he was watching me. He sighed heavily, and his pink nose twitched. I watched him until I couldn't keep my eyes open anymore.

Early morning of the third day brought me another hot loaf of black bread and a small cauldron full of stew. The sun hadn't even risen yet, and as I ate, I settled by the mirror to watch the hunt's progress. The tigers were running along the beach, taking advantage of the darkness to move freely in the open. I searched for the hunter and found him just waking up near a burned-out fire. He held a cup of liquid in his hands and looked to one side, then the other, and secretly blew some fire into his cup to warm its contents.

"That's cheating," I shouted at the mirror. "You broke a rule!"

The dragon looked up and grinned. I heard laughter and his voice in my head. *It's just a warm drink, my dear. And the rule clearly states that I won't use my powers in the hunt. I'm not* hunting *yet this morning, so this doesn't count.*

I snorted and watched him finish his drink and shoulder his gun. He tracked the tigers all day, and he was good. He never missed a broken blade of grass or a depression, however obscure, in the ground. Unfortunately, the ocean didn't wash away the tigers' tracks along the beach, so they were easy to pick up and follow. When the dragon dipped into the jungle, he stopped suddenly, and we both heard the multiple roars of big cats fighting. He quickened his pace. I asked the mirror to hurry and show me the tigers.

At first I didn't know what I was looking at. It was a close-up of furry creatures rolling, and claws slashing. When I finally got the mirror to zoom out, I sucked in a breath as a shiver ran down my spine. Ren and Kishan were in a bloody battle with a large group of jaguars. Ren had told me that big cats don't usually hunt together, except for lions, so I was surprised at the large group of cats working together. One of the jaguars was lying on its side on the ground, dead. Ren and Kishan stood back-to-back and growled at the circling pack.

I counted six more jaguars on the ground, but there may have been more. It was hard to tell because they were constantly moving. It was eerie the way they moved. They paced back and forth as one, circling the tigers. Their eyes never left their prey. One darted in and slashed its claw across Kishan's face. He swiped back but missed as the lighter, more agile cat leapt out of the way. Two jumped at Ren, one from each side. He bit the leg of one, and it limped off, but the other one landed on his back, claws extended. It bit Ren's neck and locked on. Kishan turned around and knocked the cat away, but two more jumped on Kishan.

Ren bit one in the throat and shook the cat violently. Its neck snapped, and he tossed the body aside. They bit and clawed until the spotted cats slunk off to regroup. Ren and Kishan tried to lope away, but the jaguars quickly cut them off.

They must be really hungry, I thought. They seemed to be herding the striped cats toward some thick brush.

They started pacing, circling around the tigers again. A cat snarled and darted in but ran off before the tigers could get him. Another one did the same thing. They seemed to be playing with the tigers. A moment later, two cats leapt from an overhead tree onto Ren's and Kishan's backs. They bit and held. Ren was bleeding from his chest and shook hard to get the jaguar off his back. It wouldn't budge.

The other jaguars leapt into the fray and began biting. One bit Kishan's cheek, and another his back leg. Ren wasn't faring any better. The tigers were panting from the exertion, and even with their ability to heal, I worried. *The jaguars could still take bites out of them. How would they heal from that?* Ren roared, stood on his hind legs, and banged his back into a tree. The stunned jaguar released its grip and fell off. Ren was attacking the cat on Kishan's back when a shot rang through the jungle.

The dragon had caught up. A jaguar fell dead and dropped near Kishan's front paw. The jaguars disappeared like shadows back into the verdant jungle, while Ren and Kishan mustered the strength to run.

Shots rang out again and again as the hunter pursued the tigers. A bullet grazed the top of Ren's head, and I could hear his yelp of pain. He shook the blood out of his eyes and kept running. Another sank into Kishan's shoulder. He roared angrily and staggered, but continued on, though with a limp.

Then they decided to go on the offense. Ren leapt onto a large rock and into an overhead tree. Kishan exaggerated his limp to let Lùsèlóng catch up. The hunter followed Kishan's tracks but paused when Ren's suddenly disappeared. He paced back and forth, started down Kishan's trail and then went back to where Ren was last seen. He stopped and carefully studied the surrounding bushes. A wet drop hit his cheek. He touched it and drew back his finger. It was blood.

His eyes widened, and he looked up but it was too late. The five-hundred-plus-pound white tiger had leapt out of the tree, jaws gaping and claws extended toward the throat of the dragon. Behind him the black tiger had leapt into the air also. The hunter sucked in a breath and everything froze. He stepped gingerly away from the two tigers, who hung suspended in the air, less than a foot away from mangling the hunter.

I screamed, "That's cheating! They had you!"

Lùsèlóng ignored me and walked around both tigers curiously. "I congratulate you. No one has ever gotten the jump on me before."

"Lùsèlóng! You are breaking the rules!"

The dragon laughed and spoke in my mind. *It doesn't count. My rifle was down.*

I banged my fist against the mirror in frustration, but the dragon walked off several paces, aimed his rifle, and then snapped his fingers. The tigers hit each other and rolled in the dirt. They got up, shook the dust from their coats, and the hunter fired. The shot hit the dirt inches from Ren's head. Ren and Kishan quickly broke apart and scrambled into the trees.

Fortunately, they didn't hit any traps this time. Soon the shots and sounds of pursuit could no longer be heard. They only rested for short times and kept up their wearying pace for hours. They hit the beach on the eastern side of the island and searched back and forth, looking for the castle or the hedge.

"No. No. It's not there. I'm over here. Across the water!" I shouted to the mirror, but I knew they couldn't hear me. When night fell again, I wrapped a blanket around me and sat in front of the mirror. Lùsèlóng was still searching, but my tigers were safe for the moment. Kishan's eyes closed and soon, too exhausted to keep watch, Ren's eyes closed too. I watched them wearily for a long time, and then I walked up to the mirror and traced the outline of Ren's white furry ear.

"You're not going to make it. He's going to wear you out. The dragon cheats, and there's not enough food to sustain the two of you. Do you hear me, Ren?" I slapped the mirror on the side of his face. "You're going to die, and who am I going to argue with then? I'll be a dragon's consort on a nonexistent island, and you'll be dragon kibble."

A tear plopped on my cheek, and I touched the glass with my fingertip as if smoothing the fur of his brow. "It's not supposed to end this way, you know. I didn't get to say good-bye to you. To either of you. There are so many things we left unsaid." I sniffed and felt tears rolling down my face. "*Please* live. Please find me. I'm right here."

I placed my hand over my heart and felt its beat. I could feel my connection to him, the tether that bound my heart to his. If I closed my eyes and concentrated, I could feel the steady thump of his heart as he rested. I pressed both palms to the mirror on either side of his head and touched my forehead to the glass while I cried.

My eyes felt hot and my heart heavy. Then my heart started to burn. It filled me with warmth. I dashed the tears away from my eyes and looked at the mirror. Ren was awake. He'd lifted his head off his paws, and he was staring straight at me as if he could see me. Startled, I

pushed back from the mirror and gasped softly as I saw both of my hands were glowing. When I pulled them away from the glass, the red light faded.

Ren growled quietly and woke Kishan, then began moving. He walked out to the beach straight toward me and took a few steps into the water. He stared out into the dark waves. It was foggy, and I knew even he couldn't see the island in the dark. He lifted his head as if smelling the air, then, with a few great bounds, he leapt into the water. He started swimming forward. Kishan ran back and forth along the beach, not sure what Ren was doing, but eventually, he ran into the surf as well and started swimming alongside his brother.

They were coming. I clapped my hands to my mouth, sobbed in relief, and kept talking to the mirror, encouraging them to keep coming and to not give up. I pressed my hands against the glass again, but they didn't glow like before. I tried to shoot a flare as a beacon light, but my power was still gone. The only thing I could do was stay awake and watch them swim in the dark water, using all the power of my mind to will them forward.

Silently, I prayed, asking that there would be no dark sea monster to find them. No terrible storm to overwhelm them. They swam and swam and an hour later, dragged their weary bodies onto my island and dropped down onto the sand, exhausted. They slept the rest of the night while I kept my silent vigil over them.

They were still asleep when dawn approached. I saw the dragon find their resting place on the other island and follow their tracks to the beach. He stared out at the ocean for several minutes, and then rubbed his jaw and smiled. With a deep intake of breath, he exploded into his natural form and rose into the sky. The mirror turned black.

20

a princess, a dragon, and two knights

All was quiet, and I was so tired that I dozed off. Later, I was startled awake when I felt the tower shake and heard heavy footsteps. The hunter slammed open my door and strode in. He was not dressed in his hunting clothes but in the tunic and cloak of a fairy-tale prince. He watched me speculatively.

"What happens next?" I ventured. "Did they win the first part of the game?"

"They did. Though you cheated, *deti dama*."

"*I* cheated? How?"

"You signaled them somehow. You told them where to find you. There was no way they could have discovered this island on their own. I don't know how you did it, but I'll be watching you much more closely from now on. Obviously, I underestimated them. Now I'll have to make part two harder."

"Harder? You almost killed them!"

"Yes. *Almost*. They've ruined my track record now. They've won the battle, but I will win the war, I assure you. Still, *almost* has never happened with me before. I was right in believing this would be my best game. If you hadn't tricked me into limiting myself, I would have beaten them the first day."

"*Limiting* yourself! Ha! You cheated! Twice! Maybe more. I wasn't watching you the whole time, so you probably cheated the whole way through!"

"It's my game, not yours. If you don't understand the complexities of the rules, that's not my problem. Now before we start phase two, you should be properly attired, my dear."

"What do you mean?"

"I mean, if you're going to play the part of a princess, you have to look it." The dragon circled me, appraising my shape and coloring. "Ah, I have just the thing." He snapped his fingers, and I was enfolded in whispers of fabric. The room faded to white and then started to rematerialize. I looked down and gasped. My clothes had been replaced by a beautiful gown. I lifted one hand to touch the tight sleeve that ended at my wrist.

"No, there's something missing. Ah, I know. It's the hair. Your hair is entirely too short." I pulled a short curl to the front of my face and peered at it. He snapped his fingers, and I squeaked as the hair began to grow.

"Hey!"

He hummed as my hair kept growing and growing.

"Stop it!"

The hair was now past my waist, and he was busy checking his appearance in the mirror.

"Lùsèlóng!"

"What?" His eyes met mine in the mirror. "Oh." He snapped his fingers again and my hair stopped growing, but it was now just past my knees, and it was heavy. "There. Much better. You can watch in the mirror if you like. This part shouldn't take long at all."

"Wait!"

He spun in a circle and disappeared. The door slammed shut, and I was alone once again. I pounded angrily on the door, just because it felt good, and then walked over to the mirror to check on my tigers.

A stranger stared back at me. The dragon had not only dressed me, he'd done my makeup. A bold-eyed beauty was reflected there, and I poked my cheek several times to make sure I was the same person. He'd dressed me in a blush-pink gown that enhanced my dark eyes and hair. The dress had long tight-fitting sleeves with silver embroidery at the edges and was embellished with satin ribbon. An elegant neckline, trimmed in silver, swept just over my shoulders, leaving my neck bare.

Filmy organza tippets draped from armbands and a thick silver belt hung at my waist. The skirt was tiered in alternating silk and organza, and the bodice was adorned with silver embroidery to match the sleeve edges. Twisted silver and blush piping bordered the hemline of the skirt, and I wore dainty silver slippers. My long brown hair was shiny and fell in waves from a delicate silver headband with a long pink veil. I was a beautiful, pouty-looking princess who was extremely ticked off.

I ripped the veil off my head and sat on the bed, but then grunted in frustration as my head was wrenched back because I'd sat on my stupid hair. I yanked two ribbons from my sleeve, tore them off, and braided the mass into two long French braids. I said to the mirror, "Show me my tigers."

The mirror shimmered and zoomed in. The poor brothers were still sound asleep. The air moved, and suddenly Lùsèlóng was standing next to them. He cleared his throat, and the two tigers sprang to alertness and roared. The dragon snapped his fingers, and the tigers shifted to men. Ren and Kishan stood before him angry, filthy, and dangerous. They both took a step toward the dragon, who calmly examined his fingernails.

"I've decided this next part of the game will have different rules.

Instead of giving you your weapons here, you will have to fight for them. You will find them at different places in the maze, but to take them you must overcome the guardian who protects them. Some you may have to fight. Others you will have to outsmart. If you survive the maze, you will have to scale the castle walls, overcome me, and rescue your princess. And this time, no cheating. Now, let's make sure you look the part."

He snapped his fingers and the clothing changed on both of them. Kishan wore a brown leather doublet with a long-sleeved tunic, black breeches, tall polished riding boots, and a hooded black cloak. Ren wore a white shirt that pulled through the sleeves of a green velvet doublet edged in gold. He had black leggings and thigh-high boots. His full-length woolen cloak was trimmed with fur.

Apparently I am going to be rescued by either Robin Hood or Prince Charming.

The dragon considered both of them. "Excellent. Now I imagine you're hungry. You will find food in the maze as you travel and, this time," he slapped his palm lightly with a leather glove as he considered, "I think it would be best if you didn't travel together." He leaned closer and leered. "We don't want the challenge to be *too* easy now, do we?"

He laughed and snapped his fingers again. Everyone disappeared. I asked the mirror to show me Ren. He was standing at an opening to the maze. He looked up the hill toward the castle, but the dragon had caused a mist to cover it, so it would be harder to find. Ren set his jaw and entered the maze. When I had the mirror switch to Kishan, I found him already in the maze. He was jogging down a long section, then turned left and kept going.

By midday, Ren had stolen water and bread from an angry pack of dogs and won a sword and scabbard from a gnome he'd captured and hung upside down while holding his foot. The upset gnome kicked and screamed, but Ren refused to put him down until he gave him a prize. Kishan, meanwhile, had killed a boar by grabbing its tusks and twisting violently, breaking its neck. He won the Golden Fruit and had it create food. He ate and drank as he ran.

By evening, Ren had defeated an ogre and gotten Kishan's *chakram*, Kishan had won my bow and arrows in an archery contest, and they were about halfway through the maze. Ren settled down for the night, but Kishan continued on. He moved ahead quite a ways but guessed the wrong answer when a manticore asked him a question. The creature was red with the body of a lion, the face of an ogre, the tail of a scorpion, and the wings of a bat. Kishan defeated the manticore when it attacked but was sent back to the beginning of the maze. Kishan bellowed in frustration and started walking again. Finally, he stopped around midnight and slept.

Ren was attacked in the early morning while he was still sleeping. A gang of thugs surrounded him with nets and spears. He fought them off with the sword and then with his bare hands. As a man would fall incapacitated, he would shimmer and then disappear. Panting, Ren finished off the last man and was awarded a spectacular white horse with a silver saddle. He climbed up on the steed's back and pressed on through the maze.

Kishan was far behind now, and he'd chosen a different path than he had before. He won the *gada* by wrestling with a giant snake and the trident by killing a large vulture with a golden arrow. Ren used the *chakram* to cut off the heads of three female harpies who tried to lure him with spells and seductive promises. As his prize, the Divine Scarf was returned to him.

Kishan crossed a boiling stream by skipping across on stones. While he was mid-stream, a giant crocodile attacked. He had the Golden

Fruit fill its mouth with sticky peanut butter, and it disappeared under the water again. A few steps later, Kishan found his *kamandal* hanging from a tree. Placing it around his neck, he tucked it into his tunic, and moved on.

Kishan met with the newly revitalized manticore again, and this time he answered the question correctly. The manticore moved him ahead in the maze. He was close now. Much closer than Ren. Ren stopped when he came to a dead end. The maze was blocked by a brick wall. He turned the horse around and went another way and hit another brick wall. He was trapped. Large spiders started spilling out of the hedges, causing the white horse to stamp and rear.

Ren soothed the horse and at the same time he used the Divine Scarf to make a large net. It swept up all the spiders, catching them in a filmy web. He had the Scarf roll them into a giant spider-filled cotton ball, speared it with his sword, whipped it around his head a few times, and threw it into another part of the maze. The brick wall crumbled, and Ren maneuvered his horse carefully through the broken pieces.

After some time, he stopped at a stream of water that kept disappearing as he tried to drink. The horse was able to drink, but not Ren. He stood there thinking for a while, changed to a tiger and drank his fill, and then changed back to a man. Using the Scarf, he made a water bag and filled it to take with him. His princely clothing stayed with him when he changed back. Ren and Kishan slept unmolested that night, making their beds on the soft grass of the maze.

The challenges came so often and were so difficult that I was in a constant state of horror. I'd just see one man safe and breathe a sigh of relief when the other one would be in danger. I sat on the bed glued to the mirror, thinking that if I left for one minute, I'd return to find one of them dead or horribly injured. They'd both assured me they couldn't die, but I wasn't entirely sure of that. What if something cut off their heads? Or poisoned them? Ren had scratched the bullet out of Kishan's shoulder with a claw, a gory process that I had to turn away from. Kishan had healed, but what if the bullet had gone deeper? Blocked an artery? I tried to rest when they did, but I'd wake with a start every time I heard a noise.

Early the next morning, Kishan burst through the maze and found a black horse waiting for him. The mists cleared momentarily, so he could see the castle. He mounted his horse and rode hard, urging his steed to a gallop. Ren met a giant salamander that spat poison. Using his sword, he cut off its head, and watched the dead creature reform itself. It shrank and turned golden—it became Fanindra. Ren knelt and held out his hand. The cobra wound around his forearm and hardened into her jewelry form.

He next met a man made entirely of bronze and fought him for several minutes without making any headway. The sword bounced off his skin in a shower of sparks, and the *chakram* couldn't penetrate the bronze torso either. It banged off of him like a knife caught in the garbage disposal. The threads of the Scarf couldn't hold him. Fanindra came alive and snagged her body over a low tree limb while Ren fought.

She lengthened and wound down and stealthily moved into a position behind the bronze man. Then, when the opportunity presented itself, she bit him just behind his knee. The man staggered, grunted, and fell over, dead. When Ren examined the body, I could see through the mirror that Fanindra had bitten him on a tiny patch of white skin where the man had been vulnerable. Ren's reward was food. He gave the apples to the horse, patted its head, and ate the bread. After thanking Fanindra and sliding her up his arm, he leapt onto the horse and rode out of the maze.

Kishan had reached the castle walls now and, from his perspective,

they soared upward forever. He twisted the trident and shot a series of spears into the wall. The golden darts sunk deeply into the stone. He stepped on one, testing its strength, and found it could hold his weight. He climbed up the dozen darts, shot more into the rock, and kept climbing.

Ren raced toward the castle but became lost in the dragon-made mist. Fortunately, Fanindra came alive again and moved her head in the direction she wanted him to go. When he made it to the far side of the castle, he leapt down from the horse, and used the *chakram* and the Scarf. He created a sturdy rope, wrapped it around the *chakram*, and took several steps back. Ren whirled in a circle and threw the *chakram* with all his might toward the top of the castle. When the *chakram* spun back to him, he yanked on the rope and, finding it stable, tied off the end to a tree and began scaling the wall.

At the same time, Kishan made it to the top. He ran along the battlement until he found a bridge. I asked the mirror to show me the dragon. Lùsèlóng was standing on the uppermost turret of the keep. Pressing his hands on the stone wall, he leaned over so he could see the brothers' progress below. He smiled as if anticipating the battle and ran a thumb across his bottom lip.

Snapping his fingers, he disappeared for several seconds and then reappeared in dragon form. Wrapping its lithe body around a nearby drum tower, it waited for Kishan and Ren. Kishan ran down the stone bridge and entered the keep. When he crossed the threshold, his princely costume disappeared and instead he wore a suit of black armor. He also held a golden shield with a black tiger emblazoned on it and carried a long spear. Without missing a step, he charged forward.

Ren lowered himself using the rope and dropped into the bailey. Before entering the keep, he took Fanindra off his arm and said, "Find her, Fanindra." The snake obediently came to life and slithered into the castle's darkness. When he stepped into the castle, the same thing happened to him: his clothes shimmered and changed into a suit of armor. He pulled a heavy broadsword from the scabbard at his side and picked up his shield. His symbol was the white tiger on a blue background and his armor was silver. A white cloak hung down his back.

Instead of charging ahead like Kishan though, he trailed after Fanindra. Encouraging her to continue, he followed the snake through many doors and passageways until he came to a set of stairs. I heard him call.

"Kelsey? Are you up there?"

I gasped. The call came not from the mirror but from outside my room. "Ren? Ren!" I ran to the door and pounded. "I'm here! I'm up here!"

"I'm coming!"

He started up the stairs, and I heard a voice in my head. *Tch, tch, tch. Now what did we say about cheating? Hmm? Did you forget you are supposed to slay the dragon* before *you rescue the princess? Just for that, you get a time out.*

Ren shouted, "Kel—" then the sound of his voice was suddenly cut off. I hurried back to the mirror to see what had happened. Fanindra slithered under my door and curled up in a resting position. I picked her up and put her on the dresser. Ren had disappeared from the stairs and was now tied with chains to a pillar near the dragon. Kishan ran up to the roof and stopped, shocked to see Ren there. He started toward him but was cut off by a blast of fire. *Up here, black knight. Your brother will join us in good time.*

Kishan turned, screamed out a battle cry, and lunged toward the dragon with spear raised.

The dragon knocked him down with a blow of his tail and laughed. *Is that the best you can do?*

Kishan whispered some words and suddenly the drum tower was covered in hot oil. The dragon slid off awkwardly and banged its head against the parapets, causing the tower to shake. A massive chunk of broken stone broke and dropped hundreds of feet below.

Kishan didn't wait. He raised his spear and heaved it powerfully at the green dragon. It glanced off a scaly side, but not without leaving a bloody wound behind. The dragon roared and blasted Kishan with bright reddish-orange fire that rushed toward him in a plume of heat.

Kishan brought his shield up just in time to protect himself, but the edges became soft and started to melt. The flames jumped to the pooling oil, and the drum tower burst into flame. Ren ran past Kishan and threw himself on top of the dragon. I wasn't sure how he'd gotten free. I guessed he'd either used the *chakram* to file through the chains holding him, or the dragon had released him from the penalty box.

The dragon bucked and heaved trying to dislodge Ren, but he clung tenaciously, distracting Lùsèlóng long enough that Kishan could retrieve his spear and thrust it into the side of the dragon. At the same time, Ren lifted his sword over his head and drove it into the dragon's back. Lùsèlóng screamed, piercing the air with the sound of twenty angry pterodactyls and slammed both of them against the parapet. Another piece of stone wall broke off near Kishan, who fell over the side. He yelled and gripped the crumbling edge with just his fingertips.

Ren leaned over and grabbed Kishan's hand, but before he could pull him up, the dragon turned its head and closed on the now-vulnerable Ren. It seized Ren in its jaws and lifted both him and Kishan into the air.

Lùsèlóng shook Ren and crunched on his armor with its powerful jaws. As Ren groaned in pain, he let go of Kishan who dropped to safety on the top of the drum tower. After crushing Ren's armor terribly, the dragon opened its mouth and tossed Ren to the stone roof of the next building. Ren fell with a crash and lay immobile, looking like a large can of tuna run over by a semitruck.

Kishan yelled and attacked the dragon with a vengeance using every weapon at his disposal. He launched a multi-angled assault using the Scarf, the Fruit, the *chakram*, and Ren's dropped sword.

The dragon beat him back with claws, tail, teeth, and flame until he was battered, bruised, and breathless. I knew he couldn't last much longer. Ren was still out of commission, and Kishan was hurt. Even he couldn't heal this fast. Kishan yanked off his helmet. Blood trickled down a sweaty cheek, and he was limping badly. He wiped his mouth with the back of his hand and bent over, panting.

The dragon smiled. *It's just a matter of time, you know. I've defeated your brother, and now I'll beat you. You can't possibly outlast me. You can barely stand.*

"I'm just catching my second wind. Shall we continue?"

You could just admit defeat now. I may even allow you to live on the other island. I'd hunt you, of course, but you would at least be alive.

"I'm not interested in being your pet tiger."

Very well.

The dragon sucked in a deep breath and blasted fire over the tower. Kishan staggered and ran, but the fire followed. He jumped and pulled himself up a wall, armor and all, using just the strength of his arms. He dropped over the side to land one level up from the dragon and lay there gasping for breath. Tearing off his smoking gloves, he reached for a weapon but found they all lay on the rooftop below. The dragon sniggered and wound around the turret.

Do you have any last words before I eat you?

"Sure." Kishan circled the turret to stay out of the dragon's range. "I hope you choke."

He leapt off the turret to the stone below, and the dragon bellowed and followed after him, jaws wide open. Kishan hit the rooftop and rolled but slammed his head against a broken stone. I heard a roar of triumph from Lùsèlóng as he descended, prepared to snap up Kishan in its jaws. Suddenly, it screamed, stopped in midair, and fell with a deafening crash next to Kishan. Nothing moved for a moment, and I sat on the bed with my hand over my mouth. Then something stirred near the turret.

A figure staggered away from the dragon's body and headed toward Kishan. It was Ren. His breastplate and helmet were gone. A long bloody gash across his chest had just started healing. I asked the mirror to show me the other side of the dragon. Ren had run the dragon through the heart with the spear. Not even I had seen Ren leap back to the tower, creep up, and hide in the shadows of the turret. Ignoring him had been the dragon's fatal error.

Ren unbuckled and threw off the rest of his armor, and then knelt to take off Kishan's. Kishan was alive. He moaned and blinked open his eyes.

"It's over," Ren said. "The dragon is defeated."

The body of the dragon shimmered and disappeared.

"Come on, I know where she is."

He helped Kishan stand, and then the two brothers, leaning heavily on each other, made their way down the tower and through the keep until Ren found the stairs leading to my lonely tower on the other side of the castle. They started up the steps but Kishan couldn't lift his feet after the first step.

I heard the dragon's voice. *Only the winner may claim the prize.*

Kishan braced his back against the stair wall and panted heavily. He nodded, indicating that Ren should go ahead. Ren turned and hurried up the long circular stairway. He twisted the handle, but the door wouldn't open.

"Kells? Can you hear me?"

"Yes! I'm here. It's locked. I can't open it."

"Stand back."

He took a few steps and slammed into the door. It wouldn't budge. Again and again he threw himself against it, but it still wouldn't open.

The dragon laughed. *It's not my doing, tiger. She is the one keeping you out.*

"What do you mean?" I hollered.

You aren't letting him in.

"Of course, I am!"

You aren't. The hero wins the prize, and you are a prize who doesn't want to be won, deti dama. *If you want him to save you, open the door.*

"I can't!"

I don't mean the door to the room, the dragon spoke in my mind, *I mean the door to your heart.*

"What are you *talking* about? Why are you doing this?" I sobbed.

I heard Ren's concern through the door. "Kelsey? Are you okay?"

The dragon's voice pierced through me. *Let . . . him . . . in.*

I suddenly understood. I knew what he meant, and the knowledge made me tremble. He wanted me to feel all the things that I'd been ignoring. He wanted me to unleash all of the pent-up emotions and suffering. I banged a fist softly against the wooden door, cried, and pleaded quietly with the dragon, "Don't make me do this. Please leave things as they are."

That's not how the game is played.

I can't allow myself to feel those things. It hurts, I responded mentally.

Hurt is a part of life. Now get on with it.

I dashed away my tears and pressed my hands against the door. Resting my forehead on the wood, I closed my eyes. The dragon laughed, and I felt its delight in my despondency. I'd purposely closed off the powerful connection I felt with Ren. Shutting it off like a valve, I'd done

my best to block out my feelings for him. The faucet was leaky, but I plugged up the holes the best I could and tried to shunt my emotions, redirecting the flow to other places.

As I stood there quaking, I realized that blocking my feelings was my modus operandi. I'd done it when my parents died. I'd done it when I left Ren. I'd done it when he was taken. *I can't risk it, dragon. He'll leave me again.*

Lùsèlóng replied, *Without risk, there is no reward. Would you rather stay here with me for an eternity?*

No. At that moment, I realized I was a coward. And I knew I had no choice but to press forward. *How do I start?*

Travel along your connection to his heart.

The green dragon led me. My mind summoned a vision. I stood in a white foggy mist. Lost, I turned in circles, searching for something. The dragon called to me, and I walked blindly forward, following its voice. The fog swirled around my feet, and the ground was unsteady. Then something golden appeared in the mist, a bright rope that crackled with energy.

Now put your hands on the tether, and follow it to its source.

I obeyed the dragon, grabbed onto the golden rope, and walked alongside it. Once on the journey, I hesitated and almost turned back. I heard a warm voice speak in my mind. *Please don't let go. I can't lose you again.*

The pleading in the voice moved me, and I clutched the rope as I walked. Forgotten feelings and memories rushed into my vision. The mists started to fade as my mind replayed tender moments Ren and I had shared—our first kiss, dancing on Valentine's Day, how he held me after a nightmare. The farther I walked, the more my heart opened. But letting in those happy memories also brought the evil doppelganger of pain and hurt.

My feet dragged as if I was stuck in quicksand. When I hesitated and moved a step back, the fog rose up and numbed me again. It would have been so easy to turn back, to block my feelings, but I knew I had to trudge ahead, despite the fact that each step brought more agony. Each movement forward increased the stabbing pain of betrayal, of loss, of tender first love spurned, of being left alone.

Dark fingers of jealousy, bitterness, and confusion grasped at me and tried to pull me away from the tether, but I clung to it. I could feel the pulse running through it. It was powerful, good, and . . . joyful. Something changed for me on that journey. I realized that I wasn't alone. I couldn't see who was ahead, but someone was calling out to me. Every so often a warm wind would caress my skin, and a soft voice would encourage me to press on. I knew that whoever it was loved me. Suddenly, I came to the end of the rail and stopped, confused.

Where am I?

A voice behind me spoke. "You're here with me."

I turned around and faced a smiling Ren. He held out his arms and, with a whimper, I melted into them and pressed my cheek against his chest. He held me so close that I felt I was a part of him.

"Why was it so hard for you to find me, *iadala*?"

"You left me. I had to let you go."

"I *never* left you. I have a place for you in my heart always." Ren lifted my chin with his finger. "But what about you? Do you feel differently now? Do you wish for me to let *you* go?"

I hesitated for only a brief second. My eyes filled with tears, and I held him tightly. "No. I don't want you to let me go. Not now. Not *ever*."

He held me and murmured words in his native language, soothing me. I felt safe here. Protected and loved. I'd turned the valve, and it was too late to turn it back now. The liquid drops of hurt, hope, betrayal, devotion, anguish, and love rushed through my hands, seeped through my fingers. My heart bled.

Desperately, I tried to stem the tide, to maintain control, but

stopping it now was no use. I cried, and once the tears started, I couldn't hold them back. I began to speak, telling him of my deepest, darkest fears. I described how it felt to be without him. How much it hurt to see him with another. Ren stroked my back and listened patiently and unguardedly. I sniffled wetly as I continued my confession.

"It hurt when you forgot me and when you pushed me away. I couldn't bear to watch you go. You *left* me, like my parents did. I had to shut off a part of myself to survive. Without you, I shriveled and became only a shadow of myself. I felt . . . jumbled, like broken words on a page. A poem hacked to pieces. Nothing made sense. How could you do that to me? To *us*?" I accused.

"Don't you know that I would do anything to keep you safe?" Ren argued. "I had to love you enough to let you go. It was the hardest thing I've ever had to do, and I don't intend to ever do it again. Even so, my heart always belonged to you. Surely you still felt that."

"Yes, but I buried my feelings for you so deeply that I don't even know if I can revive them," I admitted. "My strength comes from them; I can at least admit that. It's obvious that I need you. That I want you. My body burns with a golden flame when you touch me. But I can't trust you anymore. I don't want to push you away, but I'm frightened. I love you so much, I'm afraid you'll destroy me."

Ren pressed his cheek against mine and said, "For many, love is a two-sided coin. It can strengthen or stifle, expand or enfeeble, enrich or pauperize. When love is returned, we soar. We are taken to heights unseen, where it delights, invigorates, and beautifies. When love is spurned, we feel crippled, disconsolate, and bereaved. I *have* always and *will* always love you, Kelsey. Nothing on Earth or in the heavens can change that fact. Polish the coin, and you will see only requited love on both sides. I was destined to love you, and I will belong to you forever."

I took a step back and looked up. My blue-eyed prince stroked my cheek and wiped away a tear with his finger.

"How can you be so sure of all this? Of me?" I asked. "We've suffered so much in trying to be together. Maybe destiny wants to keep us apart. Maybe that would be easier."

Ren smiled and cupped my face between his hands. Sighing, he traced my bottom lip with a thumb. "If, at the end of this, I get to be with you, it all will have been worth it. 'Only a man who has felt ultimate despair is capable of feeling ultimate bliss.'"

I sniffed and smiled. "Who said that?"

"Alexandre Dumas, who wrote *The Count of Monte Cristo*. We were going to read it together, remember?"

"We've been a little busy."

"Yes, we have, *rajkumari*." He sighed and pressed his lips to my palm. "My ultimate despair was being without you. Am I without you still? Or do you belong to me as I belong to you? Do you still love me, *priyatama*?" My dream Ren trailed his fingers down my hair and tilted my chin so I looked at his handsome face.

Because I was pretty sure this was all a dream, I felt comfortable admitting things I would have held back from the real Ren. I closed my eyes and nodded. "I've always been yours. I never stopped loving you."

Ren caressed my cheek until I opened my eyes. He smiled and said, "Then I'll never let you go," and captured my lips with his. He held me tenderly, and I felt the barrier of protection in my heart dissolve completely. Now I was defenseless. My heart was completely exposed and vulnerable—a nice, meaty organ ready for crushing, cutting, or just plain old consumption.

I heard the click of a lock and felt the slight breeze of a door opening and closing, but it seemed far away and unimportant. I surrendered my newly opened heart to my prince and felt enfolded and warm and

cherished. Ren loved me. This was where I belonged. If I could have just stayed there forever in that golden world and forgotten about everything else, I would have, but I didn't get my wish.

The fog rose and enveloped us. The vision disappeared, but the awareness didn't. I felt real arms holding me, cradling me, and real lips molding to mine. Enfolded in Ren's mellow warmth, I kissed him endlessly. I whispered of how I loved him and how I'd missed him. We were locked in a golden glow as we spoke softly, and touched, and kissed. I held him tenderly and pressed his hands to my lips. He murmured endearments that I felt more than understood.

Then I was startled out of my romantic haze when I heard the door slam open. I blinked and found myself looking into a pair of golden eyes burning with jealousy.

storm

In my mind I heard Lùsèlóng laugh, and though Kishan quickly masked his emotions, I knew he was upset. With flaming cheeks, I stepped away from Ren and stood between the brothers. Both of them looked at me. Turning away to hide my face didn't help because I could still feel the prickles of two sets of eyes burning holes into my back. No one said anything, and the laughing voice in my mind became a physical laugh behind us. The green dragon was sitting casually on a windowsill in his human form. He was dressed like a prince again.

"You all have provided me a most diverting game, one I will think upon fondly for many millennia to come. Are you sure you don't wish to stay here with me a bit longer?"

"No," I replied. "We wish to return to our ship."

Kishan stepped forward. "We won. We'll take our prizes and go, dragon."

Lùsèlóng frowned. "I don't remember offering more than one prize."

"You said you would help us find Durga's Necklace if we played. You're the one who insisted on an extra prize in the game," Ren said. "I win the girl, and Kishan wins your aid."

Kishan narrowed his eyes at Ren, but said, "Fine. Let's get this over with."

"Perhaps we can bargain. If one of the tigers agrees to stay, I will give you the girl *and* help you find my brother, the golden dragon."

"*No!*" I shouted in disbelief. "You *cheated* in the hunt. It's too late to change the rules to suit your pleasure."

"Alright!" The dragon snorted and spurts of orange flame shot out of his human nostrils. "You take the girl," he said to Ren. Turning to Kishan, he said, "And you take *this*." He shot out a hand and a ball of fire burst from his palm, zoomed toward Kishan, and hit him in the face. He screamed and covered his eyes.

I cried out in alarm. "What did you do to him?" I ran to Kishan and put an arm around his bent frame.

The dragon studied his fingernails. "Nothing much. He'll be blind for a while, but it's only temporary. It is what you wanted after all."

"We didn't want you to hurt him," I accused.

"What do you care? If anyone has hurt him today, I would say you are more at fault than I. Now I'm bored with you. It's time for you to leave."

The dragon snapped his fingers, and the three of us suddenly stood on the beach of the other island alone. The boat was nearby, and we could see the yacht anchored on the ocean. Ren scrambled to untie the boat while I put my hands on the sides of Kishan's face and asked, "Can you open your eyes?"

"Yes. But it stings."

"Then don't worry about it now." I ripped the sash from my dress and tied it around his eyes. "Keep them closed. Let's get you back to the ship. Just hold onto me. Alright?"

He nodded and put an arm around my shoulder. I wrapped my arms around his waist and slowly guided him back to the boat. Ren helped steady Kishan as he climbed aboard, and I sat with Kishan and held his hands while Ren drove us back. The three of us were quiet as we headed for the ship.

When we arrived, Ren took care of getting the jet boat stowed away while Nilima and Mr. Kadam helped me with Kishan.

After we took him to his room and sat him in a chair, Mr. Kadam asked quietly, "What happened, Miss Kelsey?" To his credit, he gave our strange apparel and my exceptionally long hair only a cursory glance.

"The dragon blinded him. He said it was only temporary and acted as if that's what we'd wanted him to do."

Mr. Kadam nodded. "Very well." He patted Kishan's forearm. "There now, son, let me take a look." He gently unwrapped the sash covering Kishan's eyes and asked him to open them slowly.

Kishan blinked his eyes open a few times, and they began to tear. I gasped involuntarily when I saw that his once beautiful golden eyes were now completely black and, as we watched, small flames began to dance and build in them. He blinked again, and the flames disappeared. I covered my mouth to choke back a sob.

"What?" He turned his head toward me. "What is it, Kelsey? Don't weep."

I cleared my throat, dashed my thumbs over my cheeks, and knelt beside him, taking his hands in mine. "It's nothing. Just stress. Do you want anything? Are you hungry?"

"I could use a little something." He took my hand. "Will you stay with me though?"

"Of course."

Nilima rose. "I will get the Fruit."

"Does it hurt?" Mr. Kadam asked.

Kishan shook his head. "Not anymore. It's odd not being able to see anything, but there's no pain."

"Good. I will have Nilima get us under way, and then I will do some research on this. Perhaps it would be wise for all of you to rest. You will stay with him, Miss Kelsey?"

"Yes."

"Make sure he eats, rests, and drinks plenty of liquid. He feels a bit warm to me." Mr. Kadam smiled. "Well, warmer than usual, I mean."

I nodded. "I'll take good care of him."

"I'm sure you will. Notify me immediately if his situation changes."

Mr. Kadam left, and Nilima returned with the Fruit. Kishan said he was tired and would eat later, but I managed to get him to drink a glass of apple juice while I tugged off his boots. He pulled the doublet and tunic over his head, and I drew the covers over him but he shoved the blankets off and searched for my hand.

He wanted me near him, so I sat against the headboard and put a pillow in my lap. He lay down on the pillow and I covered him with his blanket and stroked his hair. Kishan wrapped an arm around my waist as I hummed a lullaby my mother used to sing. Finally, the lids closed over his fiery eyes, and he slept at last.

Quietly studying his handsome face, I stroked his brow and listened to his rhythmic breathing. Hearing a noise, I looked up. Ren stood in the door, watching me with a sober expression. He didn't say anything. Kishan shifted in his sleep, moved the pillow, and cushioned his head on my thigh instead. I adjusted the quilt over his shoulders, and he settled again.

When I looked up, Ren was gone. I held Kishan for another hour, spending the time thinking about what had happened. When I tried to leave, Kishan reached out in his sleep, pulled my arm across his chest, and held on to me. Eventually, I slept too, overcome by the experience of the green dragon's island.

I woke with stiff, sore muscles some hours later and managed to maneuver myself away from the heavy sleeping form of Kishan. Still wearing my princess dress, I headed through the connecting door to my own room, showered, and changed. Shampooing through my

knee-length hair took a long time, but brushing through it took even longer. I dressed, checked on Kishan, and grabbing a pair of scissors, went in search of Nilima.

I found her and Mr. Kadam in the wheelhouse. As Nilima prepared to shear my overly long locks, Mr. Kadam told me about the research he'd done on blindness and mythology.

"One of the Pleiades named Merope had a son named Glaucus who was blind. The term *glaukos* means "bluish green or gray," and from that word, we get *glaucoma*. Meropia is a physical condition of partial blindness. Another Greek oracle, Tiresisas, was blinded by the gods for either seeing them or disclosing their secrets. The three sisters, sometimes called the three spinners of destiny, or the Moirae, shared an eye among them—an all-seeing eye, it was called."

"I remember them. Hold on a second. Nilima," I pulled a lock of my now waist-length hair over my shoulder and frowned at it. "I think I want it shorter than that."

"I'm sorry, Miss Kelsey. I was given specific instructions to cut it no shorter than waist length."

"Oh, *really*?"

"Yes. Ren threatened to fire me, and technically, he has the right."

"He won't fire you. He's bluffing."

"Still, he seemed very serious."

"Fine. I'll just cut it myself later."

"*No, you won't.*" I turned at the sound of the threatening male voice. Ren leaned against the doorway with his arms folded across his chest. "I'll throw all the scissors into the ocean."

"Go ahead. I'll figure something else out. Maybe I'll use the *chakram*. You wouldn't dare throw that into the sea."

"Try it. You'll have to deal with the consequences, and you *won't* like them."

I frowned at the stubborn expression on his face until Nilima turned my head and began snipping again.

"Shall I go on?" Mr. Kadam asked.

"Please," I said, tight-lipped.

"There's also Phineas, who was punished for revealing too much about the gods. He was blinded and put on an island with a buffet full of food he could never touch."

"I remember him," I said. "Jason and the Argonauts saved him. They fought the harpies so he could eat, and then he told them how to get through the Clashing Rocks at Bosphorus."

"Correct. Polyphemus was the cannibalistic Cyclops blinded by Odysseus. I can't see a connection with that story, but I thought I'd mention it. Then there was Oedipus, who took his own eyes after discovering he'd fulfilled the words of the oracle in marrying his own mother. He found her dead after she committed suicide and gouged out his eyes with pins."

Acerbically, Ren said, "Perhaps taking a woman belonging to another would apply."

"First of all, *Mr. Subtle*, Kishan didn't *take* me anywhere I wasn't willing to go. Secondly, I don't believe *Laius* told his wife to get lost. And thirdly, I don't think the story of Oedipus has anything to do with this!" I spat hotly. "The *obvious* theme here, which you could figure out if you could control the green-eyed monster currently inhabiting your body, is prophecies and oracles."

Mr. Kadam cleared his throat uncomfortably. "I would tend to agree with you, Miss Kelsey."

I smirked at Ren, who sighed deeply and said, "So you think Kishan is supposed to become some kind of an oracle? That he'll lead us to the fourth dragon?"

"Only time will tell." Mr. Kadam rose. "Perhaps I will go check on him now."

"He was sleeping when I left," I added as he made a hasty exit.

Ren accused, "Yes. You've been the best of nursemaids. Offering him the softest of pillows to rest his weary head on."

"Umm . . . perhaps I will go with Grandfather," Nilima said. She set down the scissors, looked at my expression, and then changed her mind and took them with her. She quickly slid between Ren and the door, making her escape.

I pulled a rubber band out of my pocket and began braiding my hair. "Has anyone ever told you, you sound petty when you're jealous?"

"Do you think I care what I sound like?"

"Obviously you don't."

"You're right. I don't. And yes, I'll admit, I *am* jealous. I'm jealous of every minute you spend with him, of every concerned expression you send his way, of every tear shed, of every glance, every touch, and every *thought*. I want to rip him to pieces and purge him from your mind and from your heart. But I can't."

I swiveled in the chair, stood, and tossed my braid over my shoulder. "Kishan needs me right now, and I'm sorry if you can't accept that."

He took a step closer. "*Kishan* isn't the *only* one who needs you, Kelsey."

I sucked in a breath. "Maybe not. But his need is more immediate."

"For now. But the fuse is lit. You can run all you want to, but you leave a trail of gunpowder in your wake. There's going to be a reckoning eventually." He took another step forward and cupped my chin, tilting my head up until I looked in his eyes. "You should know that I was there in the dragon's lair too. I was in that foggy dream world with you. I heard your secret confessions. I *know* the innermost feelings of your heart. You will never belong to him. You belong to me, and it's about time you came to terms with that."

I bit my lip and stewed. He had a point, but I was irritated. "It's very bold to assume that I *belong* to you. I'm not some slave girl or

some bartered bride you can buy from her father. There's no contract governing my affections. I make my own decisions. I'm my own person, and I belong to who I *want* to belong to, for as *long* as I want to. Don't ever presume that you have the right to do with me what you will. Just because you're a *prince*, doesn't make *me* your subject. So get off your high and mighty horse, your *highness*, and find some other girl to intimidate into submission."

We stood toe-to-toe and nose-to-nose. I was breathing hard. His eyes narrowed and then darted down to my lips. He smiled dangerously.

"'Teach not thy lip such scorn, for it was made for kissing, lady, not for such contempt.'"

I was about to protest when he yanked me against him and crushed his lips against mine. I ineffectually pushed against his chest as his lips bruised my mouth. He held me in an inescapable grip. He found my hands and trapped them at my sides so I couldn't flail against him any longer. I tried to kick him, but he adjusted his stance so I had no leverage. He bit my lip softly, and then instead of trying to escape, I moaned and kissed him back feverishly. He took my braid in his hand, wrapped it several times around his wrist, and yanked my head back to deepen the kiss. It hurt but in a *very . . . good . . . way.*

When he finally raised his head, he smirked.

I gasped for air and narrowed my eyes. "If you even *think* of saying that was enlightening, I'm going to blast you overboard."

He ran his fingertips gently over my swollen bottom lip, smiled, and nudged me toward the door. "Go. Take care of Kishan."

Confused, I stepped through the door.

"And, Kelsey—"

I turned. "What?" I asked impatiently.

"I'm serious about the hair."

I screeched in disgust and stomped off, ignoring his soft laugh. I

muttered all the way down the stairs. *Imperious, smug, too-enticing-for-his-own-good alley cat! Thinks he can put his paws all over me. Strong-arm me to get what he wants.* I rubbed my hands up and down my arms where I could still feel the pressure of his grip and ran a finger across a still-tingling lip. *Bully. Might as well throw me over his shoulder and make off with me like some pirate stealing a wench.*

I suddenly imagined a long-haired Ren dressed as a swashbuckler—tall black boots, a white shirt with laces open at the throat, and a red cape. He'd be brandishing a sword and stalking slowly toward me, pinning me against the railing. While I'd be helpless, in a torn gown, with a heaving bosom and . . . *sheesh! Obviously I've read too many of Mom's romance novels.* I shook my head to clear my thoughts and was scowling when I entered Kishan's room.

"Kells? Is that you?"

I sighed and slapped a smile on my face though he couldn't see it. "Yes. It's me. How are you feeling?"

"Better."

Nilima sat next to him. "He wouldn't eat until you came," she said.

"He's a pretty stubborn cat. Okay. I'm here now. What's on the menu?"

"Soup."

"Soup? You never eat soup. What's the special occasion?"

Kishan grinned. "You hand-feeding me is the special occasion. I'm just helpless without you."

"Uh huh," I laughed. "I'll bet. You're going to milk this for all it's worth, aren't you?"

He sat back and put his hands behind his head. "You know it. How often does a guy get to be served by a beautiful girl who feels great empathy for him and would do almost anything to help him feel better?"

"*Almost* being the key word there. And as for beauty, your judgment is impaired."

He reached for my hand. When I put it in his outstretched one, he tentatively ran his up my arm until he touched my cheek. "You're always beautiful."

"Flattery won't keep me from spilling your dinner into your lap. Fine. I'll spoon-feed you, but not soup. You need something heartier. How about stew and grilled cheese?"

"Sounds good."

Nilima winked at me and left as I used the Fruit to make his meal. Between bites of potato, carrot, and roasted lamb, he asked, "Are we under way yet?"

"We're away from the island, but we haven't figured out where to go."

He grunted and sipped from the cup I held for him.

"Did Mr. Kadam come down to talk with you?" I asked.

"Yes. He told me all about the theory that I will be an oracle of some kind. I don't feel any different though."

"Hmm. Well, until we know where to go, I guess we'll just stay where we are." I set down the empty bowl and dabbed his lip with a napkin.

He took my hand, pulled me onto his lap, and wrapped his arms around me. "I just wanted to tell you, it's *okay*, Kells."

"What's okay?" I mumbled in his shirt.

"We are. I mean, I'm not mad. If I was in Ren's shoes, I would have tried to kiss you too. It's not your fault."

"*Oh*. Well . . . that's not exactly—"

"Shh. It doesn't matter. You don't have to tell me. The important thing is . . . you're with me now."

"I really think we need to talk about what happened at some point."

"We will, but let's just focus on Durga's Necklace for now. Everything's

going to work out okay. I feel it." He smiled. "Hey, maybe that oracle thing's starting to work for me."

"Oh, yeah?" I laughed quietly. "Well, it looks good on you."

"Thank you." He ran a hand up my back and kneaded my shoulder.

I let out a pent-up breath and let him rub my shoulders for a while. "Have I told you lately that you're just too good for me?"

He laughed and said nothing but pressed a kiss on my forehead and stared at the wall with his black eyes. I rested against him and wrapped an arm around his waist.

I spent the rest of the day with Kishan, taking care of him. We walked the deck, I read to him, and even fed him grapes as he teased me about being his harem girl, but we didn't speak about the green dragon's island. I also avoided looking into his black eyes because I feared that if he looked closer he would see into my soul and find out that my heart had betrayed him.

I felt immensely guilty over my relationship with both brothers. Ren knew how to push my buttons well enough that I could shove the feelings to the back of my mind, but Kishan was so patient and sweet, the guilt rose up until my heart was swallowed in billows as black as his sightless orbs. That evening I told him the stories of the blind oracles and began to cry quietly, but he just held me and wiped away the tears until I fell asleep.

When I awoke, Ren was carrying me to my own room.

At first, I snuggled against him, felt him press his lips against my cheek, and all was right with the world. Then I became semiconscious. "What are you doing?" I hissed.

"There is *no* need for you to be sleeping in his room. I'll watch over him tonight, and *you* can sleep in your own bed."

"Put me down," I whispered angrily. "You're not in charge of my life.

Kishan happens to be my boyfriend, and he's sick. If I want to stay in his room, I will."

"*You . . . will . . . not.*"

He kissed me briefly and hard and dropped me on the bed. I started to get up but he turned around, crossed his arms, and gave me a look that made me freeze.

"Kelsey . . . if you get out of that bed I will have to do something drastic, and you won't like it. So *don't* tempt me."

He shut the door softly behind him, and I threw a pillow at it just to make a point. I stewed for an hour until I was finally able to drift off again, this time with a smile on my face as I imagined using the Scarf to dangle Ren in front of the kraken, but then in my dream *I* became the kraken and wrapped my tentacles around him, pulled him into my eternal purple embrace, and stole away with him to a murky cavern in the depths of the ocean.

After I shook off the effects of my dream the next morning, I checked on Kishan. Quietly, I peeked in and saw Ren ordering his breakfast. He handed the plate to Kishan with a fork, told him where everything was, and then sat back and picked up a book of poetry. I opened the door wider, and they both looked up—Kishan moving his face toward the sound of the door.

Kishan sat up and patted the spot on the bed next to him. "Kelsey? Want to help me out with breakfast?"

"You were eating just fine before she came in. She's not a nurse, and you're not an invalid," Ren spat out.

I glared. "Stop being a jerk. If he wants me to help him, I will."

"No. If he *needs* help, *I'll* do it!"

Ren yanked the plate of food away from Kishan and started shoving forkfuls of eggs into his brother's mouth.

"Hey! She's a lot more gentle," he choked out between bites. "And she doesn't spill cold, wet stuff into my lap!" Kishan picked up something and mashed it between his fingers. "What is it?"

I laughed despite my anger with Ren. "It's fruit. Looks like pineapple."

"Oh." Kishan scooped up the pieces and flicked them toward Ren, who smacked his brother upside the head in retaliation. "Did you sleep well?"

I smirked at Ren before answering. "Yes. I dreamed I fed Ren to the kraken."

A grinning Kishan said, "Good."

Then Ren shoved a giant forkful of fruit into Kishan's mouth, and he started coughing.

"Now look what you've done," I accused. I approached Kishan, sat next to him, and smoothed back his mussed hair. Kishan stopped coughing, reached out for my hand and kissed it warmly.

"There's my girl. I missed you, *bilauta*. Did you sleep better in your own bed?"

"Well, actually—"

"Here," Ren growled and shoved the plate back into Kishan's hands. "Finish it yourself. Kelsey and I need to talk about something. We'll be right back."

Ren grabbed my hand before I could protest and yanked me through the hall to the stairs and down to the staff deck. Then he stopped and grabbed my shoulders.

"Kelsey, if you don't tell him it's over, I will. I'm going insane watching you fawn all over him."

"Alagan Dhiren! Don't you have any sympathy for him at all? Can't you understand how hard this is? You think you can just snap your fingers and make the past few months disappear? Well, you can't. I realize that

this situation is uncomfortable. It's not easy on any of us. I need time to sort through my feelings and decide what to do."

"What do you mean decide? You think this is like choosing which shoes to wear? You don't *decide* who you love, you just do."

"And what if I love you both? Did you ever think of that?"

He crossed his arms over his chest. "*Do* you?"

"Of course I love both of you."

"No, you don't. It's not the same, *iadala*." He sighed unhappily, turned, and ran a hand through his hair. "Kelsey. You're driving me crazy. I never should have picked that trigger."

"What? What trigger? What are you talking about?"

Conflicted, he tore his gaze from me, walked over to the staff dining table, and sat down. He put his elbows on the table and his head in his hands and then confessed, "Durga let me pick the trigger. The thing that would happen to help me get my memory back."

I pulled out the chair across from him and slowly sat down. "What did you do?"

"I needed to pick something that would guarantee you were safe. I couldn't just pick seeing you at the house, for example, or even meeting with Phet. I racked my brain trying to come up with something, and the image of Kishan stealing a kiss from you on the beach kept flashing through my mind. I knew he'd try to do it again, and I figured that if I was around to see him kiss you, and he felt comfortable doing it, that you would likely be out of danger. So the trigger was a kiss. Who knew he would wait so long."

My mouth fell open in astonishment. "You bet your memory on Kishan's kissing me?"

"Yes."

"Wait a minute. Kishan kissed me before the ship. He kissed me in Shangri-la. Why didn't it work then?"

"Because I was still a captive, which was part of the stipulation. I had to be free *and* see you kiss. Wait a minute—when did he kiss you in Shangri-la, and why is this the first time I'm hearing about it?"

I waved my hand in the air. "It doesn't matter. What *does* matter is, you're an idiot."

"Thank you."

"You're *not* welcome. You're an *idiot* because I made Kishan promise *not* to kiss me. He promised me he wouldn't until he knew you and I were over. He didn't touch me for months because of that promise." My mouth fell open. "*You* didn't *trust* me."

"I didn't trust *him*. And just how many kisses are we talking about here? Because if they were anything like the one I saw, I'm going to have the Scarf sew his lips together."

"For your information, he stole a couple of kisses in Shangri-la, and kissed me at the pool before we rescued you, which made me cry by the way, and that's when I made him promise. I waited for you. Even when you got back and didn't remember me and couldn't touch me, I waited for you. I didn't even *approach* Kishan until you started flaunting bimbos in front of me. I was loyal to you, Ren. I *loved* you."

"You *still* love me."

I groaned. "Why couldn't you have picked something *else* for a trigger, like getting home safely or eating my cookies again?"

"I had no idea he would keep his hands off you. I assumed he'd try kissing you at every opportunity."

"He did until I made him promise not to. This is ridiculous. I feel like we're stuck in a Shakespeare play. He loved her, she loved him, he forgot her, and then she loved the other guy."

"So is it a comedy or a tragedy?"

"I have no idea."

"I'm hoping for comedy." He took my hands in his. "I love you,

Kells, and I *know* that you love me. I feel sorry for Kishan but *not* sorry enough to let him have you. I'm not going to walk away."

I glanced up at his handsome face. "I need time."

He sighed unhappily. "Every minute we're apart feels like a lifetime. I can't watch you be with him, Kelsey. It tears me apart inside."

I let out a deep breath. "Okay, here's the deal. Give me some space, and I'll ask the same of Kishan. That will have to be good enough for both of you. We have two more dragons and the Seventh Pagoda to go through, and we really can't afford any more distractions right now."

Ren sat back and studied my face for a moment. "Alright. I'll tolerate him. As long as he's *hands off*."

"That means you keep *your* hands off too."

He gave me a hot look. "Fine." He smiled. "But you'll miss me."

"Did I ever tell you that you have an arrogant streak a mile wide?"

He got up and walked around to my side of the table, pulled me to my feet, and kissed me softly, a drowning, luxurious, knee-buckling kiss, and then took a step back. "That's just a little something to remember me by."

He left, and I pressed my hand against the wall to steady myself. *Holy Hannah, that man is dangerous.* I tried to shake off my reaction to him before I headed upstairs, but my rebellious thoughts kept dwelling on Ren.

When I regained the use of my legs, I sought out Kishan. I finally found him on the sundeck, standing at the bow.

"There you are."

He didn't respond.

"Kishan?" I touched his shoulder. "Kishan? How did you get out here all by yourself? Did Ren bring you?" He stared straight ahead out over the ocean.

I shook his arm. "Kishan? Talk to me. Are you okay? What's going on?"

He turned his head slowly, eerily, like a zombie from a horror film. His face was devoid of expression. Orange flames burned in his black eyes. "A storm is coming," he said in a low voice not his own. "I will prepare the way. Go. Warn the others."

We both looked ahead at the sea, and I saw the sky had turned gray. Dark clouds were rolling in, and waves were cresting against the boat. A stiff wind blew over my skin. It was cold and smelled like rain.

"I'll be right back," I assured him. "Don't go anywhere."

He didn't react to my comment. I turned around and ran up the stairs.

"Ren! Mr. Kadam!" I barreled into the wheelhouse and met Ren's chest with my face.

He grabbed my shoulders. "What is it? What happened?"

Between breaths, I panted, "It's Kishan. He's in oracle mode. He's standing at the bow and saying a storm is coming. I think he's going to guide us through it."

"Alright, you help Nilima. I'll go check on him."

Ren left as Mr. Kadam emerged from the back room. "A storm, is it?"

I was explaining what had happened to Kishan when Ren returned. "Kishan's not there. He's missing. I'm going to sniff him out. Stay here. I mean it."

"I get the message. Go find him already."

Mr. Kadam moved to the controls and began pushing buttons. I walked to the window. If the sea looked foreboding before, it was worse now. The gray clouds had turned black and were violently pushing and shoving each other back and forth like giant sumo wrestlers smacking and thundering together. Rain fell in fat drops and hit the window with

the noise of a thousand drums. The waves pushed the ship back and forth angrily.

Ren stuck his head into the wheelhouse. Soaked through, rivulets ran from his hair down his neck and into his sopping shirt. "He's on top of the wheelhouse," he shouted over the storm. "We need to tie him down! He's not responding to me, and he won't hold onto anything!"

"I'll get the Scarf! It's in my room!" I hollered over the noise of the storm and headed toward the door. A wave hit the ship, and I slid on some water right over to Ren.

"No. I'll get it." Ren shoved me back inside and disappeared.

I bit my lip, worried about Kishan. After another wave tilted the ship, I scurried out the door and up the ladder to check on him. The top of the wheelhouse was slick with cold rainwater. Kishan still stood, not holding onto anything. I slid over to him, grabbed him around the waist and locked my other arm around the railing.

He didn't look at me or acknowledge me in any way. The ship leaned precariously to the right, and I braced my feet on the metal bar used to tie off ropes and held onto Kishan. His body was stiff and my arms screamed in pain as I kept us both upright. The ship finally straightened, and I was able to rest for a second.

Just then, I felt Ren's arm wrap tightly around me and heard a very angry voice in my ear. "I thought I told you to stay put. Why do you always have to do exactly the opposite of what I ask?"

"He was going to fall off into the ocean!" I shouted back.

"Better him than you!"

I rammed my elbow into Ren's stomach, but he just growled in my ear, and a second later I felt the wispy threads of the Divine Scarf wrap around Kishan and secure him to the railing.

"There. Now let's get you back inside."

"No!" Rain dripped off my nose, and my bare arms trembled from the cold. "Someone has to watch over him!" I yelled over the torrential rain.

"Then *I* will. But let me take you back first."

"Can't you just lash me to the rail like Kishan?" I sneezed loudly and looked up sheepishly from behind wet eyelashes, knowing I was going to lose this battle.

Ren stared at me furiously and growled, "This is nonnegotiable! You're going back to the wheelhouse now if I have to carry you in a bag slung over my back! Come on!"

He took my hand and we climbed down the ladder together, cocooned on the descent. After I entered the wheelhouse, he closed the door, gave me a dark look, and headed back up again.

The storm gathered speed, and the cresting waves became walls of water. Now I was worried about *both* my tigers. The storm was violent. Mr. Kadam and Nilima were busy, but there was nothing for me to do except pray that the men above would be safe.

A sodden Ren appeared at the door a half hour later. He shot me a cursory glance. Satisfied that I was staying put, he said, "We're to follow the path of the lightning."

He left and almost immediately the inky purple view was lit up with twin lightning bolts that shot from just overhead and hit the ocean to our right. Thunder boomed, echoing through the wheelhouse so loudly that I covered my ears. Mr. Kadam veered right, and we started up an immense wave. Seawater splashed the windows and ran off the open decks of the ship. I'd never heard of a cruise ship this size being sunk by a storm and sincerely hoped it was very uncommon.

Lightning shot out again. This time the crackling bolts veered slightly left. We pressed on following the path the lighting showed us. About every fifteen to twenty minutes it would adjust our path. I stopped looking out the window when they lit up the ocean. The waves were so high and the clouds so dark and violent that it scared me. Not so much for my own life—I felt fairly certain Mr. Kadam knew what he was doing—but I was scared for the men standing in the open overlooking

the terrifying storm surrounding us. How helpless it must make them feel, how vulnerable, knowing one slip could snuff out their lives in an instant.

All that long, dark, terrible day and through the early evening, I sat quietly, whispering prayers that Ren and Kishan would be safe, asking that the storm would calm, that the sun would appear again, and that we would all live on through this horrible tempest. I wondered what those early mariners must have felt like on their small ships, battling storms such as these. Had they made peace with the idea that they would likely be laid to rest in a watery grave? Did they avoid connections to other people knowing they'd probably never see their loved ones again? Or did they just close their eyes and hold on like I was doing?

The ship began to settle as the rain slackened. "What's happening? Is it over?" I asked Mr. Kadam.

He peered out the window, studying the clouds and listening to the wind. "I fear it isn't. We're in the eye of the storm."

"The eye? You mean we're in the middle of a tsunami?"

"No. A tsunami is a large sea wave, usually the result of an underwater volcano. We're in the eye of a hurricane or a typhoon, depending on exactly where we are. Hurricanes occur in the western north Atlantic, but in the western Pacific or the seas of China, they are called typhoons. Incidentally, the word *typhoon* originally came from Greece. The word *Tuphōn* represents the father of the winds in Greek mythology and—"

"Mr. Kadam?"

"Yes, Miss Kelsey."

"Can we discuss typhoons, hurricanes, tropical storms, tornados, tsunamis, and cyclones later?"

"Of course."

The boat started shaking as we cleared the eye and moved back into the thrust of the storm. Mr. Kadam and Nilima were kept busy as the

lightning bolts started striking again. Several hours later, the rolling of the ocean lessened, and the rain became lighter and then disappeared altogether. The clouds stopped roiling and moved away, leaving wispy fingers in their wake. I heard a noise just as the door slid open. Ren stood there supporting the limp form of his brother. He stepped through, and both men collapsed onto the floor.

Nilima helped me drag them into the wheelhouse and began vigorously rubbing Kishan's head and arms with a towel. She threw one to me so I could dry off Ren. They shivered violently.

"It's no use. We'll have to get them out of their wet clothes."

"But they're too heavy," Nilima said.

Ren had wrapped the Scarf around his arm. It hung there dry despite the fact that the rest of his clothes were completely soaked through.

"Nilima, I have an idea. Scarf, can you remove their wet clothes and replace them with dry ones? Something warm like flannel? And don't forget warm socks and long sleeves."

The Scarf twisted on Ren's arm and slid up to his sleeve. The threads of his sleeve began to unravel, moving faster and faster as the Scarf absorbed them. In a few seconds his shirt was gone, and the Scarf moved on to his jeans. Nilima giggled at my embarrassed expression, put her arm on my shoulder, and turned the both of us to look at the ocean while the Scarf continued.

We listened to the soft whisper of moving threads for a few more minutes and then peeked at their feet. Seeing their toes safely encased in wool socks, we turned back to the brothers. The Scarf had created flannel shirts right down to the imitation fabric buttons. I picked up Ren's cold hand and tried to warm it in mine. Kishan's hand too felt like ice. I instructed the Scarf to wrap them in warm blankets and asked the Fruit to make hot apple cider, figuring a warm drink plus some sugar would do them good.

I lifted Ren's head and slid behind him to help him drink. Nilima did the same with Kishan. Kishan was delirious. He mumbled of prophecies and dragons. Ren was slightly more alert. He sipped the hot cider but kept his eyes closed. His body trembled under the blanket.

"So cold," he whispered.

"I'm sorry. I don't know what else to do." I started rubbing my hands over his, mentally willing him to warm up, and something happened. My hand symbols glowed, and a warm layer of heat radiated from my palm. There was no lightning bolt, and the heat didn't burn his skin, but his hand didn't feel as icy. I focused my energy and thoughts on warming him. I could actually feel the heat penetrate the layers of his skin and drift lower until his muscles became warm too. I moved up his arms and down his legs until his limbs stopped trembling. Unbuttoning his shirt, I pressed my hands against his chest, feeling the heat move layer by layer. I slid my hands down to his muscled belly and back up to his neck.

What started off as a means to warm him actually became something more. Something intimate. I'd never touched him like this before, and I found that the heat reflected back into my body and warmed me also. I blushed finding Nilima scrutinizing my efforts, and I moved from his neck up to his face and pressed my hands against his brow. The heat was so intense his hair began to steam as the water evaporated. Sliding my hands to his cheeks, I held very still and closed my eyes as I concentrated on warming him. I blinked, startled when I felt a caress on my cheek.

Ren had opened his blue eyes and was watching me with a tender expression. He swept his fingers across my cheek again and trailed them down a strand of hair.

"How do you feel?" I asked.

"Like I've died and gone to heaven," he said with lopsided, gentle smile. "What are you doing?"

"Giving you a deep-body heat massage. Did it hurt? Was it too hot?"

He raised an eyebrow and grinned. "It hurt in a good way. I wouldn't have minded it a little *hotter*, actually."

My eyes widened and I tried to subtly send him a nonverbal message to shut up. Puzzled, he peeked under my arm and noticed for the first time we had company. I cleared my throat and said, "If you feel sufficiently recovered, I need to work on Kishan now. Can you sit up?"

He nodded. I rewarmed his unfinished cider with my hands. "Drink this."

He shifted and frowned at the sweats he was now wearing. I teased dryly, "I know it's not designer, but it's warm."

I moved over to Kishan, who was no longer thrashing in delirium, but he looked blue. He breathed shallowly, and Nilima had been unsuccessful in getting him to drink anything. We traded places, and I began with his limbs. His body was cold, colder even than Ren's had been. I was able to warm his hands and arms, but by the time I got to his legs, I was out of juice. Ren had been watching my progress silently while sipping his drink. He set the cup aside and knelt next to me. Reaching out a hand, he stroked my shoulder, down my arm, and took my hand in his, rubbing it between his palms.

"Try again."

I summoned the heat and let it trickle out of my palm and into Kishan's thigh. It soon sputtered again but Ren moved closer and rubbed my back and cupped my shoulders with his palms. Golden warmth surged down my arms and began to warm not only Kishan but also the entire wheelhouse. I heard Nilima gasp behind us. The heat actually became visible like there was a tiny sun hidden under my palm.

I heard Mr. Kadam's intake of breath as he peered over our shoulders. "Fascinating," he murmured.

Ren stayed near me as I moved to the other leg and then to Kishan's

upper torso. I pressed my palms against his stomach and chest, and then his face and ears. His chest heaved as he sucked in a deep breath and seemed to settle into a relaxing sleep. Ren rose and picked up his brother. Mr. Kadam assured us we were out of danger and that he and Nilima would take turns keeping watch. He wanted us to sleep.

I said goodnight and followed in their wake. We tucked Kishan into bed, and then Ren escorted me to my room. I was exhausted. I felt numb and cold, like all the heat had been sucked out of me. After I collapsed on the bed, Ren came over and tucked me in the way I liked.

"Thanks for keeping me warm, *iadala*," he whispered in my ear.

I smiled and drifted off.

The next day was bright and sunny. Kishan woke me exuberantly. His vision was back; his pirate-gold eyes sparkled once again. He spun me in a circle and told me he was starving. Then he headed upstairs to take over for Mr. Kadam and Nilima. We ate breakfast together in the wheelhouse, and he talked about how strange it felt not being in charge of his own body. He could hear me and feel me touching him, but couldn't respond. The lightning bolts had apparently come from his eyes. He said his eyes still itched from the experience.

Ren showed up and kept looking at me meaningfully as Kishan held my hand and kissed my cheek or put his arm around me. I could have sworn I heard the phrase *"hands off"* quietly mumbled as Ren turned a page in a book. Kishan didn't notice Ren scowling, or if he did, he didn't care.

Kishan threaded his fingers through mine and leaned closer as he demonstrated some instrument on the panel, and Ren abruptly stood, handed me the Scarf and the Golden Fruit, and asked me to stow them away somewhere. I was about to protest that it was probably smarter to keep them in the wheelhouse when I realized his motivation was to get me away from Kishan.

I sighed, agreed, and left the wheelhouse, but instead of heading to a lower deck, I climbed. I went to the very top of the ship where Ren and Kishan had stood bravely during the storm. Looking out at the ocean, I couldn't imagine what it must have felt like. A soft breeze swept back my hair, and I leaned over the railing, twisting the Golden Fruit in my hands as I thought about what I should say to Kishan.

I loved him. I loved *both* of them. *Kishan would understand, wouldn't he? If I said I needed time to think, he wouldn't hate me forever, right?*

The Golden Fruit sparkled in the sunshine throwing rainbows in every direction like a disco ball. I held it by its stem and spun it, thinking about what Mr. Kadam had once told me about diamonds. He'd said that cutting and polishing them is how they become brilliant. "Huh, with all the cuts in my heart, it should be about as sparkly as you are by now," I said as I twirled the Fruit.

I saw a twinkle in the water below, a flash of gold that grew brighter. I stared transfixed and gasped as a large golden head emerged and rose up toward me. Flashing white teeth gleamed in the sun, and a voice with the sound of clinking coins said in my mind, *What a fancy bauble you have there, my dear. Would you be interested in a trade?*

22

the golden dragon's hoard

erhaps you would allow me to introduce myself? I am Jīnsèlóng, the voice said. *Now what brings you and that bright, shiny, dazzling, priceless trinket to my realm?*

I sighed and appraised the dragon while I tossed the Fruit from palm to palm. Its sparkling ginger eye watched the Fruit carefully as I moved it. Water dripped off its horned head. This one looked more like a water dragon. Its triangular mouth was closed but sharp white teeth overlapped its bottom lip. Its scales were made of hard golden disks that glinted in the water. The scales were variegated in tint, ranging from bright bullion, to Buddha gold, to pirate doubloon, to copper penny. The lighter colors ran along its belly while darker tones were on its back.

Instead of the horns its brothers had, Jīnsèlóng had four long spikes protruding from the back of its head and a trail of smaller spikes starting at its nose and traveling along its spine. When it opened its mouth, its long red tongue rolled out and flopped to the side. It was panting while it watched me play with the Fruit, and it reminded me of a dog waiting greedily for a treat.

"We're not really interested in trading the Fruit," I said.

Oh. How very *disappointing.* The tongue rolled into its mouth before the golden dragon snapped its jaws shut and started to slip back into the water.

"Wait!" I shouted desperately. "Maybe you'd be interested in another kind of trade?"

The dragon halted and angled its head to peer up at me. *What did you have in mind?*

"We seek information. We're searching for Durga's Necklace."

I see. And . . . what would you give me for this information? It would have to be something priceless. Not even your Fruit would be as valuable.

"I'm sure we'll come up with something," I offered dryly.

Very well. We will barter. But on my *turf.*

"Where exactly is your *turf*?"

My palace is beneath the waves.

"How do we get there?"

Dive off your ship with a piece of gold in your hand.

"How deep is it? How are we supposed to breathe?"

The depth will not affect you as long as you remain in my realm. Breathing will also not be a problem in my underwater palace. But you must hold the gold tightly in your hands until you get there. Shall we meet in say . . . an hour?

"Fine. See you there."

The dragon slipped beneath the waves and disappeared. I mumbled, "Great. I've got a date with a dragon," and went to hunt down everybody.

I headed back to the wheelhouse and slammed open the door. Kishan and Ren abruptly stopped arguing about something. I rolled my eyes and said, "Really? Now is not the time. We've got a date with Jīnsèlóng in less than an hour. Mr. Kadam? Are you here?"

"Just a moment." He emerged from the back dressed in a robe and drying his hair with a towel.

"Sorry to interrupt your shower. We need three pieces of gold and something really valuable to barter. I suspect it needs to be very shiny."

"The golden dragon?"

"Yes. We had an interesting chat not twenty feet away from these two." I crooked my thumb over my shoulder. "So much for tiger hearing," I accused.

Kishan managed to look sheepish, but Ren was gearing up to fight. "And where were *you*? Were you below deck like you were supposed to be?"

"No. I was on top of the wheelhouse, if you must know. And before you get on your safety soapbox, I *can* protect myself."

Ren growled in frustration, but I turned toward Mr. Kadam and pointedly ignored him. "So do you have any gold?"

"Yes. Let me get dressed, and we'll go through the safe."

An hour later, Kishan, Ren, and I stood at the opening to the wet garage. Kishan held a gold pen, Ren a letter opener, and I held a golden brooch that belonged to Nilima. Ren had brought his trident, Kishan the *chakram* and the *kamandal*, and I brought Fanindra. The Fruit and the Scarf were placed in a diving bag, along with precious stones, Nilima's most expensive jewels, and a golden statue of Durga.

I wasn't very optimistic about the dragon accepting these things when he'd said that even the Golden Fruit wouldn't be enough. I worried he'd want Fanindra or the *chakram*, and Mr. Kadam insisted we hide all of Durga's gifts in the bag as well. I insisted on keeping Fanindra with me, and Ren slung the bag over his shoulder and chest.

Just before we jumped, Nilima rushed in with Durga's lotus-flower lei. She placed it around my neck and told me she'd had a dream I would need it. I hugged her and then Mr. Kadam.

"If this doesn't work we'll be back in a second—wetter, but safe."

Mr. Kadam patted my back and told me to be careful. He reminded me that golden dragons are greedy, that they would do anything to protect their hoard, and that they are notoriously devious and tricky. He also cautioned me not to take anything, not even so much as a pebble, from the dragon's lair.

I nodded and warned the brothers not to drop their gold baubles, or else they'd run out of oxygen. Kishan smiled and slipped into the water. I turned to Ren. "Are you ready?"

He smiled. "Robert Browning said, 'There are two moments in a diver's life: One, when a beggar, he prepares to plunge; then, when a prince, he rises with his prize.'" He ran a finger down my jaw lightly. "I am *more* than ready, *hridaya patni*. And I intend to come back with my *prize*."

I shivered as he turned and slipped into the water after Kishan. *How could he cause a system overload with just one little touch? Actually, his voice alone could do it.* I rubbed my tingling jaw, tightened my fist around the brooch, and jumped into the water feet first.

My head broke the surface. I sucked in a deep breath and dove under. Kicking hard, I searched frantically for a sign of Ren or Kishan. They were gone. Just when I was ready to turn around and head back to the surface for another breath, my hand holding the brooch shot straight out, and the golden brooch almost jumped out of my grasp. As I tightened my hold on it, my body surged forward underwater as if I was holding onto a ski rope.

I held my breath even though my lungs were bursting. I squeezed my eyes shut as I was yanked at superspeed downward into the black ocean depths. Fanindra's eyes began to glow, and in her light, I saw a flash of white ahead of me. Ren had been wearing a white shirt. My vision was going dark. I knew if I passed out, I'd drop the brooch and die here. There was no way I was going to get to the surface. I was too deep. The last of my air bubbles rose above me. One grew. It became larger and touched my mouth and nose; it expanded and draped over my face like a mask.

I blinked several times and gasped. Cool air rushed into my lungs,

and I breathed deeply, panting hard while trying not to hyperventilate. I began to relax and, now that I could see, studied my surroundings. The rubber band holding back my hair swept away, and the long locks streamed out behind me in the water. I imagined I looked like a mermaid.

We continued deeper and deeper. Fanindra remained inanimate except for her glowing eyes. Flashing fish swam quickly away as I passed. I saw a shark feeding on something big resting on the ocean floor. I shivered and sent a mental thank-you to the universe that he was too busy to pay attention to me.

I was tugged along at a fast pace about ten feet above the ocean floor and watched crabs scurry as we passed. Sea anemones twisted in the current, and a giant lobster made its way slowly across a rocky outcropping. A stingray shook the sand off its back and swam away, its hiding place disturbed by our presence. A dim light ahead grew brighter. I gasped in wonder as we passed a bed of oysters, rose up over a forest of seaweed, and headed toward an underwater castle made of gleaming gold.

It shone with an incandescent light—enough that the ocean was brightened in a large perimeter surrounding it. The outside grounds had been carefully nurtured to look landscaped. Giant corals and anemones grew as tall as trees and colorful fish and ocean plants thrived in the area. I was sped toward the front gates, which opened automatically, and zipped through the courtyard. The brooch slowed me down as I approached the front door, which was open. Lights blazed inside, and I could see Ren standing on the other side of the door looking for me.

I hovered in the water for a moment until he saw me. He stretched out a hand through an invisible barrier. Grasping mine, he slowly pulled me forward and through. He wrapped an arm around my waist until my feet found the floor. He smiled as I touched his arm. "You're . . . *dry!*" I exclaimed. I grabbed my shirt and pulled a lock of hair over my shoulder. *"I'm* dry!"

"Yes. Come. They're waiting for us. Kishan's with the dragon now. We need to cover up Fanindra. You'll see why."

Quickly, he created a sweater with the Scarf and wrapped it around my shoulders. The sleeve was wide enough to cover Fanindra. Satisfied, Ren guided me into the opulent castle. The walls were painted in metallic hues depicting scenes of sunken ships and pirate treasure. Farther down was a portrayal of rich cities that had crumbled into the sea.

Gleaming statues stood in every corner made of marble, onyx, and jade. Hand-painted Greek vases stood on ornamental pedestals. Chests full of silver, gold, and gems overflowed and spilled onto thick Persian rugs piled one on top of the other. One wall was adorned with hundreds of bejeweled masks and precious art from perhaps every country in the world.

Ren had to pull me along, because I would often stop to gape, admiring one treasure after another. We entered a spacious, comfortable room and found the golden dragon in his human form seated across from Kishan, laughing.

"I win," the dragon exclaimed. Kishan frowned. "It's very hard to best me, you know. Don't take it to heart," Jīnsèlóng taunted.

"What did you lose?" Ren asked.

"Nilima's earrings."

"What's going on?" I asked, puzzled.

"There you are," the dragon said. "It took you long enough, my dear. Now if you would hand over the Fruit—"

"Don't move," Ren warned. "He's a crafty devil, and he means to take everything he can get."

The dragon frowned. "Spoilsport. Very well. Just give me the brooch, and we'll call it even."

Ren held up a hand. "You get nothing. If you like the brooch, we will barter for it." Ren continued thoughtfully, "Perhaps, if you would provide some refreshment for the young lady, I will let you look at it. It's quite valuable."

"Bah," Jīnsèlóng said, but peeked at me out of the corner of his eye and laughed uproariously. "Very well, I'll provide refreshments. I have a feeling you're going to be very good at this." He wagged his finger at Ren while grinning.

"I should be. I was well trained in negotiating trade for my father's kingdom."

"Ah, but I promise you, you've never dealt with one such as me." The dragon clapped his hands and a platter of strange appetizers appeared before us. "Please sit and enjoy the bounties of the sea. Do you see how generous I am?"

I sat down on a handsome golden chair softened with thick pillows. "Yes, you are the epitome of a gracious host," I mumbled as I picked up a goblet and sniffed before sipping. It tasted like a cross between prune juice and cranberry. I bit into an appetizer and found it salty and crunchy. "What is this?" I asked.

"Crispy swordfish on a seaweed cracker glazed with golden starfish butter. The drink is squeezed from the bulbs of flowering sea grass."

"Uh-huh." I dusted the remaining crumbs from my fingers, swallowed thickly, and set down my drink. "Delicious," I said with a forced smile.

Kishan leaned forward, scooped up a seaweed cracker, and chewed, while watching the man across from us. This dragon's human form was more diminutive than his brothers'. His hair was shoulder length and gray, and the top of his head was bald. A bulbous-tipped nose sat above a lip so thin it might as well be nonexistent, while his thick bottom lip protruded slightly outward. Ginger brown eyes sparkled with intelligence as he sat forward and rubbed his hands together greedily. He looked like an old principal of mine, and I wondered if his appearance was purposely divined to put us at ease in the negotiation process.

The dragon interrupted my thoughts. "Now, shall we begin?" he inquired impatiently.

Ren nodded and opened his bag, then reconsidered. "Perhaps the first item we should consider is the brooch in Kelsey's hand." He turned to me. "May I?"

I dropped the brooch into Ren's outstretched hand and saw the dragon peer at it hungrily. What happened over the next few hours amazed me. The dragon began with a surprising bid—information on the white dragon in exchange for everything in our bag, sight unseen. I would have immediately accepted but Ren sat back, pressed his hands together as if seriously considering the offer, and then politely declined. A moment later, I remembered that the Fruit and the Scarf were in the bag, and the brothers had probably stowed the *chakram* and the trident in there too, so I was glad he declined.

Ren made a counteroffer so low it made the dragon laugh—my brooch in exchange for information. After that, the two men became very serious. It was like watching a game of mental chess. Each man was considering several moves into the future while I had a hard time figuring out what they were trying to accomplish in the present. In a matter of minutes, the dragon had the brooch, the large ruby from our bag, a Shangri-la buffet, and a set of fairy clothes, and we had a guaranteed safe passage to the surface, though he wouldn't tell us how, a chest of coins, a priceless jade statue from China, and a diamond necklace.

After another hour, I wasn't sure Ren was making any real progress. Jīnsèlóng seemed overly interested in our bag now, assuming it would create any treasure we came up with. He hadn't noticed yet it made only food and things made of cloth. Ren and the dragon had a curious way of dealing with each other.

At first, I thought I understood Ren's style. He selected an item to barter, extolled the virtues of the object and shared its history and value while Jīnsèlóng shrewdly listened. Then he would act as if he couldn't bear to part with it after all. Reluctantly, he'd offer it again but only in exchange for twenty such items belonging to the dragon. The dragon would refuse and make a counteroffer, and then Ren would sneak in something else like the whereabouts of the white dragon's lair and other items.

The dragon would laugh and eliminate all but two or three of the things Ren asked for, and Ren would once again dangle the item and talk about how precious it was to his family. The dragon's lust for acquiring new objects worked in our favor, and soon we had a large pile of valuable treasures. They made several offers and counteroffers in this way until one of them would say, "Accept." Then the other one could propose a different bid or also say, "Accept." Once they'd both said "Accept," the deal was done, and the dragon would clap his hands, causing the objects to switch locations. What he won disappeared into his hoard, and what we won piled on the floor behind us.

During a break, I was admiring a Spanish sword when I asked Jīnsèlóng where all his treasure came from. He sipped from his jewel-encrusted goblet, smiled, and offered me an arm. "Would you like to see my castle?"

I peeked over his shoulder, and Ren and Kishan both shook their heads.

I rolled my eyes at their overprotectiveness. "Yes, I'd love to," I replied. "As long as you promise not to trick me out of any information."

He snorted gray smoke into his hand and held his palm out to shake. "Dragon's honor."

Ren rose, and they went through a complicated verbal dance assuring my safe return, and the dragon's promise that he wouldn't probe me for information. They both accepted before Jīnsèlóng tucked my hand into the crook of his arm and took me for a stroll.

I asked again about his wealth. He responded, "All the treasures of the sea belong to me."

"So this is all sunken treasure from lost ships?"

"Mostly. In centuries past, a wise cargo captain would throw me a trifle to appease my appetites. If they forgot, I'd have to do something about it. It's a fair trade, after all. Safe passage in exchange for a small bauble. It's not too much to ask, is it?"

"And if they refused or forgot, what exactly did you do?"

"Bah, spare me that judgmental look in your eye. I'm not a *monster*."

I folded my arms across my chest and raised an eyebrow.

He threw up his hands in disgust. "Fine. I'd harass their ship until they remembered, or I'd let the storms have them." He stuck a finger in the air. "I get paid no matter what. It's the law of the sea." He walked over to a marble statue of Aphrodite and stroked her arm. "Hello, beautiful." He cleared his throat as if embarrassed to be caught talking to a very . . . *voluptuous* version of the goddess of love and turned back to me. "In the old days, such beautiful things were carried in ships. Now I could sink a fleet of them and get not much more than a hunk of scrap metal."

I touched the delicate fingertip of Aphrodite. "That's probably true. These types of things are almost certainly flown across the sea now if they're moved at all. They'd likely be holed up in museums."

"Hmm. Every once in a while, I can catch a plane, but only when there's lots of moisture in the clouds," he mumbled.

"Catch a plane? You mean you *purposefully* make airplanes crash?"

He frowned. "Not as many as I used to. It's a big effort, you know, and very little reward. Besides, Bermuda is pretty far from home."

"Bermuda? As in the Bermuda Triangle?"

"I have no idea what triangle you are talking about. Dragons such as I waste no time on geometry except when it's used in art."

I poked him in the arm several times to illustrate each word. "You are a terrible dragon. All of you just make trouble. What's the point of your existence?"

"You want to know the point of my existence? Come with me. I'll show you."

He led me through another opulent hall with carved walls depicting the great sculptors of the world at work. They were lovely, and I felt myself softening at the sight. Surely someone who cares for the world's most priceless treasures couldn't be *all* bad.

We stopped at heavy wooden doors, ornately fashioned and polished to a gleaming sheen. He clapped his hands, and the doors opened. We stepped inside a warehouse of the most exquisite things I'd ever seen. Centuries-old paintings looked as new as if they'd just been finished. Statuary was glossy and perfect. Diamond chandeliers hung from the ceiling, casting rainbows around the room as the light bounced off jewels as big as footballs. Ancient tapestries hung as if they'd just been woven.

He let me touch everything, pleased that I took such an interest in his collection. I found a golden replica of the *Titanic*, a life-sized horse cast in bronze, a queen's tiara encrusted with diamonds and emeralds, and a perfect white pearl the size of a globe resting on a red, velvet pillow.

Each step made me gasp as I beheld the splendor of his treasure room. I lifted a hand to touch the head of a jade tiger and smiled. "It's so amazing." I turned to look at the dragon with an expression of awe. He seemed smug. "Still . . . it doesn't justify killing people," I charged.

"Doesn't preserving all of this make up for it? How many of these things remain on the surface—ruined and uncared for?"

"Too many," I admitted.

"There, you see? I'm preserving humanity's most precious contributions."

"But no one sees it but you."

He hedged, blew some smoke out of his nostrils, and abruptly turned, expecting me to follow.

I did, and the doors closed and locked right behind me. Though he was short, he strode quickly ahead. "I know . . . I know," he said through clenched teeth. "Yínbáilóng has been after me for years to stop sinking ships and downing planes."

"Yínbáilóng?"

"Yes, the white dragon. He's the eldest and has *opinions* about everything, including drowning humans."

"Maybe you should listen to him."

"Maybe. But then what would I do? It's not like I get many visitors down here, and I don't want to sleep all the time like Qīnglóng or go crazy like Lǜsèlóng. All *he* thinks about is hunting."

"Maybe you could help people. Leave a coin under their pillows like the tooth fairy."

"Are you serious? Perhaps you didn't get enough oxygen on the way down. You are nothing if not interesting, my dear. Give up my treasure? Bah! The last thing I would ever do is give up my wealth. Come. We've left those crafty brothers alone too long. They're probably devising new ways to cheat me out of more of my fortune."

"Well, it's nothing you don't deserve."

"Ha!" He led me back into the room, seeming somewhat distracted by our talk. This time during the bartering if he got particularly greedy, I'd raise an eyebrow, and he'd be distracted enough to make a bad agreement.

I would casually insert extra items in Ren's wish list, like not sinking any ships in the next century or not going to Bermuda anymore. Ren added them in without questioning me.

Occasionally, Kishan would lean over to whisper something to Ren as well, and among the three of us, we made some headway. Jīnsèlóng was scowling all the time and after a particularly bad loss, he began crying. He wept crocodile tears and talked about all the people he drowned. He seemed truly repentant, and I felt terribly sorry for him.

He asked if I had a tissue, and I scrambled around for a moment, then pulled out the Scarf and asked it for a tissue. It shimmered and changed into a beautiful monogrammed handkerchief. Embroidered on it was:

$$\mathcal{ARD}$$

I stared at it for a moment, puzzled, then it hit me. Alagan Dhiren Rajaram. I flushed and gave the Scarf a mental warning to cut it out.

"Here you go," I said to the dragon, and handed it to him just as Ren's hand darted toward mine.

The dragon snatched it away and pressed it to his wet face. Ren sighed and dropped his hand, and it took me another few seconds to realize that what I thought were Jīnsèlóng's heaving sobs were actually heaving peals of laughter.

As he wiped the tears from his smiling face, I folded my arms and accused, "You tricked me."

He pointed a finger and wagged it happily at Ren. "And *that's* why you never allow women into the bartering chamber. Your magical cloth is mine!" he tittered in delight.

Ren smiled evilly. "You don't even know what you have there. The cloth is cursed, you know. I'm actually glad you took it. The curse can only be transferred if another person willingly accepts it, and you played right into our hands."

"You're bluffing," the dragon said with a laugh and looked at Kishan. Kishan shook his head as if in pity.

"I only wish he was, dragon," Kishan added. "It's a terrible curse too. It weakens a man to the point of death, but perhaps it won't affect you in the same way."

"What . . . what do you mean?" the dragon asked.

"It makes you fall in love. With her." Ren tossed his head toward me while my face registered shock.

The automatically suspicious dragon narrowed his eyes and peered at me, as if trying to glean the truth from my expression.

"She's already tried to work her wiles on you, hasn't she?" Ren suggested.

The dragon stammered, "Well, *no*. Not . . . *exactly*."

Kishan spoke up, "Did she make you feel guilty? Make you want to improve yourself? That's part of what she does. Before you know it, you've lost yourself to her. You're not the same dragon you used to be."

"Now wait just a minute!" I threatened.

"See?" Ren interrupted. "She doesn't want to be exposed. Believe *me*. If you keep that Scarf, you will soon be besotted with her. She'll have you giving up whatever is most precious to you."

"She wouldn't."

"That's what she does," Kishan said. "Oh, you won't notice it at the time, and you'll even thank her for it. She'll make you think it's *your* idea, and she'll have you eating out of her hand in no time. Just wait. Can you feel it now? It's already eating away at you, isn't it? Festering in your gut?"

Ren elbowed Kishan. "She's probably already got her hooks into him. See? He's squirming under her gaze already. He's been making bad agreements ever since he came back into the room. He shouldn't have been left alone with her."

Kishan replied, "Yes, you're right. But it's a classic mistake. Anyone could have made it, even a dragon." He sighed. "Well, she's drained *us*

of all of our resources, so I guess she'll be happy enough to move on to her next victim."

The dragon swallowed dryly and darted a glance at me, then laughed shakily. "You three had me . . . had me going for a minute there, but I don't believe you. You're fabricating this whole thing."

"Are we?" Kishan leaned forward. "I can tell you right now, I've never loved someone as fiercely as I love her. I would do anything to protect her and keep her by my side. I'd want to kill *anyone* who took her from me."

I snorted at his obvious jibe at Ren. *Subtle Kishan. Real subtle.*

Kishan paused to study my expression but only briefly. "However, I would stay my hand *if* I felt assured that *you* were the one she really wanted."

That wiped the smile off my face. *Did he mean that?* I knotted my fingers and twisted them, tense and edgy after Kishan's declaration. I knew that he loved me, but I guess I'd never considered that he was as intense about it as Ren was. *Could I callously brush him aside the way Ren wants me to? No. I can't hurt him like that. He is good to me, a good man, and I do love him.*

Phet said they were both pillows in a world of rocks. *I could find a place to rest my head either way.* Kishan turned to me and winked. I half smiled back and bit my lower lip. *Of course there was another possibility. Perhaps Kishan exaggerated his feelings for the dragon's sake.* But his golden eyes met mine, and I knew he hadn't been exaggerating. He really loved me that much, and he really would let me go.

The dragon began to sweat, recognizing the truth of Kishan's words.

Ren had been sitting forward, rubbing his hands together in slow revolutions as he listened to Kishan talk. He glanced at his brother briefly, and then sat back and turned his head to look in my eyes. He smiled and spoke quietly. So soft was his voice that he seemed to be speaking only to me. Everyone leaned forward to hear him, myself included.

"I don't think I could be so generous. You see, I've loved her since the moment I laid eyes on her. I've been tortured to the point of death in her name. I would journey across the world to see her smile, to make her happy. When she becomes yours, dragon, and binds the threads of her Scarf around your heart, I will probably wither and die, for I am as wrapped up in her as a vine that clings to a tree seeking sustenance. She's tied me to her for eternity. She's my home. She's my reason for being. To win and hold her heart is my *only* purpose."

My breath caught as his words faded. The room became as still and as sacred as a church. It was as if he'd just taken a vow. He couldn't tear his eyes away, and I couldn't either. I didn't even question Ren's sincerity. I absolutely knew he meant every word he said. If there was anything he left out, it was that the object of his devotion wasn't worthy of him . . . that holding something as precious as his heart had almost destroyed her . . . that she was afraid that if he left her again she wouldn't survive.

As I sat there looking into Ren's eyes, I had an epiphany. The green dragon had forced me to open my heart to Ren again, to admit the depth of my feelings, and in that moment, I suddenly realized that I was the most selfish person on Earth. I was a coward. A chicken. I was implementing my modus operandi again, my fallback for emotional trauma. Keeping Kishan near me meant I didn't have to risk anything. He was my shield.

He protected me from the relationship roller coaster ride that was Ren. I loved Kishan, and I believed I could be happy with him, but I also had to acknowledge that it wasn't exactly the same. Ren's love was an all-consuming fire, but Kishan was more like . . . a space heater. Comfortable, steady, reliable. Both kept me warm, but one could burn

me. Singe me to ashes. If Kishan left me, I would cry, I would hurt, but I would move on, sadder but wiser.

Loving Ren was like loving an atom bomb. When he went off, and it was just a matter of time before he did again, he would destroy everything around in a ten-mile radius. Of course, *I* always managed to be standing in the middle of the bull's-eye. Shrapnel had mangled my heart. Twice. Kishan *tried* to pick up the pieces and hold them together by sheer will, but there were gaps. Pieces were missing.

Oh, my heart tried to fool me. It beat thickly, warmed by Ren's words, by his promises, but it wouldn't matter in the end. Something or someone would take Ren from me, or he'd once again sacrifice himself nobly, and I'd be stuck in the same place I was now, only Kishan would have given up on me by then. I'd be totally, desperately alone. Just like with Li before, I had to choose. I had to pick between the consuming love of Ren that I was so desperate for I sometimes forgot to breathe, and the steady glow, the endless kindness and comfort that Kishan offered me.

After a long moment of thick silence, Ren sucked in a lungful of air. His chest heaved as if he'd forgotten how to breathe. I responded in the same way, and the room came slowly back into focus. I shoved my thoughts to the side and tried to focus my attention on the task at hand while Ren turned his attention back to Jīnsèlóng.

"Do you doubt the truth of our words now, dragon?"

Jīnsèlóng's neck had turned purple as if the very idea was choking him. I couldn't help but giggle. The dragon turned toward me and held out the Scarf. "Take it back! I won't lose my treasure to you, you . . . you succubus!"

Ren raised a hand. "Now, now, Jīnsèlóng. Do you think us novices? We will not take it back. You won it, and her, fair and square."

"Take it! Please! I'll give you other jewels, more gold."

Ren rubbed his jaw and considered it. "No. That's not good enough.

It's quite a burden to be bound to her. You are only feeling the beginnings. Believe me . . . to take the Scarf back would cost a mighty sum."

"Anything. You can have anything." He leaned forward and whispered loudly, "She would make me give away all my treasure to . . . to humans. She'd have me," he flapped his hands in the air, "*fairy* about leaving coins under pillows. That's no life for a *dragon!* No! I won't do it! You must take it back. I *beg* you!" the dragon pleaded.

I played along with their game and kept the dragon distracted by sending him meaningful glances. He set the Scarf gingerly on the arm of his chair and sat as far away from it as possible. I whispered for the Scarf to change shape from time to time, making heart-shaped pillows, cross-stitched handkerchiefs that said "I heart dragons" on them, and a pillowcase embroidered with Kelsey + Jīnsèlóng stitched all along the edges. The dragon squealed and twisted away uncomfortably each time.

After that the negotiations progressed quickly. Ren was able to get back everything we brought with us, plus safe passageway to the white dragon's castle, some interesting information about the Seventh Pagoda and its gatekeeper, a commitment from the dragon for five centuries of safely escorting all manner of ships and aircraft, and ended with a variety of treasures, including the life-sized jade tiger. The dragon even ensured delivery. He clapped his hands and told us that all of our treasures would be found on our ship when we returned.

With the bartering complete, Jīnsèlóng abruptly stood and announced it was time for us to go. He would actually take us to the white dragon's castle, which was also underwater, give us a warm introduction, and then leave. As Kishan and I began to head out of the room, Ren asked us to go on ahead without him. Kishan automatically reached out his hand for mine. I relished the warmth of it and stepped closer.

When Ren reappeared, he had a big smile on his face, and I noticed that he slipped something into his pocket as the dragon spoke.

The dragon walked with him and whispered conspiratorially, "Of

course, of course," patted Ren on the back as if greatly relieved, and said, "And I wish you *every* happiness too." Then he hurried us to the door.

Ren's smile only stayed until he noticed I was holding Kishan's hand. He growled quietly, but I turned my head, avoiding eye contact. As Jīnsèlóng passed us, I couldn't help but flutter my fingers at him in a flirty wave.

He squeaked and, giving me a wide berth, said, "Now when I change into my true form and leave the castle, you will only have a moment before you begin to feel the effects of the ocean's pressure. Take a deep breath and swim out to me, grab onto one of my spikes and then you will be able to breathe comfortably, and the pressure will lessen. And try not to slip off, that would be . . . unfortunate."

The dragon ran a few steps and dove through the invisible barrier of his front door. He swam a bit as a man, and then the castle rocked slightly as his dragon form burst from his human skin like a tidal wave. His long tail ended in a fin and, though he had claws, there was webbing in the spaces between. His sinuous golden body sparkled in the dark water lighting the area around him with a saffron glow. He turned and appeared to be waiting impatiently for us.

Kishan squeezed my hand, dove through the barrier, and found a seat between two spikes of the dragon's back. Ren put his hand on my shoulder but I shrugged it off and dove through the barrier. He followed right behind me and soon passed me, swimming with powerful strokes. I sensed the pressure immediately. I felt as if I were being crushed like trash in a compactor.

Ren paused, noticed my distress, and turned around and swam back to me. Kishan started to swim back too but I waved him off. Ren took my hand and pulled me along quickly. I was running out of air. As a last resort, I mentally asked the Scarf to stretch around a spike and drag me closer.

The minute the Scarf touched the dragon, he bucked and turned to stare fearfully at the threads. Kishan patted his sides, shrugged his shoulders, and grinned. Ren and I finally made it to the dragon's back. I sat behind Kishan while Ren mounted behind me. He wrapped his arms around my waist and held me tightly. The pressure lessened and a bubble rose up and covered my face again so I could breathe.

The Scarf secured my body to Jīnsèlóng's spike, and after peering at the three of us, and the Scarf in particular, the golden dragon shot through the black ocean, moving like a sidewinder. Every once in a while, Jīnsèlóng would look back at us and surge ahead quickly as if it were a wriggling worm being chased by a hungry fish.

23

the ice dragon

the journey to the white dragon's underwater lair was both wondrous and frightening. The golden dragon descended lower, swimming through a sea so black I started to panic and feel claustrophobic. I saw a flash of lights from time to time and stared in fascination as we passed tiny fish that glowed in the dark. An octopus shot out from an outcropping. Its mantle pulsed with red dots, like a Las Vegas marquee, before it disappeared.

I'd expected the depths of the ocean to be silent, but it wasn't. Large animals hummed and called to one another, shocking my body with wave after wave of heavy vibrations. The water became colder. Ren wrapped his arms more tightly around me and pressed my back into his chest. A light penetrated the darkness. At first, I thought my mind was playing tricks on me but the longer I stared at it, the brighter it became.

We rushed toward the light. The dragon put on a burst of speed like a sprinter at the end of a race. It moved so fast, I almost missed the source of the light as we rose briefly above outcroppings and then descended again. I wondered if perhaps I had imagined it, but soon my brief glimpse became a reality as Jīnsèlóng sped to an underwater ice palace.

It jutted from the ocean floor like a crystal stalagmite. We rose over an incline and swam down onto an icy path. On each side of the path, frozen sculpted water plants and flowers sat in frosty beds. A crystal forest of trees rose up on either side, each tree lit from within with a different color, creating what appeared to be a neon city on the ocean floor. The dragon slowed, and I was able to glaze my finger over the leaf of a pink tree that burned with fiery orange in the middle.

I stared in wonder at the glittering masterpieces and wondered if the dragon had created them. The details—the branches and sparkling leaves, the sea-grass spikes jutting in straight points as they grew from the ice plants, the feathered fronds of underwater foliage—were so exact, they mimicked real plants and trees as if transported from another world.

The icy path the dragon followed angled up, and I saw thick steps carved into the ice. When we neared the palace, Jīnsèlóng veered to the right and entered a cave behind the castle. It slowly twisted through the tunnel, using just its tail for propulsion. All around us was a slick passageway of bright blue ice, lit from somewhere above. My curiosity about the white dragon was growing.

We headed toward a brightly lit hole in the ice, and Jīnsèlóng shot through it as if it could glide on the air as easily as it swam. It landed on a slick floor and dug its claws into the ice to keep from sliding. Ren, Kishan, and I hopped off the golden dragon's back. This time we remained wet and we were freezing. I asked the Scarf to gather itself, and the dragon slumped in relief, shaking itself like a dog.

Jīnsèlóng morphed back into his human form and said, "Well, don't just stand there. One of you strapping lads help me over to the sofa. A dragon falling on his behind is not very dignified," he huffed.

I giggled while Jīnsèlóng murmured under his breath.

Kishan slid over to him on bare feet, and together the four of us made our way deeper into the castle. By the time we entered what I

would call a sitting room, I was really cold, and my feet were sticking to the icy floor.

"We need some new clothes and shoes," I whispered.

Ren nodded. "You first."

I had the Scarf drape a curtain across the corner of the room and asked it to replace my clothes with winter gear, put two pairs of socks on my frozen feet, and a thick pair of slippers over those. While I was changing, I had it make clothing for the boys too so they wouldn't have to wait as long. Using my inner heat, I carefully ran my palms over my hair to dry. When done, I felt much better but was still shivering.

After Ren and Kishan emerged in new clothes, and the three of us were snuggled close together on a couch to keep warm, I removed a glove and tried to warm Ren's hand. His hand gently squeezed mine.

"Don't," he said. "Save your heat for yourself. We'll be alright."

I nodded and stuck my nose deeper into my wool scarf.

My teeth chattered, "Tttoo bad the Sscarff can't mmakke heating blanketsss."

I seriously pondered the possibility of warming a blanket with my hands for a minute and then discarded it. "Wwwell?" I asked Jīnsèlóng. "Where issss he? You pppromised to introduce usss."

"He'll be here in a minute," the dragon replied snootily. "It's not like he was expecting visitors." Despite his arrogant attitude, Jīnsèlóng drummed his fingers nervously against the side table made from ice.

My backside was freezing on the ice couch. I shifted back and forth uncomfortably. Quickly realizing my problem, Ren lifted me onto his lap. He moved my legs on top of Kishan and wrapped his arms and coat around me.

"Is that better?"

I sighed. "Yes." I pressed my nose into his chest.

Kishan frowned, but I held out my hand to him, and he pressed my gloved fingers to his lips with a grin.

Jīnsèlóng was very uncomfortable watching this. He squeaked impatiently, "Where can he be?" Then looked at Ren slyly and said, "I really should be getting back to my treasure. Aphrodite gets lonely without me, you see." He smacked his palm against his head. "What was I thinking? It's almost dusting time. You know what can happen to certain metals if they're not dusted every twelve hours."

Ren looked up at him; his lips had been pressed against my hair a moment before. "Relax," he said. "You made a deal, and you're not going anywhere until we get our introduction."

The golden dragon threw an angry hand in the air. "Bah! Remind me never to barter again with tigers."

I snorted, and he narrowed his eyes.

"Or females." He slumped in his seat, took out a bag of jingling coins and began counting them carefully while cleaning them with his sleeve.

We didn't have to wait much longer before a tall, white-haired man entered the room.

"Jīnsèlóng!" The white dragon's voice pummeled us like sleet against a windowpane. "You know you should never bring anyone here unannounced! It is forbidden!"

The golden dragon whimpered, "I had no choice. They tricked the information out of me. It's all the girl's fault, you see. She—"

"Stop. I don't want to hear one more word. I've told you time and again to give up your obsession with hoarding and bartering, and centuries later you still never listen. You never learn. Go away, and I will clean up your mess. As *usual*."

The golden dragon rose up quickly.

"And I don't want to see your metal hide for at least two hundred years!"

"Yes, Yínbáilóng. You won't hear a peep out of me. Thank you."

Jīnsèlóng glanced at us on his way out. I winked at him, and he

squealed and ran the rest of the way. We heard the dragon's heavy body enter the water with a splash, and it was gone.

The white dragon turned to us and smiled warmly. "He is so fun to frighten, isn't he?"

I flushed and nodded.

"That was quite a clever trick you three played on him. It was very well executed. He'll think twice before he barters again. Oh, he'll still do it, mind you, but at least he will think twice, which is more progress than I've made with him in centuries."

The white dragon moved fluidly across the room and bent his tall frame to fit the chair recently vacated by his brother. Crossing one leg over the other, he crooked his elbow on the arm of the chair and rested his head against his finger as he studied us. White hair was smoothed back from a prominent brow. His lips were thin and pressed tightly closed as he appraised us, but his wizened face was full of expression. His eyes were icy blue, almost translucent, and were full of curiosity. His demeanor and accent reminded me of a British professor.

"So," he began. "You're here for a key and not just any key. You want *the* key."

"We need to find Durga's Necklace. I don't know about a key," I ventured.

"Ah, yes. You seek the way to the Seventh Pagoda." He stared into my eyes and froze for a minute.

"Are you reading my thoughts?" I asked.

"No. I wouldn't do that without permission. Just . . . studying you. I haven't conversed with a human in a long time, let alone one so lovely."

"Thank you."

"You've had a long journey, then, haven't you? To make it this far must have been a tremendous effort." He stood as if startled. "Now what kind of a host am I? Here you sit, frozen, hungry, thirsty, and tired while I go on about things that can wait until later."

He whirled his hands and a blue fire lit in the grate near us. It crackled like ice breaking, but it was amazingly warm.

"But won't it melt your castle?" I asked.

Yínbáilóng laughed, a warm sound in a frozen room. "Of course not. My home is protected from melting. Perhaps you have more questions about dragons. I would be happy to answer them over dinner. May I have the pleasure?"

He strode over to our couch and offered his arm. Ren's arms tightened around me, and I heard a little growl from Kishan.

The white dragon chided, "Now, now, gentlemen. There's no need for jealousy. I merely meant to escort the young lady through the halls. You two may follow, of course. If you would, miss?"

"Alright. Thank you."

I took his hand, and Ren reluctantly let me go. He and Kishan immediately trailed along behind us.

We passed what appeared to be a game room with a billiard table, and the dragon asked, "Do either of you young men enjoy billiards? I haven't played a game in quite some time, but it would be a nice way to pass the hours."

"How do you differentiate the snowballs?" Kishan asked with a chuckle.

"They are colored much as my trees outside."

"How do you get them to glow those different colors?" I inquired.

"Bioluminescence."

"You mean phosphorescent animals?"

"Not exactly. Ancient men once stared at the night ocean and saw a glow. They mistakenly associated it with the burning of the chemical phosphor. What is typically called phosphorescence in the ocean has nothing to do with burning at all. It involves no heat. Living creatures called dinoflagellates create my light. Similar to your fireflies on the land, these animals glow with an inner light. Most of them are microscopic

and actually create light when reacting to oxygen above the water. I have duplicated the environment necessary to make them glow here. Feeding and caring for them gives me great happiness."

"So your plants and trees are like tiny aquariums? They're your pets?"

"Precisely. Each tree hosts a different animal that creates different colors. Jellyfish, shrimp, squid, various types of worms, some plants, and also *Cypridina*, which create the most beautiful blue color."

"What are *Cypridina*?"

"They are similar to clams, but their shells are tiny and transparent. Normally they're found in the waters of Japan."

"But don't they freeze inside your ice trees?"

"I can modify the temperature and the environment to meet their needs. In fact, you might have noticed you no longer need your winter gear."

Now that he mentioned it, I was slightly warm. I slipped off my outerwear and tucked it over my arm. We entered a large dining room made of ice. Each chair had a greenish hue, and the large table was red. I moved closer to inspect the surface and saw thousands of tiny creatures wriggling around under the ice.

"They're beautiful!"

"They are. You may all be seated. The chairs won't freeze you any longer. It will feel like you're sitting on chairs made of oak."

After we took our places around the table, the white dragon whirled his hands, and a feast appeared before us. I was starving. We hadn't dared use the Golden Fruit in front of Jīnsèlóng, and the seaweed crackers hadn't been that appealing after I found out what they were. I took a moment to study the banquet in front of me. Ice bowls held king crab legs with clarified butter and cold peeled shrimp with cocktail sauce.

Other dishes were kept warm. There was lobster pot pie, toasted flatbread with a warm cheesy dip made with artichokes, spinach, and

crab. He had platters and bowls full of stuffed sole, seafood gumbo, a julienned salad in a vinaigrette sauce, clam chowder, garlic shrimp linguini, and the biggest maple-and-cherry-glazed salmon I'd ever seen—even in Oregon. He poured us fruity drinks called electric ices that looked like snow cones.

I picked strawberry, and the dragon went to work. He poured a few drops of red syrup into the top of an amazing detailed dragon ice sculpture centerpiece and spoke a few words. The red liquid began to travel through the curvy dragon. Then, Yínbáilóng scooped up a frosty mug and held it under the mouth of the ice sculpture. The drink looked like a slushy but with more liquid and less ice. He repeated the process, making a grapefruit drink for Kishan, lemon for Ren, and cherry for himself.

Indicating the smorgasbord set in front of us, he said, "Please enjoy."

Still slightly cold, I started with the hot clam chowder. It was the most creamy, most flavorful clam chowder I'd ever tasted. I ate half the bowl before I remembered I wanted to ask the dragon some questions.

"Yínbáilóng? Your brother told me that you were all born in different oceans and that he was the Earth Dragon. What does that mean, and who were your parents?"

The Ice Dragon set down his fork and leaned forward, clasping his hands under his chin. "My parents," he said, "are whom you would call Mother Earth and Father Time."

I set down my spoon, hunger forgotten. "You mean they're real people?"

"I don't know that I would call them people, but they are real beings."

"Where do they live? Do you ever see them? What are they like?"

"I do see them though it's doubtful you could because they reside mostly in another dimension. They live . . . well . . . everywhere. If you

could train yourself to see, you could find them. Mother is a part of every living thing on Earth. Plants, animals, people, and even dragons are all her children, and she and Father Time will never cease to exist. He is the past, present, and future. He is omniscient. He knows everything that will happen but is endlessly curious to see the course of the world unfold, regardless. He told me you would be coming. My brothers would have known that too if they would ever listen. They're so young. Like teenagers, really. They think they know everything, so they never listen to our parents. But a wise child always regards parents with respect."

He sipped his drink and went on. "They're . . . retired now. At least as much as immortals can be. They've turned over the duties of guarding Earth and its occupants to us. Jīnsèlóng watches over the treasures of the Earth. He makes sure mineral deposits are created and found, and despite his faults, he inspired the industrial revolution, though his chief purpose was not entirely altruistic. He wished to manufacture goods more quickly, so he could increase the size of his collection. He does have his quirks, but by and large, he's been good for mankind.

"Lùsèlóng is the Earth Dragon, as you know. He is responsible for keeping the balance between the land and sea. He watches over growing things. Trees, flowers, mountains, deserts, and forests are all under his purveyorship. He makes crops grow. He taught the Egyptians how to create papyrus and keep records. If it weren't for him, human-kind wouldn't have any books."

"What about Qīnglóng?" Ren asked.

"Qīnglóng is the laziest of my brothers. Disasters have happened because he refuses to pay attention. He is supposed to be keeping Jīnsèlóng in check. The fact that Jīnsèlóng has so many treasures piled up is because Qīnglóng hasn't been caring for the ocean properly. His job is to provide the world with water.

"He governs the rain clouds, the rivers, lakes, and most of the

oceans, though every so often we help out our own territories. There are creatures becoming extinct in the oceans every day due to his negligence. Overfishing, pollution, and drought are largely his fault. The entire whaling industry happened during one of his naps. But, to be fair, he did inspire your early explorers to find other lands. He was young and eager to please back then."

The white dragon snickered. "Imagine! Columbus discovering land in those tiny ships on his own? Without a dragon, he would have been lost at sea in the first two weeks."

"Kelsey."

I looked over at Ren, who was pointing at my plate with his fork.

"Eat, please."

"Oh, right." To my delight, my fish was still warm. I took a bite and said, "Please, go on."

The Ice Dragon chuckled and ate a bit more himself. "Lóngjūn is the most distant. He rarely visits. He imagines himself to be above us all just because he resides in the sky."

"What's his job?" Ren asked.

"Can you guess?"

"Something to do with the stars?" Kishan suggested.

"Correct. He is in charge of the constellations. He keeps the stars lit and comets on safe trajectories. He governs meteors. Small showers are allowed, but large meteors are moved or destroyed. He's been having trouble with the ozone lately, and that's always his excuse now to miss family reunions.

"He watches over space stations and shuttles and trips to the moon. Lóngjūn was on the moon when Neil Armstrong first set foot on it. In fact, if you watch the old video, you can see his shadow hovering overhead. He is very proud of the space program. He inspires scientific discovery, specifically astronomy, was great friends with Galileo, and

actually visited him in dreams. He's also fond of mathematics. He even taught Pythagoras how to play chess."

"Well, that takes care of everyone except you. What do you do?"

"I am the eldest brother and have the most important charge. You might wonder, what could be more vital than caring for space, land, water, or minerals? Than giving humankind science, math, discovery, technology, or a green planet?"

He paused with a twinkle in his eye and waited for one of us to guess. No one got the right answer. He politely dabbed his lips with his napkin and said, "I am the white dragon of the ice. I watch over the ice caps and the poles. I turn the Earth on its axis. I whirl us around the sun. I cause the seasons to change.

"I inspire humans in philosophy, democracy, order, and the law. I cannot afford to nap. I cannot afford to ignore my duty. One mistake would send our planet whirling off into the dark universe. One misstep would damage the time line. One tiny loss of control, and the axis of Earth would shift, plummeting us into chaos. I was the voice behind the world's greatest philosophers, religious reformers, and political revolutionaries. I follow the laws of the universe—the basic fundamental truths that govern all humankind."

My fork clattered noisily to the table. I picked it up, embarrassed, but he continued.

"Of course, such things are transitory. Greed and avarice can overtake anyone, but I still have hope. It worked in Shangri-la."

"You're responsible for Shangri-la?" I asked.

"Indirectly. I can teach only basic right and wrong, so the people learn self-governance. The society then has to choose to accept it fully or in part. If even one member chooses to go another path, the system will eventually fail. The Silvanae not only accepted but also embraced the concept. They have lived peacefully in their land for millennia, and

the animals that choose to accept and abide by their laws live there in harmony as well."

"But what about the world tree? The iron birds didn't seem to follow the same law."

"The birds of which you speak were created for one purpose. They protected the Scarf. They did not wish you harm until you took the object they were designed to guard. They ceased to exist after the Scarf left their lands."

"And the ravens and the sirens?"

"They were only fulfilling their purpose. They did not mean to injure you."

"And now what do they do?"

"They have been given a choice. The ravens and bats chose to follow the Silvanae law and may come and go as they please, but the sirens preferred to leave. They found no one among the Silvanae willing to become their . . . *inamorata*. So they chose to leave the tree, which can still be found just outside the Silvanae lands. Incidentally, the invisible protector remained in Shangri-la as well."

"Interesting. But how do you know about the Scarf and the Fruit when Jīnsèlóng didn't?"

"As I mentioned, he often doesn't pay attention when important events occur. Would you like some more? You haven't eaten much, young lady."

"It's hard to eat when I have so many questions."

"Don't let that ruin your appetite. I will remain at your side and answer as many questions as you have time for. In fact, I would like you all to remain as my guests this evening. You will need a good night's sleep before you journey to the Seventh Pagoda."

We accepted and spent another hour at the table, nibbling treats and asking questions. Yínbáilóng reminded me of Mr. Kadam. He

knew about almost everything, and I could listen to him ruminate for hours at a time. He invited Ren and Kishan to play billiards with him. I perched on a seat and watched them play. The dragon was quite good. He explained the rules and commented from time to time, giving tips as they played and claimed he invented the game. It wasn't long before I began yawning.

The dragon offered to escort me to my room, but I stuck it out another half hour. He then insisted that I rest and said if I'd like to walk on my own, I merely needed to press my hand on the wall, and the little living creatures would light up and show me the way. I nodded and both Ren and Kishan set down their cue sticks to follow me. The dragon raised an eyebrow, amused, and waited for my response. I put my hand on Kishan's arm and stood up on tiptoe to kiss his cheek. "Do you mind if Ren walks me back? I need to talk to him."

Kishan said goodnight, kissed me softly, and reluctantly turned back to the game. Ren stuck his hands in his pockets and studied my expression with suspicion.

"After you."

I sighed, placed my hand on the icy wall, and said, "A guest room, please."

Tiny green creatures surged toward my hand just behind the ice and began moving forward. I clasped my hands behind my back and followed them. Ren silently paced along behind.

After we were several halls away from the billiards room, he asked, "Well? What did you want to talk about?"

I bit my lip. "Do you remember when you first came to America, and I was dating Li?"

"And *Jason* and *Artie*."

"Right. Well, when you first arrived, you told me that you wanted me to date both of you and make a choice."

"Yes."

"You also said that if I did choose Li you would support my choice. That the important thing was that you be near me. That if friendship was all I could give, you would take it."

"Yes. Where are you going with this, Kelsey?"

"I'm getting there. Be patient."

We arrived at my guest suite, and I opened the door. A blue fire crackled in a corner of the room, and a huge bed with an ice frame took up most of the space. The floor looked like it was covered with ice shavings. I bent to touch it, and it felt like a deep shag carpet. I kicked off my slippers and wiggled my toes. Little creatures under the floor drifted toward my feet and massaged my toes. Experimentally, I picked up my foot and they disappeared. When I put it back, they began massaging again.

Impatiently, Ren leaned back against the doorjamb. "What are you trying to say, Kells?"

I turned to him, but lowered my gaze, afraid to meet his intense expression. "I'm trying to say that I knew then that we belonged together, and I chose *you*."

"Yes, I remember," he agreed softly.

"But you promised that if I *had* picked Li, you would always be there for me. You would always be my friend. Is that true? Even if I'd chosen someone else?"

"You know it is." He took a step closer and picked up my hand. "I would never abandon you."

I took a deep breath. "That's good because I don't think I'd like life much without you in it. You know that I'll always be your friend too, don't you? That I wouldn't desert you?"

Puzzled, Ren tilted his head back to study my face. He paused before answering hesitantly, "Yes. I know that you're my friend."

"And the most important thing is that we're a family, right?"

"Yes."

"Alright. Then I'm going to tell you something, and I need you to understand I've given it a lot of thought. I want you to open your mind and listen."

Ren folded his arms across his chest. "Alright. I'm listening."

"First, I need to clarify something. When you and Kishan were declaring your feelings to Jīnsèlóng, did you mean everything you said?"

"Yes. I meant every word."

I blew out a breath. "That's what I was afraid of," I muttered.

"Why do you say that?"

"Okay, here goes. You're my first love. You're more important to me than water or air. Thanks to Lùsèlóng, you already know that, but I can at least confirm it. I wish I could have spared you the hurt and torture you endured. I wish that Lokesh had never found us, and we were still in school. Everything was easy then."

Ren raised an eyebrow.

"Well, *easier*, anyway. I wish that we'd never been separated, that you were the one with me in Shangri-la."

He pressed his palm against my cheek and stroked it lightly with his thumb. "You know I wish for those things too."

"Yes, I know. But it doesn't change anything. I've thought about this for a long time. Really, ever since you forgot me." I looked away and twisted my hands. Stammering, I continued, "This isn't easy for me, and I don't say this lightly. But weighing everything in the balance, it's just what makes the most sense."

"Just spit it out, woman. What are you trying to say?"

I took a deep breath and looked him in the eye. "You've been trying to get me to admit that I'm still in love with you. You were right. I am. I'm *crazy* in love with you, and I don't know that my feelings for you are *ever* going to change but—"

"*But what?*" His face darkened slightly. I even blinked, thinking it was a figment of my imagination.

"But . . . I can't choose *you* this time. I'm choosing . . . *Kishan.*"

He dropped his hand from my cheek and took a step away. He looked at me with disbelief, and then his expression turned angry. The anger rolled into self-doubt, and then a kind of coolness stole over his face. Ren said nothing for a long minute.

I couldn't tell what he was thinking, and anxious, I stretched out my hand and touched his forearm. "I need you to understand. This doesn't mean that I don't need *you*. I'll always—"

Ren drew himself up and nodded politely, reminding me of that long ago day in the jungle when I rebuffed him after he'd asked for permission to kiss me. Tightly, he spoke, "Of course. I understand." He edged through the open door and started to leave.

I dashed to the door. "But, Ren—"

He turned his head slightly so that I could see his profile. As if it pained him to look at me, he dropped his eyes and said softly, "The white tiger will *always* be your protector, Kelsey. Good-bye, *priyatama*."

24

the ocean of milk

ood-bye? *I never do this right! Why do I always screw up everything?* I'd meant to tell him *why* I wasn't picking him. I wanted him to understand my thinking . . . or at least hear me out. Honestly, I thought he might actually stick around and talk me out of it. Tell me I was an idiot. Tell me I was just letting my petty fears scare me out of something wonderful, something perfect.

I thought it would be easier, more practical, if I just picked Kishan. *No. Practical is the wrong word.* Safer. *That's the right one. Ren* took risks. *Ren* surrounded himself with beautiful bikini-clad girls. *Ren* subjected me to Randi. I know *why* he did it, but the fact remains that he still did. And if another opportunity to "save me" came along, he wouldn't hesitate. He'd once again sacrifice himself, and I'd be alone. I'd almost had the man of my dreams. But almost doesn't count.

Almost winners aren't remembered anyway. Nobody cared if you *almost* made a touchdown. *Almost* had that three-point shot at the buzzer. *Almost* made a triple play. What counted was the final score. I was a coach who'd just benched the all-star rookie player. I had my reasons, but the fans didn't care. All they'd see was a coach who'd made what they felt was a very bad decision.

But, to be fair, do you throw the rookie into the championship game, hoping his showy enthusiasm will get you points? Or do you put in your slower but steadier guy? The players who've proved themselves all season. They may not hit three-point shots but they can go the distance. *Sheesh! Was I just thinking of a sports analogy? I must be desperate.*

Besides, who took care of me when Ren nobly let himself be kidnapped? Kishan. Who told off Randi when she was insulting me? Kishan. Who lets me wear my hair the way I want to? Kishan. Who said he'd be willing to let me be with another if that's what I really wanted? Kishan. Who never argues with me? Kishan. Who kept his hands off when I asked him to? Kishan. I got distracted for a moment thinking about a fight with Ren that resulted in him putting his hands *on* me and me *liking* it, and then shook it off. *What was I thinking about? Oh, yeah. Kishan.*

Kishan was a safe bet. Loving Ren was a gamble.

Hmm . . . maybe I should join an Anonymous group. I could picture it already.

Hi. My name is Kelsey, and I'm an addict.

Hi, Kelsey.

It's been two minutes since I let Ren walk away, and I think I'm going to fall off the wagon.

No! Stay strong, girl! We're here to support you.

Right. But you don't understand. I can't live without him.

Sure you can. You just take it one day at a time.

You mean I have to go a whole day without seeing him?

My fellow addicts would laugh. *Try a whole lifetime, girl. You've got to go cold turkey. Completely expunge him from your life. Mementos will just tempt you. You're an addict, and you're in denial. Now let's repeat the serenity prayer:*

Grant me the serenity to selflessly forgo my relationship to save humankind;
To accept that the man I love cannot and will not change;
The courage to let him realize his potential and fulfill his destiny;
And the wisdom to stay as far away from him as possible.

I sighed and slid under the blue ice-palace covers. *Maybe I need a sponsor.* Could I really expect Ren to hang around and watch me be with his brother? It would be cruel, like he said. *I couldn't do it if the situation were reversed. Maybe Lokesh would kill me, and then everyone would be better off. Seems like my disappearing would solve everyone's problem.* I fell asleep and dreamed of Lokesh hunting me in the jungle, just like when Lùsèlóng hunted the boys, only I didn't have any claws to protect myself.

I woke feeling displaced before remembering I was in the Ice Dragon's palace. I turned to my side and buried my fist beneath my cheek. The bed rolled slightly and glowed softly as tiny creatures surged to the surface, warming and massaging everywhere my body touched the mattress. My thoughts picked up right where they'd left off the night before. I was not feeling very confident that I'd made the right decision, but I was determined to follow through on it regardless.

Attached to the strange bedroom was a private bathroom. The clear shower taps turned easily, and blue water cascaded from a series of jets. It was hot and steamy despite its crystallized appearance. I used a cerulean ice gel to shampoo my hair. It tingled and smelled like mint.

There were no towels, but when I turned off the shower a series of air blowers turned on. I stood there shocked, feeling like an old car in a gas station car wash. Warm air pummeled my body from every angle, and once I got over the surprise, I actually enjoyed it. *Huh. Now I understand why dogs stick their heads out of car windows.*

Thoroughly dry, I stepped out and, with dismay, tried to run my fingers through my hair. I had giant cotton-ball hair. It would take forever to comb out, so I left it and turned to the Scarf for more clothes. Then I sought other humans. Well . . . the closest thing to humans anyway. I found my tigers breakfasting with the dragon.

"Mmm . . . smells good."

"Won't you please join us, my dear?" the dragon asked politely. Then he looked up. "My, don't you look . . . fluffy."

I groaned and pulled a poofy strand of hair over my shoulder to stare at it. Kishan looked up and started laughing. I narrowed my eyes. "It's not *that* funny. You don't happen to have a brush or comb, do you?"

Kishan snickered. "Nope. Sorry, Kells."

"Yínbáilóng?"

"We dragons don't need such accessories."

I sighed and sat down.

"I have one," Ren said quietly from across the table. I'd been avoiding eye contact with him. Trying to ignore his presence hadn't really worked, as I was ultra aware of him, but I'd made a good effort. Resigned, I looked up, but he'd already turned aside.

He reached into his treasure bag and pulled out a golden comb. Rising from his seat, he came around to my side of the table to set it gently near my plate, and then he abruptly left the room. I picked up the delicate treasure and wondered how I could use something this priceless to tame my unruly nest of hair. It was narrow, about the size of my hand, with long tongs. The top was carved mother-of-pearl and showed a knight on horseback slaying some kind of beast.

Kishan speared a slice of melon and said with a grin, "I kind of like it the way it is now."

After breakfast, I followed Kishan and the dragon to the sitting room. Ren was already waiting for us. Picking up the comb, I began working on my hair as Yínbáilóng told us about the ice caves and the hidden key that we would need in order to access the Seventh Pagoda. He said the key could only be accessed by one with the blood of the gods running through his veins.

I listened with half an ear. My mind was distracted, which wasn't good considering it would probably take all three of us to retrieve Durga's Pearl Necklace and make it out alive. Thankfully, Kishan seemed to

be paying attention. I smiled and daydreamed a little as I methodically combed my puffed up hair.

My mind drifted to another time, a balmy Indian night when Ren had combed gently through my hair. My scalp suddenly felt tingly, and I shivered slightly remembering his sweet, hesitant touch. I glanced up and found Ren intensely watching me. I blushed, wondering if he was thinking about the same thing. He quickly tore his eyes away and went back to listening to the dragon. When I'd finally tamed my hair and braided it, the three of them had come up with a plan. It was time to go.

Grabbing my bag and sliding Fanindra up my arm, I trailed Kishan, Ren, and the white dragon through an icy door. We stepped into a huge room with no furnishings. Clear ice surrounded us on every side, and the dark ocean was lit outside the cube. Strange creatures of all kinds swam lazily all around us.

"I call this room the fishbowl," announced the white dragon.

I snorted. "Only we're the fish."

I wandered closer to one wall, with Kishan following. A sausage-shaped diaphanous sea cucumber moved along the glass, leaving a trail. Snails and starfish also clung to the translucent wall. I looked beyond the starfish and jumped back, seeing a hatchet fish, the size of a beanbag chair, with giant glowing eye lenses and a gaping mouth.

Other types of fish made me squirm. Gulper eels with huge heads and wide jaws big enough to swallow fish larger than themselves; angler fish with big teeth and a bobbing headlight; and lantern fish with a row of tiny strobe lights running along the bottom of their bodies swam by, ready to snap at our fingers. Viper fish with curved fangs so long the fish couldn't close its mouth, albino lobsters and crabs, colorful jellyfish, and what Yínbáilóng called vampire squid also came in for a closer look.

A huge dark shape slid past the icy box and bellowed.

"What was that?" I asked, shaken. "Please tell me that wasn't a giant shark."

Yínbáilóng laughed. "It was a sperm whale. They're the only large creatures that can make it to this depth. They like to stop by for a visit once in a while."

"Oh," I said somewhat relieved. "Uh, exactly how deep are we?"

"Well, let's just say, normally, you wouldn't be able to survive here. The pressure would kill you. Fortunately, you are protected as long as you remain in my realm. Dragons can withstand any pressure. I could even survive in the Mariana Trench, the deepest trench of the ocean, though it's not a very pleasant place to be. I much prefer the bottom half of the bathypelagic zone."

"What's that?" Kishan asked.

"The oceans are divided into four zones according to depth. Jīnsèlóng lives in the euphotic zone, which comprises the top five hundred feet of the ocean. Plants grow there, and it's full of a variety of marine life. He does leave, though, to seek treasure in all the zones. The mesopelagic zone is next. It doesn't have plant life, but numerous animals still seek sustenance in its depths. That is where you find most species of shark." The white dragon smiled at me briefly and went on.

"We are between three thousand and ten thousand feet, the bathypelagic zone, where the only large animal, like I mentioned, is the sperm whale. Food is scarce, but I provide for those who choose to share my realm. It's feeding time soon, and that's quite a sight to behold. Below this level is the abyssal zone, which continues on to the bottom of the ocean. There isn't really all that much going on down there. But the Seventh Pagoda *is* located in the upper part of the abyssal zone. It's not really that much deeper than you are now, and once you reach the Ocean of Milk, you should have smooth sailing—if you'll forgive the pun."

I elbowed Kishan. "The Ocean of Milk? Did we talk about that already?"

Kishan leaned over and whispered, "I'll fill you in."

"Thanks."

The dragon asked, "Would you like to see me feed the fish before you go?"

"If you don't mind, dragon, we'd like to get under way," Ren said, looking restless.

"Very well. Make sure you keep warm, my dear."

"Umm, okay." *Note to self: next time I'm hanging out with a white dragon at the bottom of the ocean, pay attention!*

Kishan used the Scarf to make me a down parka and snow gear. He slipped the jacket over my arms and shoulders and handed me a pair of gloves so thick that they rendered my hands useless. He wrapped a scarf around my neck, and topped the whole outfit with not one, but two hats.

"Don't you think you've gone a bit overboard? I feel like a snow-woman."

"It's cold where we're going," Kishan explained. "And—"

"Stand back," the dragon interrupted. "I need to take my natural form to open the doors."

I didn't see any doors except the one we came in through, but Kishan pressed me up against a wall while I pretended not to notice the hungry fish with giant teeth that knocked uselessly against the ice trying to take a nibble. Yínbáilóng cracked and splintered into a thousand shards that gleamed and disappeared, and a sparkling white body spilled onto the glassy floor. Its dragon claws were blue, as were its eyes. Its underbelly shimmered like the aurora borealis. The scales on its back looked like white diamonds and sparkled as it moved.

The white dragon's long face stretched toward me with a smile, and its blue forked tongue curled out as I heard it chuckle in my mind. The two horns on the back of its head looked like long icicles, and it had more on the end of its tail. A white mane stretched from the top of its noble head all the way down its back.

I pulled off a glove and stroked the dragon's nose, finding it smooth and warm, not icy at all. "You're beautiful!"

Thank you, my dear. I like to think so. Now stand back so I can open the door.

Yínbáilóng angled its head to peer at a wall. Its mouth gaped open to reveal long rows of pointed teeth. Its body began to shine brighter and brighter until I had to look away. The light seemed to move toward its head until it concentrated in its eye. Blue light shot out from its unblinking orb and penetrated the wall. Layers of thick ice peeled back, as if melting away. I squinted and saw a door where there was none before. When the dragon was satisfied, it shuffled back, snorted a frozen breath, and shifted back to its human form.

"It is done. Through this door is a path that will take you directly to the Ocean of Milk. Once you cross it and find the guardian, she will guide you to the key and the Seventh Pagoda. Listen carefully to her instructions. Now, shall I stay to help you strap in?"

"That would probably be a good idea," Kishan said.

"You first, my dear. Let's make sure you're comfortable."

Just as I started to ask what everyone was talking about, Kishan guided me through the door and onto an ice sled. He quickly piled thick blankets on top of me and strapped me in.

"We're traveling by sled," Kishan explained.

"Yeah. I can see that. Where are the dogs?"

The dragon patted my head and answered, "Your young men will pull the sled."

"What? How? They'll freeze."

"They'll be perfectly warm. Gentlemen?"

Ren's hair fell across his cheek as he bent to secure his bag to the sled. He was so close his warm sandalwood scent washed over me. My fingertips itched to smooth back his hair, but he rose without looking at me, nodded, and he and Kishan morphed into their tiger forms. I watched in shock as the dragon strapped them into the sled harnesses.

"They don't need to pull me," I stammered. "I can walk."

The dragon immediately dismissed my suggestion. "This way will be much faster. Besides, it's best not to linger too long behind the ice. The animals here *do* get very hungry. These walls are thick, but you never know when they might break through."

"And by break, you mean . . . break through the ice?"

"Yes. I've recently solidified the tunnels, but there is tremendous pressure in this part of the ocean. Of course, remember that you will not always be vulnerable in the ocean; the ice tunnels lead to caves that wind through rock as well."

"Fabulous. So how do I drive this thing?"

"That's the beautiful part. You don't need to. Your tigers will do the driving for you."

"Wonderful," I murmured sarcastically.

"Good luck to you all. I wish you the best."

With that the dragon closed the door, and we were plummeted into blackness. Fanindra wrapped herself around the handle of the sled and lit up the little cavern with her green eyes.

"Alright, boys. Mush, I guess."

Ren leapt first and the sled swayed dangerously from side to side for a time until the brothers fell into rhythm. I watched the tigers run, claws digging into the ice, and kept a wary lookout for hungry fish. At one point, a fish the size of Ren's Hummer took an interest. It raced along with us for several minutes and even nudged the ice tunnel, scraping it briefly with its long, pointed teeth before swimming off—much to my relief. Ren and Kishan seemed to have endless amounts of energy and ran for several hours, stopping only for brief rests.

Somehow, somewhere along the ice tunnel I fell asleep—only to be awakened by a sudden bump along the path. Blinking into the darkness, I wondered how far we'd traveled. The smooth ice tunnel through the ocean had changed to a snow-like crushed-ice path with jutting rocks and I realized that we were surrounded by earth not water. I insisted we stop so the brothers could eat and wished up a whole pot roast for each. I sipped a steaming hot chocolate while they ate and rested.

It was cold. I felt like the tin man. All my joints were frozen in whatever position I'd fallen asleep. I shifted and tried to find a more comfortable position and fruitlessly tried to remove my safety strap so that it wouldn't dig into my shoulder. Frustrated, I yanked off my glove and immediately felt the temperature difference. The cold was so frigid it was painful. It was the kind of cold that seeped into bones, and even the hottest of showers wouldn't be able to warm them again.

After another few hours of running, Ren and Kishan decided to stop for the night. I unhooked the boys from their harnesses, asked the Scarf to make a tent and dozens of blankets, and then crawled under all of them. My tigers snuggled right next to me, one on each side, and like little super heaters, they kept me toasty all night.

We continued the journey the next day. Around midmorning, the rock cave opened into a larger cavern with a frozen lake. The tigers cautiously walked onto the ice, sniffing as they moved. A few more cautious steps, and they began running again, though more slowly. I had no idea how they knew where to go, but they went on, both heads aimed in the same direction. Maybe it was a tiger sixth sense. Or more likely, they knew where they were going because they listened to the white dragon while my mind had been occupied elsewhere.

We entered another tunnel on the far side of the lake. It wasn't long before we came into a carved-out room. The ice path ran in a circle around it; in the center was a tall stone fountain. Ren and Kishan stopped, and I asked the Scarf to make them clothes while I unbuckled them. When they were free, I turned my attention to the fountain, which was about twenty feet tall, had four basins, and was covered with ice.

Kishan shrugged into a thick coat and walked over to me. "It's up to you now, Kells. Free the guardian."

"What? What do I have to do?" I asked nervously, wondering what new kind of scariness I'd be facing next.

"Melt the ice," Kishan replied, nodding to the fountain.

Relieved, I relaxed and smiled. "That I can do. Flowing water, coming right up."

I peeled off my gloves and raised both hands. Starting at the top of the fountain, I slowly worked my way down. Each inch I melted uncovered the most beautifully detailed carvings of fish, dolphins, starfish, crabs, and turtles. My power started to wane when I was only a third of the way finished.

"What's wrong?" Kishan asked.

"She's cold," a warm voice behind us responded. *One that I tried desperately to ignore.*

Kishan took my hand and rubbed it between his palms. "Is that better? Try now."

I did, but the heat soon sputtered again, and what was worse, the water I'd defrosted was glazing over.

"Maybe you just need to rest for a while," Kishan suggested.

Ren walked up and silently held out his hand. I glanced at it and shook my head.

"Don't be stubborn, Kelsey."

I rubbed my palms vigorously. "I can do this myself, thanks." I tapped my inner core of fire and threw everything I had into the blaze, determined not take Ren's hand and allow myself to succumb to the burning I felt when he touched me. I could finish without him.

I pushed heat out until the cavern thrummed with it. The ice melted faster and faster. I started to sweat as the fire flamed down my arms. When I finally thawed the bottom of the fountain, I had about two seconds to marvel at the life-sized mermaid I'd uncovered before I collapsed at Kishan's feet. He picked me up and set me on the lip of the fountain to rest. Ren scolded me, despite my verbal assurances that I was fine and my admonition to zip it.

Now that the water was moving freely, I saw how beautiful it was. The water wasn't clear or even blue. It was milky white and sparkling. Dolphins at the top of the fountain shot water into the second basin while stone fish peeked out of the third tier and dribbled water into the next. Turtles lay as if sunning themselves on rocks, and the mermaid wriggled her tail and combed through her long hair with her fingers and . . . *wait* . . . the mermaid was *alive*!

She giggled and twitched flirty fingers at Kishan. "Aren't you a lucky girl to be carried around by such a handsome man?"

"Yep. My luck runneth over. Are you the guardian of the key?"

"That all depends," she leaned forward and whispered conspiratorially. "Just between us girls, can I keep one of these two?"

I frowned. "What, exactly, would you do with one of them?"

The mermaid tittered. "I'm sure I could think of something."

"They do have claws and tails, you know."

"And I've got scales. So what?"

"Yes, indeed, you do have scales," Kishan grunted appreciatively.

I slapped his arm lightly. "Stop looking."

"Right." He cleared his throat. "We really do need the key to the Seventh Pagoda. Umm . . . What is your name?"

She pouted prettily. "Kaeliora. Alright, you can have the key. But you'll have to get it yourselves. If I can't keep one of the men, then there's no good reason for me to get my hair wet again." She frowned and peered at her reflection in the water. "It's been covered in ice so long all the roots are drying out," she exclaimed. Picking up a comb made of coral, she began delicately combing out her mounds of long blonde hair.

When she picked up the section covering her right upper body, I gasped softly. She had scales alright. They were all over her. Her arms, face, and back were human, but the scales from her fish tail traveled up most of her torso and banded around her neck like a halter top. When she turned to look at her reflection in the water again, I saw that the whole front of her upper body was encased in cat-suit-style scales that seemed somehow more provocative than her being nude. Kaeliora's scales were a kind of purplish-green and gray like those of a rainbow trout. She was gorgeous and seemed to be seeking Ren and Kishan's attention.

Turning my eyes deliberately to the snapping turtle, I said, "So? The key? You won't have to get your hair wet. I'll do it."

"Fine, but first, where's my present?" She fluttered her fingers.

"What present?" I asked.

"You *know* . . . something bright and living?"

"Uh . . . sorry. We didn't bring you anything."

She pouted. "Then I guess I can't help you after all."

"Wait," Ren said. He opened his bag and took out Durga's lotus lei. "The prophecy said to lay the wreath on the Sea of Milk. Is this what you want, Kaeliora? Flowers?" He placed the flowers on the milky water, where they floated to the mermaid's outstretched fingers.

"Oh!" She picked up the wreath and cradled the blossoms to her face. "I haven't smelled a fresh bloom in thousands of years. It's perfect."

She settled the lei around her neck and splashed her tail happily.

We stood around for a minute waiting for her to notice us again. The mermaid admired the reflection of herself, the flowers, her hair, and so on.

Finally, I said, "The key?"

"Oh! You're still here? Very well," she mumbled as she studied her hair for split ends. "It's back there at the bottom of the lake."

"The bottom of the lake! How do you expect us to get it?" I asked.

She raised her head and grinned. "By swimming, of course. What a silly question."

"But the water is frozen, and it's too deep!"

"It's not *that* deep. Only twenty feet or so, but it is cold. Whoever goes in will probably freeze before getting back to the surface."

"I'll go," Ren softly volunteered.

Something snapped inside me, and I couldn't stop it from bursting out. "Of *course* you'd say that!" I yelled. "Always willing to put yourself in harm's way, aren't you? Can't resist a worthy cause, no matter how dangerous! Why not? He's faster than a speeding bullet, able to leap tall buildings. *Naturally*, you want to go."

"Why should I stay?" he asked quietly.

"No. You're right. You have absolutely no reason to keep yourself safe. It's just another day at the office for you, isn't it, Superman? No, Iceman would be more appropriate in this case. Why not? Go ahead! Fly off and save the day, like you always do. Just make sure you don't come back as Mr. Freeze. He was the bad guy."

Kishan stepped in. "I think you're overreacting, Kells."

"Sure I am. But we all have our roles to play, don't we? I'll play the part of the irritating girlfriend who holds everyone back. You can be the

nice guy who stays behind, consoles the girl, and pats her hand, and Ren can go off and save the world. That's how all this works, am I right?"

Ren sighed, and Kishan looked at me as if I was out of my mind, *which I was*, and the mermaid wrinkled her nose and giggled. "Isn't this fun?" she said. "But it doesn't matter anyway. *He* can't go. Only this one can." She pointed to Kishan and then became fascinated with her fingernails.

"What? Why him?" I asked.

"Because *he* drank the *soma*. If this one tried to enter the water," she pointed to Ren, "it would kill him immediately."

"Drank the *soma*? You mean that drink at Phet's house?"

"I don't have any idea where he drank it. I just know he did. The power just shimmers on his skin. Can't you see it? It's very enticing."

I peered at Kishan. "Nope, can't really see his power."

"Well, the water is full of it. Power, I mean. My job is to stir it once in a while so it doesn't settle to the bottom. Dip a finger in, and you'll get the shock of your life. An arm, and your brain shuts down. Your entire body? Zap! You're just nutmeg floating in the eggnog."

"Great," I mumbled.

"But the water does do wonders for a girl's scales. Milk baths are all the rage when your tail dries out. Don't *you* try it, though. There's not just creamy goodness in *that* lake. All kinds of special powers are in there, and only an elite few can access them. You might call it the swimming pool of the gods, and only those who have a pass can enter. It's a members-only kind of thing. Neither of you belong to the club. He'll probably still freeze anyway, but at least *he* has a sporting chance. Oh, and I forgot to mention, you'd better make it quick. My toes are freezing already, and if the fountain refreezes before you get back, you can't enter or exit the lake, and I won't be able to tell you how to get the Necklace."

We stood there dumbfounded.

"Shoo. Go on now. Hurry up."

The three of us took off at a run, slipping and sliding back through the tunnel to the lake. I heard the soft complaints of the mermaid whining about her tail not getting enough moisturizer. Then we turned the corner, and I couldn't make out her words anymore.

Kishan threw off his coat and slipped out of his shoes while I used my heat to make a hole in the ice big enough for him to enter.

We could faintly hear Kaeliora shouting, "It's gold! Shines in the dark! Can't miss it!"

Kishan shook out his limbs, kissed me hard, and dropped straight down into the ice. He stayed down several minutes before his head cracked the thin glaze now covering the hole. Taking a deep breath he said, "Don't see it yet."

I stood there stewing, biting my lip, and trying to think of a rational excuse for why I didn't act the same way with Kishan diving in the dangerous water as I had with Ren. I was soon able to convince myself that it was just because I hadn't had the time to process my feelings.

Two more times Kishan surfaced. On the last time, he said, "I saw it, but it's pretty far. I'm sure I can get it though." His teeth chattered, and his lips were blue.

Kishan submerged again, and the mermaid called out in a loud but still-bored voice, "He won't make it. He's freezing to death. You can help him, you know."

"How?" I hollered back.

"You already *know* how."

I let another few seconds go before ripping off my coat and yanking off Ren's. He didn't say anything, and he already seemed to know what I was going to do. I pushed up the sleeves of my shirt and threw my firepower at the lake. Ren pulled me back into his chest, pressed his

cheek against mine, and slid his hands down my arms. I felt the hot flames lick my skin as golden fire burst from not one of my palms, but both of them. He twined his fingers with mine, and the heat intensified.

Steam rose from the lake and the hole grew quickly and began to expand across the entire surface. A head emerged halfway down and Ren whispered, "He's alright. I can hear him breathing. Can you do more?"

I nodded and continued to warm the lake until I could no longer see ice and Kishan started swimming toward us in the milky water.

He got closer and shouted, "Hey! This feels pretty good. Almost like a sauna! Too bad you two can't try it!"

Seeing he was safe, I jerked myself away from Ren, who raised an eyebrow, but otherwise said nothing, and asked the Scarf to make towels.

Kishan stood up, waded out of the water, and shook himself like a dog. He grabbed me, gave me a very soggy kiss, and pressed the key into my hand. While Kishan stayed behind and changed into dry clothes, I ran down the now muddy path back to the fountain with Ren following along silently behind me.

I slid to a stop by the half-frozen mermaid, gave her a blast of heat, and then showed her the key. "We've got it. Now what?"

25

the seventh pagoda

"**G**ood. Now listen to me very carefully. You obviously seek the Necklace and have Durga's favor." Kaeliora paused to delicately sniff the lotus blossoms again. "Otherwise I wouldn't be helping you. Continue to follow this path. The tunnel will lead you back to the ocean. I suggest you move through the ice quickly, because some of the world's most ancient creatures make this realm their home, and they aren't too keen on intruders."

"The white dragon didn't tell us about that," I commented as Kishan caught up to us.

"Yes, well, he hasn't been down here in a long time, and what doesn't faze a dragon can be deadly to a human. Some of the ocean's most terrifying predators are mere pets to one such as Yínbáilóng. Once you arrive at the pagoda, use the key to open the doors. The Necklace will be found inside the shell of a large oyster in a pool of milky water so make sure only he," she nodded at Kishan, "goes in to search for it. That's the easy part."

"Wonderful," I muttered.

"The hard part is—" she wiggled her tail and softly grunted. "I seem to be frozen again. Would you mind?"

I sighed and lifted my hand but nothing happened.

"She can't. She's exhausted," Kishan explained.

Ren removed his glove and caught my bare wrist before I could move out of range. Golden light surged out from my palm to warm the entire fountain. Steam rose from the water, and the mermaid sunk deeper, sighing with pleasure.

"*That* is absolutely lovely. You don't know how long it's been since I've been truly warm. Thank you."

"No problem." I lowered my hand and tried to inconspicuously jerk my wrist away from Ren's grip. Sheepishly, I took a step closer to Kishan, who seemed shocked. I glared at Ren, who just looked away. It's not like I was exactly *cheating* on Kishan, but I felt like I'd just been caught lip-locked with Ren. There was something different, something special, about the golden flame, and I didn't want to explore the uniqueness of it.

"It's nothing," I whispered.

The mermaid disagreed. "Oh, I'd definitely say it's something. I haven't seen a connection that strong in millennia."

"What do you mean by connection?" Kishan inquired politely but with an edge in the undertone.

"That light. It's more powerful than she can make alone. He acts like . . . well, like a filament. She pours her energy into him, and he heats it. Then he sends it back into her just like a light bulb. They create a kind of vacuum between them; that is the connection I am referring to. It's very special and rarely seen. When they're touching, nothing else exists outside the two of them. All they are aware of is each other."

My first reaction was shock. *That explains a lot.* The mermaid was dead-on accurate. There was only one problem with her theory. Ren didn't *need* to touch me to create a vacuum. I could feel him—all warm and powerful—*all the time*. All I needed to do was close my eyes, and he could wrap me in a bubble so strong I'd forget everyone and everything else. Ren was just *that* potent.

My connection to Ren was *cosmic. Makes sense.* We were destined to find each other to break the curse. That's all. And if I just avoided touching him, I could probably do a better job at being Kishan's girlfriend and, as a result, be less plagued by guilt. I might even be able to forget *what's-his-name* and love Kishan completely with my *full* heart, which was my goal.

Kishan looked at me with hurt and confusion, probably misunderstanding the emotions that were crossing my face. I took Kishan's hand and downplayed the parts I didn't want to think about.

"Well, I guess that explains why we can create the golden light together, *if* you can take an ice mermaid's word on the whole light bulb analogy. As if she would know. Like she's changed a lot of bulbs down here in the ocean." I laughed though no one else did. Clearing my throat, I stammered on, "It's definitely a handy tool though. Saved your life a little while ago, Kishan."

I squeezed his hand, a silent message that we would talk later, and asked Kaeliora to continue with what she was *supposed* to tell us. I also sent her a warning look not to mention other things that should remain unmentioned.

"Oh, yes . . . what *was* I talking about?"

"The hard part," Ren furnished.

"Oh, right. The hard part is not getting in. It's getting out. The Necklace will help you escape. Just ask it for a way to the surface. It can manipulate water, much as your other item manipulates cloth. But a great predator lurks outside the Seventh Pagoda. It doesn't eat. It doesn't hunt. It doesn't sleep. Its only purpose is to prevent you from doing what you are going to do."

"Will it be able to break through the ice tunnels?"

"It won't have to. You cannot return through the tunnels."

"Why not?"

"Because once you pass the threshold into the pagoda, the tunnels will melt to prevent any potential thieves from escaping. The only way to the surface is through the ocean."

"But the pressure will kill us!"

"Not if you have the Necklace. It's still very dangerous though. Understand that before you make your choice. You can still turn back if you don't want to risk it."

Both men looked at me.

I bit my lip. "We'll go on. We've come this far."

"Very well. Before you go, I have a gift for you, Keyfinder. You may fill your flask from my well," she said with a grand flourish.

"My flask?" asked Kishan curiously.

"Yes. A flask. A container of some kind. Don't you have one? Durga should have given you one."

"Durga?"

"Yes, yes."

"A container from Durga? It's the *kamandal*," I burst out excitedly. "Are you wearing it?"

He yanked on the thong around his neck and pulled the conch shell out of his shirt. "You mean this? But it doesn't have a stopper."

"That doesn't matter," the mermaid said. "Just dip it into my fountain. You won't need a stopper. Not a drop will be spilled unless you wish to use it."

He held the conch shell under a stream of milky water. "What am I supposed to do with it? Kill people?"

The mermaid laughed—a bubbly, happy sound. "No. Its properties change once it leaves this place. It won't hurt you any longer. The nectar of immortality is to be used when you are the most desperate. Trust your instincts. To use it liberally is to change the course of destiny. A *wise* man sees the path all must walk and embraces the free will of humankind, even if to watch it unfold causes him pain."

Kishan nodded and placed the *kamandal* under his shirt.

"If your decision is to move forward, I suggest you go quickly."

Ren and Kishan prepared the sled while the mermaid called me to her. She plucked a bloom from the lei and pressed it into my hand.

"You're a lucky young lady. Love can overcome many challenges. It's a precious treasure—worth more than all of these other miraculous things. It's the most powerful magic in the universe. Don't let it slip through your fingers. Hold onto it. Tightly."

I nodded and left to strap in the tigers. After I was seated and buckled in, I turned to look at the mermaid one last time. She was splashing contentedly in her fountain. I patted Fanindra and tied one of the bags more securely, and then we started off.

As the boys circled the fountain, I gasped in shock. The mermaid and the entire fountain were already frozen. Milky droplets hung suspended in the air, trickling from the mouths of frozen fish. Kaeliora had dipped her head to smell the lei and had iced over with a glistening smile on her face. The boys started running, and I shifted to watch the path looming before us.

It wasn't long before we shot into the ice tunnel again, running through the ocean. The black water surrounding us suddenly made me fearful. As we raced along, I couldn't help but hum the song from Willy Wonka's scary paddleboat ride. Creepy neon fish darted up to take a look but mostly left us alone. They weren't really big enough to break through the ice, but it wasn't very long before something large took an interest.

I didn't see anything except a gray shadow at first. I thought my mind was playing tricks on me, but then I looked down over the side of the sled and saw a giant eye peering up at me. I screamed, and the tigers slid to a halt. Something about us stopping spurred the creature to action. It nudged the ice tunnel from beneath. The sled popped into the

air abruptly and crashed down, knocking the air out of my lungs. Kishan and Ren fell in a tumble of legs and tails, and the sled tilted and slammed into the side wall. I pushed against the ice and righted us again while the boys scrambled to their feet.

The creature swam to the right and scraped its scaled side across the ice. We bounced into the other side, and a large crack appeared. Ren and Kishan broke into a run, with the creature giving chase. I started calling out its positions, so they could brace themselves when it hit. Cracks were forming all over the tunnel. I knew the ocean could easily rush in and kill us. We had no dragon air bubbles here—all we could do was run.

Faster and faster the tigers sprinted, but the creature easily outswam us. At one point, I couldn't see it anymore and had just breathed a sigh of relief when I looked to the right and saw something swimming toward us at top speed. It looked like a prehistoric crocodile. Its long snout gaped open as it headed right for us. It was going to bite the ice tunnel in half!

I screamed again and braced for the impact. Closing my eyes and covering my head, I felt the tunnel shake violently as the creature hit. Kishan and Ren slid to a stop and dug in their claws. I'm sure they were wondering, as I was, if it would be smarter to turn around and go back.

As we waited for the shaking to stop, I looked deeply into the maw of the beast. The only thing preventing us from being fish food was the tunnel. Its teeth were each a foot long and jabbed into the ice with a terrible crunch. Water started leaking in where a tooth pierced the top. Kishan nudged Ren, and they began running forward again.

The creature wrenched its head up and bellowed in frustration as we moved away from it. More huge cracks appeared in the ice as its body pounded over the top of the tunnel trying to catch us. Its noise must have attracted attention, because it was soon joined by another beast—an eel that had a long tail ending in a fin. It wrapped its tail completely around the ice tunnel and started squeezing. I heard several pops and water streamed in, coating the walls and making the ice slippery. The tigers slid and had to slow down to dig in their claws for traction.

A vibration shook the tunnel as the crocodile bellowed and started to fight the eel for the prize. The eel creature bit the crocodile's tail while the latter slammed its body against the tunnel, pinning the eel. The ice crackled before they swam off in a flurry of fins. The tigers took advantage of their absence to press on.

We turned a corner and saw a rocky outcropping and a glint of gold ahead. The Seventh Pagoda! We were close. Through the ice I made out the temple. We were headed for a mountain of stone that rose from the bottom of the sea. Carved into that mountain were tall pillars and smooth dark panels that looked like glass, though I knew the pressure here would implode windows. The tunnel led right to its golden door.

The tigers doubled their speed, but the first creature was back, slamming its head violently against the tunnel. Water sprayed against us as more cracks appeared. The frozen rivulets dripped into the thick layers of my clothes, making me shiver. Icy water hit my face and my hair, instantly freezing it and causing my breath to hitch. A thin river ran under our feet making the path slicker, even for claws. Ren and Kishan scrambled as best they could, knowing it was going to be a close race. A cold fear crept into my stomach and grew, creating sharp icicle daggers that shot through my limbs.

Another impact, and I saw terrible claws rake down the sides of the tunnel. Shards—dangerous spear-sized icicles—dropped and shattered around us. A section of tunnel opened and a wall of water slammed against the sled, spinning us around. We were only twenty feet from the door, but the tunnel was filling with frigid seawater. The beast bit the

tunnel again. The horrible crack sounded like a pocket of ice breaking off a glacier. I wrenched off my ties to the sled and unstrapped Ren. He changed quickly and began helping Kishan.

"Run, Kelsey! Get the key into the lock."

I waded as fast as I could, but my clothes dragged me down. The water was up to my waist now. I tried to gulp in air, but the shock of the frozen water on my body was overwhelming. My lungs tightened and wouldn't expand or contract normally. Prickles of pain raced through my limbs then faded to numbness. Ren and Kishan were coming up fast behind me. The crocodile beast bellowed again and a rush of freezing water slammed me into the golden door. My hand shook as I pulled the key out of my pocket with frozen fingers. The keyhole was underwater, and thanks to my panic and fuzzy depth perception, I couldn't get the key in the lock.

Hands covered mine and guided the golden key. We twisted it, and the door opened just as a surge of ocean threw us into the Seventh Pagoda. I spilled out onto the floor next to the bags Ren tossed in and scrambled to my feet as Ren and Kishan threw themselves against the door, trying to shut it against the weight of the water. A shiny object hit my shoe. I reached down to pick up Fanindra and cuddled her against my chest. Grateful that Ren had thought to retrieve our bags and my golden pet, I stroked her coils and apologized as best I could.

The brothers somehow managed to shut the door and lock it, and then slumped to the wet floor, panting. I positioned myself between them and slid to the floor too.

Leaning my head on Kishan's shoulder, I said, "We made it. The Seventh Pagoda."

At first, I was aware only of our breathing. Then I began to shiver. We stood and by mutual decision chose to change into warm clothes, eat,

and sleep. Ren and Kishan had used all their energy. I remembered
Ren's circus trainer, Mr. Davis, had once told me that big cats sleep
most of the day and use up their energy in quick bursts. These two had
been running for quite some time, and Kishan had been swimming like
a polar bear. I knew they were exhausted.

We explored the shrine a bit, looking for a place to camp, and found
it smaller than the other two underwater castles. It wasn't cold like
Yínbáilóng's palace. Instead, it was warm and dark.

I hastily dried off and set up a tent and sleeping bags while the Scarf
created warm clothes. Everyone made their own dinner using the Fruit.
Kishan ate three pizzas, I chose Grandma's biscuits and gravy with hash
browns and eggs, and Ren ordered stuffed pasta shells, breadsticks, and
salad—the first meal I'd ever made for him. When I gave him a look, he
raised an eyebrow and nonverbally dared me to do something about it.
I decided ignoring him would be better, so I turned my back to him and
scooted closer to Kishan, who was already on his second pizza.

"Want a slice?"

"Nah, I've got plenty, thanks."

Nobody said much of anything else. It was awkward. We ate in
silence and then prepared to sleep. I sipped my hot chocolate and
wondered what I was going to do about sleeping in such close proximity
to Ren as a man. Kishan didn't seem to have a problem at all with
our sleeping arrangements. He just crawled into his bedroll and began
snoring.

Ren turned to me. "You coming?"

"I'll . . . be another minute."

He watched me thoughtfully for a moment, and then finally ducked
inside the tent. When I couldn't put it off any longer, I pulled open
the flap and sighed at the very obvious empty place for me between
Ren and Kishan. Hoping not to disturb them, I quietly picked up my

sleeping bag and tugged it to the other side of Kishan. There was only a tiny space available so I asked the Scarf to widen the tent, crawled into my bag, and turned to face the tent wall.

"It's not like I'm going to attack you in your sleep," Ren said softly.

"I get too hot between the two of you," I lied.

"I could have switched with you."

"I wouldn't want Kishan to get the wrong message."

I heard a deep sigh. "Goodnight, Kelsey."

"Goodnight."

I stared at the tent wall for several hours, and, though he was quiet, I didn't think Ren slept much either.

When we woke or, in my case, decided to move, we packed up and further explored the Seventh Pagoda. The structure was still dark, and the light Fanindra created worked only in a small area. We found rooms full of treasure. Gold, precious gems, and priceless statues littered the floors and shelves of each room.

We entered a cavernous area and paused as the sounds of our voices echoed in the space. I could hear a waterfall and smell the ocean, and I imagined the brothers smelled something else as well, because, at the same time, both brothers moved in front of me. We inched forward slowly and came to a large basin filled with sand. Boxes of long sticks rested on a side table.

"What is it?" I asked.

Ren picked up a stick and studied it. "Incense. They're used in shrines."

I gathered a few sticks, placed them in the sand the way Ren had done with his, and used my power to light them. Delicate smoke rose up, smelling of pine. Kishan opened a box of red sticks and began filling the basin with them. I lit them, and my nose twitched as I smelled sweet blossoms. As the incense burned, we noticed the room became brighter.

The pagoda was stunning! We hadn't been able to fully appreciate its splendor before. We were in a room so huge hundreds of people could have fit in the area comfortably. Golden pillars three floors high supported the painted, domed roof overhead. Thick arched windows displayed the sea in such a way that I felt I was looking in on a series of exquisite aquariums. Detailed scrollwork and murals were framed on the walls, but otherwise the walls and ceiling were painted red with lacquered dragons spurting flame.

The floor was made of polished black tile. A small fountain trickled into a wide pool that took up most of the space. The water was white like the mermaid's pool, impossible to see through. I made a mental note not to touch it no matter how beautiful it was. Kishan and I joined Ren, who was studying one of the murals.

"There it is. The Necklace. See how it rests in the oyster?" Ren said excitedly upon spotting a mural depicting Durga's Necklace surrounded by hundreds of oysters.

"Hmm . . . yes, but we can't see anything in the water. It's too cloudy. How is Kishan supposed to find it? And what else is down there?"

"According to the mural, nothing. Only an oyster bed. He'll have to open all the oysters to find it." Ren patted Kishan on the shoulder. "Glad you drank the *soma* instead of me."

"Thanks. Well, no time like the present. You two sit poolside, and I'll toss them up." He peeled off his shirt and kicked off his shoes.

As I turned back to the mural, Kishan wrapped his hands around my waist from behind. "Want to go for a swim, beautiful?"

"The water will kill her," Ren said dryly.

I glared at Ren, turned around to hug the bare-chested Kishan, and smiled. "Maybe later." I patted his chest and ran my hand down to his waist. Poking him in his rather fine abs, I said, "I really think you need to be working out more, Kishan. You're getting all flabby in your old age."

"Where?" he demanded, as he tried to pinch the skin at his waist.

Laughing, I said, "I'm being sarcastic. You could grate cheese on your abs. I'm just lucky there aren't any other girls around. They'd all be swooning at your feet."

He grinned. "One girl swooning is enough for me. Besides, a guy's got to be strong enough to save his damsel in distress, doesn't he?"

Ren frowned and interrupted. "What will you use for a knife?" he asked.

"I'll use the *chakram*. How are you going to wedge them open?"

"We'll think of something." He gave Kishan a debatably friendly shove toward the milky pool. Kishan squeezed my hand and carefully slipped into the water. A few seconds later, we heard a wet thunk as a heavy oyster the size of a pancake hit the tile. I left Ren alone for a few minutes to figure out how we were going to pry it open and wandered around the outside of the pool.

The waterfall was lovely. The milky water fell over black tiles into the pool below. Steps led up to the top of the fountain, and I climbed them. At a level above the falls, I noticed an alcove with another fountain and some marble statues.

I peered down at Ren and heard him tell Kishan to keep the oysters coming. He was using his trident to open the oysters, and, not having a weapon of my own, I decided to take a minute to study the statues.

The marble and gold statues depicted three people: two men and a woman. The woman draped her arm over one of the men who offered her a beautifully detailed carving of a pearl necklace. The other man looked on jealously. A thick curved wall of marble stretched behind the fountain on either side.

"Ren? I think I found Parvati and Shiva! Indra's here too!"

"I'll come up and look in a minute," he called out.

There was something else. Indra's one hand was tightened into a threatening fist but the other was pointing behind the fountain where

Shiva and Parvati stood. *Maybe it meant something. Something else might be back there. Another statue maybe.* I climbed down the fountain steps, walked all the way around the long wall, and then gasped in shock and horror. A giant shark lay dead on the floor.

"It can't be," I whispered.

Its pointed nose jutted into the air, and its mouth gaped open loosely. Though it was made of marble, I shivered, imagining it bearing down on me. Its mouth was big enough to bite through a dragon, let alone a puny human such as me. Mesmerized, I reached out a finger to touch a sharp, serrated tooth, but pulled back at the last moment. Mumbling to myself, I said, "It's impossible. I've never seen anything this big on *Shark Week* before." *Maybe it's prehistoric.*

I cleared my throat. "Ren?" No response. I called out a little louder, "Ren? Can you come up here? Please!"

"Just a minute, Kelsey. Almost got this one open."

I slowly backed away from the nightmare creature until my backside bumped up against the alabaster railing. Freezing there, I stared at the length of a creature that frightened me more than anything I'd ever faced. The Kappa were kittens compared to this thing. The Stymphalian birds? Canaries. I started shaking as waves of fear poured over me, obscuring everything except the monster I couldn't look away from.

I shook my head, and little mewling sounds spilled from my lips. Stumbling quickly down the steps, I stopped at the waterfall and froze again. All I could think was the word *no*. I chanted it over and over in my mind—*no-no-no-no*—and didn't realize I was repeating the words out loud until I heard the word echoed in another's voice.

Ren appeared in front of me as if by magic, put his arms around me, and held me close. He lightly massaged the back of my neck and asked, "*No . . . what, Kelsey?*"

"It's impossible," I whispered against his shirt like a zombie.

"Come on. Show me what you found."

A part of my brain registered Kishan who shouted, "Hey! Where is everybody? Guess I have to do everything myself, then." I heard him prying open the oysters. Knowing he was in no danger, I continued to bury my nose in Ren's shirt.

"It's alright," Ren soothed. "Let's go take a look. I'll go with you."

He stepped away from my clinging form and took my hand. I grabbed onto it with both of mine and pressed myself against him. He briefly touched his lips to my temple before climbing the stairs. We passed the waterfall. When I saw the first statue, I started shaking again.

He stopped at the top and studied the forms. "I don't understand. What's wrong, *strimani*?"

I lifted a shaking hand and pointed in the same direction as Indra. "It's—" my voice shook, "it's too big."

Seeing I wouldn't take another step, he let go of my hand and began the long walk around the marble wall by himself. I watched his face register shock and then grim determination. He crouched down by the beast's head and studied it.

I grimaced thinking that, compared to the shark, Ren looked like a tasty cream puff dipped in chocolate. *He'd be delicious, decadent even. But even he was just an appetizer. Me? Maybe a celery stick. Not the tastiest, so I might as well douse myself in ranch dressing to save the shark the trouble of spitting me back out. Kishan was perhaps a little meatier. He'd be more like a taquito or an egg roll. Even if the shark ate all three of us, it's likely it would have to go back for seconds and thirds. It was just . . . that . . . immense.*

Ren paused to study the statues briefly, and then turned to me.

"It's going to be alright, Kelsey. Try not to worry."

"Try not to worry? It's a giant shark!"

"Yes, but—"

"Ren! Spider monkeys are to King Kong as great whites are to that thing!"

"I know, but—"

He was interrupted by an irate Kishan on the floor below us. "Where *are* you guys?"

I walked over to the railing and waved down to him. "We're up here. Be down in a minute."

"Fine." He sulkily went back to opening oysters while I turned back to Ren.

"But what? Don't you get it? That's the great hunter who doesn't sleep or eat—the thing the mermaid told us about. Its only purpose is to prevent us from reaching the surface!"

"We don't know that this creature and the one she spoke of are the same."

"It looks bloody likely to me!"

"That's your fear talking. I know you're scared, but there's no use panicking about something that hasn't happened yet and might not ever happen."

"I don't want to be eaten by a shark," I whimpered softly.

Ren wrapped his arms around me, smiled, and said, "*You* are much more likely to be eaten by a tiger. Remember?"

I nodded weakly and sniffled as a tear dropped onto my nose. He kissed my forehead and pressed his hands against my cheeks. "We're going to be alright. I promise. Okay?"

"Okay," I replied quietly.

His thumbs traced my cheekbones lightly, and my breath hitched. Nervously, I stepped away from him before his comforting progressed to the next level, and I walked up to the statue of Parvati. Ren watched me quietly, not moving from the place where he'd embraced me.

Poor Parvati. You had to choose between two men who risked their lives for you too. You had to worry and wonder if either one of them would survive the monster. I wiped away a tear from my cheek and reached out to touch her hand. The statue shimmered and disappeared.

"Ren!"

"I saw it!"

The statues of Indra and Shiva shimmered and disappeared also, but what was worse was that the giant shark also began to shimmer. I cried out in horror as it disappeared. At the same time we heard a bark of triumph come from below us.

"Hey, guys!" Kishan hollered. "I found it! I have the Necklace!"

26

surfacing

"Whoa! What's happening?" Kishan shouted.

After the statues disappeared, a shimmering cloud descended around us. When it dissipated, both my clothes and Ren's had changed. My mouth fell open. He looked like an Indian god.

The only piece of clothing on his body was a white wraparound *dhoti* that tied at his waist and ended just above his knees. He wore a golden headdress, armbands, and ankle and wrist cuffs. Around his neck hung an intricate golden necklace. His bronze muscled body glistened.

"Are you," I swallowed thickly, "*oiled*?" I couldn't help but stare incredulously at his broad chest.

Ren didn't answer. He just gaped back at me with a very strange expression on his face.

"What? What is it?" I asked nervously.

"You . . . you're the most beautiful thing I've ever seen."

"What?" I looked down at my costume and tentatively touched the thick golden belt that hung at my waist. "Wait here a second."

I headed over to a sea-blackened window, hoping to catch my reflection. "Huh." I was looking pretty goddesslike. A thick, heavily embroidered white skirt draped from my waist all the way to the floor. My hair was intricately braided and coiled at the nape of my neck,

and loose curls tickled my bare skin. A *dupatta* scarf wrapped over my tight beaded top and draped in folds from the belt. The golden belt cinched tightly at my waist and hung over my hips, accentuating their curves.

I, too, wore golden jewelry—a sparkling tiara, many lengths of golden chains, heavy earrings, bracelets, and even anklets. Though the sheer, white *dupatta* hung down my back and covered the front of me, the top under it was very tiny. When I moved, I could feel the silky dupatta brushing my waist and back. I crossed my arms, trying unsuccessfully to cover my bare skin.

It didn't help that when I turned around, Ren was still staring. To my utter amazement, he dropped down on one knee, took my hand, and touched his forehead to it. Nervously, I stammered, "Uh . . . Ren? What are you doing?"

"Kneeling before a goddess."

"I'm not a goddess."

"You are. A goddess, a princess, a queen. As a soldier, I pledge myself to your service. As a prince, I grant you any boon within my power. As a man, I ask to sit at your feet and worship you. Ask me to do anything for you, and I will do it."

He raised his eyes and captured both my hands in his. "*Sundari rajkumari*, my heart quickens to see you adorned as a royal princess from my time. If I had met you then, if you had visited our palace, I would have immediately knelt at your feet just like this and begged you to never leave me."

I blushed and said, "I think you may be exaggerating or perhaps you're suffering from narcosis."

Ren smiled a brilliant knock-every-girl-off-her-feet-within-a-ten-mile-radius smile and added, "Your modesty makes you even more becoming. You are the loveliest of women, Kelsey."

I stopped squirming and studied Ren's expression. He was serious. *Who knew I could bring a man to his knees?* Not able to resist, I smiled at the beautiful man kneeling in front of me and smoothed his hair away from his face. He turned his head, kissed my palm, and held my hand to his lips.

Kishan approached and turned a stormy gaze on Ren. "I generally like to give you the benefit of the doubt because I know you lost your memory and all, but can you please step away from my girlfriend and tell me what's going on? Why did our clothes change?"

Ren moved back to let Kishan approach me—but Kishan also stopped in his tracks.

"You are gorgeous!" Kishan exclaimed.

"*Gorgeous* is too crass a term to use to describe her," Ren added quietly. "She is . . . divine, ethereal, stunning—"

I held up my hand. "Right. Okay, if we could all stop staring at Kelsey now, I'd feel a lot less self-conscious."

Incredulously, Ren said, "Self-conscious? Why on Earth would you feel that way?"

"Because I'm uncomfortable displaying this much skin. Can we please turn our attention to other things?" I asked in an un-goddesslike way, which seemed to help snap them both back to reality.

Ren and Kishan blinked, and Ren reluctantly turned to tell his brother what we'd seen. I caught them both stopping from time to time to admire my exposed skin. A soft growl from one brother at the other usually brought their attention back to the discussion.

Kishan wore some kind of wraparound loincloth, had several lengths of beads around his neck, and armbands. Half of his hair was pulled back in a bun and wrapped with jewels, and the other half hung down, brushing the top of his massive shoulder. He wore a thin cord belt that hung from his waist, and an attached horn rested at his hip. Golden

hoops in his ears clinked when his head moved, and a third eye was painted on his forehead.

I quickly realized something. "Wait a second!"

The boys paused in mid-sentence, and I walked around both of them, scrutinizing their costumes. "Our clothes aren't random. We're them! I'm Parvati."

They both turned to look at me, and Kishan shrugged.

Ren studied me closer. "You're right. You're wearing her clothes."

"Then that must mean that this belongs to you." Kishan smiled at me and held out a necklace.

I mentally corrected myself. Not *a* necklace, *the* Necklace—the Black Pearl Necklace of Durga. Because all I could do was stare at it, Kishan stepped around behind me to snap its clasp. Instead of a chain, tiny diamonds set in silver arcs crossed over each other with tips overlapping. Hanging from each tip was a shiny black pearl the size of my thumb. A cluster of black and white pearls hung from its center to form a lotus flower. The Necklace draped heavily across my neck. I gently fingered the lotus flower.

Kishan brushed his lips across the sensitive skin under my ear and whispered, "They suit you."

I heard the click of the clasp just as Ren shouted, "Wait!"

Immediately, I was sucked into a tunnel of wind that deposited me in white space. The amulet burned at my throat where it rested. Confused for only a moment, I relaxed my stance and watched as a flash of blurry scenes tumbled into view.

At first, I was back on the *Deschen* listening to Mr. Kadam and Nilima as they studied maps. They couldn't hear or see me, though I tried to communicate with them for several minutes. Then the vision fragmented, and I was whisked away to another ship with what looked

like Mr. Kadam's ghost. Fins broke the water and then disappeared. A twenty-foot great white raised its head above the surface, snapping its powerful jaws and making a horrible sound. Lokesh stood above the fierce creatures, hand to his amulet.

I stepped to the side and gasped when I recognized Captain Dixon. His right eye was swollen shut, and he had bloody lacerations across his chest and arms. I listened to Lokesh question him, but the noble seaman remained defiant, refusing to reveal our whereabouts or our destination— even when held over the rail where the sharks waited hungrily below.

"Perhaps you need further motivation?" I heard Lokesh politely inquire.

The dark magician waved his hand and an unseen force nudged one of his crewmen overboard into a melee of feeding frenzy. His screams were quickly silenced, but the sounds of the sharks feasting were terrible—the chomping, the crack of bones breaking, the splashing of slick torpedo-shaped bodies as they rushed after torn body pieces, tails swishing back and forth as jaws ripped flesh off in chunks to swallow whole.

Lokesh smiled at the sound. "Last chance, Captain. Have you no care for your life?"

The captain answered, "Since I was a young boy playin' in de water, I know'd dat ma bodee wood be laid ta rest far away from de shores. Ma bones wood lie on de bottom of de ocean. De sea, you see . . . she is ma wife and yon sharkies are ma childr'n. I go ta her arms ta die in her embrace. I hab no regrets."

Frowning, the sorcerer flicked his fingers. "Then, so be it."

With another wave of his hand, Lokesh sent the prisoner over the rail. Silently, the captain fell, dropping slowly as he turned in the air. He descended toward the black water and when he at last touched it, the waves folded over him like a dark blanket.

Without making a splash, his body sank and was quickly sought after by sharks. I gasped in horror, unable to make a sound. Their fins disappeared, and soon the water was as black and as still as the soul of the man at the rail watching.

I saw Lokesh's evil visage crystallize in an admiring glance before turning his back on his doomed captive—and then he froze.

It was as if we had somehow stepped out of time and were ghosts in a white ethereal world.

I saw both Lokesh and Mr. Kadam look behind me and turn. Ren was silent, holding my limp form in his arms while Kishan murmured endearments and smoothed back my hair.

Lokesh addressed me for the first time. "Interesting. I assume you heard my recent exchange as I heard yours." He studied the vision behind me. "I see you've captured the hearts of both brothers as my beautiful Yesubai did. How very . . . *Machiavellian* of you, my dear *Kelsey*."

"You will not speak to her," Mr. Kadam's form proclaimed.

"Ah," Lokesh smiled evilly, "and has the young one caused even *your* ancient heart to smolder with jealousy, my friend?"

Lokesh turned his gaze back to me, and his eyes burned with an intensity I hadn't seen before. "I must admit," he laughed casually but his hungry leer belied his pleasant demeanor, "she's captured *my* interest as well."

"She is my ward and thus falls under the protection of the Rajaram house," Mr. Kadam warned. "Do *not* look upon her in that manner. I forbid it. She is an innocent and not meant for one such as you."

Not meant for him? *Lokesh wanted . . . me?* I felt sick, and the way he was looking at me made me want to scrub my skin with lye, gouge out my eyes, and pour bleach in my brain to cleanse him from it.

"Murderer!" I spat. "You killed Captain Dixon!"

"Come, come, my dear. It's the fault of your precious tigers. They thought I was so feebleminded, so old, that I wouldn't find the ship

named after their mother? They are stupid. Weak. Like their father. Rajaram ran away rather than face me. He hid his family in the jungle and left his people to fend for themselves. They will leave you in the same way."

"They will never leave me." I clenched my teeth to keep from sobbing as hot tears ran down my face.

Lokesh thoughtfully considered me. "Think of all we could accomplish together, my young one. With the amulets united, I could rule the world, and you would stand by my side as my queen. I would lavish you with the luxuries of the ages. You have merely to wish for something, and whatever you desire would be granted. I am a handsome man, young." The area around him shifted and blurred. "Young enough for a woman such as yourself to find . . . pleasing."

Startled, I studied his features. He was right. He *was* young and handsome. *Why did he seem older before? Is this some kind of trick?* He was thinner and his hair was slicked back. He still had rings on each finger but instead of stubby digits, his fingers were long and tapered, and his body powerful and muscular.

"It's an illusion, Kelsey. Ignore him," Mr. Kadam pleaded.

Lokesh went on, "I could give you a good life."

"What do you *want* from me? Why me?" I asked. "Surely you can have any woman you want."

"Just *any* woman is not *worthy* of me. As to what I want," he laughed suggestively as his gaze traveled slowly up my body to settle on the amulet, "there is one thing even a man of my power cannot do alone. Can you guess what it is?"

When the answer came to me, I sucked in a breath. "A child. You want a child?"

"Yes. I want a son. I choose you because you are strong and brave. Yesubai's mother was weak. Only one other woman has ever affected me in the same way and sadly, she inconveniently disappeared."

"Deschen," Mr. Kadam whispered incredulously. "You wanted Deschen."

"Yes. She was beautiful and fiery. Deschen would have given me a fine son, an heir. He would have been splendid—as tall and courageous as Dhiren, as brawny and powerful as Kishan, but with my own wisdom, cunning, and thirst for power. A son of my own blood."

"But you," the sorcerer addressed me, "are the better choice. Not only are you bold, but you are also passionate and filled with power. Perhaps it only comes from wielding the amulet, but I think not. There is something special, something . . . different about you. And whether you want it or not, I *will* have you."

"No," I whispered quietly. "*No*," I affirmed as I shook my head in denial.

Lokesh tilted his head and considered me. "Perhaps, if you came to me willingly, I would allow your tigers to live, albeit on a tiny island far away, in a place where they would be of little consequence. I assure you, though, that once I choose a course of action, I am rarely thwarted."

"That is enough! She will be under my protection, and you will never touch her as long as there is life in my limbs," Mr. Kadam threatened.

Lokesh smiled. "Then we will have to see to it that life does not remain in your limbs much longer, my friend. I look forward to the challenge. Be forewarned, I am coming for you."

"And I'll be waiting." Mr. Kadam finished.

Our bodies started to fade, becoming ghostlike.

I turned my worried eyes to Mr. Kadam, and he smiled, trying to reassure me.

"Oh, one last thing," Lokesh added with a smooth leer. "I'm sure if he could, Captain Dixon would have expressed his sorrow at being unable to serve you any longer. His new position is one that is . . . interminable."

Lokesh noted the tears slipping down my cheeks and laughed madly. The terrible sounds rang in my ears as the scene before me disappeared.

I woke with tears on my face. Kishan reached for me, and Ren reluctantly let me go.

"What is it, my sweet? Can you tell us what happened?"

Brushing away the tears, I leaned back against Kishan's chest and told them I'd seen Mr. Kadam and Lokesh in a vision. When they asked what Lokesh had said, I lied.

"Just the usual," I hedged. I didn't want to burden either of them with the knowledge of what Lokesh wanted. It would serve no purpose for them to know. It would only madden them to the point of insanity, and I thought they had enough to deal with for the time being. I'd tell them about Captain Dixon later too.

For a fleeting moment, I considered the offer Lokesh had made. In a tiny part of my heart, I thought, *What if? What if we lost and accepting Lokesh would save them? There was no reason for them to know that I now held tightly onto a trump card. If, in the end, the only thing that would save them would be my sacrifice, then so be it.*

The tigers were anxious to leave. Strong enough to stand, I took a step away, adjusted my *dupatta*, and patted my hair. When I looked up, I found Ren staring at me and blushed, remembering him kneeling at my feet, but this time his face was stricken.

"What is it?" I asked. "What's wrong?"

"Kishan. He . . . he's Shiva. He has to be with that third eye, his clothes, and then the way he presented you with the Necklace—" he trailed off.

"And that makes you—"

"Indra," Ren declared wretchedly.

"Right. So what does that mean? What are we supposed to do?" I asked.

Ren's face tightened. "We do what we came here to do. *Indra* slays the beast and *Shiva*," his eyes darted to my face briefly, "claims his bride."

Kishan had moved up behind me and cupped my shoulders. I felt both of us stiffen at the same time. Kishan relaxed first and squeezed my arms without saying anything. Ren walked over to the window and studied the black sea beyond. I turned, smiled at Kishan, and patted his hand, and then walked over to Ren and touched his arm. I bit my lip, thinking I was right to keep the desires of Lokesh hidden. They could barely tolerate the idea of each other as rivals let alone adding their nemesis into the mix.

"*You* aren't Indra. You may be dressed like him, and I may be dressed like Parvati but I'm not her. I'm Kelsey, you're Ren, and he's Kishan. If there *is* a beast to slay, Indra won't do it. Kelsey, Ren, and Kishan will do it together. We may be trapped in a myth, but we will make our own story. Okay?"

Ren nodded and grabbed me in a fierce but brief hug, and then set me aside. I could tell he didn't necessarily believe me, but he was trying.

"I'll get our things," he said softly.

I watched him walk off then went back to Kishan, who wrapped his arms around me in a hug of his own.

"He's upset," he said.

"Yes. But it's more than the Indra thing. I had a talk with him in the ice palace. I told him that I couldn't be with him anymore and that I was choosing you."

Kishan froze. "You did?" He asked hesitantly, "What did he say?"

"He said that he will always be my protector and friend."

"Really? That's it?"

"Yes. Did you expect something else?"

"Honestly? Yes. I've been expecting you to break up with me for a while now."

"Well, I'm not going to."

"I see." He rubbed his jaw and frowned.

"Do you . . . not want me anymore?"

"Not *want* you?" he asked incredulously. "There is nothing I want more than to belong to you. To remain with you. I guess I have to admit, I'm surprised. Why didn't you go back to him?"

I thought about what would be the appropriate thing to say for a second, and then snuggled against his chest and wrapped my arms around his waist.

"I stayed with you because . . . I love you, and you make me happy."

"I love you too, *bilauta.*" He tucked my head under his chin and stroked my back.

I could tell Ren had returned when I heard the bags thump to the floor. I stepped out of Kishan's embrace, straightened my skirt guiltily and heard Ren say, "Let's get this over with. Kelsey, if you wouldn't mind."

"Pearl Necklace," I said, "please create a way for us to rise to the surface and don't forget about the ocean pressure and that we need oxygen."

The Necklace sparkled and began to glow so intensely, we had to look away. After a few seconds it faded, but nothing had happened.

"What are we supposed to do?" I asked.

"I'm not sure," Ren replied.

"Something's coming closer. Do you see that glow?" Kishan pointed at the black window.

Sure enough, something was moving closer. Globs of pulsing white light came into view. "They're jellyfish," Kishan said. "Only they're giants!"

They were giants alright. Each one looked bigger than a hot air balloon. An idea struck me, I sucked in a breath, and said, "I think they might be our transportation."

"I don't think so, Kells," Kishan said. "How would we breathe?"

"Stranger things have happened," I answered.

He grunted, and the three of us pressed our noses against the glass window, staring at the approaching globes. They were fascinating. Moving slowly but surely toward us, the pulsing domes puffed up and expelled water as they danced toward us like fleshy puppets on strings. They had long trailing tentacles that hung from their bodies like ribbons from a piñata.

Their round hoods were bell-shaped, diaphanous, and luminescent. And dangling from the centers of the creatures were feathery arms that reminded me of wisteria hanging from a tree but instead of white or soft lilac like those blossoms, these feathery fronds were bright orange and yellow. The arms fluttered in the water and could also be seen through the hood. It made the jellyfish look as if they glowed with an inner fire.

A jellyfish approached us, hung there for a moment, and then lifted several thin tentacles and touched the window. They trailed over the shape of the glass, feeling the surface delicately, like a blind man touching a shrine. Then, finding a chosen spot, the thin fingers actually pierced the glass and moved toward us. All three of us backed up, startled. The creature angled closer, while we stood frozen like statues. Somehow it had crossed the barrier of the window without breaking it.

No ocean water surged in. Not so much as a drop trickled down the window. A tentacle reached Kishan and wrapped gently around his arm. He could have pulled away, but the creature was so delicate, to move back might have injured it. Softly it pulled on Kishan's arm until he took a step forward. More tentacles surged in and wrapped around him, drawing him closer to the window. The creature pulled him into its gentle embrace, reminding me of a frail old grandmother trying to hug her strapping grandson.

The jellyfish began to back away from the window, pulling Kishan along with it. His arm disappeared through its black surface and

reappeared in the water outside. He sucked in a breath and with a gentle tug the creature carried him through the glass, gathered him close, and held him tightly. Creating a bower, it nestled him so his head rested just under its hood. He gave us a thumbs-up sign and showed us he was breathing.

Kishan's jellyfish moved away and another one moved closer. As its tentacles entered the pagoda window, Ren adjusted the straps of his pack.

I touched his arm and said, "I'll go next."

Nodding, Ren stepped out of way as the tentacles reached for me. He watched as the creature slowly enfolded me. He seemed so sad, and he looked at me as if he was never going to see me again.

As the jellyfish began to tug me slowly toward the window, Ren took my arm, pressed his lips to my ear, and quoted, "'Like as the waves make toward the pebbl'd shore, so do our minutes, hasten to their end.'" He softly kissed my temple and whispered, "Remember, I love you, *priyatama*."

I was about to respond when the creature sucked me through the window and into the freezing ocean. I was only cold for a moment, because as soon as the animal pulled me into its feathery embrace, the temperature changed. My head was drawn up into the hood and was nestled against a warm rubbery pillow that glowed softly in the darkness like a flickering candle.

From my shoulders up, I was suspended above the jellyfish's interior water line and heard a rush of air like a bellows. I laughed as I realized the animal was making oxygen for me. The rest of my body hung in a sort of hammock created by the tentacles and a surge of warmth cycled around my body. It felt like I was lounging in a hot spa and, as if the jellyfish could read my mind, its body began to hum and vibrate. I sighed and relaxed in the capable "hands" of my abyssal-plain masseur.

When I cracked open my eyes a moment later, I saw Ren had joined us. I could easily make him out through his transparent balloon, and slightly behind and above me was Kishan. The lights dimmed to a faint glow, and I felt the great pumping of my jellyfish as it began to move upward in the dark water. The Seventh Pagoda disappeared beneath us in a swirl of shadow and then was gone.

Our couriers moved steadily if not quickly, and I didn't feel the pressure of the surrounding ocean or even see any deep-sea creatures, though I kept my eyes peeled. The jellyfish gracefully swirled around each other in an ocean ballet. When mine rose slightly above the others, I felt like a lady with full lacy petticoats and a parasol swinging above a stage oblivious to all except the men who came to see the show and who watched me from below with hungry eyes.

I could sense when we left the abyssal plain and moved upward through the bathypelagic zone and into Jīnsèlóng's realm. I began to see fish. At first, they were the scary long-toothed type, but then the water brightened slightly, and I saw a sperm whale. As we rose higher still, the first shark appeared. I panicked, but it was only a hammerhead that ignored us. A school of tuna with flashing scales passed us, and I took a deep breath, relieved. We were going to make it. I estimated we had roughly a thousand feet to go. More animals swam by us, some curious, but the jellyfish continued to make their way upward.

Excitedly, I was pointing out the first cluster of plants to Kishan when I felt a disturbance in the water. Kishan's eyes widened, and I searched for what had caused him alarm. I trembled and prayed that it wasn't what I feared. I pressed my hands against the flexible skin of the jellyfish hood and looked into the ocean. At first I saw nothing, but then the jellyfish spun, and I saw the fearsome shape of the giant shark from the Seventh Pagoda. It moved lazily along, patrolling the water.

The shark swam with its mouth slightly open, and, even from a

distance I could see its rows of sharp teeth. Other sharks, probing, approached and then rapidly sped off. Even a pod of dolphins swam quickly away from it while screeching a warning in the water. I watched them disappear and wished I could do the same, but I knew this shark wouldn't bother the surrounding sea life. It didn't eat. It didn't sleep. There was only one purpose it had been created for—preventing the Necklace from reaching the surface . . . and the Necklace was on me. The good news was that it still hadn't seen us. The bad news was that we still had around five hundred feet more to go.

The shark swam parallel to us for a while and then passed out of our visual range, but it soon returned and swam around us in a wide circle. At about that time, the sun came out from behind a cloud and the water turned from gray to a bright blue. My jellyfish shifted, and the gold belt I was wearing cast a sparkling reflection in the water.

Though the shark was below us, it rolled slightly and peered up with a giant black eye. It swam in and made a close pass. I could almost see the spark of recognition in its cold eye as it looked me over. In a flash of speed, it was gone. I searched the ocean frantically and soon saw with horror that it was surging up from the black ocean below. I screamed as I saw it open its jaws and head, not for me, but for Ren. I put my hand over the pearls at my throat and whispered, "Pearl Necklace, please move him."

A surge of water shifted Ren's jellyfish, and the shark rushed past him, biting off only a few tentacles. The shark circled for another attempt, and I clutched the pearls again. "We're almost to the surface. We'll need something to rest on."

The Necklace gleamed, and the shadow of a small watercraft appeared on the surface of the ocean. The shark swam closer. It was like a semitruck with teeth. Its jaw unhinged as it extended it for a bite. Taking its time, the giant shark approached Kishan's jellyfish and, like

a snobbish gourmet, bit almost delicately into the hood of the creature just as I was whispering for the Necklace to move Kishan. I was too late.

Some kind of jellyfish fluid squirted out and clouded the area around them. The tentacles began to flail against the shark's body, and Kishan jerked in the water as the jellyfish quickly expelled him. He took a moment to look at me. The shark hadn't seen him yet. I pointed to the shadow on the surface, and Kishan started to swim. The giant fish chomped messily through the delicate jellyfish until all that remained was a long tentacle hanging from one of the shark's teeth. Its eyes rolled forward, and it scanned the water. With a great swish of its crescent tail, it disappeared.

Ren had disengaged himself from his jellyfish and patted it on the hood. It began moving off. Terrified, I peered through the shadowy water. A formidable shape materialized in the dark ocean behind Ren. I screamed and bucked against the wall of my jellyfish as I frantically pointed.

Ren spun in the water, pulled out his trident, and shot a succession of spear darts at the shark. One dart lodged in its mouth, some glanced off its tough skin, and some pierced its side. Unfortunately, it probably felt like acupuncture to a creature of that size, annoying, but not life threatening. Still, it bothered the shark enough for it to veer away from Ren. It dove, and Ren rose to the surface for air. He threw his backpack onto the boat the Necklace had created for us, and then I was alone in the water.

My body shook, and I twisted every which way in a turbulent panic. I could feel my vulnerability to my very core. I bemoaned several things at once—the fragility and transparency of my jellyfish, the darkness of the water, the sparkle of my costume. All of these things made me an easy target. I was practically a bull's-eye, a tasty morsel holding a sign that said, "Eat me!"

The shark had moved into the darker water below and was most likely preparing another assault. I knew that the longer I hovered in the ocean, the more danger I'd be in. Using the Pearl Necklace, I asked the jellyfish to take me to the surface faster. We rose higher, but it was taking too long. The shark was still somewhere out there. I hoped that Ren's dart would bother it enough to leave me alone as I neared the boat.

Ren and Kishan swam down to meet me. Suddenly, I saw the shark rushing toward them. They clasped hands and pushed off each other, kicking so the shark passed between them. As it did, Kishan drew the *chakram* and Ren the trident. Ren shot spear darts all along one side, while Kishan sliced open a long gash on the other. The shark swam off in a cloud of blood.

I wiped the rubbery wall of the jellyfish hood, but the water was too agitated and the area too bloody for me to make out much. Shapes darted quickly past the jellyfish, and I realized they were other smaller sharks that were looking for lunch. They'd obviously been attracted by the mighty struggle and caught the scent of blood in the water.

In a full panic, dreading to leave but too petrified to stay, I asked the jellyfish to release me. I thought perhaps in the confusion I could make a break for the surface, but instead of expelling me like Kishan's had done, the jellyfish drew my body closer inside itself and jerked back and forth. That's when I felt a sharp pain and a tug on my leg. The jellyfish and I were yanked through the water at a frightening speed. At first, we moved horizontally in the ocean. Then we started descending.

Hot knives jabbed into my skin. I looked down at my leg and screamed. Desperately, I kicked my other leg and flailed my arms, but I knew I couldn't escape. The huge shark had returned and now had my left leg in the side of its jaws. A part of my brain registered that it didn't sever the limb. In fact, it seemed intent only on dragging me back down to the bottom of the ocean.

When I managed to kick its side, the shark slowed down and whipped the jellyfish and me from side to side. I thought the bite on my leg was bad enough, but when it jerked me around, my body experienced a level of agony I didn't think was possible. Its serrated teeth had not only pierced my leg but also were slowly shredding it. I felt a snap as my tibia broke, and my sharp scream tapered off into a horrified whimpering noise. A bright red cloud rose around the hood of the jellyfish, dimming my vision. Realizing it was my blood this time rather than the shark's, bile rose in my throat, and I almost passed out.

I saw the flash of the trident in the water. Then, suddenly, my leg was free. The jellyfish pumped wildly to get us away, but it was injured. It quivered on one side and water filled the interior of the hood. A surge of adrenaline swept through my body and cleared my petrified mind. Touching the hood, I thanked the dying animal and sucked in a breath. It expelled me, shuddered, and began twirling in a slow descent as it died.

Slick torpedo-shaped bodies gave chase, and I soon lost sight of the gentle creature. I swam using only my arms, dragging the dead weight of my injured leg behind me. I had no idea if my leg was still attached or how bad the damage was. I knew I was bleeding and only had a few moments, if that long, to reach the surface. I couldn't see anything around me and hoped I was swimming in the right direction. Lungs on fire and getting nowhere, I tried kicking with my good leg too. That helped some, but I made little progress. Something touched me, and I jerked back but I quickly realized the touch was human. Kishan.

He wrapped his arms around my waist and swam with me to the surface. Water rushed into my lungs. Somehow he pulled us up onto the watercraft created by the Pearl Necklace. He pounded my back violently. I choked and vomited over the side. I heard him tear the backpack open and murmur words to the Divine Scarf. Hearing the whisper of threads was somehow comforting, and I felt them bind what was left of my

leg in a tight tourniquet. Ren scrambled aboard, breathing heavily and dripping blood from a long gash on his arm.

"How is she?" he asked.

"She's . . ." Kishan hesitated. "She's bad."

"I have to go back," I heard Ren say. "I have to kill it. It will just come after us."

Ren looked at me, and though I could have mistaken his expression, dazed as I was through the loss of blood, I imagined I could see his heart break. He picked up my hand. *At least I think it was my hand.* I couldn't feel anything. My body was numb. My eyes closed though I tried to keep them open. He clutched his trident and whispered, "Take care of her."

"I will. I love her, you know," Kishan said.

"I know," Ren replied softly and dove into the sea.

Kishan's body shook, and when I cracked open an eye, I saw him dash tears away. He lifted my head onto his lap and stroked my wet hair away from my face. I could hear the splash and the displacement of water as the shark moved past. The giant fin broke the surface and circled our craft widely.

Alarmed, I managed to shove aside the darkness threatening to engulf me and watched the gray sail the size of a windsurfing rig angle toward us as it came to finish us off. It dipped under us, and we rose into the air on its back before slipping with a splash onto the ocean. Somehow, our little boat remained upright. Then the waves stilled, and I heard nothing. I closed my eyes and focused, but not even the splash of a small fish could be heard.

Suddenly the shark breached the surface twenty feet away like a giant submarine. More than half its body rose out of the water, and I twisted to see it, screaming as I knocked my leg painfully against the side of the watercraft. High in the air, on the back of the shark's head,

Ren hung from his trident, which was deeply embedded in the gray flesh. With water streaming from his body, he looked like Poseidon riding the back of a sea monster. I whimpered in pain. I was dying. I knew I didn't have much time left, but my mind screamed that I could help him. My last act could be saving Ren.

I raised my hand, used the other one to hold it still, and concentrated. Kishan quickly figured out what I wanted to do and lifted me higher against his chest. White light burst from my palm and hit the giant shark in the belly as it turned to the side. Though I was weak, it would have been impossible for me to miss a target that big.

Blackened flesh melted like hot wax before a flame. The skin split widely, and the contents of the shark's belly spilled into the ocean. The shark snapped its jaws shut and shook violently as it started to descend, trying to dislodge the man and escape the pain. I noticed other, smaller fins rushing past our boat toward the dying shark. As Ren and the monster shark sank under the water, my eyes rolled back, and I collapsed.

bedlam

Voices. Whispers of sound roused me. *So thirsty.* The sun beat down on my body. *Pain. Throbbing pain.* A cool hand stroked my forehead, and I wished whoever it was would give me water. I heard the desperate words, "You're not the only one who loves her," but I couldn't tell who had said it. My cracked lips parted, and a cup was pressed to them. Cold, *ice* cold liquid dripped into my mouth. It was delicious and seemed to spread coolness through my limbs. *Not enough. More. I need more.*

Again the cup was brought to my lips. Mere drops, only a teaspoon of the soothing liquid was given. I licked the remaining drops from my lips, and my head lolled back against a warm body. I slept.

I woke thirsty again, but the heat was gone, and a cool breeze wafted over my feverish skin. I opened my mouth to ask for water, but only a whimper came out.

"She's awake. Kelsey?"

I heard Kishan speak, but I couldn't open my eyes or move.

"Kelsey? You're going to be alright. You're healing."

Healing? How was that possible? The shark bit through my calf. The lower part of my leg was hanging on by only a few tendons. I hadn't meant to look at it after I'd gotten in the boat but I couldn't *not* look.

"Give her some water," Ren suggested.

Ren? He was alive. Somehow he'd escaped from the feeding frenzy.

"Do you need some too?"

"Her first. I'll survive."

He'll survive? What happened to him? Instead of questions, my body produced moaning sounds.

I felt a light touch at my neck and heard Kishan say, "Pearl Necklace, we need some drinking water."

Gently, Kishan lifted my upper body so my head rested against his chest. I blinked woozily, but couldn't focus until I saw a cup brought to my lips. He held it for me as I swallowed gratefully. "It's a good thing we have the Necklace. The Golden Fruit can't make water."

When it was gone, I whispered raspily, "More."

He filled the cup four more times before I nodded that I was satisfied. I'd even had the strength to grip his arm as I raised my head. He refilled the cup and handed it to Ren. It was evening, and we were floating on an ocean bathed in moonlight. I practiced keeping my eyes open, watching Ren as he drank. By the time he was done, my eyes had adjusted, and six Rens had become one.

"You're hurt," I said.

Ren's grimace became a smile though I could still see the pain he tried to hide. "I'll be fine."

I squinted at his chest. A strange scar arced from his shoulder to his stomach. My eyes widened.

"The shark bit you? Those are puncture wounds!" I started wheezing, which turned into a wet cough.

Kishan held me as my body spasmed painfully. Ren waited until my coughing stilled to answer.

"Yes. It bit me almost in half. Broke all my ribs on the left side, my left arm, shattered my spine, and I think it may have pierced my heart and kidney."

"How . . . how did you get back to the boat with all those sharks in the water?"

"After the monster shark died, thanks to you and a trident to the brain, most of the others went after him. A few came after me and bit my legs, but they weren't in attack mode. A quick jab with the trident caused them to leave me alone. Kishan saw me and instructed the Scarf to make a rope. He tugged me back to the boat before they could take off any of my limbs."

I shuddered and reached for his hand. He wrapped his fingers around mine, and I sank back against Kishan, weak as a daisy after a thunderstorm.

"You said I was healing. How? I should be dead by now."

Ren made eye contact with Kishan and nodded.

Kishan cleared his throat and explained, "We used the Nectar of Immortality—the drops of liquid collected from the mermaid's fountain. You *were* dying. You were bleeding to death, and the Scarf couldn't stop it. Your heart slowed, and you lost consciousness. Your life was slipping away, and there was nothing I could do to prevent it from happening. Then I remembered the mermaid's words. She said the nectar was to be used when I was the most desperate. I couldn't let you die . . . so I used the *kamandal*.

"At first, I wasn't sure it was working. There wasn't enough blood for your heart to pump. I could hear that it wasn't filling between beats. Then your heart rate increased. You began healing. Your leg slowly repaired itself before my eyes. Color returned to your face, and you slipped into a deep sleep. I knew then that you would survive."

"Does this mean I'm immortal now? Like the two of you?"

Kishan looked at Ren. "We don't know."

"Why is my skin so hot?"

"It could be a side effect." Kishan offered.

Ren countered, "Or she could have a sunburn."

I groaned and poked my arm. It turned white, then pink. "I vote sunburn. Where are we?"

"No idea." Ren grunted, shifted, and then closed his eyes.

"Is there anything to eat? I could use some more water too if you have any."

Kishan used the Golden Fruit to make tomato soup, which was nourishing, but not too heavy for our weakened bodies to handle. Then he instructed Ren and me to sleep while he kept watch. Kishan cradled me in his arms while my exhausted body obeyed.

It was dawn when I woke. I was lying on my side with my head resting on Kishan's thigh. My hand was pressed against the cold, slick floor of the boat. *Fiberglass? How had the Necklace produced that?* Rubbing my hand back and forth against the smooth surface, I felt the sides of the boat curve up. Gingerly, I shifted my leg and felt only a twinge of pain.

"How are you feeling?" Ren asked softly.

"I feel . . . okay. Not going to be running any marathons today, but I'll survive. Can't sleep?"

"I traded off with Kishan an hour ago."

I ran my hands over the outer edge of the craft and found the bumpy ridges on the outside. The center of the boat was a hot pink that faded to light pink and then alabaster around the outside. Kishan was asleep, an arm covering his eyes, as he rested in one of five vertical folds.

"It's a giant clam shell," Ren explained.

"It's beautiful!"

He smiled. "Only you would find something beautiful in our situation."

"That's not true. A poet can always find something good to write about."

"A poet doesn't write only of beauty. Sometimes he writes of sorrow—of the ugly things in the world."

"Yes, but you make even the bad things sound lovely."

Ren sighed and ran a hand through his hair. "Maybe not this time." He sat up with a determined expression. "We need to check your leg, Kells."

I shook my head slightly. "Can't we wait until we get back?"

"We don't know how we're getting back, and we need to watch for infection."

I started hyperventilating. "I can't."

His expression softened. "You don't have to look. Why don't you tell me a story while I unwrap your bandages?"

"I . . . I can't think of any. Ren, I'm scared. What if my leg falls off? What if it's just a stub?"

"Can you wiggle your toes?"

"Yes. At least, it feels like I can, but that could be a phantom foot tricking me. I don't want to lose it."

"If that happens, we'll deal with it. The important thing is you're alive."

"But I'd never walk normally again. How could I ever have a normal life? I'd be crippled forever."

"It doesn't matter."

"What do you mean it doesn't matter? How could I help you finish the tasks? How could I—" My words cut off abruptly.

He paused. "How could you what?"

I blushed. "How could I marry and have children? I wouldn't be able to chase the kids around the house. My husband would be ashamed. And that's only if I could convince someone to marry me."

Ren watched me with an indiscernible expression. "Are you finished? Are there any more fears you haven't shared?"

"I guess that's it."

"So you're frightened that you won't be normal, you won't be attractive, and you won't be able to properly fulfill your responsibilities."

I nodded.

"I can identify with not being normal, but if the decades at the circus taught me one thing, it's that normalcy is an illusion. Each person is utterly unique. A standard of normalcy is something that most people of the world simply will never access. A husband ashamed of his wife doesn't deserve her, and I will personally make sure such a man never makes your acquaintance.

"As far as you being attractive or attaining a man's interest, I can guarantee that even if both of your legs were removed, I would still find you beautiful, and I would still desire you." Ren smiled while I twitched. "And children are a responsibility of both parents. You and your husband would balance the work between you in a way that was comfortable for both of you."

"But I'd be a burden to him."

"You would not. You'd lighten his burden because you love him."

"He'd have to wheel me around like a grandma."

"He'd carry you off to bed every night."

"You're not going to let me wallow are you?"

"No. Now can I check your leg?"

"Fine."

He smiled. "Fine. Now hold still."

He whispered a command to the Divine Scarf to gently remove the blood-crusted bandages from my leg and make new, soft cloths. He asked the Pearl Necklace to create a basin of warm water. My toes emerged first, and I was relieved to see them healthy and pink. But as the threads disappeared around my calf, I shut my eyes and turned away. Ren said nothing, but dipped a cloth into the water and began cleaning my leg. It felt like my leg was all there, but I didn't want to risk looking.

"Can you talk to me? Distract me so I won't think about it," I asked tightly.

He pushed my once beautiful but now salt-crusted skirt over my knee and gently wiped under and around my kneecap.

"Alright. I wrote a new poem recently. Will that be sufficient?"

I mutely nodded and whimpered as Ren swiped a tender spot.

"It's called 'The Caged Heart'." He began and his warm voice washed over me, soothing me the way it always did.

> ### The Caged Heart
>
> Does the caged heart diminish?
> No! It beats more fiercely.
> It paces
> Bound not by locks and iron bars
> But by his own hand.
>
> He crushes his heavy heart.
> He holds it back
> Molds it to an orderly shape
> Uses his great will to contain it
> And yet it strains against his grip.
>
> Feral and untamed
> It can only find rest
> In the jungle.

A place where it is free
A place where it is welcomed.

There it finds peace
As he is embraced
By her leafy arms.

But the path to the jungle is lost.
So he moves
Circling his cage anxiously.
He watches
Waiting for the moment
When his hungry heart will be set free.

Ren finished and squeezed out the towel. "You can look if you want to. Your leg is going to be fine."

I cracked open my eyes and looked down the long white length of my leg. A thin pink scar ran from the top of my calf to my ankle. Ren touched it lightly, tracing it from the beginning down to my foot. I shivered.

He misunderstood my reaction. "It's not that bad. Does it hurt?"

"No, not really. It's just a little sore."

He nodded and cupped the back of my calf, squeezing lightly.

"That actually feels good. Maybe a massage will help, after I've healed a little bit more."

"Anytime."

I put my hand on his arm. "Thank you. I . . . your poem . . . it was lovely."

"You're welcome," he smiled warmly, "and thank *you, dil ke dadkan.*"

Saddened, I shifted closer and rested my palm against his heart. "Your 'Caged Heart' poem wasn't about Lokesh, the circus, or forgetting, was it?"

"No." He placed his hand over mine and held it against him. "And before you ask, it means, 'my heartbeat.'"

A tear plopped onto my cheek. "Ren . . . I—"

Kishan grunted as the sun rose over the horizon and hit him in the face. Sitting up, he rubbed his sleepy eyes and scooted closer to us. Then he wrapped his arms around my waist and slid me back into his chest.

"Be careful with her!" Ren hissed.

"Right, sorry. Did I hurt you?"

"No. Ren cleaned my leg. Look. It's much better."

He inspected my leg closely. "Looks like you're out of the woods." He nuzzled my neck despite the soft growl coming from the other side of our shell boat. "Good morning, *bilauta*. What did I miss?"

"Just a poem."

"Glad I slept through it," he snickered.

I elbowed him lightly. "Be civil."

"Yes, my sweet."

"That's better. How about breakfast?"

We ate heartily after Ren and Kishan agreed that we all were almost back to normal health. When we had finished, I repositioned myself stiffly in the naturally curved clamshell seat.

"Okay. Now what do we do?" I asked.

"Maybe we call a dragon for help," Kishan suggested.

Ren replied, "I have a feeling they won't help us anymore. Besides we don't want Lùsèlóng to come along and offer us another challenge, *do* we?"

"No!" I shuddered, remembering how both of them were almost blackened dragon kibble. "One thing's for sure. I need to stay out of the

sun today." I fingered the side of the shell where a small hole had been hollowed out, and an idea started to form.

"Ren? Can you use the trident to make three more holes like this one? I want them spaced evenly like a box."

He knelt next to me and thrust his finger through the hole. "Do you want them the same size?"

"Yes. We need them big enough for a thick rope to pass through."

He grunted and got started.

Kishan shifted over next to me. "What's your plan?"

"I think we should try to use the wind to carry us back to the ship."

"Good idea. It's better than just floating here in shark town."

"Shark town? I hope you're exaggerating."

"Exaggerating?" Kishan's brows knit together when he saw the fear on my face. "Right, exaggerating."

"No, you weren't. They're all around us, aren't they?"

He winced. "Yes. There's still a lot of shark meat in the water. I heard them splashing all night."

I made an involuntary sound and closed my eyes, praying my little experiment wouldn't flip us over into shark-filled waters. I asked the Scarf to create a kite-like parachute and attach it with ropes to all the holes Ren made. Then I asked the Scarf to gather the winds softly into the parachute and blow us back to the *Deschen*.

A breeze picked up, and Ren and Kishan fed the parachute like a kite into the wind. The strong cloth ballooned out and tugged us forward. We bounced on the water, and the wind whipped us around, but Ren shifted quickly to keep our shell boat balanced. All things considered, it was a pretty comfortable ride. Ren even made a sunshade using a canvas courtesy of the Scarf and oversized peppermint sticks embedded in hollowed-out wheels of cheese, which the Golden Fruit provided.

We snacked on wedges of salty Romano cheese on crackers and

talked as we kept our eyes peeled for the yacht. I relaxed knowing we were now miles from the shark buffet and even trailed my fingers in the spray of water. I dozed off and on.

The morning passed into afternoon, and still there was no sign of the *Deschen*. Clouds rolled in, and soon we were surrounded by a fog thick enough to block out the sun.

"Maybe we're near the blue dragon's island," I said.

We decided I should send up a flare every fifteen minutes or so, and it was after the fourth one Kishan said he'd heard something. They pulled on one of the ropes to angle us to the right and told me to send up another flare. This time, I saw a faint sparkle in answer. The wind suddenly died, and our parachute floated onto the water.

Ren dragged it back into the boat as another flare went off directly above our heads. As the red sparks faded, our clamshell struck the smooth side of the yacht. Kishan tied us off, and I was so happy I practically cried.

"Hello?" a familiar voice called out into the fog.

"Mr. Kadam? Mr. Kadam! We're here!"

Then out of the fog Mr. Kadam's beloved face appeared.

He smiled hugely and helped Kishan pull the boat closer. "What in the world type of craft are you in?" he laughed.

"It's a clamshell," I explained. "It was created by the Necklace."

"Well, haul it aboard. May I help you, Miss Kelsey?"

"I've got her." Ren scooped me up in his arms and somehow managed to get us both up the ladder to the wet garage while Mr. Kadam and Kishan maneuvered the shell boat onto the ramp and dragged it in.

"Miss Kelsey, you've been injured again."

I nodded. "I think I died. Kishan brought me back. We have so much to tell you."

"I can imagine. But first, allow me to send Nilima to help you get comfortable. Can she walk, Ren?"

"She hasn't tried since the injury."

"Put me down. I should be able to stand, at least."

He carefully stood me on my feet and lent me his arm for support as I practiced walking. I limped a little. The muscles felt cramped.

"I think I'll be alright, especially if I can get a nice calf massage later."

"I can do it," both brothers spoke at the same time.

I laughed. "Lucky I have two legs then." I bent over, traced the pink scar, and compared my legs. Sighing, I saw that I now had a scar on each leg, one from the monster shark and one from the kraken. "I think I can manage with Nilima. You two can take off. I want to catch up with Mr. Kadam."

"I'll stay with you," Ren offered.

"No. I'll stay with her," Kishan challenged.

"I'll be fine. Don't worry about me. I'll see both of you later."

Reluctantly, both men left, and I leaned against Mr. Kadam's shoulder. He put an arm around me and sighed.

"You haven't told them yet."

I knew exactly what he was talking about. I shook my head. "There was already so much danger; I didn't want to burden them. Knowing would only spur them on to confront Lokesh."

He nodded. "They need to know though . . . soon."

"I know. They just need a good night's rest first. 'One battle at a time' is my new motto."

"You're tired too. You need rest."

Mr. Kadam insisted we save the explanations for later that evening and left me alone in my room. I turned on the shower and took off my jewelry. Nilima appeared and helped me with the clasp on the Pearl Necklace. She made a sound of admiration as she held it in her palms.

"It's lovely, Miss Kelsey."

"It is. It makes water and summons creatures of the ocean, sort of. We'll need to figure out what else it does."

"May I try it?"

"Knock yourself out."

"Please fill the tub with hot water for Miss Kelsey."

The tub immediately filled, and Nilima clapped, delighted.

I smiled. "It looks nice, but I'd like a shower to get all the salt off first."

"Of course. You can soak afterward."

I shuddered. The thought of soaking made me nervous. I wondered if I'd ever be able to scuba dive again. Images of the giant shark flashed through my mind, and I could easily picture its extended jaws opening for a bite.

"I'd like to soak another time if that's okay. I think I'll stick with the shower for now."

Nilima shrugged and helped me out of my dress. She clucked at the ruined material and ran her hands over the beadwork. "It must've been so beautiful."

"It was pretty," I admitted, "but it made me a little uncomfortable."

"Why?"

"The top was too short."

"Ah, the *choli*. There are many different styles, some modern, some ancient. They are not short to expose a woman's body but to keep her comfortable in the heat."

I raised an eyebrow, and Nilima laughed.

"Okay. I admit that sometimes it's worn to catch a man's eye."

"Then it definitely works. *Too* well," I mumbled.

She removed the jewels from my hair and marveled at each piece with appreciation. Steam rose from the shower. After she loosened my

choli, she left me alone, and I took my time soaping through my hair and scrubbing my skin. When I sat at the vanity in my thick robe, she returned with an armful of clothing. She brushed out my long wet hair while I rubbed lotion into my sunburned arms and legs.

"Nilima?"

"Yes?"

"Will you cut my hair shorter? Please?" I hurried on as I saw her shaking her head with apprehension. "It's too long. It's unmanageable. You don't have to cut it all—just to mid-back or so."

"He'll be mad."

"I don't think it matters anymore."

"Why not?"

I sighed. "Because we've broken up. I've told him that I'm with Kishan now."

She paused, mid-brushstroke, and then continued slowly. "I . . . *see*."

"Kishan doesn't care what I do with my hair and even braided, it's too much for me to manage when it's this long."

"Alright, Miss Kelsey. But if he asks, you did this yourself."

"You've got a deal."

She cut my hair to just past my shoulder blades and braided it for me. I pulled on a soft T-shirt and a pair of worn jeans and set off barefoot to find everyone.

Nilima stayed on watch in the wheelhouse while Mr. Kadam joined the three of us in the sundeck lounge. We ate and took turns catching him up on what had happened. He took copious notes and frequently asked us to repeat the dragon's instructions as precisely as we could. I showed him the Pearl Necklace, which he turned over in his hands and sketched a very accurate resemblance in his notebook. He documented the different ways in which we'd used it and wanted to begin a battery of tests as soon as possible.

"I find it interesting that you didn't heal from the shark bite while in this realm, though you healed quickly in Shangri-la from the bear attack," Mr. Kadam commented.

"Remember, I didn't heal in Kishkindha either when the Kappa bit me."

"But you did heal from the kraken bite, though somewhat more slowly. A few possible explanations come to mind. One: It could be that there is something special about Shangri-la. The law of doing no harm might apply. Two: Perhaps only the actual guardians of the objects can cause mortal harm. Three: Healing only occurs when the wound is not mortal. Whatever the reason, I believe you need to be very careful, Miss Kelsey.

"Even in the realms of the other worlds, you can be killed. We are fortunate that Kishan was blessed with the *kamandal*. I feel we can no longer afford to believe that your amulet protects you from injury or that being in a magical realm will help you to heal." He reached forward and patted my knee. "It would be unthinkable to lose you, my dear."

Mr. Kadam widened his gaze to include everyone. "We will all have to be more vigilant regarding Miss Kelsey's health."

The brothers nodded in agreement.

When we finished giving our accounts, Mr. Kadam sat back and pressed his hands together. He tapped his lip in his usual style and said, "I believe that is just about everything. Except I feel I should share with you that the five dragons have disappeared on Lady Silkworm's design. Nilima and I could see the dragons change as you entered their realms, so we knew when you left the waters of their dominion. Two days ago all five of them vanished."

I blinked. "That was about the time we entered the Seventh Pagoda."

He nodded. "We still have the sextant and the disk, but I believe those will disappear when we reenter our world. Nilima and I have

speculated that there is a passageway of some kind similar to the Ugra statue and the Spirit Gate that will take our boat back into normal time.

"Tomorrow we will head to the location where we first met the red dragon and hope that it will lead us back to the Shore Temple. However, before we proceed, I would like to stay at anchor tonight and allow everyone to get a good night's rest. I have reason to believe another battle looms in our near future, and I want us to be ready. Miss Kelsey? Perhaps it is now time to share what happened in the vision."

I swallowed thickly and turned to face Ren and Kishan. "When you asked me before what Lokesh said, I downplayed it."

"What do you mean?" Kishan asked.

"I . . . I lied."

Ren leaned forward. "What really happened?"

"First of all, Captain Dixon is dead."

Mr. Kadam waited a moment for them to absorb the news and then explained, "Lokesh caused the death of my friend. We watched it happen, and I feel great sorrow for his loss. My first reaction was that we should seek the rest of the crew and make sure they are all safe, but we cannot risk going back to Mahabalipuram, knowing that Lokesh was, and possibly still is, there. It's very likely he has already murdered our entire crew. I can only hope that some of them survived, but in my heart I don't believe they did. Still, when we are safely away, I will send agents to look for them."

"What else?" Ren said.

"Umm . . . it seems he wants more than just our amulets," I stammered and choked.

Mr. Kadam smiled in sympathy and took over. "He made overtures to Miss Kelsey. He . . . desires her."

Ren abruptly stood up, and Kishan's fists tightened.

"I will kill him," Ren swore. "He'll never touch her."

"I don't believe it is merely lust for a woman that is driving him, though that's certainly a part of it. He sees power in Miss Kelsey, and he wishes to . . . sire a son from her."

The reaction from the two men was very different. Ren was seething. His hands clenched, and his fingers curved as if he still had claws and wanted to rip something to shreds.

In contrast, Kishan despaired quietly. His face fell. "This is my fault," he said.

I touched his arm. "Why do you say that?"

"I goaded him, pushed him when I fought him on the Baiga lands. He saw me wield the *chakram* when I was disguised as you."

"I don't believe that is entirely the reason," Mr. Kadam assured. "But perhaps that adds to his perception. If I may be so bold as to hypothesize, I think he has always seen the Rajaram family as powerful, and he wants to absorb that power. He has never defeated you. You have escaped him many times, and he doesn't like to lose. Having a son is something he's desired for a long time, for centuries even. Back in our day, he had the same wish but with a different woman."

"Mother," Ren choked softly.

"Yes. He would have taken Deschen if we had not escaped, and now he seeks to take Miss Kelsey. He is on a boat, and I suspect he will be watching for our return."

"He won't lay a finger on her," Kishan promised.

Ren added, "We need to hide her."

"Wait a second," I interjected. "You need me. I have power, and there are dozens of Lokesh's pirates to face. We saw them."

Mr. Kadam tapped a lip. "I concur with Miss Kelsey. I believe if we are to win a fight without losses, we'll have to hit them quickly and hard. I don't believe that they will try to kill us. Most likely, they will use stun weapons again. We'll use the framework of the boat as a shield and use

your power from a distance first. Hand-to-hand fighting will be a last resort, and Miss Kelsey is a good distance weapon. I will come up with a specific plan of attack while the three of you sleep. Get as much rest as you can. We will hope to escape his notice but we will prepare for war. Tomorrow we need to be battle ready."

Ren turned to face a dark window and asked, "Why did you keep this from us, Kelsey?"

Rubbing sweaty palms against my jeans, I answered, "I didn't want to distract you. If we didn't make it to the surface, it wouldn't have mattered. I hoped there would be plenty of time to tell you later."

He turned to face me. "Next time, just tell me. I can handle disturbing news better when everything's out in the open, and you are honest with me."

"Okay," I agreed but broke eye contact uncomfortably.

With the meeting adjourned, I headed back to my room with Kishan at my elbow and Ren trailing along behind at a discreet distance.

"We have the Necklace. You two can be men for eighteen hours a day now. Only one more task to go."

Kishan nodded distractedly, kissed my forehead, and stopped at my door. "Eighteen hours, huh? That sounds like a lifetime." He smiled. "Ren and I need to talk." He brushed a finger across my cheek. "I'll see you in the morning, okay?"

Confused, I nodded and went to bed.

Kishan never returned to my room, and it was just as well because I woke repeatedly from nightmares. I ended up turning on a soft light so that I'd stop imagining I was under the black water again. When I opened the connecting door, I found Kishan lying on his stomach, sleeping deeply.

Softly, I closed the door and headed to breakfast. Mr. Kadam and Nilima had already eaten and told me to make a plate up for myself.

I settled across from them at the table just as a freshly showered Ren turned the corner. He heaped a plate high with pancakes, spread peanut butter over the tops, sliced up a banana, and doused his whole plate in maple syrup.

I hid a smile by sipping milk. He sat next to me, and we bumped shoulders.

"Did you sleep well?"

"Yes. You?"

"I've slept better," he said and smiled as if remembering a specific incident. "But it was good enough. Where's Kishan?"

"Still sleeping. I didn't want to wake him."

He frowned. "He should be more vigilant where you're concerned. He should have woken when you stirred."

I shrugged. "It's not like I was in any danger, and I don't think he was sleeping deeply. That's how he sleeps as a tiger too. Besides, it's possible he didn't hear me."

"Why wouldn't he hear you?"

"He slept in his own room last night."

Ren grinned. "Had a fight, did you?"

"No. And where he sleeps isn't your business."

"It is if he doesn't take care of you."

I sighed and picked up my plate. "Do you know if we are under way yet, Mr. Kadam?"

"Yes. We should arrive at our chosen coordinates in a few hours. Relax for now. I'll alert you with plenty of notice before we get there."

Ren polished off the last bite of his pancakes and asked, "Would you like to play a game of Parcheesi while you wait for . . ." he frowned, "while you wait?"

"Sounds good. But no Parcheesi. I need to teach you the train game. We do have that one, don't we, Mr. Kadam?"

"Yes, and the others you recommended as well."

I threaded my arm through Ren's. "Come on. I'll let you be blue."

An hour later, Ren analyzed the board, slapped down a wild card, and placed his last train. "I win," he announced.

"Not so fast. We need to count the score."

"I think it should be obvious without counting that I win."

"Not necessarily. I have the longest connection and big segments. You aren't afraid to use your math skills, are you?"

"Are you implying that I cannot add?"

"No. But it's been a long time since grammar school. Feel free to whap your paw against the table like a horse if you need to." I grinned wickedly.

"Apparently, you need to be taught a lesson in respect."

"Are you going to write a law against teasing the *High Prince and Protector of the Mujulaain Kingdom*?"

"That's *Prince and High Protector of the Mujulaain Empire* and, yes, perhaps I should write a law."

"And what would you do if I broke your law? Cut off my head?"

He smirked. "I was thinking more along the lines of devising a way to keep you from talking, but you might enjoy the punishment too much." He rubbed his jaw. "I could throw you into the pool, I suppose."

He smiled, but then his expression changed when the blood drained from my face. "What's wrong, Kells?" Quickly, he slid the game board across the table and took my hand. The little train cars spun off the board every which way, messing up our scoring. "What is it?" he asked softly and stroked my cheek.

"I don't know if I can ever go back into the water. I couldn't even sit in the Jacuzzi last night. All I see is giant teeth coming after me. I had nightmares all night."

"I'm sorry, my *anmol moti*. Is there anything I can do to help?"

"No. Not really." I sighed. "I'll get over it eventually, I hope. I enjoyed diving before this happened."

He nodded and stood, then held out his hand. Grinning slyly, he said, "Then perhaps your punishment should be cleaning up the game while I watch."

"That's a terrible punishment. A definite teasing deterrent."

I began scooping the trains into their little bags, and despite his edict, he helped. My braid flopped over my shoulder as I bent to retrieve the box lid, and he tugged on it.

"You thought I wouldn't notice?"

"I knew you probably would. I'm surprised you didn't say anything about it last night."

"I did notice but . . . I'm sorry, Kelsey. I shouldn't have been so adamant about it before." He twisted my hair ribbon around his finger thoughtfully. "When you cut your hair right after we broke up, I felt as if you were cutting away all your ties to me. When you and Nilima prepared to cut it again, I panicked. It was very difficult for me. I know it's just in my mind, but I feel as if the long-haired version of you belongs to me, and the short-haired version belongs to Kishan."

He sighed. "But your hair is attractive no matter which way you wear it, though I've always been fond of your braids." He set the thick braid down and trailed his fingers from my jaw down the side of my neck then took a step closer. I stopped breathing, transfixed by the beautiful man intent on kissing me.

"Kelsey? Kelsey, where are you?" Kishan hollered as he leapt down the stairs and onto our deck.

"In here!" I shouted back with a panicky edge to my voice as I took a step away from Ren.

He ran over to my side, oblivious to the thick tension I felt with his brother, and pecked me on the cheek. "We're almost there. Mr. Kadam wants us in the wheelhouse."

Kishan took my hand to lead me from the room. Ren followed along behind us. I felt him watching me and tingling goose bumps shot down

my arms. I listened for his footsteps, and he shot past us on the wide stairs.

As we walked around the outside deck to the wheelhouse, Ren asked, "Kishan, will you sleep in Kelsey's room tonight?"

I peered at Ren who looked like he'd just swallowed something bitter.

Kishan openly gaped at his brother, then straightened and folded his arms across his chest suspiciously. "Why?"

Ren quickly explained, "She's having nightmares. She sleeps better with a tiger around."

I frowned. "Ren, you don't have to arrange—"

"Just let me help with this, Kells."

"Fine. Whatever. You two work out your plans." I started up the stairs and heard Kishan and Ren whispering below. Rolling my eyes, I entered the wheelhouse and plopped into a comfortable chair. "So what's going on?" I asked.

"We're getting ready to enter the red dragon's waters."

"Okay."

Half an hour later, the brothers and I watched as Mr. Kadam and Nilima deftly guided the ship in a circle around the waters of the red dragon. Nothing happened. We couldn't see a passageway or a marker indicating what we were supposed to do. Lóngjūn didn't make an appearance either. By mid-afternoon, I was restless and thought I'd go crazy if I had to stare at the ocean any longer. My fingers brushed against something soft as I turned away from the window. It was Lady Silkworm's kimono.

I traced the star on the front, which was now complete. Turning it over, I saw that all five dragons had indeed disappeared from the back, but that their elements were still there. I ran my hand over the clouds, traced the lightning bolts of the green dragon, and then flipped the

kimono over again and drew a line to the Shore Temple with my finger. "Take us home," I whispered.

I heard the slick pulling of silk threads and felt the ship lurch.

"What happened?" Mr. Kadam shouted.

"I touched the kimono and said, 'Take us home.'"

Nilima and Mr. Kadam backed away from the controls that were now blinking wildly. The sextant and the sky disk shimmered and disappeared. Ren and Kishan abruptly changed into tigers and sat at my feet, one on each side. The movement of thread against my fingers caught my attention, and I showed Mr. Kadam a tiny stitched boat traveling along the new line of thread ending at the Shore Temple.

"It would appear as if we're moving in normal time again. Though none of our instruments are working," he said. "I believe Lady Silkworm is pulling us home."

I sat abruptly and let out a breath. "Does that mean we have time before we get back?"

"I believe it does. It took us approximately twelve hours to travel between worlds before."

"So we'll arrive early tomorrow morning."

"It would appear so."

"Considering what's waiting for us, that's probably a good thing. Ren and Kishan need to be tigers for six hours." I patted Ren on the head and scratched Kishan behind the ear, amending quickly, "Not that they aren't equally as formidable in battle when in their *feline* forms." I grinned and gently twisted Ren's ear. Leaning over, I said, "Can't punish me for teasing you now, can you, pretty kitty?"

Ren growled at me in a way that let me know he'd remember my jest and make me pay for it later. I giggled.

Mr. Kadam turned distractedly back to his maps while I smoothed the kimono on my lap. When I flipped it onto the other side, I saw

the five dragons were back. The blue one snored softly, the white one nodded and smiled warmly, the red grinned, the green winked, and the gold panicked and ducked his head into a pile of gems.

"Nice to see you all too," I laughed.

I shared dinner with my tigers and snickered when both of them preferred hand feeding. I'd missed this version of them and teased about their being giant spoiled kitty cats while they licked the juices between my fingers from the meaty chunks I was feeding them.

Later, I read to them from *Grimms' Fairy Tales* while reclining against Ren's back. Kishan lay along my side with his head resting on my leg. It wasn't too long before I shifted uncomfortably and asked him to move his head to the floor.

"Sorry, but my leg still hurts a little."

Ren growled softly in response.

"You shush." I slapped the white tiger playfully on the shoulder. "He didn't know, and now he does."

They both settled down, and I spent another hour reading out loud the stories of *The Frog Prince*, *Tom Thumb*, and *The Lady and the Lion*, which was my favorite version of the *Beauty and the Beast* tale. After that, I stumbled my way sleepily to my room followed by both tigers.

Kishan jumped onto the bed, and Ren lay on the floor. I changed into my pajamas in the bathroom and slid between the sheets. Kishan was already asleep, but Ren lifted his white head off his paws so I could scratch his ears.

"Goodnight," I whispered and fell into a dreamless, healing sleep.

Just after dawn, the ship lurched so suddenly and violently that I rolled off the bed and landed on top of Ren. He changed to a man and pulled me quickly out of the way as an entire shelf of books fell heavily onto the floor where we had just been a moment ago.

Kishan leapt to the floor as a tiger and immediately changed to a man. "Meet me in the wheelhouse!" he called out as he barreled out the door.

Ren gathered our weapons while I changed clothes. I emerged from my walk-in closet with a bump on my forehead. Another wave had hit the ship, and I smacked my head into the robe hook.

"It's strange." I made my way over to him while the ship straightened itself and commented, "It seems like the waves are timed rather than random. It doesn't feel like a storm."

"You're right. It's not natural." Ren slid Fanindra up my arm, attached the Pearl Necklace, tied the Scarf around my waist, slid the Fruit into the top of my quiver of golden arrows on my back, and handed me my bow. The trident hung from a loop at his waist, and he carried the *gada*.

"Got everything you need?" I asked as I braced myself in the doorway.

He smiled and touched my cheek softly. "Yes. Everything I need is right here."

I folded my hand over his, and he brought it to his lips. I leaned toward him when another wave tossed me into his arms. "We need to go," I said.

"Yes." He made no move to leave.

I pecked him on the cheek. "Come on, Tiger. We'll . . . *talk* later."

He grinned and tugged me out of the room. We ran as fast as we could up the lurching stairs to the wheelhouse.

"Are we under attack?" I asked. "Another sea monster?"

Before Ren could reply, we stepped onto the sundeck, and I stood there for a moment shocked. "The Shore Temple! We're home!"

The city of Mahabalipuram stretched out before us on the shore. In just a few moments, we flew past the city, continuing to follow the shoreline. Wherever we were going, we were headed there fast.

"Kelsey! Come on!"

I caught up to Ren and grabbed his outstretched hand just as another wave pummeled the ship. I lost my footing as the ship tilted dangerously to the side. Ren braced himself on the rail and yanked me up until he could wrap his arms around me.

"Thanks," I murmured against his chest as my feet found the ground again.

"Anytime." He grinned and squeezed my waist.

We stormed into the wheelhouse where a frantic Mr. Kadam explained, "We've been discovered. I had no idea he had this kind of power."

Giant waves rushed toward us, one after another, each one threatening to founder us. Black clouds moved out of nowhere and darkened the bright Indian sky. Wind whipped the ship so hard the windows rattled.

"It's Lokesh?" I shouted over the noise.

Mr. Kadam nodded. "My calculations were wrong! We arrived at the Shore Temple at dawn—sooner than expected. I decided to give the city a wide berth, just in case. But he was waiting at the temple and launched an attack! We've got to try to disable his ship before he destroys us!"

He had found us.

I headed for the roof of the wheelhouse with Ren. Kishan caught up to us. The first thing I did was secure the three of us to the railing using the Scarf. Then I told Ren to use the Scarf, Kishan the Fruit, and I would use my firepower if Lokesh's ship came within range and try something with the Necklace.

I focused on the black ship that was quickly gaining on us. It was still too far away for lightning power so I whispered to the Necklace, telling it to pummel their ship with rain and catch them in a whirlpool. Next, I asked for any creatures of the ocean that would heed the Necklace's

call to come to our aid. Ren created a giant tarp to drop down over Lokesh's ship, and Kishan covered its decks with oil and weighted every free space in its hold with cream cheese.

I grinned as I imagined the panic we'd caused, but frowned when the wind whipped off the canvas and screamed when I saw large fins rushing toward our boat. Ren touched my trembling hand.

"What is it?"

In a barely audible voice, I whispered, "Sharks."

His hand tightened over mine. "Don't look at them."

But I couldn't help it. I stared at them circling our boat and froze. I heard Ren speak to Kishan though I couldn't process his words.

Then Kishan answered back, "I dumped a thousand pounds of rare steaks nearby, but they won't go for it."

Steaks? Oh. He was trying to distract the sharks. *Of course it wasn't going to work. They don't care about food. They want us.* Heavy raindrops plopped on my cheeks and head. The waves stopped, but Lokesh was whipping up a terrible storm. I snapped out of my shark fixation and directed the rain back to the other ship. That's when I felt the power of Lokesh touch me. Rain met rain. His power nudged against mine, and I pushed back. It felt . . . intimate. Invasive.

I pushed harder, and so did he. The rain caressed my cheek roughly as if he were physically touching me, and I could almost hear his laughter in the sounds it made hitting the decks.

He pushed so hard, I whimpered, but Ren put his arm around me, and I felt renewed strength. I shoved the power of Lokesh away using all my mental energy and felt him break off, though a part of me knew he was delighted at my show of bravery and that he had *let* me win. Suddenly, the rain stopped, and the clouds broke. The sun streamed over us, and I tilted my head up, willing the warmth to strengthen me during our brief reprieve. Their ship broke free of the whirlpool to pursue us again.

My thoughts flitted wildly as I tried to find a new course of action. I tried to sink him by flooding his decks with water, but he deflected it and sent it back into the ocean along with a few of his men. He gained on us, flying forward at an impossible speed. *How could we beat him?*

Kishan checked in with Mr. Kadam and returned grim-faced.

I touched his arm. "What is it?"

"We're almost out of fuel. We won't be able to outrun them."

"How long have we got?" I asked.

"Half an hour. Maybe an hour at best."

The three of us huddled together and discussed other options. Kishan wanted to ground the ship and fight him on land. Ren wanted to turn around and ram the yacht into his ship. I thought the land option might be better because at least we'd be rid of the sharks. Our quiet planning was interrupted by the sound of several erupting geysers. Whale spouts!

I shaded my eyes and made out at least a dozen gray whale humps heading for the black ship. They surrounded it and pounded with their heavy bodies, effectively slowing the ship's progress.

"Let's run for it," I said. "The whales will slow them down. We go as far as our fuel takes us, and then take the jet boat ashore and disappear in the jungle."

They agreed, and Ren ran down to tell Mr. Kadam when something caught my attention.

"The sharks! Kishan, where are they?"

"There." He pointed to the ocean, and I saw several large fins heading back to the black ship. "He's having them attack the whales."

"No!" The water quickly turned red as a baby was separated from its mother and killed. "Stop it!" I screamed. I touched the Pearl Necklace at my throat and sent the gentle creatures back to the depths of the ocean. It wasn't long before the sharks returned to swim in the wake of

the yacht. Ren returned and I told him dejectedly, "The whales are gone. I couldn't allow them to be killed."

"I understand." Ren gently squeezed my arm. "We'll fight him hand to hand. It seems that's what he wants."

I nodded. "He wants me alive."

"He'll never take you."

We looked into each other's eyes for a brief moment, and I nodded, praying that his determination was enough.

"They're coming fast!" Kishan shouted. "Get ready!"

Lokesh's ship was close enough now that I could make out figures on the deck. It wasn't as big as ours, but it was still a ship of some power, and it was fast. A large harpoon was fitted on the upper decking. Men scrambled over rigging and around the decks and ducked down behind boxes for protection. Only Lokesh stood tall and unafraid as the boat approached. When he spotted me, his image blurred to show him younger again. Brash and bold, he grinned at me and held out a hand, beckoning me to come to him.

I stepped between Ren and Kishan and shook my head. Lokesh frowned and issued a command. The boys were ready. Kishan threw the *chakram*, and Ren used the Scarf to tie up men and dangle them over the sides of their boat within chomping range of the sharks. Unfortunately, the sharks stayed focused on us. Their open jaws snapped as they breached the water. The *chakram* cut off a foe's arm and sliced open a chest before it returned.

Ren had eyes only for Lokesh, who smiled and invited him aboard with a flourish. I nocked and released a series of arrows, one imbued with lightning power. I hit two men and caused a minor explosion in the back of the ship, but I'd been aiming at Lokesh. He seemed to use the wind to divert the course of our weapons.

Lokesh moved his arm, and his vessel surged forward. The yacht

rocked violently as the black ship rammed into the back in an explosion of splintered wood and screeching metal. A ramp was quickly attached to our ship and a battle cry rose in the air as men streamed up onto our open deck.

Ren leapt off the wheelhouse and dropped twenty feet to land in a crouch on the deck below. Kishan followed after, and another battle cry rang through the air—the battle cry of the house of Rajaram. I scrambled down the ladder and raced after them. Kishan used the *chakram* and claws, switching from tiger to man just in time to catch and throw between blows. As a tiger, his ears lay back flat and his teeth were bared as he roared. Seeing the ferocious black tiger, some of the men stumbled to a halt, deciding to confront Ren instead and moved to challenge him, but he was equally as dangerous.

Ren separated the trident into Sai knives and leapt into the fray, slashing through bodies like a bull in a chicken coop. His knives spun so fast he looked like a man-sized blender, slicing through anything that came near. I hid behind some decking and took out men with either arrows or lightning. Lokesh was missing. I searched for him, but he was hiding somewhere.

We'd taken down dozens of men and still more emerged from the ship. They weren't armed with dart weapons this time, which puzzled me. Lokesh knew Ren and Kishan couldn't be killed. And though these pirates were modern, they fought with knives, machetes, and other older types of weapons. I didn't see a gun anywhere. It wasn't a battle so much as carnage. The sheer number of the pirates was the only reason we hadn't won yet.

Mr. Kadam and Nilima joined me on the deck. She was armed with a knife and he with a Samurai sword.

"Who's driving the boat?" I whispered as I let loose an arrow and smiled at the screech of pain from the pirate about to stick a knife into Kishan's back.

Mr. Kadam answered, "There is no need. We're almost out of fuel anyway. We put down the anchor and decided that we will help to rid the ship of these brigands."

"But Nilima—"

"Is fully trained in martial arts and weapons. She will be fine. And it's about time this old man stopped sitting on the sidelines while the younger men have all the fun." Mr. Kadam grinned.

The three of us surged ahead into the fray. Nilima was lethal. Men actually stopped when she approached and smiled at the beautiful woman. She took down man after man as they fell dead at her lovely feet.

I snorted. "At least they die with a smile on their faces."

Mr. Kadam fought as a master swordsman. He was dignified and graceful as he slid away from his attackers before they could touch him. He did not linger over a fight. He simply disabled a man as quickly as possible and moved on to the next one, his bright sword flashing in the sun.

As we dispatched the pirates, I found myself back to back with Ren. Again, I puzzled over Lokesh and his plan. There was something I wasn't seeing. The pirates had obviously been given instructions not to harm me, though several of them tried unsuccessfully to carry me off. Bodies lay piled at our feet. *Why aren't they using tranquilizers? This battle is almost child's play.*

Ren defeated a huge opponent and hissed, "I don't want you up here. We're doing fine. Move back where you were before. It was out of visual range."

"You need me."

"I will always need you. That's why I want you to be safe. *Please* move back." He turned his back on the man attacking him and pleaded with his eyes. I sighed and blasted the man rushing at him then nodded my head. The battle would soon be over anyway. With Nilima and Mr. Kadam involved, there was little for me to do.

"Alright, but save some for me."

Ren grinned. "No problem. And, Kelsey?"

"What now?" I said exasperated as he elbow punched a guy in the face without even looking at him.

"I love you."

My lips twitched into a lopsided smile. "I love you too."

Ren turned back with a whoop into the melee. I shouldered my bow and jogged back to my little alcove then pulled out an arrow and searched for another target. I relegated myself to being the backup, taking out men who came too close or were getting the edge on someone. I still felt involved with the battle though I stood apart. My golden arrows flew straight, and my lightning power was on target.

Closing one eye, I sighted along the top of the black ship and gasped. I yelled, but it was too late. The man I'd been sighting had set the harpoon and fired. The giant shaft shot toward Nilima. It would kill her.

Mr. Kadam saw it too. He shouted, "Nilima!" and stepped directly in front of her, hugging her to his chest.

I screamed, "Look out!" and dropped my bow, staggering out of my hiding place.

They were gone! I scanned the deck for their impaled bodies, but they weren't there. The harpoon struck the deck and sunk deeply into the splintered wood, but Mr. Kadam and Nilima had vanished.

A voice behind me said, "There she is!" Three pinpricks hit me. One in the shoulder, one in my thigh, and one on my arm.

"No!" I staggered to the wall and pressed a shaky hand against it to balance myself.

Angrily, I wrenched the darts from my body. Heavy arms picked me up and threw me over a beefy shoulder. I tried to call out, but my voice was a mere whisper in the windstorm of noise from the battle.

Three stealthy pirates made off with me to the other side of the

boat. The big man climbed, with me still over his shoulder, precariously down the makeshift ladder they'd used to board. I tried to blast him, but already my power had fizzled. I flailed, but he just laughed at my feeble struggles.

Lokesh wasn't with them, which was a relief, but I knew my relief would be short-lived. I would be seeing him soon. Now I knew why he'd disappeared and why the battle, though bloody, was a bit one-sided. It was a trap. He didn't care if all those men died. My body felt heavy, and my eyes started to close. Time was running out.

After shooting me with three tranquilizers, the men were smug enough not to tie me; instead, they busied themselves starting the boat and beating off sharks with oars. Apparently, the sharks were going to be my personal escorts. Trembling, I slowly raised my hand up to my neck and, when the boat jumped over a small wave, yanked the amulet off. I whimpered and turned to my side as if I was falling asleep and whispered instructions to the golden snake on my arm.

Slowly, carefully, I slid Fanindra off my arm and wrapped the amulet's chain around her neck several times. My arm was heavy and lifting her to the edge of the boat seemed impossible. I tried and failed; my deadened arm jerked.

"Hey there! What are you doing?" A pirate twisted to investigate, grabbed my elbow and squeezed it painfully. His eyes lit up when he saw the flash of gold. He leaned closer, and Fanindra came alive, opened her hood, and hissed.

"Snake!" he bellowed and scooted to the far side of the boat. Taking advantage of his distance, I focused my eyes on Fanindra and swallowed thickly, trying to clear the waves of blackness lapping at my consciousness. With a monumental effort, I pushed her golden body over the lip of the boat and smiled as I heard the splash she made when she hit the water.

"The boss isn't going to like that," one man said.

"Then we won't tell him, will we? I don't have a mind to be shark bait."

"Agreed. Let's keep this to ourselves." The man leaned over and a cloud of his stale breath washed over my face. "No more tricks, little missy. The boss told us all about you."

I couldn't reply though I thought of a few choice words to share. We went over a wave, and my paralyzed body slammed hard against the bottom of the boat, yet it felt like the softest of pillows to me. I couldn't even begin to understand what had happened to Mr. Kadam and Nilima; so instead, my last thoughts were of Ren and Kishan.

I knew they'd survive the battle, and they'd probably be wily enough to get away. At least I'd helped to give them back eighteen hours. A tear squeezed out from my closed eyes and spilled over my cheek. Another fell on the other side. I thought it was only right that I shed one tear for each of my tigers, for I loved them both.

Phet said that I had to choose. Something I'd agonized over for months. But I didn't understand then. Now I knew what he'd meant. I didn't have to choose *between* them. I could just choose to *save* them. Both of them. They would live if I offered myself to Lokesh. Not that I wouldn't struggle or try my best to escape, but if escape wasn't an option, it was the last gift I could give my tigers.

Durga had said, "Regrets are only felt by those who do not understand life's purpose."

I know my purpose now, and I have no regrets. If they live, my sacrifice will have been worth it. Somehow my lips twisted into a smile, and I relinquished myself, sinking into oblivion.

taken

The two men sped across India, stopping to rest only when necessary to refuel and eat. They slept only when the beast took over. They were relentless, both desperate to save the woman they loved. Both knowing it was unlikely they'd be able to save her in time. Still, they had to push on. They had to try.

By mutual decision, they pulled off the road and parked their motorcycles in the brush, far enough away that passersby wouldn't see them. Ren pulled bread from a knapsack, tore the loaf in half, and threw a section to his brother. They chewed in silence, and it wasn't long before they both reached for their cell phones, looking for the GPS dot that was all they had left of Kelsey.

"He's moving her again," Kishan said. "She's traveling fast. Maybe by plane."

Ren grunted in agreement. "Can you see Kadam?"

"No. Still nothing on him."

With a sigh Ren slipped his cell phone into his bag and shrugged out of his racing jacket. His brother secured his helmet to the bike and kicked off his heavy boots. With his clothing neatly folded and placed in the motorcycle's leather satchel, Ren finally allowed the tiger to take over his body.

The burning started in the pit of his stomach and spread to his limbs. Tremors shot down his arms. As his center of gravity shifted, his upper torso fell heavily to the ground. At the same time, his fingers curled up into his palms. Fur covered his body, and his whiskers emerged. The feeling always made him want to sneeze.

His claws were always the hardest change. They emerged like daggers from the skin between his knuckles—a weapon that was always a part of him, embedded in his tissue. Though he'd used and trained with weapons all of his life, Ren didn't relish war or fighting like Kishan. He'd rather wage war verbally, around a table of advisers. He enjoyed games of strategy and clever battle tactics, but in his heart he craved peace. He longed for the life his parents had had before Lokesh. He wanted to make a home with the woman he loved and finally raise a family.

Ren circled the ground, pacing, as his restless mind worried about his lost woman. For the white tiger, it was simple. She was his mate. She belonged to him, and he wouldn't rest until he found her and destroyed the threat that had taken her from him. For the man, the situation was more complicated. Despite her admitted love for him, she had decided to be with another. He couldn't wrap his head around it, and it wearied him.

With a sigh he dropped to the ground and rested his head on his paws. He thought back to the time when they were together in Oregon. It seemed so long ago. She loved him then without reserve, without complication. So much had happened to them since. Ren closed his eyes and let his thoughts drift to her. He could still feel her though she was far away. The connection to her heart called to him as it always did across the long, lonely miles.

If only he could somehow reach through the wide expanse and pull her close into the safety of his arms. As he drifted off into a restless

sleep, Ren thought he smelled her sweet scent surround him and felt the ghost of her touch as she kissed his nose and pillowed her head on his paws. Her beloved voice whispered softly on the breeze, *"Mujhe tumse pyarhai*, Ren." He caught the wisp of the thought, clung to it, and slept at last.

ACKNOWLEDGMENTS

I would be greatly remiss if I did not thank my mother, Kathleen, and my sister, Tonnie, for their hard work in promoting my books. Mom started her own fan club at work, hung posters, learned how to e-mail and Facebook, and sold earrings, bookmarks, T-shirts, and books to everyone she met. She's even come up with crazy ideas such as belly dancing at my events or selling the books on the sidewalk on Saturdays. If we would let her do it, she would be out there every weekend.

I don't think there is one person in, or near, Forest Grove, Oregon, who has met my sister and not heard about the books. This includes the mail carrier, the bus driver, her kid's teachers, the checkout lady at Safeway, her clogging group, people at church, and every soccer mom in the neighborhood. Together, my mom and my sister are personally responsible for the sale of more than four hundred books, which is quite an accomplishment.

I'm also grateful for my husband, who still loves me even after all of our editing arguments, and I still love *him*, even though he likes to try to sneak in drastic changes on copy edits. He is tirelessly supportive, and he's always willing to take a leap into the unknown with me.

Thanks to my fabulous editor, Cindy Loh, who has been constantly at my side for months as we've worked on the nearly insurmountable task of getting three books out in one year. I have learned a lot from her and am a better writer because of her influence.

I want to especially acknowledge my agent, Alex Glass, who scooped me up a week before I self-published *Tiger's Voyage*, much to the dismay of my early fans. Though he was called the devil in disguise by some, I still think of him as my personal guardian angel and am always grateful for his wisdom, expertise, and patience.

Hurrahs for Jared and Suki, my brother and his wife, for their tremendous efforts on my behalf. They work for a pittance and spend much of their free time trying to answer my questions and talk me through my technology emergencies. They are part of my early-reading group, and all of their comments keep me laughing.

Most of all, I'd like to express my appreciation for my fans. It's finally here! In the past few years, I've received hundreds of letters filled with encouragement, support, and desperate pleading for any details that I'm willing to share. *Tiger's Voyage* would not have been published this quickly or perhaps at all, without their support. They've opened their hearts to my tigers and to me, promoted the series, and embraced their inner radishes.

Thank you. Thank you. *Thank you.*

An Exclusive Author's Note By
colleen houck

Dear Reader,

I first came across the story of Mahabalipuram and the City of the Seven Pagodas when I was researching sunken cities for *Tiger's Voyage*. The whole story of a jealous Indian god sinking six of the temples in a storm while leaving one lone temple behind was fascinating to me, and I knew I wanted to add that myth to my book.

Layering real historical events and places mixed together with fantasy elements is something I really appreciate in novels. It's fun to imagine a special site that could serve as a gateway to another world. The wardrobe where Lucy Pevensie slips into Narnia, the rabbit hole that Alice falls through, and the doorway leading to the chocolate room in Willy Wonka's factory are all examples of magical entryways that take beloved characters from our world into magical lands where anything can happen.

The City of the Seven Pagodas in the real world is just as mysterious as the fantasy realm I created. Marco Polo mentioned the beautiful city in his writings, but some wondered what location he was referring to. Local people spoke of temples that had been swallowed up by the waves, but it was assumed that their stories were simply the exaggerated tales of superstitious fishermen. The City of the Seven Pagodas just didn't exist.

Not until a tsunami hit the eastern coast of India in 2004 and the waters receded far off the shore was any credence given to the legend.

Witnesses saw something amazing. The ocean stirred, the sand shifted, and long-sunken temples appeared once again, as if they'd been lifted from the rocky ocean floor by the hand of a sea god. Myth became real. The forgotten was remembered. What was lost had been rediscovered.

This incredible story fired up my imagination. What would it be like to dive below the surface and explore these undersea ruins? What hidden treasures lay submerged in the deep? What dangers lurked in the dark underwater corridors? My mind was flooded with possibilities.

In *Tiger's Voyage*, I wanted to use this unique threshold to create a magical place full of mystery and peril. I crafted an assortment of supernatural guardians, ranging from the ethereal to the monstrous, who would serve as barriers, protectors, and even reluctant guides as my heroes progressed through the realm of the Seven Pagodas, seeking the prize of their goddess.

The ocean is full of life; it's essential to our world, and yet a vast portion of it is unexplored. Perhaps my tale is not as fantastical as it would seem. Perhaps a realm exists where dragons rule, where sea creatures of myth thrive, and where the treasures of Earth are gathered.

I hope you enjoyed traveling with Kelsey and her companions on their journey and discovering a whole new world full of danger and excitement as you unraveled the secrets of the Seven Pagodas.

Colleen Houck

A DISCUSSION GUIDE TO
tiger's voyage

1. Do Ren and Kishan have a good reason to distrust Wes, their Texan diving instructor, or are they merely jealous?

2. What do you think Phet means when he calls Kishan "the father of many" (p. 42)?

3. At the beach party in Trivandrum, Ren makes sure that Kelsey sees him dancing with a number of beautiful women—including Nilima. Since the series reveals little about Nilima's interior life, do you think that she has hidden feelings for Ren? What is her role in the series?

4. Why is the length of Kelsey's hair such a point of contention for Ren?

5. What is Lady Silkworm trying to say when she shares her own sad history with Kelsey?

6. Even after Ren recovers his memory, Kelsey chooses to honor her promise and continue dating Kishan. But even if she loves him, she's not "in love" with him. Would you accept Kelsey's affections under those conditions?

7. At first, the dragons appear to be quite fierce, but eventually Kelsey discovers their weaknesses, and they actually seem quite childish. What is the metaphorical significance of the dragons?

8. After Kishan located Durga's Black Pearl Necklace, Kelsey found herself "transformed" into Parvati. Kishan became Shiva, and Ren, Indra. Given the fact that Shiva cast Pavarti out—much as Ren did to Kelsey—why isn't it Ren who is transformed into Shiva?

9. If you were to undertake the adventures faced by Kelsey and her tigers, which of Durga's weapons would you choose to arm yourself with for the journey?

10. Although Kelsey battles dragons and the monstrous kraken, sharks are what terrify her the most. Why?

11. Kelsey tells herself that "if another opportunity to 'save me' came along, [Ren] wouldn't hesitate. He'd once again sacrifice himself, and I'd be alone" (p. 454). Is Ren more concerned with behaving heroically than keeping Kelsey happy?

12. Ren quotes liberally from Shakespeare's *The Taming of the Shrew* throughout *Tiger's Voyage*. Is it an apt analogy for their situation? Is Ren and Kelsey's relationship a comedy or a tragedy?

READ ALL THE BOOKS
IN THE BESTSELLING
tiger's curse SERIES

Author photo by Gabriel Boone

COLLEEN HOUCK's *New York Times* bestselling Tiger's Curse series has received national praise. Colleen is a lifelong reader whose literary interests include action, adventure, science fiction, and romance. She has worked as a nationally certified American Sign Language interpreter for nearly twenty years. Colleen lives in Salem, Oregon, with her husband and a huge assortment of plush tigers.

To find out more, visit
www.tigerscursebook.com.

GO MOBILE!

To access bonus content for the TIGER'S CURSE series, download Microsoft's free Tag Reader on your smartphone at **www.gettag.mobi**. Then use your phone to take a picture of the bar code below to get exclusive extras about Kelsey, Ren, Kishan, Mr. Kadam, and other characters from the TIGER'S CURSE series, as well as more information about the books and author Colleen Houck.

1. Download the free tag reader at: **www.gettag.mobi.**

2. Take a photo of the bar code using your smartphone camera.

3. Discover the spellbinding world of the TIGER'S CURSE series!

SPLINTER

An imprint of Sterling Publishing Co., Inc.

New York
www.sterlingpublishing.com